# PACAZO

ALSO BY ROY KESEY

*All Over*
*Nanjing*
*Nothing in the World*

# PACAZO

a novel

Roy Kesey

Jonathan Cape
London

Published by Jonathan Cape 2012

2 4 6 8 10 9 7 5 3 1

First published in the US in 2011 by Dzanc Books

Carlo Ginzburg's essays (trans. Martin Ryle and Kate Soper)
quoted with permission.
All other in-text translations by Roy Kesey

The author would like to thank the editors of the publications in which
excerpts of this novel were first published: *McSweeney's, Mississippi Review
Online, Backwards City Review, PRISM International, Los Angeles Review,
mudluscious, RE:AL, Stamp Stories* and *Ninth Letter*

First published in Great Britain in 2012 by
Jonathan Cape
Random House, 20 Vauxhall Bridge Road,
London SW1V 2SA

www.vintage-books.co.uk

Addresses for companies within The Random House Group Limited can be
found at: www.randomhouse.co.uk/offices.htm

The Random House Group Limited Reg. No. 954009

A CIP catalogue record for this book is available from the British Library

ISBN 9780224094023

The Random House Group Limited supports The Forest Stewardship Council
(FSC®), the leading international forest certification organisation. Our books
carrying the FSC label are printed on FSC® certified paper. FSC is the only
forest certification scheme endorsed by the leading environmental
organisations, including Greenpeace. Our paper procurement policy can be
found at www.randomhouse.co.uk/environment

Printed and bound in Great Britain by
CPI Group (UK) Ltd, Croydon, CR0 4YY

*para mi pacaza, y mis dos pacacitos*

"It is an ever-living, ever-working Chaos of Being,
wherein shape after shape bodies itself forth from
innumerable elements."
—Thomas Carlyle, "On History"

> "The foxes of the Sechura Desert howl like demons when
> night falls, and do you know why? To break the silence that
> terrifies them."
> —Mario Vargas Llosa, *The Time of the Hero*

"The solution is elegant—but how laborious, how
costly, and how fragile!"
—Paul Ricoeur, *Time and Narrative*

> "It's good to laugh," he said, "but there are some
> things one must never forget: that even the mouths
> of children will one day fill with maggots, for
> example, and that the house of the master will be
> turned into a cabaret by his disciples."
> —Julio Ramón Ribeyro, *Men and Bottles*

"It is often overlooked that the conviction that one
can make sense of history stands on the same level of
epistemic plausibility as the conviction that it makes
no sense whatsoever."
—Hayden White, *The Content of the Form*

> "The terrors, what a luxury for the imagination."
> —Julio Cortázar, *Hopscotch*

"The oldest act in the intellectual history of the
human race: the hunter squatting on the ground,
studying the tracks of his quarry."
—Carlo Ginzburg, "Clues: Roots of an Evidential Paradigm"

I.

# 1.

HERE YOU MUST BE SO CAREFUL. SCAN EACH OF THE SHADOWED branches that intertwine above you. The pacazo is waiting, will wait as long as necessary.

Reynaldo says that the pacazo is nothing but an uncommonly large iguana. I prefer to believe that it is some imp of history, coincidence made scaled flesh, a god no one worships anymore, not magnificent in its fury like the gods of the Wari or Moche or blood-smeared Chavín but some petty, bitter, local god who hates fat pale pillaging strangers. Reynaldo also says that in some places pacazos live on the ground, that here on campus they live in trees because of the foxes that come from the desert at night. This cannot be true. The foxes are the size of house cats. The pacazo is seven feet long, and if a fox were to pass too close by, the pacazo would seize it by the head and crush its skull.

Out of the trees and into the sun, across the grass to a bench in thin shade. As I sit down, the bench bows. I wait, release my breath, let my weight settle to all sides. Place my briefcase beside me. Take out a handkerchief, daub at the sweat in my beard.

The nearest building, sharp white. I close my eyes. There is the smell of decomposing leaves, of heat and wet grass. I have been this tired before but do not remember when and a ship drifts south along the coast toward the mouth of a river. A shout goes up. The men gather at the port gunwale. There is a Tallán mending a net on the bank. He is the first human they have seen in two days, perhaps of use. The men drop anchor, lower the skiff, go to get him.

The Tallán sees them coming, stands and stares. The sunlight flashes from their metal skin. Then a sound, the rasp of the skiff as it slides up onto the sand. The Tallán drops his net and runs.

It does not take long for the others to chase him down. They drag him back up the beach and throw him into the skiff, row him to the ship, pull him aboard. They stroke his black hair. The captain comes, looks, comes closer. He lifts the man's chin, gestures at the shoreline and speaks.

The Tallán watches the captain's lips as they move, understands nothing. When there is silence he looks from one bearded face to another. Again the captain gestures, and the Tallán guesses that a name is required, but a name for what? The captain takes hold of the hair at the man's nape. The Tallán blurts out the name of the river, Virú, but there is no response and he panics, stutters, tries his own name, Pelu. Now the captain smiles. He draws his dagger and cuts the Tallán's throat, rolls the corpse overboard, settles on something halfway between the two words, and thus the most famous saying here: An Indian misspoke, a Spaniard misheard, and Peru has been fucked ever since.

Someone says hello and I open my eyes. It is a former student, pleasant and smart and I do not remember her name. She looks at the bench as though hoping to join me. If I shifted to either side there would be room for her. Instead I smile.

She smiles back, nods, finally walks away. Still half an hour before my next class and a murmur rises and ebbs in the closest building. It is called Administration, is in fact a mix of offices and classrooms, History department on the ground floor. The dean is not unkind but has no use for me though I know more about the Conquest than anyone else on campus, and this version of the naming of Peru, I wonder where I heard it.

Reynaldo, probably. In other local versions the native's name is not Pelu but Belu or Beru and he is not Tallán but Inca or Chimú and he is not killed but enslaved or released. These versions are all plausible and likewise false: 1522, six years before any Spanish ship made it this far down the coast, and Pascual de Andagoya searches east from Panama City, then south into Colombia. Gold and pearls taken from the tribes he encounters and now his Chochama guides point farther south. Birú, they say, and this is the name of a province or perhaps the curaca who rules it. Birú is very rich, they say, and each full moon the warriors come north to kill us. Soon this province too and its pearls and gold have been claimed. The curaca is brought forward, and Andagoya asks, and the curaca points still farther south—an empire, unthinkable quantities of gold, and this is the error that will occur, the name misaffixed and morphing into Perú, and Andagoya goes, or tries to. He makes his way to the coast with the curaca in tow as guide or hostage or ally, explores portages in a large canoe. And one day well up the San Juan the canoe overturns. The curaca catches hold of Andagoya, lifts him onto the back of the canoe and I remember the feel of that water, warmer than you would think, Andagoya's clothes slow to dry in that humid heat and soon he is sick, bronchitis or pneumonia. Is carried back to Panama. Tells his stories to all who will listen, Pizarro in the back of the room and more students now, they stop to say hello, and I nod to each.

Again the handkerchief. I wipe my forehead, my face. Reynaldo says there are several pacazos living on campus, but

I have only ever seen the one: long thin scar down its left side, missing the second toe on its right front foot. I have seen it nine times in my four years here. Most often it was gray, but once it was brown, once green and once black.

Its color depends on the light, I suspect, and there was a day when it chose a branch too thin for its weight, came crashing down in front of me. Fat and gray and ugly. Stared at me, then stepped toward the nearest trunk, its head up, crest erect, eyes narrowed against the sun. It stepped slowly, as if it were ancient, as if it might never die.

That was early in my first year. Reynaldo said, Yes, ugly, but harmless. Eight months later shit sprayed down from the trees, a pint of rancid molasses across my head and shoulders and perhaps it is not that the pacazo gods hate all foreigners but that this one has been assigned to me personally. Intestinal parasites, Reynaldo said, or the stool would have been odorless and less viscous. This did not help. It took weeks to wash the smell from my hair. All but one of my students moved to the farthest rows.

A similar smell: the mixed air of offal and urine and sweat that wells up from the open drain near my house. Most of the city's drains collapsed fifteen years ago in the storms of the last El Niño, and have not yet been repaired. There are also the smells of garlic and sweat in every kitchen in Piura. Of mushrooms and sweat in the brothels. Of jasmine and laurel, plumeria and sweat in the streets late at night. It is always hot here, always, and the physicist who runs the university weather radar says that this year will be hotter still, that El Niño is coming back.

My wife smelled of mango and cypress and sage between her shoulder blades.

Fifteen minutes to class. Reynaldo, my friend and colleague, botanical chemist, and he is the reason I know the names of trees: zapote, charán, matacojudo. Mata, from matar,

6

to kill. Cojudo means imbecile, and only an imbecile would walk beneath a matacojudo tree in April, which in Piura is the middle of autumn. The matacojudo fruit looks like an immense potato, the kind that certain people marvel at, and save on their mantels. They can weigh twenty pounds apiece, can bash through bone if they fall from high enough. So far I have been lucky.

Matacojudos have no commercial use. Neither does pacazo shit, but it is in one sense essential. *If you do not stop screaming, the pacazo will shit on your head*—according to what I have read, it is okay to say this to your baby daughter as long as you use a voice empty of agony or rage, and full of love. They only understand the tone.

Reynaldo lives with his aunt across the river in Castilla, a district named for what once was the richest part of Spain. Here it is the driest and dustiest section of this small dry dusty city, and his aunt is enthusiastic but often ill. Reynaldo will only date women from other countries, anywhere but Spain. This year women have come from Canada and Holland and Mexico to give conferences and seminars, and he has failed with all of them. His most beloved possession is a motorcycle that has never run properly, and at the university he mixes things, creates, teaches botanical and other kinds of chemistry.

I teach English, and mix nothing with anything else. My students learn to conjugate, to skim and scan, to curse appropriately and forgive my lapses, to write resumes and reports and love notes, to ask favors without giving offense, all in English, as if this will help. I would like to tell them the truth, but they are too beautiful.

Ten minutes now. The other professors still look at me with expressions of pity and concern, still invite me to parties at their houses. I no longer go but when I did there were women with long legs and short skirts and tight colorful blouses, the rooms smelled of rum and perfume and sweat, and everyone

drank and danced beneath the Sacred Heart of Christ, chest
cut open and heart bound in thorn, the small red bulb at the
bottom of the frame and Pilar's hair hung almost to her waist.
Her eyes gathered all light. When she danced, the air went
slick and sweet with her movement and I leaned against the
wall to keep from falling.

Piura is a city nagged by time, insulted and degraded by
time, perhaps allied to it as well. It floats in the heat, chaotic,
indifferent, a gathering of things that are hard to understand.
One often eats seafood for lunch, but rarely for dinner. When
it rains hard and long, fires start and the water to all homes is
shut off. There are porcelain figurines of puppies and rabbits
and chickadees on most countertops, even those of people who
should know better.

Twenty years ago an exchange student from Abancay
arrived at my high school in northern California. He told me
that in Peru even fat ugly men can marry attractive intelligent
women who love to swim and dance and love, as long as the men
have blue eyes and foreign passports and are not totally cojudo.
I know what this makes me, do not have to be told what this
makes me, but Pilar sat in the front row alone and made me
promise never to leave Peru. Not a matter of passports, then,
and she saved me or would have. Reynaldo said that dating a
student was manipulative, unethical and repulsive, though not
an uncommon phenomenon. I told him that he was right. He
said she would break my heart. I did not listen.

Perhaps I would have listened if he had said, She will
alter what it means to be in the world, she will go late to the
outdoor market to buy mangos, she will peel them and cut
them in slices, she will allow you to run the slices across her
bare stomach and thighs and between her shoulder blades, the
juice will become one of her many scents and flavors, and four
weeks after giving birth to your child, she will be taken into
the desert, will be raped, strangled, left for dead, will regain

tortured delirious consciousness, walk the wrong direction, and die of heat stroke the following day.

And this will be your fault.

There is a shout that ends with *colorado!* I look up, but the word was meant for someone distant. Colorado, red or reddish brown, the word used to call to any Caucasian, and when I first came to Piura I confused it with colorido, brightly colored. There are few Caucasians here, and most are foreigners who turn many colors and are many colors at once; who start boll-white, and become pink when we go secretly, unethically, repulsively to the beach with the student we are dating. Some time later our arms are the color of weak tea, our neck and forehead are still pink, and the rest of our body remains boll-white.

Now I am used to people naming one another according to race: negro or negra, chino or china, indio or india. The majority here—mixed native and Spanish blood, short of stature and dark-skinned, straight dark hair and small dark eyes—are called cholo or chola. The Spaniards meant it as an insult, and threaded through the history I came to research is other history still happening, times and tenses washing over me.

In Spanish, tense and time are a single word, and in Piura it is the taxistas who call most often. They follow me down the street and shout Colorado! or Mister! They honk repeatedly, beg me to need them, and asking them to stop honking does not help. Screaming at them and pounding my fat fists on their hood does not help either.

There are hundreds of taxis here, perhaps thousands—many more than are needed for a city this size. To become a taxista one does not need a driver's license or insurance; one needs only a car and a taxista sticker. The stickers are sold for thirty cents apiece in the same outdoor market where one goes to buy mangos and galvanized tubs and llama fetuses in big clear bottles.

That evening Pilar tried to sneak out for fresh mangos, a gift for me for later that night, but I was coming up the sidewalk, just back from work, pronunciation and meaning and use, bat and vat, seen and sin, bread and breath and breadth. I caught her as she stepped to the curb, and I held her, smelled the cypress of her, the sage.

I asked where she was going, and she smiled and told me. She said that I should go to Mariángel and gather her up, that she would be so happy to see me. I said that Mariángel was still far too small to be made happy by anything but the smell of milk. Pilar said that I was mistaken, that soon I would learn. Then she stopped the first taxi that passed by.

It was an old yellow Tico. I said that I had a surprise for her, said she should hurry back. She laughed, mouth open, lips bright, promised that she would. She told the driver where she wanted to go, and the two of them worked back and forth on the price. I watched the driver as he talked. He was a thin, dark, brown-eyed man, like so many here.

Pilar got in and the taxi slid away. Out of habit I glanced at the license plate. An hour later I had forgotten most of it, knew only that it began with P, ended with 22, and yellow Ticos are the most common cars in Piura.

The handkerchief, hands and eyes. Class in five minutes. I pick up my briefcase, push up off the bench, walk to the white building and along it. Snatches of lectures ending— the feathered cloaks of Paracas, Manco Cápac's golden plough, Salaverry and the firing squad. Around the side of the building to a parking lot, the sun beating down into it. Distant trees are held shimmering in the heat. I pull a leaf from the nearest zapote. The leaf is perfect, broad, a bright dark glossy green.

Through the parking lot, the leaf shading my eyes, the trees steadying, resolving. A path leads out the far side, and up ahead it will split, deer pen to the left, Language Center to the right. Beyond both is the back edge of campus. The wall there is not yet finished, a stretch of fifty or sixty yards unprotected, and that is where the foxes enter, the scorpions and snakes and smaller lizards, and still the parameter is clear. Inside is the oasis with its canopy of trees, its lawns, its forty-four species of nesting birds, a triumph of money and hydraulics and gravity and distant aquifers. Outside are scattered stands of algarrobo, cacti, scrub and sand for miles.

The deer in the pen are crucial to many of Reynaldo's experiments. Reynaldo, light-skinned, almost colorado; he walks beside me, teaches me the names of trees, no longer asks why I do not go back to California. He would go to California if he could. If the conditions were right, he says, he would travel to California and visit Disneyland. He would make love to a tall blonde woman on the beach. He would learn to speak English, would play basketball every Saturday, would teach chemistry at a university where the classrooms look onto the ocean and have ceiling fans that work at several speeds. He says this, and this is how I reply: What is the name of that tree, Reynaldo, the one over there? You told me once before, but I have forgotten.

Up the right fork, into my office, take a folder of handouts from my desk and leave the leaf in its place, up the stairs and into the classroom as the bell rings. Smell of chalk dust, smell of sweat. These are my Intermediate students. They ignore me or pretend to, continue their discussion of last night's match between Cienciano and Alianza Lima. I set my briefcase beside the lectern, take silent roll as I wait for calm. Eighteen of twenty-four are present, neither good nor bad. Still they talk, marvel at the game's final goal, and I concede the moment.

- Who scored it? I ask.

- Waldir Sáenz, says a student named Milton. Beautiful, he says.

I ask him to come to the board, to diagram the goal and

label its parts in English. Milton takes the chalk. He shows chaos at midfield, a pass to Muchotrigo on the wing, a cross in to Sáenz and the shot, straight at the goalkeeper, the ball seeming to slip through the man's body. Only the final label gives Milton trouble.

- Por la huacha, he says. Between the legs, and beautiful.

- Huacha, yes. In English we say nutmeg.

As good a warm-up as any. I put the word on the board, have the students drill it as if it will be of value. I describe the spice as well, and Milton asks for the historical connection. The students are focused now, stare at me, and I smile.

- I have no idea. But speaking of history.

The students moan. I nod, shrug, walk them through preparatory vocabulary. Next the text, Daniel Boone, skim and scan. Comprehension questions, and finally the writing assignment, a national hero and his or her flaws.

The students' heads lower. I shuffle through the folder. For any time left over I have a crossword about vegetables. I lean on the lectern, stare at the back wall, and here is what will happen tomorrow, or the next day, or the day after that:

I am walking home from work. The sky catches soft fire in the west, and the smells of jasmine and offal settle over the city. As I pass the park not far from my house, a taxi slows beside me. The driver honks and I do not look up: looking up only encourages them. He honks again, pulls closer to the sidewalk, says, Oye colorado, taxi?

I shake my head, but as the cab glides away I glance at the license plate. It begins with P and ends with 22. I freeze, then shout and wave. The old yellow Tico pulls over beneath a matacojudo tree. I step slowly toward it, look in through the window on the passenger's side, and the driver's face is almost familiar.

- It was you, wasn't it? I say.

- Mister? he says.

And I believe I know that voice. I wipe my hands on the front of my shirt, put my handkerchief on the door handle, open the door and drag him through and out of his taxi. I slam him face-down against the hot hood. He twists and swings at me and misses, blood streaming from his nose, spattering my hands and face and clothes. I reach up, grab one low matacojudo, strike the man's head but the fruit is overripe and breaks. I reach up again and rip a vine loose, garrote the taxista, the vine tighter and tighter, the man's body at last still.

No other cars have passed, but my neighbors may well have heard or seen from their open windows. I let the body fall, walk to my house. I hear Casualidad and Mariángel in the kitchen, slip past them to my room, shower and dress.

Back to the kitchen, and Casualidad smiles, asks how I entered the house without her hearing. The elastic band of her eye patch is askew, a sharp diagonal across her forehead, holds a shock of black hair vertical above one ear. I tell her that I am tired of instant coffee, that from now on I will only drink real coffee, and send her to the supermarket. I kiss Mariángel, turn on cartoons for her to watch. Out in the back yard, I spray the bloodstained clothes with lighter fluid, burn them in my new galvanized tub, and bury the ashes in the flowerbed.

Then I remember the police lieutenant, his catalog of uncertainties. We have only part of a license plate. The taxi was a private car, like most taxis here, and there are thousands of possible matches throughout the country. No way to know where or even if it is registered. The plate could have been false or stolen, the car itself stolen. These cars are constantly resold. There are thousands of dark-skinned black-haired brown-eyed men in this city alone. My poor eyes do not always see the differences.

I walk back into the house, am washing my hands when the doorbell rings. My skin comes alive with sweat. Silence. Then a voice calls hello. Reynaldo, only Reynaldo.

He sits and watches as I help Mariángel with mashed yams. He looks in my eyes, and he knows. He asks anyway.

- What happened?
- I killed him.
- The taxi driver?
- I think so.
- You're not sure?
- It is hard to be sure. I think so.
- Did anyone see you?
- I don't know.
- I have friends in Bolivia.
- What would I do there?
- From there you could fly back to California.
- And there? What would I do?
- I don't understand. If it was him, you are free.
- And if it wasn't?

Reynaldo nods.

- And so?
- If no one comes, I'll see you at work tomorrow.
- Would you like me to stay with you?
- No. Thank you, but no.
- All right, Reynaldo says. Until tomorrow.
- Until tomorrow.

He leaves, and is back twenty minutes later with the painting of the Sacred Heart from his aunt's house. He hangs it on an empty nail and plugs the red light into a socket.

- This may help, he says.

I don't answer. He shrugs, turns to go, turns back.

- Come by the laboratory tomorrow. I've planted a new tree beside the walkway. A lucuma, from the Tarma Valley in Junín.

I say that I will, watch as he walks out the door, and Milton is staring at me. I know what has happened. Some shudder or wince and Milton saw it, knows he was not meant to, is afraid. Once I twitched so hard as I broke the man's neck that I pulled a muscle, and the whole class noticed, and the students discussed it for days.

I walk to Milton's desk. He has misunderstood the assignment, has written about his mother. I praise his paragraph structure, explain the difference between moreover and however, have imagined the encounter in many ways— many places, many weapons, many angles of light. It is only recently that the fantasies have curled in on themselves in this way. Reynaldo has begun hinting that perhaps it is time to give up. An odd phrase, to give, and up. My wife has been dead for three hundred days. The police have ended their search, and I am emptying, yes, but I fight it and do not always fail.

# 2.

OUT THROUGH THE UNIVERSITY GATE, AND THE SMELLS OF jasmine and offal are settling over the city. The sky catches soft fire in the west and my thesis advisor looks up as I walk into his office. He swivels in his chair, leans back, says that he's just had a call from Dr. Williamson. I say nothing. He asks me if he's heard right, if I truly intend to switch topics and frameworks yet again. I nod. So! he says. All hail the new Todorov! Incas instead of Aztecs, Pizarro instead of Cortés...

I say nothing, and he nods. Then again, he says, given that the old Todorov is still alive and writing, I guess technically speaking we don't need a new one just yet. Plus he had the codices to work with. You've got knotted string.

Again I say nothing. He has been generous with his time and hypotheses, particularly after I embraced his hermeneutics, and with luck at some point his anger will become frustration and then detachment. He chews his lower lip. Right, he says. Okay, he says, look: you've only been working the yanacona subaltern line for a few months, and naturally—

They cannot be considered subalterns, I say. He guffaws

and says, What the hell kind of skeptic are you? Anything can be considered anything! And if you really are going to abandon the yanaconas, well and good, but why not return to the Chachapoya? You were already so far along, did well on the LASA panel, even landed that article in *The Americas*.

I tell him that I have finally figured out what I want to do, which is precisely what I have said at each previous switch. He does not point this out. Instead he says that if I go through with it, the department won't be able to give me any more funding, not even for the October trip I planned months ago. I say that I will fund it myself. Well okay! he says. And if it doesn't work out, I'm sure you'll make a terrific junior high teacher!

I wait for him to remember that my mother has been a junior high teacher for decades. Finally he does, shrugs, apologizes, says that sooner or later I'll have to start finishing the things I begin. Then he tells me that the dean has my letter ready, and wishes me luck, however it turns out.

I nod, shake hands, walk to Dr. Williamson's office. He has been less than easy on me at certain points—So you're going to essentialize Barthes? Which one? Early Barthes? Late? Mid-early, mid-late?—but does not trouble me now. He gives me a generic letter of introduction, warns that it may not always work, says that he hopes he will see me again.

Another nod and handshake, an hour at Financial Aid arranging deferrals, and I am freed from Irvine. Out to an old white sedan in the parking lot, my father's car, always and ever my father's though he died nine years ago and a taxi slows beside me. The driver honks and I glance at the license plate. It begins with C and ends with 46. He honks again, pulls closer to the sidewalk. I shake my head and now the colored wisps in the sky are more feather or tendril than flame.

Casualidad waits at the front door, Mariángel in her arms and reaching out. I nod hello to Casualidad, take Mariángel and kiss her. Casualidad says that my dinner is waiting, that she must leave early for a meeting with her son's teacher, that she will wash all of the dishes in the morning.

The band of her eye patch divides her forehead perfectly in half, and she is rarely this talkative. Perhaps something good or bad has happened. I hold Mariángel out so that Casualidad can tweak her chin, then close the door and carry my daughter to the bathroom. I hold her in one arm, rinse the sweat from my face and neck. To my bedroom, set her on my bed and strip down, put on a pair of shorts.

Now to the dining room. I put Mariángel in her high chair and work quickly through dinner, offering her a bite from each layer of the causa—mashed potato, avocado, tomato, shredded chicken. As always she spits out all but the mashed potato.

Afterwards we traverse the house. Mariángel, eleven months old, and she is learning to walk but does not like to fall. She holds to my leg as we bisect each room, and takes things up, invents sounds to name them, Hegelian analogue or Spitzerian mimesis or Barthesian disassociated code, and I propose each in turn, then shift to the words themselves: saucepan, telephone, pillow. She repeats her own inventions. I ask when she plans to begin using words I recognize. She shakes the objects, drops or throws them. I ask her to pick the objects up and put them back in place but she is not interested in this.

She finds my briefcase, pulls at the latch and I remember the zapote leaf. It is no longer perfect, has gone limp, but is still a beautiful green. I hold it out. She is not impressed. I agree that it is only a leaf but in ten or a hundred years someone working from photograph or chronicle will type "John picked a zapote leaf" and it will become both leaf and *leaf*. Mariángel frowns. Semiological apparatus and linguistic performance, I say. She does not believe me. I tell her that I would never lie about such a thing: history a meditation not on the past as alleged but on present trace and sublimation, its form a mediated portrayal, a damming of time's destructive might, change frozen into tableaux, *leaf* now allegory, partisan teleology, plausibility defined as truce between conscience and libido, as ethical horizon, as determinant paradigm and certification of praxis, as means by which ruling interests define what can reasonably be desired, contemporary society and its moral strictures thus united as guarantors of our integrity, challenged only at our peril.

Mariángel tears the leaf in half, drops the pieces, claps twice, yawns. I warm her bottle, take her to the living room and turn on the television. The first few minutes are commercials, and she makes her way up and down the double-stack of crates that lines the near wall—dozens of notebooks, dozens of folders, a shoebox full of computer disks. One half is historical research, and the other half documents my search for the taxista.

Now she comes for her milk, and I lift her, set her on the couch beside me. She hums to herself as the Foreign Ministers of Peru and Ecuador exchange threats about border incursions. She curls up and quiets during a montage from Lady Diana's funeral last month, rouses herself only to point at the bouquets still mountained at the palace gates. A moment later she is asleep on my chest. I ease the bottle out of her hands and set it on the end table.

The footage switches to an earthquake from earlier today, ten people killed in Assisi, the Basilica of St. Francis in ruins. Then a live report on an airplane crash in Sumatra. Two hundred and thirty presumed dead. Mariángel flinches and wakes when the reporter's voice goes sharp to describe the smoke in the air, not the result of the crash but its likely cause: this is burning season for the farmers there. I turn the volume all the way down and sing her a lullaby medley of Nat King Cole and Aerosmith. She is asleep before the first chorus. I have a wonderful voice.

I look again at the television and now there is a green

man running naked through a fountain. He has a kind and thoughtful face. At the base of the fountain are pigeons that flutter up each time he passes by. Around and around and who is this man, and why has he has painted himself, and why green? Then I remember that I do not really care.

I work my weight forward and reach for the remote and the green man falls face-down into the water, does not rise. I wait. The man is unmoving. I hold my breath and the image goes dark. The newscasters return and smile and shake their heads. Then they are sad, and show pictures of a bus crash in Sullana, the pavement stained, blankets over two bodies.

More commercials: Cristal beer, Hamilton cigarettes, Always tampons. A dog barks outside and Mariángel wakes again.

- It's okay, I say.

She yawns, looks at me.

- Really. Everything's fine.

I trace her eyebrows. Pilar's eyebrows. Pilar's brown skin, brown eyes, black hair. Only the contours are mine, the broad forehead and strong chin. I place my palm flat across Mariángel's stomach and she wraps one hand around my thumb, another around my forefinger.

More silent national news—an aquarium at a hotel in Lima, and the dolphins do not look well. I begin another song and Mariángel frowns so I tell her a story instead, keep talking even after she falls asleep:

- Once upon a time there was a prince, a Malaysian prince, who had lots of money and beautiful clothes and a hundred hats. His only problem was that he had no real home anymore, had to travel from place to place without ever stopping anywhere for too long. One day he got on an airplane to fly from Cape Town to Khartoum—hour after hour of bad food and worse films, and his seatback wouldn't recline. Finally he changed seats, and this one went all the way back. He was just about to fall asleep, but then there was a storm, a huge storm, lightning and thunder and all of a sudden the plane dropped thirty thousand feet, straight into Lake Victoria. The locals got into their boats and headed out to search for survivors, but they didn't expect to find any. Who could have survived a crash like that? Then they found one: the prince from Malaysia. A miracle! said the people in the boats. They brought him ashore and took him to the hospital, and the doctors and nurses were astounded to find that aside from a minor concussion, a black eye, and two long rows of cuts on one leg, the prince was fine. They bandaged him up, and protected him from the television crews for as long as they could, but on the second morning the reporters forced their way in. The doctors and nurses shouted that they were going to call the police, but the prince said to let the reporters stay, that he had a story to tell. They set up their cameras and he began: the flight, the storm, losing consciousness as the plane fell, waking while still in the air, unconscious again as the plane slammed into the water. He woke a second time, was lying across some floating bit of wreckage, was terrified, had never learned to swim, and he felt something pull at his leg. He turned and saw a crocodile, was ripped into the water, and then for no reason the crocodile flipped him back up to the surface and let him go. All the world watched this interview on television, all the world marveling at the prince's extraordinary good luck, all the world except for a middle-aged woman sitting in a small dim office in Kuala Lumpur. This woman recognized the man from pictures in her files and knew him for what he was, guilty of fraud and embezzlement, convicted in absentia years before. Two months later the prince was in jail back in Malaysia where he belonged, and that, that, that is why we watch television. Because you never know who you will see. We stay vigilant, you and me, we scan the faces in the background of every shot, and then some day we see the taxista. And go find him. And when we have found and cornered him we draw our swords and cut off his hands and feet. Then we sheath our swords. We draw our daggers. We put the tips of the blades softly against his eyes, and plunge them in.

Mariángel shifts, lets go of my hand, wraps her fists in my beard. I lift her higher on my chest. The news ends with what looks like a new coach for the soccer team in Arequipa. Still more commercials, and Woody Woodpecker. Here he is called El Pájaro Loco. I am not sorry the sound is turned down. I do not miss that laugh.

The man had not been royalty, may not even have been Malaysian though it sounded right when I said it. Most nights are like this one, and the taxista has almost surely left Piura. There will be a prayer said at campus Mass for those who died in the Basilica. Another prayer, perhaps, for the dead in Sumatra, or a single prayer for the tragedies combined. I have no opinion either way and smooth my daughter's hair as El Pájaro Loco turns his beak into a staple gun, staples a Wanted poster onto a telephone pole, the escaped convict heavy-set and bearded.

My first year here I had a Pre-Intermediate student named Lady Diana. I saw her on the street last week, expressed my condolences. She said that it didn't matter to her but that her parents were distraught. I complimented her on her progress, on her use of that word, distraught—a good word.

The escaped convict tiptoes across someone's yard and El Pájaro Loco turns his beak into a sledgehammer, beats the man to the ground. Mariángel shifts, whines. It is most likely the heat and I carry her to her bedroom, set her down on the cool sheets of her crib. Draw the mosquito netting across the top. Point the fan away, turn it on, close the curtain. Whisper to her, not words, just the sound of whispering. Pull her door nearly shut behind me.

A glass of carambola juice from the refrigerator, and back to the living room. Standing, and looking at the couch.

The size of the impression my body has made is surprising even to me: the central two-thirds of the couch cratered deeply, the fabric discolored, nearly black in this bad light.

El Pájaro Loco is gone, replaced by a soap opera. I sit down in the crater, turn the sound up. A beautiful blonde woman is cutting carrots with a butcher knife. She starts to cry, turns away, stares out the window too long.

A handsome man comes into the kitchen. He and the woman begin to argue. The movements of their lips are not quite right for the words, the dialogue dubbed in Spanish but the program Brazilian and thus the mouths moving in Portuguese, the argument itself a thin hiss that rises and abruptly lowers as if perhaps there is a child asleep in the next room, and this hiss, its spectra of volume and tone, familiar to me though I do not know why and then yes. Daly City. Seven years old and sitting on the floor of my room, plastic dinosaurs, but then outside hours earlier and blood down the front of my shirt, dried stiff in my nostrils and on my cheeks.

The houses are identical except for the varied pastels. It is a subdivision where nothing could happen and thus where nothing has ever happened. The blonde woman raises the knife and lunges but the man catches her wrist, squeezes until the knife falls, pulls the woman close. She fights him at first, then slumps. My house, light blue. Across the lawn, in through the door, my mother already home and her smile twists but does not disappear when she sees the blood.

She leads me to the bathroom, paints the cuts with mercurochrome. I pull away, cry briefly. She blows on the cuts, brings down a tin of bandages, asks what happened. The other boy started it, standard gibes about my weight; he was thin and quick and vicious and unafraid and I tell her I fell off the monkey bars. The woman puts her finger to the man's lips. My mother's smile twists wider. She says to be more careful, knows I have no interest in monkey bars.

I nod, go to my room and here are the dinosaurs. An hour, two. My father home, quiet discussion in my parents' bedroom. Dinner, homework. Hissing in the pantry, rising and lowering, the very same spectra and then television.

My parents sit on the sofa and I stand at the set. I click past news from Vietnam, past Mayberry, pause at a football game so this must have been a Monday. The woman's head falls to the side as the man kisses her neck. My mother clears her throat. I click to the one remaining channel, the narrator just finishing his sentence, something about the thinness of the air and on the screen is a reenactment, men in armor trudging up a mountain path, leading their horses by the halter, the blonde unbuttons her blouse and this was, yes, this the very night:

The ascent at Vilcaconga. I lie on the floor, draw closer, am hauled back by the ankles and marvel at my father's strength. Soto has the vanguard too far out in front, has ignored Pizarro's orders in the hope of becoming sole conqueror of Cuzco, and his men and horses are exhausted, starving, drugged by the noon heat.

Already the slaughters at Cajamarca and Jauja. Already the slaughter at Vilcas, hundreds lanced, dozens of women taken, two daughters of Huayna Cápac himself, the old emperor already dead of smallpox or malaria spreading down from the Caribbean and I knew none of this then. The empire convulses, says the narrator, its celestial mandate in doubt, and we nod, the actor unnameable but known to us by his voice. Step by slow step, the Spaniards halfway up the mountain now. The man lies back across the bed. Soto glances up at the nearest ridge, then commercials, laundry, my father hurrying to the bathroom and back. The blonde whispers a name, and yes, the man says, yes. I scratch at the bandage on my cheek.

Lady Diana, lovely, both of them.

Soto now stares at the ridge. He goes pale as four thousand Inca warriors pour down the mountain toward him. They envelop the Spaniards, attack with maces and axes, split six skulls and

Gaspar de Marquina, his will in the Harkness collection, the archivist watches over me, watches me, watches, turns away and I remove a glove, run a finger down a crumbling edge.

The surviving Spaniards regroup on a hillock and build camp. A sharp sound, metal striking stone, and I sit up. Nothing more comes. I settle back into the crater. A hospital room, a beautiful brunette flatlining, and a much older woman crying into a handkerchief. The hillock, surrounded. Half the Spaniards are wounded. I close my eyes and they know they will die in the morning. No one bothers to unsaddle the horses, and no one sleeps. I pick at the scabs on my forehead. My mother asks me to stop. Then a new sound. The Spaniards listen, unbelieving, but yes: a trumpet.

Almagro and thirty cavalry, says the narrator, sent ahead by Pizarro not to rescue Soto but to slow him down. The trumpeter in question is Pedro de Alconchel. He is not in fact calling to Soto, is unaware of the vanguard's position, means only to halt his own party for the night. Soto's trumpeter answers from the hillock. This is Juan de Segovia, says the narrator. It takes me a moment, but yes, of course yes, a form of my own name. I look back at my parents. My mother, expressionless. My father stares at his hands.

Soto and Almagro embrace. At dawn the Spaniards mount. The Incas stare. The Spaniards set their lances. The Incas whisper to one another. The Spaniards attack, and the warriors who hold their ground are ridden down, and those who run are saved by the fog that comes to hide them.

I open my eyes. A funeral, a chase, men beaten with bouquets. The battle is done and blood trickles bright down the side of Soto's face. I twitch, shift in the crater, and my father clears his throat, tells me that conquistador blood runs in my veins.

It is not the kind of thing I would ever have imagined him saying. I ask him to repeat it and he nods. Juan de Segovia?

he says. Your ancestor. We named you after him.

Unfeasible—my luck has never been that good—but needed. My mother will not look away from the set. My father, too, again focused on the program. I get up, sit on the couch between them, watch as the Spaniards take Cuzco and replace the Inca empire with their own. Neither of the trumpeters is ever mentioned again.

The beautiful blonde woman is now asleep in bed. The handsome man opens one eye, looks over at her, draws back the covers. To the best of anyone's knowledge Juan de Segovia died before fathering any children, is thus the ancestor of no one and Mariángel wakes crying. She pauses for breath and I wait. She cries again and I go, find her arm caught between the mattress and the side of her crib. I free her, calm her, hold her until she sleeps. Then I go to the bathroom and masturbate to a memory of the woman and her knife.

Back to the couch. Find the remote, flick through the possibilities, stop at an old movie. Cantinflas rides his motorcycle in tight circles, spins to face backward, stands on the seat, on the handlebars, anything to impress the captain and win a spot on the motorized unit.

I have seen this movie before, do not remember what it is called, and this morning on my way to work I saw five people riding a single motorcycle. A baby about Mariángel's age was sitting on the gas tank, a middle-aged man was steering, and behind him were a middle-aged woman, a thin young girl, and a boy about five years old. It was not a large motorcycle, but the people looked happy. I flip through the other channels. When I hear the bell of the garbage truck, and the grunts of the workers as they sling bags into the air, it will be time to go to bed.

# 3.

My PATIO CHAIRS ARE VAST, HEMP AND REBAR, DELIGHTFUL, AND there are small birds in my almond tree. The birds are mainly brown. I have seen them many times before but do not know what they are called.

Mariángel sits on the tiled floor beside me. She stares up at the awning, then out at the birds, points as they all take sudden flight. She looks at me to make sure I saw them too and I lift her onto my lap, say that of course I saw, that the birds were outstanding, and already they are back in the tree. Mariángel wriggles away, takes a seat again on the floor.

For a time I watch the birds and watch my daughter watch them. I love the attention she pays them, but do not understand the nature of the noises she makes—she is imitating or calling to them, or possibly giving orders. Then I take up the newspaper.

Most of the papers here devote themselves to sports and extraterrestrials and nearly naked women. Their headlines are scandalous, or would be if the editors were not so inventive. Ass, tits, pussy: new words for them are created each week and

27

abandoned the next for other, newer words.

*El Tiempo* should in theory be more useful. It is Piura's non-tabloid newspaper, named for time and tense, yes, and also for weather. Today there are stories about the earthquake and the plane crash, a burglary at a paint store, a protest against rising gasoline prices. First page to last, and nothing. The photographs now, all faces foreground and background. Nothing. A third time to look for code-shift or tic, for any gap showing through to the unwritten or unpublished or both, and this is useless, is driving nails with a screwdriver, and of course again nothing, like yesterday, like all other days.

I am or was an above-average carpenter. Many people find this surprising.

Mariángel has made her way to the tree, sits in the dead leaves at the base of the trunk. She stares up and speaks to the birds, tips over backwards, rights herself slowly. The birds ignore her, flit to the top of the wall as Casualidad comes out the back door bearing a basket of laundry, return to the branches when she turns for the lavadero.

Casualidad sets some of the clothes to soak in the new galvanized tub at her feet. The rest she scrubs piece by piece and most often her eye patch is beige but today it is blue. She hums as she scrubs, a single note, sharpening and flattening from time to time but never enough to reach the next note up or down. She knows the names of most species of birds, hates all of them equally, chases them from the yard unless I am present and watching, and what little I know is inexplicable: thirty years ago a hummingbird flew straight into her face, and its beak plunged into her eye, almost deep enough to touch her brain.

I have never otherwise heard of a hummingbird doing such a thing, but I have no reason to doubt what she has told me, and her real name is not Casualidad. It is Pilar. The day I hired her away from the university cleaning staff, I told her that I needed something else to call her as my wife's name was the same and I wished to avoid confusion. She said, Qué casualidad. I smiled and thanked her—in addition to Lady Diana I have had students named Conception and Welcome and Hitler, so Coincidence did not seem too strange a name. Then a few weeks ago her son, Fermín, who comes twice a month to tend the yard, asked why I called her that. She said that it made no difference and told him to watch where he was watering. For several days I tried calling her Pilar, but it was an impossible thing.

Fermín is twelve but looks ten except for his gaze. Casualidad lifts the patch to wash the sweat from her face, and I catch a glimpse: the iris and pupil are covered by a layer of tissue that glows opalescent. She turns off the water and dries her hands on her apron. I call to her, ask if she knows what these small brown birds are called.

- Arrozeros, she says. If they could choose, they would eat nothing but rice. They will even come into the kitchen if you leave a bowl uncovered. It is a mistake I will never make again.

I tell her that there is nothing to worry about, and ask about her meeting with Fermín's teacher.

- It is not a serious problem, she says. Only that he will not speak in class.

In most senses she is the best maid I have ever had, though lately she is moving more slowly, and yesterday I found four clean plates stacked in the refrigerator. When I ask, which is not often, she says that she is happy working for me, would not want to work for anyone else. Reynaldo says that I pay her too much, that it will make her complacent and greedy. I do not know what to think about that. I also do not know how to repay her for the first months after Pilar's death, and have not truly tried.

Dead leaves fall thickly now, but by summer the tree will again shade the yard, and the house of my adolescence also has an almond tree. No one has ever gathered the almonds, and the tree does not grow well, but my father dug drainage for it each fall, took space heaters out for each cold snap. My mother still lives in that house, not Daly City but Fallash three hours to the north, old brick fireplace and overgrown back yard. Of course Pilar and I did not buy this house for the almond tree alone, but it pleases me most days.

For a year my parents had talked of how the Bay Area exhausted them; we left a week after my eleventh birthday, and Fallash, eight thousand inhabitants on the shore of Clear Lake, I hate and then love its quietness. Duck flocks, dry hills, oak and manzanita. My mother teaches social studies at a school in Lakeport and my father starts an insurance company. Late on certain nights I walk to my parents' room, see my mother twitching in her dreams and my father watching infomercials, tears slipping down his cheeks. One morning I ask. My father denies ever crying and my mother says the dreams were only grade books come alive and dancing, alive and dancing.

Here in Piura, saints are used instead of insurance policies. The plasticized images are carried in purses and wallets, given away to bring good luck. The arrozeros are gone. Mariángel stands with both hands against the tree and sways. In recent days Casualidad's skin has gone still darker, and I have no idea why, and the telephone rings from the living room.

As I reach for the receiver my hand brushes a bookend and there is a cascade—Baudin and de la Riva Agüero and Porras Barrenechea across the floor. Casualidad comes in at the noise, stands quietly as I answer the phone. It is Arantxa, my boss, director of the Language Center and head of its English Section, a large woman from Bilbao. On days when she receives packages from home, her office smells of chorizo, and she is buoyant, receptive to new ideas, even bad ones.

- You are wanted, says Arantxa.

- No. You can't. Not on the weekend.

- The archaeologist needs an interpreter for dinner with the rector. Jacket and tie, the Pórticos Hotel, in an hour.

- What archaeologist?

- You got the memo about the conference, says Arantxa.
I saw you reading it, and you should have gone, you would have
liked it, but the point is that I need you tonight.

- Why don't you do it? You're much—

- I did all of yesterday's sessions and the dinner with the
History department last night, but there was something wrong
with the pork chops, I think, or the salad. I can't get out of bed.

- Have you been vomiting? And the diarrhea, is it
greenish or brownish? And is there any blood?

- John—

- Because if there is blood, that means your intestines are
ulcerated. Amoebic dysentery, probably. You'll need antibiotics,
clean water, maybe antiparasitics, plus the—

- John.

- What?

- I just need you to be at the Pórticos Hotel in an hour.

Casualidad is gathering the fallen books. I cover the
mouthpiece, ask if she can work late. She nods, says she can
stay all night if necessary, but she'll have to call Fermín to let
him know.

- Sorry, I say to Arantxa, Casualidad is unavailable.

- I heard your question, John, and I heard her answer.

- You've got twenty other English professors on staff.
Any of them could—

- You're our only native speaker. Also, I already called
them all, and no one else answered the phone. You owe me,
John. Please be there in an hour.

I squeeze the receiver until the plastic starts to crack,
then hang up, thank Casualidad, say she can call Fermín now.
She asks if I would mind making the call myself. I nod and dial.
She was born and raised in a mountain village called Frías, and
her house had no running water, no electricity, no telephone;
she still occasionally forgets that the receiver must be placed

on the table, not back in its cradle, before alerting whomever the call is for.

Fermín answers, and under the sofa I see a book Casualidad has missed. I pass on the message and wish Fermín well, then slide the book out—the Means translation of Pedro Pizarro's *Relación*. I open it at random and the page is thick with underline. Pizarro at the Inca storehouses, the hundreds of leather trunks, and he asks what is in them. Everything Atahualpa ever touched, he is told. Every piece of clothing the emperor ever wore and every reed mat he knelt on and every corncob and meatbone he held, all here, saved so that at the proper time it might be burned to ash and scattered in the air that no one else might touch it.

At history conferences in the United States, overlong and unrelated papers are read hurriedly, prepared comments are vague, unprepared comments are off-topic, and when the panel concludes everyone hurries to the cash bar where graduate students strive to chat up funding agency appointees who strive to chat up publishing stars who strive to chat up members of the graduate student subset with whom they hope to sleep.

I was never part of any such subset, and the conferences here in Piura are leisurely and thoughtful. Until Pilar was killed I went to all of them. Once I even offered to organize a symposium, and the dean was polite and appreciative but did not think the timing was right. This is the same thing he said at my interview four years ago. On both occasions he meant, Why is your thesis unfinished?

There are important methodological differences between translation and interpretation, distinct means by which the two processes attempt to palliate their tendencies to pervert already unstable meanings beyond recognition, and I have learned that no one cares. People just want to know what was said, believe that such a thing can be known. I arrive ten minutes late and find everyone already seated at a long table in the middle of the hotel restaurant. The rector and the archaeologist are face to face at the center, with other university administrators spread out to either side.

The archaeologist is a small thin man with a neatly trimmed goatee and a Yale pin on his lapel. I am introduced in English as the American interpreter. I shake hands, sit down, rearrange my silverware. The first time I referred to myself here as American, Reynaldo held up one hand policeman-style: Stop. We are all Americans, he said, from Ellesmere to Tierra del Fuego. He told me to use norteamericano, and I pointed out that this too was imprecise. Estadounidense, then, said Reynaldo. A rough-edged word, I said, and ugly in the mouth. Reynaldo agreed but said it wasn't his fault.

The shrimp cocktails are served, and mine has only one shrimp; the rest is avocado and sauce. I do not much mind. The avocados from this region are superb, and I would not have finished the dish regardless, as interpreters can only take a bite when the speaker takes a bite, and must take smaller bites than the speaker does, in case the speaker thinks of something to say as he or she begins to swallow.

Usually the first course is accompanied only by small talk, but tonight the archaeologist holds court immediately, laments that these administrators were all too busy to attend his conference, recaps his research on what is left of Piura la Vieja in Morropón. He speaks quickly, his hands skittering through the air. Most of what he says is plausible but simplified to the point of falsehood. The university has a number of administrators who speak beautiful English but none of them are here tonight so I interpret only the barest bones.

I went to Piura la Vieja twice before Pilar was murdered,

spoke with those running the dig, and with farmers hired to help sift dirt. It is a rich site, and the local archaeologists are generous with their time and data. I could have been the first historian to turn the adobe into narrative, but of course that is not possible now. The true story of a single night, less than a night, of a few hours only—this is all I can allow myself to want.

I hold this thought in my head as the waiters come, as the archaeologist stuffs three last shrimp into his mouth, as the empty dishes are borne away. Infantile empiricism, is what my ex-advisor would call it. I know full well the inadequacy of the signifier to the signified but do not see how this can help or be helped and wince as the archaeologist repeats an old local joke as if new, that Piura should be nicknamed The Flying City, not because it moves in any direction but because it has been moved so often: from where Pizarro founded it in the Tangarará Valley to Morropón, from there to the coast, and from the coast to its present location.

I sip the sharp wine and think of villages in perpetual slow movement, the houses of matted reeds pushed by the wind, shifting each year a few feet farther away from the mountains that should shade them but no longer do, and the fish is served, sole, hard and dry. Piura is famed for its seafood and this restaurant is among the city's best but tonight it is too busy. I finish my wine, order a glass of bourbon, smile at the archaeologist and nod for him to continue.

- Morropón was a good place for a city, he says, as if he just now thought of it, and is the first ever to think it. It was up high enough to be easily defended, he says, and had plenty of water, plenty of land below for crops.

My bourbon comes and the archaeologist orders one as well. He reminds the table that it is his mission in life to find dead things in the desert and imagine them alive. I take a long drink, let them wait as I swallow, let them wait as I gaze at the wall. The archaeologist smoothes his goatee, leans forward, describes the hours he has spent photographing the site from the air.

- The wrong hour, the wrong altitude, the wrong bearing, the wrong angle, and Piura la Vieja is invisible, he says.

I turn this into Spanish, and the rector leans forward, asks what it is that one sees when everything is right.

- Also the wrong weather, says the archaeologist. The sky must be cloudless.

The rector nods, leans farther forward still.

- You would see nothing but a wasteland of sand and thorn, says the archaeologist, but I see a marvelous city.

In my interpretation I change You to The untrained eye. When I tell Arantxa about this small act of diplomacy it will make her very happy. Then I remember that I should have had today off and don't care if she is happy or not.

- Sand covers everything, says the archaeologist. Hundreds of years' worth of sand. But what is left of the buried walls of the church, the mayor's office, and the jail form infinitesimal swells that when seen from above can be known by the shadows they cast.

There is a pause as the archaeologist finishes his fish. I ask a waiter for another round of bourbon. The archaeologist cheers. The rector glares. There are several thin young women moving from table to table, but they are not wearing the hotel's quiet taupe uniform, are wearing black miniskirts instead. All but one wear white blouses. The other's blouse is red, and perhaps she is their leader.

While everyone waits for dessert, the archaeologist continues. The original move from Tangarará, he says, was for reasons of sanitation. Forty-four years after building Piura la Vieja, the Spaniards moved to what is now Paita. Could unsanitary conditions have struck again?

As I interpret this, the university authorities nod and smile as if they'd known already but are fascinated nonetheless, and surely this is the case. Then the archaeologist presents an alternate theory: that the mayor of Piura la Vieja had a Tallán mistress on the coast, and moved the whole city to be near her.

The rector frowns because this is doctrinally unsound. I frown because it is idiotic, though not necessarily false—history is full of idiots and I order another round.

- As you all know, the archaeologist says, ten years later Piura moved to its present location. Most historians believe that the Spaniards had grown tired of attacks by English pirates, but you must be vigilant against easy thinking. Perhaps the mistress wasn't interested in seeing the mayor anymore. Perhaps she was unamused, or unamusing.

I am saved from having to interpret this by the arrival of lemon sherbet in crystal bowls. One of the young women stops at a nearby table, and I see that she is a Gillette Girl. There are dozens of companies here that pay young women to wear miniskirts and give away small samples of their product— Cristal Girls and Hamilton Girls, even Halls Girls. Many Piurans consider Halls lozenges to be candy. I tell them the truth, but no one listens.

Another round. Most of the Gillette Girls are light-skinned and thin and pretty and tall, and wear their hair very long or very short. Only the woman in the red blouse is somewhat different. She too is quite pretty, but is neither tall nor short, neither chola nor colorada but something in between. Her brown hair is of medium length. Her eyelashes are long and her eyebrows are very fine. Her posed smile shows only her bottom teeth, though occasionally she slips and smiles fully.

Someone kicks me under the table. Everyone is staring at me. Apparently the archaeologist has been speaking.

- He has something very interesting to tell us, I say. We will all be charmed and enthralled.

I look at the archaeologist, encourage him to continue. The small man crosses his arms, closes his eyes, misquotes

Edward Ross' misunderstanding of Ranke's wissenschaftliche Objektivität, and that is quite enough.

- He wishes us to imagine, I say, that one of these Gillette Girls is here for a different reason than the others.

The archaeologist continues, George Bancroft on democratic histories and Von Holst on aiming for the sternest of truths.

- Imagine, I say, that instead of handing out disposable razors, these women are offering to shave the clients of the hotel. Imagine that they come round with steaming towels, and gleaming silver bowls of hot water, and of lather. Imagine that they bear leather strops and straight-edged razors, and that for a price they will shave all those who wish to bare their throats.

I pause to let the archaeologist speak again, watch the man's fluttering hands, do not listen to the words.

- Imagine that one of the women—this one here, the one in the red blouse—has come to the restaurant knowing she will see a client of hers from long ago. She walks to his table, and their eyes meet, and she realizes that he doesn't recognize her. He is thin and sleek and wears a thousand-dollar watch. She tucks a white smock beneath his chin. Hot towels are applied. She draws the open razor back and forth along the strop.

The archaeologist squints at me, clears his throat as if ready to continue, and I smile and do not stop:

- Imagine that as the towels are drawn away, she slides the razor carefully up from his collarbone, then slashes to one side, and we drown, all of us, we drown in a sea of blood.

The woman in the red blouse is staring at me, laughing at something, my tone or bulk or words. The archaeologist goes to speak, but now the rector is calling for the bill and the vice-rectors and fiscal officers are reaching for their coats, searching for their cigarettes, pulling out their keys. The man thanks the rector for dinner and grins at me. He does not yet understand that he will not be asked to return.

The bill is paid and the archaeologist is led to a taxi. I wait for the rector to thank me, to apologize for calling me in on short notice, to offer me a ride home. Instead he gets in his car and drives away.

The streetlights are improbably bright. I look back for the young woman but she is nowhere so I walk out into the street. Down the center for a time. To the far sidewalk. A trellis covered with bougainvillea, and the Plaza de Armas.

Tamarinds, ficus, Reynaldo would be proud of me. The plaza is beautiful during the day and I avoid it as I no longer have the energy to fight off the shoe-shine swarms, grab your elbow your hand your shirttail and now I see one asleep in the grass. His head rests on his wooden kit. At first I think I am going to kick him in the stomach but then I tuck a little money into his pocket. Beyond is City Hall and this means I am going the wrong direction.

I turn and walk lines of crotons and poincianas to the statue. Here is La Pola's face and here is one limestone breast loosed from her limestone gown and here is a lion's head pinned beneath her foot. She is holding a limestone parchment declaring independence but the words will not hold steady.

I step back, walk, march briefly. Soldiers come every morning to raise the flag and every evening to lower it and most nights to clutch their girlfriends in the shadows but there are none here tonight and across the street is the cathedral. Its paired yellow towers are gray in this light. Twenty columns and matched scenes from the Vía Crucis and I came here weekly with Pilar. Señor de los Milagros inside. Señor de la Agonía, Señor Cautivo, Señor de la Divina Misericordia. A gilded Virgin of Fátima. Silverwork on the main altar. A seventeenth-century pulpit with Immaculate Conception in high relief and Pilar takes her place, hears Mass while I work in the parish archives. Afterwards she comes, takes my hand, says that she prayed for me. I thank her and we go for Chinese food, another

Piuran custom I do not understand, always Chinese food after Mass and I am happy and then staring empty-chested and angry and time to go.

Along the sidewalk and smells rise up: laurel and urine, plumeria and beer, sweat. The street cleaners are already at work. They wear blue aprons, sweep slowly, never rest. Taxis stop beside me, none of them the right one—the drivers raise their eyebrows and I shrug or shake my head. In the doorways of the banks and shops and hotels are uniformed guachimanes. Some have pistols and some do not. A few are asleep, slumped against doorjambs, and the others smoke and stare into the street.

I stumble on a curb and there are waves of perfume in the dark heat. The prostitutes on the corner all have long hair and small breasts and lovely legs, and it is hard to tell if they are men or women. I have heard that the men apply their make-up with greater skill. I wave to them, and they wave back, blurred and now clearer.

I cross the street. Then I stop, turn to read the street sign, am careful not to think the thought. Three blocks west and I arrive.

There are two men sitting in plastic chairs in front of the old green house. They slouch as if reminiscing but do not smile. The living room curtains are drawn but there are lights on inside. Soft music from the second floor. I nod to the men and they stare at me.

- For Jenny, I say.

I cross my arms and tilt my head, nearly fall. One of the men stands and goes inside. The other continues to stare at me. I look away, look back, nod again as if this time it might mean more.

The first man returns, holds the door open. I walk into the living room, sit down on the couch, look at the collection of porcelain puppies on the mantel. Decide that there's nothing wrong with porcelain puppies, that a porcelain puppy is a fine thing in the world. Decide that the archaeologist wasn't evil, was probably just tired from all his fieldwork, should be forgiven, and in comes Ms. Alina.

- Mr. Segovia, a pleasure. Did you forget to make a reservation?

I acknowledge that this is the most likely scenario, observe the woman's eyebrows, viciously plucked, scimitars, perhaps a clue.

- Jenny will be free shortly. Would you like something to drink? Some coffee?

I spread my arms to show that I lack nothing, that all is fine, in perfect order. I compliment Ms. Alina on her haircut, say that I believe it is relatively new, that I hope I am not mistaken, that in any event it is a flattering haircut indeed. She smiles, says that Jenny will come for me when she is ready.

She walks back to the kitchen. Smell of mushrooms, of garlic, of sweat. There is no Spanish word for Ms. and I do not know why she chose it. Again the porcelain puppies. Time passes in odd amounts, each amount at a different speed.

My first time here was two months ago. Reynaldo organized a party for my birthday. An hour after it ended he and I finished a bottle and he was muttering about gifts, his gift, a plan. We came in a mototaxi. When I figured out where we were I walked out, walked home, could not get my door to open, fell asleep on my front steps. The second time was the next night alone. I did not know who to ask for, got Jenny by luck. She asked if her tits were big enough for me, if her ass was round enough. She was not impressed by my historiographical acumen, not put off when I started to cry, not surprised by my requests, hit me and spit on me until I gave up and said she could stop.

An older man, early fifties, well dressed, he comes through the front door and is led straight up the stairs. Reservations, reservations. There seem to be more puppies now.

Other guests, up and down the stairs, no one I have known. My third and fourth times were progressively closer to the mean and now she arrives.

Jenny is not her real name. I am glad I do not know her real name. Her face seems thinner than before, her hair dyed blonder. There is embroidery down the front of her robe—the Nazca lines, monkey and hummingbird and extraterrestrial. She takes my arm, walks me upstairs and into the closest bedroom, says that this time we'll have to hurry just a little.

I say that it is nice to see her, and she smiles. I sit down on the bed. Remove one shoe, have trouble with the other and she comes to help. She turns the lamp down, asks what I would like this time, and I say we will do what is usually done. She nods, takes off her robe and hangs it on a chair, and the camisole underneath has the same embroidered figures.

- Monkeys, I say.
- Music?
- No. But sing if you want. Sing me something.
- I'm not a very good singer.
- I love that about you.

I let myself fall back onto the bed. It seems to take a very long time to reach it, and the sound of my head landing on the mattress deafens me. I open my eyes, and Jenny is straddling my hips. I reach, lift her camisole as high as I can, and she raises her arms, pulls it up and off. She swishes her hair back and forth and lowers to me, brings her breasts one after the other to my mouth.

After a moment I push her softly back, say that I want to see it.

- Already?
- Now please.
- Okay.

She stands on the bed, looms and wavers, draws down her panties and there it is, the hair shaved in the form of an

41

exclamation point. And I laugh. And she laughs, and says she's glad I like it.

She goes to work on my clothes, socks first, then my tie, slow on the buttons of my shirt, a struggle with the belt. I lift to help her remove my pants and boxers. She turns to fetch a condom from the vanity and I catch a glimpse in the mirrored closet door, the great white mass of myself.

From there everything is fast. Jenny takes hold of my beard, tugs my face left and right as she bounces and groans above me. I grab her arms, squeeze and explode and subside but do not let go. Squeeze harder and harder. Then a sound around me, Jenny asking please and I breathe, let go of her, apologize.

She kisses my cheek, says it's all right, but fifty extra soles for make-up to cover the bruises. I nod, wipe my face, try to tell her about Pilar. Jenny says she is sorry but there isn't time.

I nod again. She rubs her arms, nudges me. I get up and look for my clothes.

- I like you, I say.

- I like you too. Next time make a reservation, and you can tell me anything you want.

I stop by the kitchen to thank Ms. Alina, ignore the men in the plastic chairs, step to the street. The night, hotter, more humid. Will do penance tomorrow, yes, the worst of the search.

I walk and Atahualpa, Atahualpa in his cell. Still the women come. A cloak made from the wings of vampire bats, the softest cloak ever known and now a tiny owl in the air in front of me. Piercing call. Flies ahead, one block at a time, always one block ahead.

The sight of my street surprises me. I stop on the sidewalk, look at my house, the strangeness of it, swaying. Up the steps to my door. Push it open, and the streetlight glow flows past me, illuminates a swath of the floor, the polished stone gone liquid, bottomless, still and then roiling before me.

I could throw rocks at the light until luck does its work,

but the last time I did this my neighbors called the police. Tonight I try something new: I stand as tall as I am able in the doorway, block the light with my bulk, jump at an angle toward shadow but one foot catches on the frame and I twist as I fall, land hard on my hip.

Something about owls—Chavín or maybe Moche. Casualidad surely heard the noise and will come. I wait. No one comes. I work to my feet, limp forward, my shirt stuck wet to my chest. Quietly through the dark to Mariángel's bedroom, find her stretched tight along the side of her crib, tugging on her ear in her sleep. I lean down to kiss her and she turns, reaches for me, rolls away from my smell.

To the kitchen, dark here too but Casualidad awake and sitting at the table. I ask why she didn't come, and she asks what I mean. I say it doesn't matter. She nods, asks if I want her to boil water for the morning. I say yes, then no, that I will do it myself.

Casualidad lets herself out. I limp to the window, open it, sniff around the stove. Propane leaks are common, my lights are badly wired, and I have seen disconcerting pictures of blackened remains. I turn on the light. Gnats and mosquitoes flit around the naked bulb. I stand perfectly still, try to remember what comes next.

A gecko moves onto the ceiling. Its skin is nearly transparent. I don't know where this one goes during the day, but at night it appears here whenever the light comes on. There are other geckos too, many others. At times there is one in each room.

I watch the gecko, and at first its movements are too slow to see. Do the mosquitoes notice it at all? How good is their vision? Now the gecko is close enough and its movements are too quick to see. A mosquito is gone, swallowed, dead. There is so much to learn in this world.

# 4.

THE BUS PULLS ONTO THE FOURTH BRIDGE, AND BENEATH US the causeway, thirty feet deep and fifty yards wide, almost empty because it is spring: the river is now a sordid thread. Clustered in the riverbed tight against the far bank are half a dozen shanties. Gaunt chickens skitter through scattered trash. The only green of any kind is a line of points in the loam, melons or maybe gourds.

My head and hip ache and my stomach roils and farther down the bank something moves along the top edge. It is long and black or dark gray, too thick for a snake and now out of sight, the bus jolting off the bridge onto the roadway. Mariángel climbs into my lap, points out the window at a speck in the sky. It is either a hawk or litter lifted by wind.

In two or three months the summer rains will start. The shanty owners will harvest their crops, move up onto the banks as the causeway fills. For a time it will be beautiful here along the river. People will come to the edge to watch the water move and to be calmed.

Then I remember the physicist and his prediction.

I was not here in 1983 when El Niño last came, have heard that calm was no part of it, that instead of calm there was dengue and drownings, that flooding destroyed highways in all directions, that there were shortages, no kerosene or gasoline for sale, no bread, no canned milk or bottled water, no rice or sugar, no candles, no plastic sheeting, no concrete or tar or lumber. There was beer, however, for a time. It was brought by army helicopters which were scheduled to return but never did.

South now, through Miraflores and Castilla and down into the Sechura, a strip of desert that holds the Pacific and the Andes apart for twelve hundred miles. Two tiny patches of it are my central texts. Marks in the sand are the sentences, their meanings unstable, altered daily by wind or rain, by footsteps including my own. I read looking for patterns, the better to see what does not fit them—traces of what was written one night ten months ago.

Of course I do not know if any traces still exist. Stunted algarrobo, thorny scrub, a single candelabra cactus spread-armed in a clearing. The coastal plain is Peru's cholo present, and the mountains are its indio past, and the ocean its future: this is something I have been told many times, usually by drunks in bars. To the extent it is intelligible, it is as much false as true, but there is rarely any point in disagreeing.

Mariángel stands in my lap, plays with the barrettes of the girl sitting in front of us, pulls her hair. The girl turns and smiles. I fight off a wave of nausea, and smile back.

A pacazo on the bank—I will have to remember to tell Reynaldo. I think about the odds of walking beneath one just as it began to defecate, about coincidence. It does not take long to pull up another, the taxi's license plate starting with the first letter of Pilar's name and ending with her age, and when mistaken for causes they can waste years of your life. Even worse, yes, the unrecorded cause that distorts a chain of events like buried ore misleading a compass, and still worse that despotic distance between lacunal source and referential past, between evidence and the act itself, and Mariángel grabs my beard, pulls my face down, forces me to look at her, and at the string of mucus she has extracted from her nose.

The barrette girl has seen and laughs. I catch Mariángel's hand. I hold her finger up to the light. I acknowledge that as mucus goes this is an excellent specimen, wipe it from her finger onto my own, lower the window and flick.

Still half an hour away. No need for sunscreen yet but once I remembered too late and it was two bad days and nights. I take the tube from my knapsack, cover her face and neck. She does not like the smell of coconut, smears as much as she can on my pants. My own face and neck, my arms, more pointing and looking at things in the sky. She cries for a moment, the reason unclear. Then she settles, closes her eyes.

Often Reynaldo accompanies us into the desert. He hopes to find an unknown species of plant or bush or tree, has never yet found one but sometimes finds other things of interest. This weekend he is reforesting somewhere to the east. The university's Outreach Office runs several such programs—solar panels, health clinics, rural education for the poorest. Most weekends they invite me along. I always agree to participate and no one is surprised when I do not.

The foothills are not far away but cannot be seen though the gray-brown haze. In a sense this haze ensured Pilar's death. If the air had been clear she would have seen the Andes and known she was walking the wrong direction.

Here the highway parallels Pizarro's route to Cajamarca. One hundred sixty-eight soldiers, hundreds of enslaved porters, a few interpreters, a few guides. In my first years here I was certain that what was needed to finish my thesis could be found in Cajamarca. Later it was simply a location where work could be done. My last visit, a few months before the wedding, and as we check into our hotel Pilar tells me she has never seen the Ransom Chamber.

The tourist board calls it the city's sole remaining Inca structure: a chaos of old ashlar blocks and new cement. I have already been twice and it is small and bare and today I need other places but Pilar does not want to go alone and so we walk out and along, across and down, then up stairs cut in a gray stone base to the door. We buy tickets, receive brochures. While she looks at the entrance paintings–Atahualpa captured by the Spaniards, imprisoned, proposing terms for his ransom and release—I take out a pen, correct the brochure's facts and phrasing, hand it to a guard.

The guard nods but does not understand, returns the brochure to its stack. Pilar slips in among the other tourists and gazes with them at trapezoidal niches. I follow, push only when necessary, my bulk unwelcome and stared at. Pilar is sad but delighted. I tell her that the actual ransom chamber no longer exists and was not located in this building. Now she glares, turns away.

Mariángel twists in my lap and I interrupt the nearest guide, Atahualpa a hostage yes but also a collaborator, looting his empire to save himself—eleven tons of gold, tooled masks and statuettes, jeweled pitchers and jars, irreplaceable and vanished. But of course he was also hoping for escape or rescue, says the guide, and perhaps believed the Spaniards when they promised him a throne in Quito. How could he have believed them? I say. Yes, says the guide, but desperate men will believe anything.

He nods to me, turns back to his group, my stomach now weak again. I lower the window further, lean my head against the frame and squint into the wind. It is rumored that Rumiñavi is on his way in answer to Atahualpa's call, leads two hundred thousand Inca warriors and thirty thousand Caribs. If this is true then by Spanish lights Atahualpa is guilty of treason, and his execution is thus necessary, justified. Soto is sent to find out, has not yet returned when Pizarro offers Atahualpa a choice of deaths: burned at the stake, or baptized and garroted. Friar Valverde leads the Spaniards in prayer as the cordel tightens at Atahualpa's throat. When it is done Pizarro simulates a state funeral, and already the execution works backward in time, causality reversed, the Inca not a criminal but a fallen king.

The haze thins slightly, the foothills visible but blurred, my headache sharper and then fading and Pilar is missing. I push through a group of Swedes, see her at the door, not leaving, just standing, waiting. I call to her, ask for a few minutes more. She looks away and I find the guide, take his arm. Rumiñavi's army? I ask. Perhaps en route, the guide says, but still distant, or Soto would have seen them. All right, I say, and Soto's lead scout, did he fall off the cliff, or was he pushed? The guide nods. One of many unknowables, he says. Like slivers under our fingernails, I say, and he nods again.

Pilar still waits and I lift Mariángel as she turns, ease her head back down to my knee, wipe the sweat from her temple, from her cheek. I crook my hand above her face to shade her eyes. Blackbirds on a powerline, dunes into the distance. Occasional patches of satuyo lace. A burro pulling a cart loaded with firewood, and competing teleologies, tectonic plates of blame shifting in the historiography. At first Pizarro is the only villain. A decade later he is innocent and fault is split, half for the natives who first spoke of Rumiñavi and half for the interpreters who questioned them. Forty years further along Garcilaso names eleven Spaniards, says they spoke up to stop the execution but few of them were truly in Cajamarca at the time and perhaps Porras is right and Garcilaso brought the story in from Valera who invented it to make Herrada not the knave who murdered Pizarro but the hero who avenged Atahualpa and there is a stench.

I lift slightly, look out the window and back at something

dead on the road, a deer, and the guide leads his group out the door. For a moment the room is empty. I sit on the rough stone floor. Atahualpa, that leather cloak, the skins of vampire bats, in his hands a chalice made from the head of Atoc, his half-brother's general, Atahualpa's captor and torturer but then the escape, the civil war, Atoc falling and later beheaded, the skin dried tight to the skull, a golden bowl mounted and filled, the chicha de jora draining out through a silver spout clenched in his teeth. The guards laugh from their posts at the door of the cell. Atahualpa will never be freed and now knows it. He drinks deeply, offers the chalice to me and someone steps on my hand. Apologizes. I stand, and the man apologizes more thoroughly. I wave it away, should know better than to try to be alone in such places and Pilar, I look, she is gone and I go to the door, out to the sidewalk, and she is nowhere.

I walk quickly down Amalia Puga, a block, two, still nowhere. More quickly still, back up and past the Ransom Chamber and on toward the Plaza de Armas. Dense blue sunlight, thin dry air and I am wheezing, light-headed. I slow, cross the street, and in the shade it is twenty degrees cooler, cold.

Pilar sits on a bench and stares at the Cathedral. I join her. She does not look at me. I wait, lean forward, say that there is time for one more site before lunch, a convent archive on Jirón Ancash, closed the last several times I came and she can help me, or can do something else, whichever she prefers. She still does not look at me. I wait. I say that there is also the Departmental archive in the Belén complex. The earliest files in their Causa Ordinaria subset are from the 1590s and I have worked through most of them already but was hurried and perhaps missed something of importance. The complex is splendid, I say, a seventeenth-century hospital and church, stone carvings, and she holds up her hand. I have been to the Belén complex, she says. You sent me there last time, she says.

There are many small groups of people walking slowly through the plaza, circling the fine fountain in the center. A few palms, and stretches of grass edged with shrubs I recognize but cannot name. A very long and very steep staircase rises up the front of Santa Apolonia to the south. Halfway up the hill is an old blue and white chapel. On the summit is the stone throne from which the Inca observed his massed troops and the view is superb and I will never climb those stairs again.

I look at Pilar, wonder if that is what she wants, to climb. Wonder if I should tell her that she is sitting on or near the spot where Atahualpa was strangled. Wonder who Amalia Puga was, and what she accomplished, and Pilar says that she wants to go to Mass. I think about this. I say that we can exchange our current suite for separate rooms, if she prefers. She looks at me. I ask who Amalia Puga was. A writer, says Pilar. I wait for more. Nothing comes. So, I say. Not everyone has to know everything, she says. It's okay to just come and look. There's nothing wrong with just coming and looking. I say that I am sorry and she says that she knows but that I need to stop.

She is right and I love her for this. A light breeze rises, stirs her hair, and we begin to arrive. I wipe my face, put on my knapsack, lift Mariángel to my shoulder. I do not remember ever asking Pilar about Amalia Puga, and Friar Valverde repents his role, protects the natives as best he can, flees Peru after the second Almagrist coup, is eaten by cannibals on Puná. I get to my feet and wince. I limp forward, and the barrette girl reaches out to touch Mariángel's shoes as we pass.

We come to stand beside the driver. He is not one I have seen before. Mariángel points at the burn scars on his arms and I lower her hand, ask him to stop at the stand of algarrobos ahead. The man looks at the trees, asks if I am sure. I say that I am. The man says that there is nothing in any direction for some distance. I tell him that he is wrong. The man says that getting back to Piura won't be easy. I lower my face to his. I tell him that we will do what we have always done, flag down the first car or truck or bus that passes by. The driver shrugs, slows the bus, stops just past the algarrobos.

Nausea rises again as I step down onto the asphalt shoulder. I take three quick steps, set Mariángel on the ground, turn and vomit into the sand. Wait. Vomit again. A third time. Wait. Mariángel is crying. I spit and wipe my mouth, take her up, whisper until she stops crying.

The day's heat is only beginning, and there are certain clouds. I put on a sling months too small for Mariángel, work her slowly into it, arrange the sunshade over her head and tuck her bottles into their straps. I check my camera's batteries and film. I take a drink from my canteen and start walking.

The path through this mile of desert was faint at first, used only by occasional goatherds. They are the ones who found Pilar. On each trip I clarify the trail to the best of my abilities: I cut notches in cacti, stack rocks, plant crosses.

Along and along through shallow dunes, scattered scrub and grasses. The noise of highway traffic fades. A cabuya low to the ground but eight feet wide, sawtoothed and fleshy, sharp at the tips. More dunes, and the ache in my hip lessens, disappears. Then sudden movement to my right, a lizard five inches long, thin and fast, dark stripes down its side, the head a bright red. It stops, raises up, looks back. A patch of blue on its chest, and I once choked on a lizard of similar size. It was a Western fence lizard. I caught it with a long grass noose and Joel dared me to eat it. Joel was my best and for certain long stretches only friend in Fallash and I can still feel those small claws digging into the sides of my throat. My father administered the Heimlich maneuver and the lizard popped out and ran.

Immense silence now. Scattered low palo santo, ghost gray and leafless, the smell of myrrh thick in the hot air, and I remember the curandero at Huancabamba fanning the smoke in my face, hoping to heal, hoping to cleanse. Tracks here and there—goat, squirrel, ground-dwelling bird. A thicket of faique, the thorns as long as my fingers.

Mariángel starts to cry, and I bring out her juice, but that is not it, and her milk, and that is not it either. Then I check her diaper. I change her in the unsteady shade, put my knapsack back on, push forward. The dust is thick in my eyelashes. More dunes, more scrub, and a hualtaco tree explodes as we pass by, shrieking and wingbeats, the caracara lifting off, black body and mottled chest, white at the throat and wingtips, naked red on the face. Mariángel crying again and the bird arcing back toward us. I hunch down, cover her head with my hands, look around for a nest but do not see one anywhere.

Thirty feet away the bird flares, lands on an outcropping. It rolls its head and snaps it forward, rattles at us. I stand, rattle back, and Mariángel quiets. I rattle again and she smiles. We bluff a charge, Mariángel laughing as she bounces against my chest, and the caracara lifts, shrieks, flies toward the highway.

- They will eat anything, I say, my voice thin and hoarse, strange to me.

Mariángel does not look up.

- Anything, and alive or dead. I have seen them dig for turtle eggs, dig for worms, have seen them attack pelicans over and over until the catch is disgorged.

Now she looks, smiles, reaches back to take hold of my beard.

- They will even chase vultures off of roadkill.

She squints and I fall quiet. The algarrobo grove is a hundred yards away. I slow down, step carefully, search the dunes to either side. Smell of heat, sweat, sand. Smell of rotting meat that fades too quickly to have been real, was some sort of olfactory mirage.

Still slower. Look again. Thirty yards. The trees are threadbare, sparse and thin. Twenty yards, ten. The path widens as it enters the grove. The sand here is no longer stained, no longer bears witness to the night my wife was raped and beaten and left for dead.

Sweat gathers in my beard, on my chest, down the center of my back. I take another drink. Then I weave through the trees, scanning the ground as I go. To the cairn I have built at the far end of the grove. I look out along another trail I have clarified to the best of my abilities. This is the path Pilar walked the next day, walked until she fell and could not rise.

Back to where I entered the grove. Begin a circle. Mariángel twists against my chest, whines, and I put a hand across her forehead, sidestep a columnar and its spines. Again to the starting point, and another circle, this one slightly larger. I must find something, anything, before we can leave. That is the arrangement.

A third circle. Into the densest part of the grove, and now more vegetation underfoot—strands of bichayo, withered borrachera. Halfway around there is a small overo, the broad leaves covered with dust. Mariángel is crying yet again and I squat in the shade, bring out her juice, bring out raisins and crackers, wait as she eats and drinks.

The sand at the base of the trunk is oddly patterned, rivulets as seen from a mile in the air, beautiful. I stand, smooth the rivulets with my boot. My hip has stiffened but does not hurt. Mariángel points, a huerequeque, sprinting away.

Farther and farther out. Mariángel pulls again at my beard and I push her hands away. Deer tracks. A low gray maze of some woody plant, and Reynaldo once told me the name but I have forgotten. I pick my way through. On the far side I find a hard patch of ground three feet across, almost perfectly round, a glittering disc of sand and dried mud.

I walk past it, turn back, step closer. Mariángel whines and I sweat and she whines and I threaten and she whines. The disc is nearly gold from this angle—another sun. Mariángel whines again and I curse her, curse myself, whisper.

The search, curling in on itself as well. I wipe the sweat from my face, neck, hands. Turn away from the disc and walk. Walk and look. Only bushes, grass, only sand and heat. I am so very tired, and there are so many good reasons not to have brought Mariángel. In the future I will come only when I can leave her with Casualidad.

In front of me now is a wide ravine. There is loam in the bed, smooth and dry, and for a few months each year water must come fast from the mountains. I have never yet walked it and not found tracks. At times the species that made them is clear to me and at times it is not. When it is not, if it is early enough in the day, I sketch the tracks as well as I am able and research them the next day at work. Along and along and perhaps today will be the day there are no tracks but then ahead I see the loam disturbed, the thin bands of darker soil. Closer, and it feels as if I already know. Closer and there is no question, dog tracks, a dozen sets or more, intermingled, down and across and disappearing.

I want to move, to walk, but don't, can't, my fault wholly and inexcusably and the dogs found Pilar three miles east of here. She was dead by then, the mortician promised me this, but late at night I have seen it otherwise, Pilar too weak to move, and she can hear the dogs as they come, the lead dog loping up and others and they snap at the backs of her legs. She tries to fight them off but the lead dog seizes her wrist in its jaws, pulls her flat and another sinks its teeth into her face and I scream, gasp, Mariángel screaming too.

I am on all fours in the sand, Mariángel hanging beneath me, fighting at the cords of her sling. I breathe, deeper, slower. Push myself upright. Mariángel cries and I stand, hold her, whisper to her, only sounds. I turn away from the ravine and walk, gather it all around me, the old guilt and the new as well, my fading, my emptying, I gather it and bear it.

The heat stronger, this expanse, the haze. I walk and stare and stop and walk. Nothing. Mariángel still crying and I walk, whisper, walk. Then a copse of palo verde. The trees are twenty feet tall and at least as wide, their green trunks dust-stained brown, their lowest branches reaching almost to the sand, the copse a dense interlocked mass. I know those thorns, have come too close before. I stare, and the mass flattens into latticework, a myth of geometry, of structure, intricate and beautiful and pointless but then a flaw, a crack in the surface at last: half-buried in the sand at the base of one of the trees is a small smooth chunk of black, its curves wrong for natural stone.

I hunch down, gauge the distance, won't be able to reach it from here. I pull Mariángel out of the sling and set her in the wispy shade. I take off my knapsack, go onto my stomach, the sand burning my chest as I crawl forward. The branches bend, strain against me, catch at the sling and my clothes, hold me. I reach and a thorn scrapes down my forearm, draws blood. Mariángel screams and I reach again, stretch, one finger, have it, pull back and take her up.

I whisper to my daughter as I look at what I have found: a flat rubber heel. It could be from either a man's or woman's shoe, is old and worn and weathered, seems unlikely to be relevant but it is something and therefore sufficient. I tuck it into my knapsack and walk back to the algarrobo grove. I search for a loose stone, find one the size of my fist, carry it to the cairn. I set it in place on top, and turn for the highway.

# 5.

THE SHEEP RUN TO THE MIDDLE OF THE PASTURE AND STOP.
Dog or coyote or mountain lion or nothing. I am a hundred
yards away but the moon is full and I can see them clearly.

# 6.

NAKED AND DAMP AND IMMENSE AND MANY-COLORED, I TOWEL
dry and survey the damage. The scrape is infected. I run a
bead of cream along it as if caulking a seam. The sunburn is
minimal, a single parallelogram on my left arm. The bruise on
my hip has eased from purpled black to a blend of browns and
greens and the pain is almost gone.

Trousers, collared shirt, tie: the growing heat is irrelevant
to the university dress code. Then to the kitchen, where
Casualidad has prepared my breakfast and Mariángel's bottle.
I take my daughter, hold her in one arm as I eat. As always
she drinks quickly, perhaps more quickly than she should. I ask
Casualidad if she seems dehydrated or otherwise unwell, and
Casualidad looks, shrugs, says some babies simply drink fast.

When Mariángel is done I set her in her chair and twirl
her hair around my fingers. She pulls away and I nod, bring my
face in close. She hits me in the head with the empty bottle,
throws it and laughs and I think of calling in sick today, every
day, waiting to hear that laugh again but now she reaches for
Casualidad. I kiss her, pick up my briefcase, turn back, then go.

On the far side of the street, a neighbor is finishing the second floor of her house. Barefoot men carry square metal cans of wet cement. They climb bamboo ladders with the cans balanced on their shoulders, never waver as they climb, never fall. There is a tense sweaty peace about them, and the loose mesh of rebar above has been in place for years. Many houses here are left unfinished in this way, most often to avoid certain taxes.

To the corner and across. A glass-encased statue of the Virgin waits as ever on the overgrown traffic divider. Her peace too is tense though it has nothing to do with builders or with roofs except of course the First Rebellion.

The puppet ruler Manco Inca Yupanqui finally understands that the pillaging and torture and rape will never end unless he ends them. When the rains cease, he sends messengers. By Easter the army is too large to conceal. Most of the Spaniards are off inspecting their lands or on new expeditions. Hernando Pizarro sends out seventy mounted soldiers, Manco harries them back and the siege begins: Cuzco surrounded, the Sacsayhuamán citadel occupied, canals destroyed to flood fields, holes dug and camouflaged to cripple horses. I pull out my handkerchief, wipe my neck and hands. There are the smells of roses and brine and if Manco attacks in force—but instead he waits for more warriors, gives the Spaniards time to prepare defenses and supplies. In May at last the Incas come. They load their slings with heated stones and set fire to the thatch roofs of the city. The wind rises. Soon all of Cuzco is aflame, all except the enclosure where half the Spaniards hide, and this is the legend, the Virgin on the roof of Sunturhuasi, putting out the flames.

Stench of the open drain, and no eyewitness mentions her. Titu Cusi writes instead of slaves with buckets, but Garcilaso gives her as fact, and Guaman Poma de Ayala draws her riding a cherubim, water spraying from her palms, the

Incas falling back in terror. A cloud now, and easier walking. The siege weathered three more months. Fish and lizards from Piura dried underground by the Tallán and paid years before in tribute, stored against famine in mountain caches, now spirited into Cuzco. The Spaniards counterattack, retake Sacsayhuamán, Manco's honor guard slaughtered, the natives swimming out into Chincheros Lake to escape and lanced there in the water or captured, the women's breasts and the men's hands cut off.

When the Spaniards are reinforced, Manco runs. The Chachapoya offer refuge, but something is not quite right. They had welcomed Alvarado, fought often on the Spanish side, are perhaps still aligned. Manco turns, spins, settles finally in Vilcabamba and a taxi honks and slows.

The license plate starts with P but ends with 81 and the driver is an old man. Behind it is a garbage truck, two boys hanging off the back, bandanas across their faces. Then a mototaxi, the front half that of a motorcycle and the rear a sort of chariot, plastic and vinyl stretched over a metal frame, and the mototaxi too honks and slows. They are slightly cheaper than regular taxis, slightly slower and much louder. I shake my head and the matacojudo ending is among the finest I have imagined, but now here at the park I look at the empty vines and they seem too thin, too fragile for that sort of work.

Additional means of transportation: combis, which are vans, and colectivos, which are old sedans converted to diesel and often missing several windows. Unless the distance is unreasonable I walk so that taxis will stop, and I have heard that there are restaurants here where small lizards are still on the menu. Ceviche de lagartija. With luck pacazos are sometimes used instead.

Along the edge of the park, and on the far side teenage girls are gathering on the grass for their walk to school. They are dark and bright and lovely, wear the uniform chosen thirty years ago by General Velasco. Few schools still use it. White blouse and black shoes, charcoal skirt and socks, it is the perfect uniform and the girls surely detest it.

Velasco also seized the vastest encomiendas here, gave the land and equipment to cooperatives of the local poor. This was the center of his attempt to redress the past four hundred and sixty years. It failed in most ways but not everyone is sad that he tried, and there is movement far down the street, someone thin and dark and waving perhaps at me.

Closer, and yes, Armando, assistant professor of History, expert on eighteenth-century patterns of inheritance. He is sitting at a table on the patio of Neuquén, a restaurant I have sometimes found useful for beer and grilled meats in the evening. He was helpful in my first years here, had a good sense of what was to be found in each Peruvian archive, was rarely wholly wrong in any respect. He waves each time he sees me, is ebullient in regard to most things.

- Juan de Segovia! he says.

Somehow it still amuses him to call me this. The first time he did so was years ago. He had not known of the conquistador, had transliterated my name for the simple pleasure of hearing it in his language, and the waitress brings his breakfast—a plate of cold cuts, a basket of bread.

- Hello, Armando. Ceviche de lagartija?
- But we would never have ceviche for breakfast!
- I know.
- A joke!
- Of sorts, yes.
- How is your thesis progressing?
- Fine, I say.

This is what I always say. If I am not mistaken, Armando has already had today's first drink. I tell him that I will see him on campus, and he waves again.

A bit faster now—my first class does not begin until

nine, but I am required to be present in my office by eight-thirty. Nothing urgent or important has ever occurred in the course of that first half hour; none of the Peruvians in the English Section have their own offices, and none are paid as highly as me though most are better professors. I wonder why they do not resent me more than they do, and when I first came to Peru I had not planned to stay in Piura for any length of time, meant only to visit the ruins in Morropón, but as I waited for my bus to Cajamarca there was a tug at my arm and I turned, turned back, and my backpack was gone.

Smell of balsam, smell of sweat, and how I would love to find those thieves and squeeze their heads until they burst but then another man, large and clean-cut and friendly: Reynaldo. He was waiting for a bus to Trujillo, saw me spinning, has come to ask if he can be of help. I say that he cannot. He stays regardless and together we confirm that I am here because Peruvian history interests me, that I am from the United States and have been robbed. He speaks slowly and clearly so that I will not misunderstand, requests a phone book at the counter, and while we wait for one to be located he asks me multipart hypotheticals about Michael Jordan and the future of the NBA.

The phone book is brought. Reynaldo copies down for me the address of the police station. Then his bus arrives. He asks what I plan to do. I tell him that I do not know. He looks at me, gives me his card, says that he can promise nothing but the university where he works is often looking for more English professors. I ask about the History department and he shrugs, says that perhaps it is also a possibility. We shake hands. I watch his bus pull away. I possess nothing but my passport and a little money, and my research trip is otherwise over. I walk to the sidewalk, and hand Reynaldo's card to the driver of the first taxi in line.

The smell of turned earth. I thank the History dean for his time, walk out of his office and ask, follow along the white building and across a parking lot and up a path, am led to Arantxa. I ask if she is in need of professors. She says that God has sent me. Not God, I say, but a man at the bus station. Arantxa insists, a dog barks, sun sharp again in my eyes, and I see no reason not to agree. I give her the answers required: native English speaker, M.A., teaching experience, not a felon. She does not care that I do not have a TEFL certificate as long as I plan to get one at some point. I say that I have just been contemplating that very option. She tells me that the summer term starts in two weeks, that she can give me a full load, will pay me hourly for now but switch to a monthly salary in the fall if things work out. I agree though all this makes no sense to me, and won't until I learn that the week before she had to fire her only native speaker, an Uzbek-Canadian named Shukhrat. I will later hear about Shukhrat from many at the university. The things I hear will be meant as warnings. He was polite and smart and pleasant and stole office supplies, smoked marijuana on the roof of the water tower, wrote a weekly underground newsletter comparing the Pope to Stalin.

The work was and is simple. The students are lively and kind. Then Pilar, and three years move past, and perhaps I will see the taxista pull up to the pump at the Texaco station, will approach quietly, strike a match.

Unlikely, ungraceful. I will have to come up with something better, and Sancho's chronicle, Atuahualpa standing in the square, asks Pizarro to watch over his children, and Pizarro promises, steps back, signals the executioner. Months later he sends Atahualpa's brother Quilliscacha to fetch the children from Rumiñavi in Quito. Quilliscacha and his men arrive bearing Atahualpa's body. Rumiñavi welcomes them. The wake begins. He feeds them, bids them drink. Bids them drink more. Bids them drink more and murders them, these collaborators, these rivals. Quilliscacha's bones are crushed and a single incision made, the bone shards extracted, head and hands and feet embalmed as if he'd been a criminal, his body made into a drum and perhaps the process can begin while the victim is still alive.

Two more taxis pass. One of the drivers is too young and the other's face is not dark enough. I turn onto Ucchuracay, and here the sides of many buildings have been left unfinished: broken brick-ends, rough mortar. There are a few finer structures with completed sides, red bricks painted red, whitewashed cement spacers at regular intervals. It is a means of differing.

Across the Panamericana to the Texaco station, check my watch, have only thirty seconds to allot. Taxistas in Piura can rarely afford more than a small amount of gas at a time and so circle the stations like moths. It is not the case that I despise them all. Of course I do not. It is only the one. The others work hard and earn little, like so many here. Most were once shop owners, teachers, engineers. The last taxi I took was driven by a former architect. He told me of a partner who absconded, of bankruptcy, of months of rice and water for him and his wife and their son, of two years selling off-brand soft drinks at stoplights. The weight of the cooler, the rope cutting into his back, fifteen hours a day under this fat despotic sun. Then the move up to brand-name soft drinks—a wonderful day, the man said. Another year, and enough saved to rent a taxi from someone else's fleet. Two years of driving it and then that very week his own taxi, second-hand but solid, a decade of debt but a means now up and out, and he smiled at me, swept his hand from window to window as if showing me a ballroom in a palace.

This morning all the taxis are clearly wrong. I wait thirty more seconds, forty, forty-five. Then past the Río Azul Hotel, across the street, and another hundred yards of heat and pavement along a wall bearing a mural: the establishment of Piura, first Spanish city on the Pacific coast, Francisco Pizarro, his drawn sword.

The mural has faded, the paint flaking in places. The figures are drawn simply, childlike, cardboard armor, plastic sword, a basement full of these things, my old Halloween costumes and my father walking among them, walking and falling, that great heart beating as ever, then ceasing to beat. My mother sees the door left open. Calls down the narrow staircase, knows already, must have known. I drive up from Berkeley. He was still warm when I found him, she says, collapses against my chest. Bearing the coffin. I'd thought it would be lighter. Aunts and uncles, cousins. Grief like whitecaps.

My final night I ask my mother why he had gone down to the basement, what he had intended to do or hoped to find. She says she isn't sure. She asks why it matters and I say that of course it does not.

The drive back to Berkeley, empty. My room, empty. Another week of nothing, then classes and that wild whipping powerline, certainty of the absence of certainty and Juan de Segovia is listed among the founding citizens of Cuzco in March of 1534, returns to Jauja with many of the other conquistadors, and Pizarro parcels out the right to extract tribute from the native populations. Segovia receives no such grant, and here the fog lowers. Has he fallen from favor? Is he planning on returning to Spain with his fortune and health intact? Is he already dead, and if so, how? Disease, battle, accident, so many ways and by the end of the year his death is fact. He has left no will, appears to have left no progeny. He disappears from history and I think of my father's small and absurd lie of love. Perhaps he forgot ever telling it. I wish I had told him: a useful narrative. Carried me at times. Also made me preposterous in new ways and I am now five minutes late.

I check the trees quickly on my way to the Language Center, squat to untie and retie my shoe in front of Arantxa's open door, wave to her, enter my office. I set down my briefcase and lean for a moment against my desk. I scratch the scrape

on my forearm. Then I clutch my stomach, murmur loudly
about intestinal difficulties, walk out and past the bathrooms,
past the deer pen, across toward the chemistry laboratory and
Juan had an uncle, Diego, also a trumpeter. Diego arrives from
Spain, lives for a time with Pedro de Alconchel, attempts to
claim Juan's fortune and is unsuccessful—the Crown's fist once
closed does not open. Stays in Lima. Dies there. His widow
sells his trumpets to natives brought from Mexico to play at
festivals and Reynaldo is standing outside, his hands covered
with wet soil. He is looking at a newly planted tree. If I am not
mistaken, it is a lucuma.

- Hello, Reynaldo. From the Tarma Valley?

Reynaldo squints.

- Or the Mantaro—

- They grow anywhere warm these days. I got this one
from the tree people down at the market.

There is a line of mud across Reynaldo's forehead, dark
circles under his eyes, and perhaps his aunt's health is worse
than usual.

- It is a fine tree, I say.

He nods. Lucuma fruit is not often eaten fresh. Instead
it is sold powdered and used in desserts. It is most Peruvians'
favorite flavor, something like maple syrup, and in the branches
of an algarrobo not far away there is a bird, white and brilliant
yellow across the breast, black wings and tail and face. Its song
flutes up and down the scale. I ask Reynaldo what it is called.

- Chiroca, he says. I think it is some kind of wren.

I have seen many wrens, and none of them looked like this.

- Perhaps you should stick to trees.

The bird flies away. Reynaldo walks to the algarrobo,
runs his hand along the lowest branch. This tree is one of the
first whose genes he helped design, and each generation grows
straighter, faster, with smaller spines, larger pods, more of the
seeds that will become flour or oil or a liqueur that women like

better than men do. He has explained his research processes several times. I do not yet understand the chemistry as such but the processes themselves involve old women and small children, scarification and sifting screens, a gravimetric separator, an immense refrigerator and the eight deer in the pen.

Reynaldo asks what I am doing after work. I say that I have no plans, and he says he will try to think of something for us to do. I know already that he will not be able to think of anything, and that this will not be a problem. I ask how his aunt is doing. He says that she is improving. I nod and ask if a matacojudo vine would be strong enough to garrote a full-grown man.

- I doubt it, Reynaldo says, but there is no harm in trying.

My class will begin late and because it is not my fault I do not care. I stand just outside the classroom door, my Pre-Intermediate students in loose groups around me. I stare in at my friend Günther, who is hunched over the lectern and is pleading, or so it seems from his intonation, pleading in Elementary German.

The bell rings and he continues to plead, his abnormally large hands clenching and unclenching. He is the coordinator for all of the German courses at the Language Center, and teaches them all as well. There are also French and Italian courses, one coordinating professor each. The Italian classes never have more than three or four students, and lose a good deal of money. This is not a problem, is what Arantxa says. It is all part of the university's market share strategy, is what she says.

At last Günther gathers his books and snaps his briefcase shut. He smiles as he comes striding out, envelops my hand in his, walks away. Perhaps what I took to be pleading was something else entirely. I wait for his class to exit, step through to the lectern, fiddle with my notes, watch my students take their seats.

There are brief impromptu warm-up discussions regarding judicial systems and cheesecake. Then as per our coursebook schedule I introduce one possible relationship between the past simple and past continuous tenses when combined in a single sentence.

- It is easy, I say.

My students always believe me when I say this, even when it should be obvious that I am lying.

- The past continuous clause is for background, for context, for fundamental narrative. Then something, some event, interrupts that narrative. This event gets its own clause, past simple.

The students nod, and write in their notebooks. When they are all looking up again, I continue.

- Either clause can come first, as you will see in a moment. There is also the issue of the two relevant subordinating conjunctions, when and while.

I turn, jot two examples on the board, turn halfway back.

- Look here: "The phone rang while I was shaving." Past simple, then *while* plus past continuous, you see?

More nodding, more writing.

- Good. And now with the clauses reversed. Past continuous, then *when* plus past simple. "Manco was playing horseshoes when Méndez stabbed him from behind."

Still more writing, and Juan Carlos raises his hand. He is one of my best students. I nod to him, and smiling broadly he says, The past is never simple.

The students, they have such splendid smiles. I tell them to take out a clean piece of paper and write four hundred words on the disadvantages of happiness. Then I walk out of the classroom. Stand in the hallway. Limp to the nearest bathroom, the nearest stall and sooner or later Arantxa will hear of the essay topic. She will corner me, ask about its role in the curriculum, its immediate pedagogical purposes. My answers will not be good ones, though not as bad as when she asks about what happened at the Pórticos Hotel. She will know that a story of Gillette Girls and blood is not one an archaeologist is likely to tell under such circumstances. She is a smart woman, my boss. She feels sorry for me, and wishes I could be happy.

If my answers are bad enough, it is possible that she will consult with the rector and then fire me, but not probable, as on average my classes outscore all others in the English Section, and we are too close to midterm exams for her to replace me comfortably. More likely she will shout at and forgive me. What she said over the phone is true: I owe her nearly as much as I owe Casualidad. I sometimes regret being so much work for her but she often took hold of my hand before I started dating Pilar, and if I were less work for her she would now perhaps start taking my hand again. She would of course fire me instantly if she ever learned of Jenny but that will never be the case. Arantxa is as incapable of imagining her professors visiting brothels as the Incas were of imagining gunpowder.

I squeeze my stomach with both hands, knead at the rolls of fat. Diego Méndez. Sides with Almagro the Younger against the Crown, imprisoned but escapes, one of seven who beg Manco Inca for sanctuary, are taken in, his guests for nearly two years. Then a new Viceroy in Lima—a chance for the seven to work back into royal favor. Manco's turn to throw and Méndez comes in behind, slides the dagger into his back. Titu Cusi, nine years old, watches his father fall. The seven surround him as well. They cut but fail to kill him, ride for Lima not quickly enough. I trace the scrape on my forearm, the warm red line; I knead again at my stomach, wait and hope. Twenty years later the seven heads still on display and I do not understand how it is that my students do so well. When other professors ask, which is not often, I tell them that it is surely not a matter of the late sixteenth century once again, not natives filling churches because they think Dios has conquered Viracocha, that my students were most probably the strongest to begin with, sought and seek me only for the accent.

This may or may not be true—I have not done the relevant regressions. My students study as if they believe that English will save them. I do not know why they would believe this. I have never implied such a thing.

# 7.

Romeo says, Alas, that love, whose view is muffled still, should, without eyes, see pathways to his will! Where shall we dine? Oh me! What fray was here? Yet tell me not, for I have heard it all. Here's much to do with hate, but more with love. Why, then, o brawling love! O loving hate! O any thing, of nothing first create! O heavy lightness! Serious vanity! Mis-shapen chaos of well-seeming forms! Feather of lead—Dost thou not laugh?

Then Benvolio says, No, cuz, I rather weep.

Piura has only one cinema. The cinema has only one screen. The screen offers three showings per day but all of the same film, that film being all that is shown for days or weeks and in some cases months.

We arrived an hour early as always. Mariángel drank her milk and I scanned license plates and failed. If I had seen and recognized the taxista, I would of course not have confronted him. We would simply have taken the next taxi to come along, followed for as long as was required to obtain all necessary details.

The woman who sells tickets at the window in front works rosary beads back and forth. Her lips continue to move even as she takes bills, makes change. The lobby is lined with posters but they are not necessarily for films that have come to Piura, or ever will. Mariángel leans back against me, and Capulet tells Paris that Juliet is too young to be married.

What he says is true, anyone could see it, though things may have been different in Verona, and Peruvian girls often marry at her age or younger. The manager who tears tickets carefully in half is as big around as I am but shorter by half a foot. I have never seen him smile. Perhaps this is because we always come on Wednesdays, when two persons enter for the price of one.

Here deeper inside I searched faces and failed and the air smells of ammonia and mildew and sweat. Mariángel yawns. My students have told me that this film is very good, so I assume it will be bad, though this is not always the case. *12 Monkeys,* for example, was a film they liked, and it was a fine film.

I believe that the ammoniac smell is the result of bats. The cinema is full of them. Mariángel and I do not mind. They eat the mosquitoes that also dwell here, and make horror movies more realistic.

Today was hotter than yesterday. Tomorrow will be hotter still. As is the case with all cinemas with which I am familiar, it is a few degrees cooler inside than out, and Benvolio attempts to convince Romeo to attend Capulet's party. He leers as he tells of the women waiting there, and a bat flies across his forehead. This is a complicated coincidence: the Spanish word for bat is murciélago, and the word for womanizer is mujeriego. Their roots have nothing in common, but I once made the mistake of saying Womanizing Man when I meant to say Batman. Everyone smiled, and for weeks I repeated the mistake as a joke.

Lady Capulet speaks of delight writ with beauty's pen. Mariángel turns, curls in toward my chest. Unless this film is unlike all others she will sleep through to the end, a remarkable thing given what is certain to come—our fellow spectators' angry whistling every time the projector breaks down, their excited discussion of each unexpected shift in plot, their shrieks and screams at bats.

Mariángel and I arrive early not only to search and scan, but also to get the best seats. The films here start precisely on schedule. They are the only events in Piura that do.

Mercutio wears a curly white wig, a mirror-sequin miniskirt, speaks of Queen Mab and goes manic. Of all rows the eighth is the best. It is far enough from the front not to cause nausea, far enough from the back that the teenagers who sit in the balcony would need better aim to hit me with the things they throw. I am thankful that baseball is not popular in Peru.

This film was released in the United States a year ago and arrived in Piura last Thursday. Watching it is thus somewhat like reading the newspaper in a remote highland village. The newspapers arrive months late, and not always in chronological order. One walks to the store on the plaza—even the smallest village has a plaza, and even the smallest plaza has a store—and asks for whichever day's newspaper has arrived. They contain not news but history, and perhaps the residents keep extensive diaries, check them against the horoscopes.

Let lips do what hands do and yes some hands pray lest faith turn to despair. Pilar and I came to the cinema monthly or nearly so. At first I thought that I would be fired if anyone learned I was dating a student, so Pilar and I would come each with a separate group of friends, would sit at the inside edges of our respective groups, as close as possible to one another such that during scenes of great dark intensity we could safely hold one another's hands.

I believed we were hiding successfully but she knew

that everyone knew, and now the balcony. Romeo uses the same words as in the play, though fewer of them. This should feel wrong but for some reason does not and there are of course Romeos and Juliets in all places and times. Even the Incas had them or seem to have: the end of *Miscelánea Antártica*, Cabello Balboa's telling of Quilaco and Curicuillor, forbidden and unlikely love, families at war, corpses piling higher and again love.

The man sitting to my right has a camera in his lap. If at any point a naked or half-naked woman appears on the screen, he will start taking photographs. He will not be the only spectator to do so, an inexplicable thing given how easily pictures of nude women can be obtained from most newspapers here. It is not strictly speaking a problem, as Mariángel will sleep through the flashes and clicks as well.

*12 Monkeys* was the last film Pilar and I saw together. We were hiding nothing by then, were married, Pilar seven months pregnant. We held hands throughout, held them even for the whore-and-dentist scene, and Father Lawrence says, O mighty is the powerful grace that lies in plants, herbs, stones, and their true qualities: for nought so vile that on the earth doth live but to the earth some special good doth give, nor aught so good, but strain'd from that fair use revolts from true birth, stumbling on abuse. Virtue itself turns vice, being misapplied; and vice sometimes by action dignified, and the projector breaks down as Romeo arrives. Our fellow spectators whistle predictably loudly. Mariángel shifts but does not wake. I have yet to see a film here during which the projector did not break down and Father Lawrence is right— there was the ayahuasca.

There are perhaps as many fleas in the cinema as there are mosquitoes. It is a shame that bats do not eat fleas as well and the civil war between Huáscar and Atahualpa has not yet begun. Quilaco is a handsome young officer, blood relation to both men. Atahualpa sends him as emissary to Huáscar and in the Queen Mother's house he meets Curicuillor, most beautiful of Huáscar's daughters, raised here in secret to keep jealous courtiers from poisoning her as they had her mother.

Quilaco and Curicuillor, instant love, of course, but Huáscar rejects the peace offering, murders most of Quilaco's men. Quilaco promises to return as soon as he is able, and for four years Curicuillor waits, holds herself chaste. Then she dresses as a man, joins the army, goes to find Quilaco and the projector is repaired but the film has skipped forward: Romeo stands between Tybalt and Mercutio.

Mariángel flinches at each gunshot, nearly wakes, and before we entered the cinema tonight I was for a moment sure that I had seen Jenny. The bad light went momentarily bright in long blonde hair. The sharp curve of an eyebrow. A smile almost certainly hers but then a group of students, some mine and some otherwise.

I was obliged to greet them. When they were gone so was Jenny or the woman who resembled her and that is as it should be. Curicuillor finds Quilaco bleeding to death on a battlefield near Jauja, nurses him toward health and brings the news: Atahualpa victorious in the civil war but taken prisoner and murdered by foreigners, and one of them, Hernando de Soto, is lodged nearby.

She convinces Quilaco that there is no reasonable option except to seek Soto's favor. Quilaco does, and it is granted; Soto even sponsors their baptism and marriage. Bliss, of course. Then two years later Quilaco dies, Curicuillor gives herself to Soto, and a daughter, Leonor, is born to them. All this Cabello Balboa gives as true story faithfully told and of course it is as false and true as what we watch, Romeo climbing in through Juliet's window, and I am suddenly exhausted.

Camera flashes here and there as clothing sloughs off. Mariángel shifts and sweats, heavy against my shoulder, then wakes, unprecedented thing. She flails but I sing to her, Deep Purple. Slowly she calms and Cabello Balboa's work is all but done, the Incas fitted in time and place and teleology as descendents of Noah. He has added the story of Curicuillor and Quilaco to complete the book with love, he says, but of course he also had a king to please, and the Conquest's violence to reframe.

Something else, Woody Woodpecker, a gathering noise, and I wake as Romeo barricades the doors to the cross-filled crypt. He walks to where Juliet lies. Her hand twitches. He doesn't notice. His grief rends him and he speaks of everlasting rest. He takes out the vial of poison, and it is unclear why he needed it as he already had a gun.

One by one those around me begin to suspect that in this version too, Juliet will not wake soon enough. They watch Romeo open the vial. Oh no! they shout. This is actually what they shout, the very words.

# 8.

The days pass by like cattle. They stare at you, draw close if they think you will feed them. They smell of grass and sweat, and bring flies.

# 9.

Mariángel sits in the flowerbed at the base of the garden wall. She clears leaves from a spot in front of her. She pats the mud smooth, molds it into hills, takes up a stick and cuts tiny terraces as if hoping to grow tiny corn.

Now she stands, stomps the hills flat and from the street comes a blaring of car horns. I wait, know the next sound to come and it comes: the hoarse chorus of strays in the streets. My neighbors' dogs answer, rage from rooftops, strain at chains in front yards. On bad days the dogs bark at every child, every maid, each car and bus and bike. Today one by one they fall quiet, and because it is a Sunday what comes next is not silence but vendors.

An hour ago it was men selling tanks of propane from the bed of a truck. The men called loon-like, echoing each other sadly through the neighborhood. Then a knife grinder, and the screech of his stone wheel against steel. Now fruit vendors. At least three, maybe four. They circle through the streets, their microphones rigged to speakers hanging from the tarpaulin roofs of their carts. Buenos pepinos! they shout, and the windows of my house begin to rattle. Buenos melones pepinos melones, hay limas hay piña hay plátanos de seda, pepinos plátanos naranjas, plátanos pepinos buenos plátanos.

More barking. The conquistadors brought dogs with them, wolfhounds and mastiffs bred for war, and found other kinds of dogs already here. One native species is hairless and thin and rat-tailed. It is blotched pinkish and gray in the winter as if diseased, and dark brown or black in the summer. In Tallán it is called viringo, in Quechua ccala, in Spanish among other possibilities calato. All of these words mean naked. The Chavín and Moche and Wari and Chimú put its likeness on their jewelry and ceramics. The Huanca offered its meat to their gods. The Incas kept them as pets, believed in their magical ability to calm stomach pain.

Mariángel scratches her face, leaves a stripe of mud down one cheek. Curanderos still prescribe drinking the dogs' blood fresh to calm asthma, applying its saliva to cuts and its urine to freckles, embracing its warm cadaver to cure typhoid and pneumonia, the powdered ash of its skull as cure for gangrene, its brains raw to repair stroke damage, and one such dog wanders past my house from time to time. It fights often and poorly. It bleeds at the mouth, limps from corner to corner, sleeps in the shade of the Virgin. When I first moved here I thought it was the ugliest dog in the world. In fact it is not even the ugliest dog on my block.

I go to my daughter, wipe the mud from her face. Then there is movement at the back door. Fermín is waiting just inside. I welcome him into the yard, ask why he didn't come yesterday with Casualidad as usual, ask if perhaps he had a soccer match, and if so, did it go well? Fermín stares at the ground. There is no point but I repeat the question. Fermín murmurs unintelligibly, and from the street a fruit vendor sings Plátanos piña pepinos, hay limas pepinos papayas, hay plátanos de seda.

I return to my chair. Fermín takes up the rake, tears at the lawn's skin of dead leaves, and Mariángel begins another set of terraces. She finishes well before he does, takes hold of his pantleg as he passes by, points to the hose. He smiles, tells her that he cannot water yet, that it is not time, that first all the leaves must be gathered and borne away. Mariángel pulls herself to her feet, points at the hose again. Fermín shakes his head but she will not have it, squcals, and finally I suggest a new sequence for today: water this one flowerbed, finish with the leaves, water the rest of the yard.

Fermín first hesitates to let me know that this seems wrong to him. Mariángel watches as he covers the terraces with water, claps when they collapse and Fermín laughs, says they were the best terraces he has ever seen. I listen for the fruit vendors. Instead I hear an ice cream cart, the bicycle horn worked ceaselessly and the dogs start up again.

Now the newspaper. Page by page and as always there is nothing of use. Then Mariángel is at the radio, reaching with her muddy hands and I stretch, too late, the radio on, salsa flaring from the speakers. I turn it off and wipe the mud from the console. I explain to Mariángel that Piura is already so much louder than a city its size should be.

She starts to cry. I pick her up and she pushes at my face, cries louder. I surrender though I know I should not, turn the radio back on, dance with her tight against my chest, take her by the wrists and swing her back and forth.

The next song is merengue. I bring her again in close, and we spin madly. Finally I am sweaty and she is tired and Fermín is done. The lawn is a leafless lake. He stands at the spigot, coils the hose sadly: watering is his favorite activity. I offer him a sandwich and some orange juice, and he nods without looking up, waits on the patio, eats and drinks in silence, murmurs what is most likely thanks.

I give him twenty soles and he smiles at the tree. Mariángel and I walk him to the front door, thank him, wave goodbye. Mariángel waves goodbye to me as well, and I watch as she toddles toward her bedroom. Hay pepinos hay piña, pepinos y piña y plátanos. I wait for the vendor to call out that he has mangos as well, but of course he does not. Mango season does not begin for another month.

I start the bathwater and go to Mariángel's room but she is not there. Now I hear splashing outside. I run to the patio. She stands in the corner of the flooded lawn, the water above her ankles. She is holding a doll not quite her own size—a plastic Inca princess, golden-skinned, bald and naked, her hair and clothing lost to a stove burner weeks ago.

Mariángel ignores me when I call to her. She ignores me again when I curse and step toward her, throws the doll as I lift her. She screams all the way to the bathroom, quiets when she sees the water running, laughs as she plays with the small bright water rings, screams again when I lift her from the tub, and I finish drenched and bitching. Then I remember to sing, Chabuca Granda, softly. At last Mariángel calms. I set her in the crib, bring her bottle. I watch until she closes her eyes, and return to the patio.

The sun strikes the water, the glare hits me full in the face, but there is something near the far wall, something shining, a tiny figure. And of course—the doll somehow upright in the shallow water. But in the instant before I knew this, it was something else: Punchao.

The doorbell rings. Whoever it is will leave soon enough if I make no sound but Sundays are bad days for doorbells. Punchao, Quechua for daybreak, the sun's first ray striking in through Andean peaks. Punchao, God of Day. Punchao, a gold statue, the form of a ten-year-old boy but the size of Mariángel.

Again the doorbell and perhaps it is the man who collects empty bottles. He comes most Sundays and is at times insistent. Pachacutec expands the empire, revives the sun cult, claims a dream or vision: a shining child, Punchao. The statue's sandals and circlet also gold. Sits within a silver pavilion. From the pavilion extends a cloud of gold medallions. When the sun strikes the medallions, the reflections are so bright that the figure can barely be seen.

Statue and pavilion rest on a cloth of iridescent feathers, this cloth on a golden disc six feet across, and the statue's chest is hinged. Inside the chest cavity is a gold chalice. Inside the chalice are the rough-ground hearts of past emperors and again the motherfucking doorbell.

I go, look out the peephole, see no one. This means it is either children or Hugo, a deaf midget who holds a piece of paper saying, "I have nothing to eat, and one sol would be fine, or ten soles if you wish." I open the door half an inch. The stoop is empty and I walk back to the patio.

For one hundred and thirty years each Inca seeks the Punchao's guidance, claims to hear it speak. It is carried on a litter for all ceremonies. It sleeps in the company of princesses. Spread out before its altar are gold and silver vessels filled daily with maize and meat and chicha de jora and one morning the conquistadors arrive at the gates of the Coricancha. They push the Inca priests aside. They walk through the temple to the central garden: silver cornstalks, and the corn ears solid gold. Beyond is another room, the altar tended by mamaconas and here the cloud of medallions, the silver pavilion, Punchao.

The Spaniards post guards but somehow the statue is slipped out past them, borne first toward Chachapoyas and then to Vilcabamba. This final Inca fortress so distant, so nearly inaccessible, and the Spaniards come all the same. In the end it is Hurtado de Arbieto leading two-hundred fifty mounted soldiers, two thousand native auxiliaries. Battle at Coyao-chaca, battle at Huayna Pucará. Túpac Amaru and his retinue chased down into the Amazon basin. His son captured. His brothers, daughters, and now the Punchao is taken. Túpac Amaru and his wife still uncaught. Deeper and deeper into the jungle, they run and run but his wife, and a dog barks once, again, quiets.

Others who have not yet come but surely will: those seeking donations to help street-children return to school; to help the French Alliance arrange more and better concerts; to help feed the men and women at the Centro de Reposo San Juan de Dios, a lunatic asylum up the street whose acronym for unclear reasons is CREMPT. Some who come sell bittersweet candy at twice its true price. Some only hold out their hands.

The medallions are cut off, and the statue is shipped to the king as a gift for the Pope. It might still exist, hidden in some Vatican storeroom or palace vault. Hay limas hay papayas, plátanos piña naranjas, hay limas pepinos y plátanos. I dream the vendor on his three-wheeled cart, his water bottle in a dirty plastic bag suspended from the handlebars, the tarp stretched taut across the bamboo frame. The papayas here can grow to the size of watermelons. The sun now behind a cloud, the doll only a doll. My garden wall, smooth and white and fifteen feet tall, lined with broken glass and useless.

Behind the wall is a warehouse of some sort. It appears to be and perhaps is abandoned—it has been years since I've heard the sounds of storage. I suspect that the burglars come through or along it, climb ladders, lay empty rice sacks over the broken glass, vault across into my yard.

The cloud slips east. The shards of glass go bright with sunlight caught and colored. In truth the burglars do little damage: my few appliances were bought secondhand and cheap, there is a roving market where they can be recovered still more cheaply, and I do not keep much cash in the house. All the same it pleases me to think of them seeing me on the street, noting the color of my skin and imagining me rich, following me home and breaking in only to discover that Mariángel and I possess mainly books and plush toys.

Even if I wished to, I could not hate them as much as I hate the huaqeros. Like me the huaqeros read the desert as text, but they are searching for clues to a far simpler narrative.

They come with shovels, iron rods, kerosene lamps. They dig into each dirt mound, prod at the sides of the tunnels. If they have read correctly the mound is a burial site and the rod slides cleanly into the cache. The archaeologists arrive days or months later. They preserve the scraps, study the fouled context, the fouling itself now part of history and how I would enjoy gathering the world's huaqueros and beating them to death with a mattock, one by one.

At times there is little or nothing for them to sell. Farmhands search for fresh pasture near Laguna de los Cóndores, glance up at limestone cliffs, see a row of Chachapoya tombs. In a week Pilar will be murdered. They climb, secure themselves, draw their machetes and slash at the bundled remains. No precious metals, no gems. The farmhands shrug and climb back down. Later a museum will be built in Leymebamba to house the mutilated skeletons, textiles, quipus. I have not yet gone, hope to at some point, have not yet decided if I must.

At other times there is a great deal to be sold. Early 1987 outside Sipán, a slumping set of pyramids thought to be Chimú. A tunnel into the smallest pyramid advances down through two layers of guardians: one of canine skeletons, another of humans with their feet amputated to forestall abandon. The huaqeros hit a vein of ceramic pots once filled with food and drink for the dead. Then a first tomb, four skeletons covered with semiprecious jewelry.

Still deeper, and lateral tunnels branching. A layer of stonework, another of soil blended with cinnabar. Ernil Bernal, the lead huaqero, sees an unlikely textural variation in the tunnel wall. He prods at it, and the wall collapses, and he is buried in dirt, silver, gold.

His brother pulls him out. The others reinforce and extend, begin filling their sacks, are crazed by their sudden fortune. Night after night they return. But Sipán is too small for such a secret, and other rumors start as well—betrayal, kidnapping, murder. A week later the police raid the Bernal house and find a single sack of artifacts. The rest is gone, on its way to the private collections of rich men here and elsewhere.

Midnight. The police look through what they have found. They call an archaeologist, the director of a local museum. He has bronchitis, has not slept in three days. He tells them that whatever it is can wait until morning.

The officers say, No, no, we do not believe that it can. They describe the objects they hold and the archaeologist is out of bed and dressing. Arrives at the police station. Lifts the pieces, one and then another. Not Chimú but Moche, seventeen hundred years old, a discovery like none since the Conquest and impossible, the Spaniards and yanaconas so thorough in their scouring, impossible but here the pieces are.

Hay limas pepinos melones hay manzanas. I shift in my chair, my own breath loud from my chest. The police lead the archaeologist to the site and word has spread: huaqeros swarm the pyramids. The police have machine guns. The huaqeros run, stop, turn back. The archaeologist watches and knows there is no time for proper channels. He must simply start digging.

I have not yet finished my coursework, lack the proper background, watch my colleagues devour the discovery and the police raid the Bernal house a second time. Ernil runs, is gunned down, or so the story is told. Smell of sewage, of jasmine, keen of a hawk that circles too high to be seen. Half of Sipán is camped around the site. The villagers claim all artifacts as ancestral inheritance. They claim Bernal as martyred saint. They threaten to kill the archaeologist if he continues.

The archaeologist knows this calculus. He hires the loudest villagers as guards. In the main chamber he finds another body, and beneath it another chamber, a copper-banded coffin, the royal tomb. A gold death mask. A gold headdress. Pectorals and necklaces of scarlet chaquiras and gold.

The doorbell rings and I twist, cough, and already the

plan is failing: more villagers each day. One morning they surge, are barely driven back by tear gas. The archaeologist walks to the edge of the dig, cuts a hole in the barb-wire fence. He calls one of the villagers forward. He grabs the man by the lapels, drags him in through the hole, tells him to go get his inheritance.

The man does not move. The hundreds lean in toward them. Smell of dust and heat and the archaeologist takes hold of him again, drags him to the very pit. Puts a shovel in the man's hands. Dares him to dig.

The man drops the shovel, steps back. The hundreds fall quiet, but soon they will begin stoning the archaeologist and his team as they arrive each day. Limas naranjas pepinos papayas, plátanos limas pepinos and of course a new museum is worth little when one's village has no school and the roads are mainly unpaved. Broken glass glints at the top of the wall. I hear a slight sound, something soft brushing against something softer. I wait. Nothing more comes, and it was my imagination or else the curtains moving in the breeze of a fan, and now a flash of color in the tree.

It is a putilla, lovely bird, tiny bright point of red. I see them often on campus, always in pairs. I wait for this one's mate to come. Nothing moves. The putilla rests on a low branch. It looks at me, then flies away.

The closest city to Sipán is Chiclayo: the city where Pilar was born and raised. From Piura it is an easy bus ride south. Two years ago she took me to meet her family. Her three brothers all teach English at local institutes, and during lunch that first day we discussed methodology and technique, but there was an oddness to their talk, a straining after sentences.

Pilar and her mother left for Mass, and the rest of us went to the living room—the father and I in overstuffed chairs, the three brothers on the couch in descending order of height. There it was made clear that an interrogation was forthcoming, that all would be made known and judgment rendered, but there had been pisco sours before lunch, and beer with lunch, and now there was whiskey. Before the first question had been clearly phrased, all five of us were asleep.

We woke when the women returned. The oldest brother then said, I hope, John, that everything is perfectly clear between us. I assured him that it was and the next morning we went to Sipán. The father drove slowly in their ancient sedan. Pilar sat beside him, me beside her, the mother and brothers mountained in the back seat.

At first it was absurd. The mother gasped at each piece. The brothers pulled at my elbows. But the work: the paired necklaces of goldplated copper, one of joyful faces and one of faces caught in death; the high priest's crown and its owl, the wings spread wide; the earspools, deer of turquoise with antlers and hooves of gold; and over and through it all the degollador, the executioner, his fangs, degollar, to rip out someone's throat.

Back to the car, and to the dig. The archaeologist himself at work. I send my letter of introduction in with a guard and the archaeologist does not come but lends us an assistant. We all walk together. Pilar and her family suffused with good pride and the owl, yes, another Moche executioner. I have since seen a ceramic pot bearing scenes of human sacrifice and the coming rain, the sacrifice causing the rain or else celebrating it, and the owl presiding, god of warriors, displaced later by condor and vulture but now in the night air before me and Jenny, her exclamation point, the owl and I open my eyes.

Silence. Broken glass, arrozeros, silence. Then plátanos piña pepinos, hay limas hay pepinos hay plátanos de seda. When the voice quiets I hear something from inside the house, not soft but sharp and flat, not curtains or my imagination so I go.

Mariángel is sitting on the floor beside a bookcase. It is not clear how she has gotten out of her crib without hurting herself, or why she has come here instead of seeking me. She is chewing on the corner of Basadre's *Perú: Problema y Posibilidad*.

Perhaps it is a matter of teething and this book is the perfect size.

The teethmarks would bother me more if the text had better weathered time. She yawns, was likely only feigning sleep before. I walk her back to her room, and lower the crib mattress to its final setting. I check her gums and see no swelling; I take her up, turn in slow circles and sing, Mercedes Sosa this time, "Si se calla el cantor." When Mariángel appears wholly asleep I poke her to make sure, then lay her down, work the book out of her hands and a stuffed alpaca into them.

I gather the other books she has dislodged, put them back in place. Domingo Angulo, Rostworowski, Ginzburg, Pérez de Tudela and my father's lie working: not a popular child, fatter and fatter each year but also stronger and stronger, not unagile, no longer afraid. I believe I did not lose another fight, and once or twice even sought them. My parents heard me tell other children of my ancestor the conquistador and said nothing. I think that at first they saw the lie as doing too much good and too little harm to correct, and surely my needs would wither.

Instead they grew, branched, became beautiful. In the Berkeley stacks it was no longer the Spaniards but their allies— Huanca, Cañari, Chachapoya. To this day there are regions in Peru that celebrate not the Incas but the local culture they destroyed, and there is a final book to put away, Prescott's flawed classic. It was among the many my mother mailed down when I said I was staying. One box had a letter taped to the top, the house so empty now, but the flowers in the garden and the ducks by the lake, and sitting on the bookcase is the old rubber heel I found last week in the desert.

I do not know why it is here. It should not be here, should be boxed with the rest. There is no reason for me to have left it here but I cannot simply store it now: it has been too long since I did the right work.

For the moment Piura is silent. If Mariángel wakes

before I am done I will not have the strength to sing her back to sleep. I get the key from its hook in the kitchen and go to the linen closet. I open the padlock, turn the knob, step forward as the stack of boxes tilts.

I ease the top box to the floor, bring the second one down, the third and fourth, spread them around the doorway. I lift the fifth, carry it to the center of the room. If I still had all I have found, I would need another closet, another padlock, but in the early months I took what appeared most salient to the police. They thanked me on each occasion, and smiled. I took them less and less over time. When they closed the investigation last month, I went to reclaim what I had given. They said they had no idea.

The oldest box first. I take its objects one after another. I hold and observe each for a moment, then set it on the floor. Slowly the grid is formed. Working down through the box in this way comes always to feel archaeological, the mattocks of my hands digging from one soil horizon to the next, but of course it is not, can never be, the artifacts' stratigraphic context here not that of their proper events but of my finding them and therefore nearly useless.

For a time I gathered fewer artifacts than specimens. There were many labeled bags in my freezer: hair, bloody bandage, used toilet paper, a fingernail clipping found on a bar counter. A month ago my freezer failed as all things fail and the evidence turned to rot.

I am left with twigs broken at unlikely angles. Paper towels blotted with motor oil. Shreds of cloth, lengths of thread. Filthy combs and brushes. Wads of aluminum foil filled with dirt of unnatural colors. Bits of plastic that I cannot readily identify—three dozen from the first box alone.

The doorbell rings, rings, another box and another, through to the fifth, and in addition to the artifacts there are photographs. Shots of streaks of yellow paint on trees and fence posts and the sides of buildings. Shots of yellow taxis missing streaks of paint. Shots, often blurred, of men who in some way resemble the driver whose face I believe I remember.

Now, finally, the new heel. I hold it and close my eyes and ask impossible things of it: a superstition, stupid, and nothing comes. I look more closely. The rubber is hard and scarred, cracked and flaking. Small holes where nails once were. Bits of failed glue. The heel is worn thin on the outside, indicating that the wearer supenates. The rubber is darkest black deep in the cracks, indicating nothing at all.

I count across the floor. This is the ninth black rubber heel I have found. I place it in the farthest corner. I climb onto the table and scan the grid for pattern or path the way a police officer might, a detective or judge. I look for anything that might cohere or correspond to a truth from that night. For some remnant of the tissue that once connected anything to anything else.

And nothing. As always, as every time I have done this, once a month since Pilar's death and every single time there is nothing. I close my eyes. The table creaks. Limas pepinos melones plátanos, hay manzanas y mangos but there is no vendor, I listen and there is no vendor.

I look again at the grid, stare until my eyes ache. The room laid out like this in squares, the colors shifting and now the floor is plots of pasture as seen from the air. Autumn or winter or spring; early morning or late afternoon. Cloudless sky, approach from the south. Oblique angle to the ground, shooting and looking for soilmark, cropmark, shadowmark, frostmark, and for a moment it is there, the pattern, it fades but then returns, and an intimation of something, something opening as the legs snap and the table collapses, throws me to the floor, the evidence scattered, twig and cloth and comb, the same goddamned hip as before and Mariángel screams from her crib.

# 10.

THIS MORNING ARANTXA'S OFFICE SMELLS ONLY OF SWEAT AND talcum, and the talcum is visible, a faint blur in her cleavage. I hand her the exams I have prepared for the upcoming midterms. She drops them in a drawer, tells me to close the door and sit down, asks about the Pórticos Hotel.

I am tempted to ask for her sources and to argue for their epistemological instability, for the impossibility of uniting outside of time a fact and its documentation, of mapping a memory to the instantiation of its content, but the chair she has set out for me is unpadded and narrow and this is not unintentional. I explain about bruising. I exchange the chair for a wider one from the far side of her office and sit gently. Then I tell her three truths among dozens: the archaeologist's idiocy, my boredom, a drink or two too many.

- Sooner or later, she says, the rector will find out, and you will be fired. I won't be able to protect you. It will be out of my hands.

Arantxa is nearly always right, and her use of idiomatic expressions is in general impeccable. Impeccable: an odd word in English, but not in Spanish. Pecado is Spanish for sin. There must be some relation.

- And if you ever do it again, she says, I'll fire you myself.

Arantxa does not threaten often or idly. I tell her that I will try to be more careful.

- It's not a question of being careful. Why would you do a thing like that?

I tell her that I am not sure, and that it does not matter, as my story was more amusing than any of the archaeologist's anecdotes. She asks if I wish to speak with a doctor or counselor or priest. I say that I have nothing against doctors or counselors or priests, and also no desire to speak to them. She says nothing. I stand. She shakes her head and I sit back down.

- Also, two weeks ago you gave an essay assignment that could be understood as an attack on Catholic doctrine and university principles.

- Yes. And given the students' level of English, it was also far too long. Has your diarrhea cleared up?

- Please don't do it again, she says.

- It was really more a case of lesson plan confusion than—

- Don't do it again.

I thank her, say pointlessly that I need to get back to my office. She turns to her paperwork and I stand again and go. There are only twenty minutes before my next class, but here, within limits, if one is not at the lectern one is expected to be in one's office, to be perpetually welcoming. Arantxa chastised me when I first attempted to block off specific hours for student appointments. I pointed out that it is only the relatively fixed positions of stars that allow us to navigate, however poorly. She began a sentence, smiled and walked away. I have since learned what she nearly said: assigning specific hours has no bearing whatsoever on what time students arrive.

My students come often and rarely wish to discuss class. They come to ask for donations to help their department buy the flower arrangements they wish to present to the Virgin on the days such things are done. They ask me to aid with the transcription and translation of the songs on the tapes their cousins send them from Los Angeles or Trenton. They ask for my assistance in filling out applications for scholarships and graduate study in the United States or Europe, and do not understand how little I can help, and are frequently successful in spite of me.

To fill the hours when no student happens to come, I first put my name on the waiting list to use the one computer in our office that is connected to the internet. Then I write quizzes and take-home exercises. I correct essays and read the newspaper. I imagine ways to enrich the Resource Bank, and once a week I visit the deer pen.

This is a remnant of a custom from before Pilar and I were engaged but after we had begun. She would be waiting, and I would come to stand beside her, unbearably, and she would smile. One day there I told her of the last great Inca hunt. Manco Inca and Pizarro allied for the moment, Quisquis routed and fleeing for Quito, and to celebrate Manco brings ten thousand warriors, sets them in a circle ten miles wide, and in the course of eight days they draw inward toward a single valley. The enclosure tightens and tightens until the warriors can join hands. Manco invites Pizarro and fifty other Spaniards to watch or join in, and they do so but mounted and in battle gear, afraid they are meant as prey.

Inside the circle are thousands of deer and hares, vizcachas and chinchillas, vicuñas and guanacos, foxes and pumas and bears. The Incas kill and skin the predators. They shear and release the vicuñas and guanacos. Of the rest they begin with the sick and weak and old, supplement these with healthy animals as needed for meat or fur, eleven thousand head of game in all, beat them to death and free the rest.

I told Pilar all this and she was intrigued or pretended to be. Then I asked her to marry me. She asked me why she should. I said that she probably shouldn't. She said she knew and would regardless.

These deer are the size of goats and no more or less friendly than penned deer elsewhere. I feed them handfuls of random grass, which they seem to enjoy more than the algarrobo pods piled in the corners. The pods are being tested as fodder, and the seeds like so much in this world are indigestible, pass cleanly through the deer, are ready for screening and scarification. It is the best way to obtain them, says Reynaldo. Running the pods through grinders can damage the seeds, he says, and waiting for the pods to rot takes unreasonably long.

When the deer are satiated or bored I walk back to the office, read in silence. In early years I occasionally reread chronicles of the conquistadors to make sure I had missed nothing. I disguised some of them in unrelated bookcovers, as Peruvians have long memories if only in certain respects. Reynaldo is not my only friend to own and wear a t-shirt bearing a filthy Spaniard in sixteenth-century armor, waves of stink emanating as he says, My culture for your gold?

Reynaldo does not wear this shirt to the university, of course, and Arantxa is among his closest friends, and before I read little that was recommended by others. Now I read little that is not. The next book on my desktop stack was brought to me for unclear reasons by Armando: the poems of Carlos Oquendo de Amat. Oquendo wrote only one book, *5 Metros de Poemas*. It is a single page that unfolds accordion-like to a length that I assume to be five meters, though I have not measured and do not intend to.

Arantxa's secretary comes looking for me, and for a moment I think I am in for new and difficult questions, but Eugenia only wishes to remind me that my current visa extension expires in two weeks. She is very good about reminding me of these things. She has had four years of practice.

I should have begun residency paperwork as soon

as Pilar and I were married. After her death, the clerks at Immigrations told me that I had waited too long. They said this sadly, as though wishing they could do something to help. Eugenia later told me that this was not wholly true, but by that point it was easier to apply for a regular work visa. Seven months ago I sent in my papers. I ask Eugenia how much longer I will have to wait.

- Not much longer, she says. Everything will be ready soon.

- How soon?

This is a question one must never ask most Peruvians, and before she can answer I tell her that it doesn't matter, that I am grateful for her help. I gather my materials and head to the cafeteria for a hurried coffee. Reynaldo is there, asks me to join him. I order and sit down at his table. He is drinking an Inca Kola.

Inca Kola is the national soft drink of Peru. Nearly all Peruvians believe it is the perfect accompaniment for Chinese food, and for many other kinds of food as well. It is the color of urine and tastes like bubble gum.

His order is however only marginally worse than mine. Here in Piura most coffee is either instant or made from esencia. Esencia freshly prepared is what many would call strong coffee, but is not drunk as such, not here. Instead it is poured into tiny pitchers and left out to cool, to be mixed with hot water and sugar at some point hours or days later. I have tried to explain the unnecessarily unpleasant results of this system to my students, my colleagues, the men and women who work in so many of Piura's restaurants. I have pointed out the high quality of the coffee grown in the highlands of this very region, the ease with which this coffee could be served properly here in town, and my students, my colleagues, the men and women of the restaurants, they all nod, and pass me the tiny pitcher.

I smooth the tablecloth with my hands and smile briefly.

Only professors are allowed to sit at the tables with tablecloths—it is one of our several privileges. Reynaldo stares out at the desert, asks again what Berkeley was like when I was a student. I have told him many times that I was there a decade too late for the stories he hopes to hear. In the early Eighties we were all between one thing and another. We didn't know whether to wear our hair long or short, so we wore it medium, and had medium-sized combs in our pockets. We took drugs when we could, but it was hard to know which drugs were the right ones, and we lived in fear of being wrong or perhaps it was only me.

- Free love! says Reynaldo.

He knows that if he says this I will tell him that no love is free, though some loves cost less than others.

Out the gates, and the street names near the university are mainly those of saints—Miguel, Felipe, Cristóbal, Ramón. Elsewhere in the city they have the names of trees or foreign countries. There are also sections where the streets are labeled by letter or number, and in the center they are named after departments: Cuzco, Ayacucho, Arequipa.

By department Peruvians mean what others mean when they say province, and by province they mean something like county; there is a rumor that soon departments will be called regions and no other change will be made. Departmental capitals often share the name of their department—again Cuzco, again Ayacucho and Arequipa—but this is not always the case. The department of Junín has a province called Junín whose capital is the city of Junín, but the departmental capital is Huancayo, which is the world capital of suicides caused by unrequited love.

In the park maids play with infants on blankets, take the infants up whenever dogs are seen. Junín the provincial capital was the site of the second-most-significant battle in the War of Independence, a late counterattack led by Suárez beating down Canterac's royal troops. The city has since been of little importance to anyone who does not live in or very near it, but at least it has not been erased. There are towns nearby that have. Yungay was twenty thousand people in the Callejón de Huaylas, a valley that runs between the ice of the Cordillera Blanca and the dark shale of the Cordillera Negra. Ten miles southeast is El Huascarán: twenty-two thousand feet high, the tallest mountain in Peru.

May 31, 1970, mid-afternoon, and most of the town is home watching the opening match of the World Cup, Mexico against the Soviet Union, a dull tie but the first match ever broadcast in color. A few hundred children are instead attending a circus in the local stadium off to one side of town. There are flowers and small rodents painted on the children's cheeks. There is cotton candy stuck in their hair. The older children have tied balloons around their wrists. Their baby brothers and sisters rub dirt in each others' faces and smile at the trained bears insane in their cages.

Then the earthquake. When the ground is done shaking, Yungay is ruins: houses and stores collapsed, the Plaza de Armas split open, survivors stumbling into the streets. And they hear a sound. A roar. They turn.

The northwest face of El Huascarán, a chunk of rock and ice half a mile wide and more than a mile long, has broken off. The slide gathers speed, hits small lakes and reservoirs, adds their water and mud to its mass, is moving at more than a hundred miles an hour and this is what the people see: El Huascarán strange now to them, diminished, and below it the foothills beneath which they have ever lived, and leaping toward them a monstrous flood of ice and rock and mud. The children at the circus, they came running out of the stadium when the earthquake hit. They stand, their cheeks painted, their bright balloons, ice and mud and rock sweeping past and Yungay is gone from this earth.

Some adults survived as well—the few maids and parents at the circus, the few widows who had chosen that afternoon to visit the graveyard on the far side of town. The entire zone is now a national cemetery. The taller palms on the Plaza de Armas were buried not quite to their tops, and their fronds still somehow grow. The nation's schools have earthquake drills yearly on the day.

There have of course been other earthquakes here in Peru, thousands, but none so lethal and only one as well known: the conquistadors built the Church of Santo Domingo directly on top of the Coricancha, and in 1950 an earthquake destroyed the church but left the temple foundation intact. Tourists love this and consider it symbolic. Most Peruvians learn of it in primary school and even at that age are unsure whether or not to be ambivalent.

In primary school I was taught to hide under my desk during earthquakes, and also during nuclear attacks. Doorways were a secondary option, and once an earthquake came while I was at the Fallash library. I stepped to the closest door, watched adults run in circles. The shelves tumbled. A man's leg was broken, and a woman's ribs. My picture was in the newspaper the next day.

At last home, and the only death now is a dustpan full of geckos on the kitchen counter. There is also a lack of noise. I find Mariángel asleep in her crib, and Casualidad in my bedroom sliding the curtains carefully open. She has not heard me enter, and when I speak she whirls and falls. I am not quick enough to catch her. She hits her head on the side of the bed, and there is a bit of blood.

I bring her a towel, and she tells me that there are geckos everywhere. I remind her that she does not have to kill them, that I do not want her to kill them, that I like them very much and want them in my house, alive.

- But the baby, she says.

By this she means that geckos are poisonous and evil, that they will climb onto the ceiling above the crib and drip venom onto Mariángel's face. I do not know why she believes this, and have assured her many times that they have no reason or capability for doing so, that in fact they help by eating mosquitoes and flies. I have even told her that they bring good luck, though I have no proof of this. And she wants to believe me but cannot. She sees only the bulging yellow eyes, the heaving sides, the nearly transparent skin and the dark curl of entrails inside.

When the bleeding stops she goes to lie down on the couch. I serve myself a glass of papaya juice and the lunch she has prepared. It is a fine salad of avocado and tomato, and a plate of lomo saltado: strips of beef and potato and tomato and pepper sautéed. It is served with boiled white rice. Everything in this country is served with boiled white rice, and lomo saltado is one thing that can safely be eaten in most restaurants. So is roast guinea pig, which is tasty but unattractive on the plate. Most cooks do not remove the feet, which look like tiny human hands, or the head, which looks exactly as one would expect if one has had a guinea pig for a pet, except the mouth is open as if screaming.

Nearly all who come to Peru experience diarrhea for two or three weeks upon their arrival, regardless of what they eat. I was told repeatedly that this is not a concern. One set of beneficial microbial flora is simply being exchanged for another, I was told, and no given set of flora is better or worse than any other.

At the moment dessert is the only problem. It is cherry gelatin. Mariángel and I do not like gelatin of any flavor, and I have told Casualidad many times, but she forgets. Perhaps it is one of her favorite things. I have told her that she is welcome to buy it with the regular grocery money and make it for herself alone. I will have to tell her again but not today.

There is crying, Mariángel awake, and I go, lift her out and sing: Zambo Cavero, "Alma Traicionera." She stops crying halfway through the first verse. I walk, living room entryway dining room patio yard. At the end of the chorus she puts her hands over my mouth though it is a very good song and I have not finished.

Cavero is a splendid singer and almost as fat as I am. I pretend to eat Mariángel's hands and she laughs. She still has not spoken any proper words. Her first birthday is less than a month away and now Casualidad comes. Her head is bandaged, her eye clear. She offers to take Mariángel, and I say that she is welcome to rest for half an hour more instead, but first I need to know how old Fermín was when he first spoke clearly.

- Because of Mariángel?
- Yes.
- Ten months, or nearly so.
- And why did he stop?
- What do you mean?

I think uncharitable thoughts and she frowns, perhaps has sensed them.

There is a tremendous splattering of pacazo shit, white and gray and black on the sidewalk outside the library. I skirt it carefully, walking well out onto the grass on which one must not walk. I scan branches thoroughly but also quickly as I am late, and nearly trample Dr. Guardiola.

He is the Dean of Economics, is old and thin and always wears a hat. He has been here since the university's founding thirty years ago, and in some ways he is the university, which he himself calls a cactus: surviving impossibly, flowering in absurdly bright colors. I ask if he has seen the pacazo, but he doesn't hear. He takes me by the arm, asks if I wish to join him and several other professors for a prayer retreat over the weekend.

I explain to Dr. Guardiola that I am very busy this weekend, which is what I have explained to him every week since I arrived in Piura. As always he is disappointed and polite. Then I ask again if he has seen the pacazo. He says that he hasn't, nods and backs away, says that he hopes I will be less busy next weekend, and never stops smiling.

My five o'clock class is Upper Intermediate and the students ask questions I cannot answer. I never lie to them where matters of grammar or vocabulary are concerned. This is among the first things one learns teaching English as a foreign language: there is always one student who knows the correct answer but will not speak up unless you lie.

Today we are scheduled to study the third conditional in its simplest form. I explain about alternate histories—things that did not happen and their nonexistent consequences. I write an example on the board, careful to keep my writing from slanting downward: "If Atahualpa had not slaughtered the Cañari for siding with Huáscar in the civil war, the Cañari would not have sided with Benalcázar against Rumiñavi."

I finish writing and step back. It is a preposterously complicated example. With luck one of my stronger students will help the others to make sense of it.

- No necesariamente, someone says.

It is Claudia. She is an accounting major, is not much of an English student, and I have no reason to believe she knows anything about history. Perhaps her day has been difficult. I smile and ask her to please stick to the target language.

- Túpac Yupanqui killed them too, she says. It was years before. He threw ten thousand bodies in Yaguarcocha.

This is true. Yaguarcocha means Lake of Blood and I had forgotten. I bow to Claudia. She puts her head down on her desk and closes her eyes.

    - Another example, I say.

    I write, "If Admiral Grau had had more boats, Peru would have won the Battle of Angamos."

    I wait for someone to challenge the veracity of this, but no one does. I wait for someone to comment on the timeliness of the example, as just yesterday we commemorated the battle, Grau's death, and the loss of the War of the Pacific. Again no one does. I wait. Most Peruvian heroes were killed in battles subsequently lost. Admiral Grau was born in Piura, was by all accounts gifted and wise and humane. Peruvians consider him the greatest hero of all times and places. His house is now a scant museum and though the concept is not supposed to be introduced until next week, I explain that one can also use the third conditional to express regret. If I had. If I hadn't. I wish I had. I wish I hadn't. I put the students in pairs and force them to regret things they would otherwise never have considered.

    It is time again. I stand across the street from the Sánchez Cerro bridgehead, waiting for the stoplight to turn. I will find my place, sit and watch and wait for him to pass by. For the first time I will be waiting not alone but with Mariángel: Fermín has bronchitis and Casualidad could thus not stay late.

    It is an unlikely way to find the taxista. All ways have always been unlikely. I have chosen the Sánchez Cerro not because it is the most heavily transited of Piura's four bridges but because it is next on my rotating list and Mariángel tugs sharply at my sideburns.

    I have all the milk that she might require, and all the diapers, and as much of everything else as I can carry. The light turns and I walk to the apex of the bridge. There is a slight widening of the sidewalk here, and this is my place. I lay down my piece of cardboard and sit. There is a weak breeze, so I pull a blanket from my knapsack, draw it over my shoulders and tuck Mariángel in beneath.

She will not lie still, twists and twists in my lap. I change her diaper and prepare a bottle of milk. She pushes the bottle away, then wants it intensely, grabs and pulls it to her. Pedestrians pass. I look only at the faces of the men, and they look back, stare, perhaps wonder. I open my thermos and pour some coffee, most of it in the cup and a bit on the sidewalk and a few drops on my trousers. A taxi, old and yellow but the wrong make of car.

I listen through the traffic for the sound of the river, but there is no such sound, no such river, hardly even a creek at this point. Ambient light leaves the stars invisible. The smells are of exhaust and sweat and a flower I do not recognize and sewage.

When the bottle is empty I put Mariángel beneath the blanket again, and again she struggles against it. I bring her back out. We play the blinking game, wherein we blink at one another and laugh. I scan traffic between blinks and gradually she tires.

Now I sing, Silvio Rodríguez, verse and chorus and verse and chorus about unicorns. It is a beautiful if stupid song and she closes her eyes, lies motionless but unsleeping, perhaps another game. A taxi, red. I draw the blanket up over her, bring out another and drape it as well, minimally better protection against the lights and noise.

An hour passes, and another. Then the sound of birds, a small flock low overhead and fast, by the time I look up they are gone and very near the beginning: ducks for Pizarro. The Inca noble sent by Atahualpa to gather information on the violent strangers meets Soto scouting at Cajas. Soto has seen dozens of bodies hanging from trees, locals who hadn't surrendered to Atahualpa during the civil war just now ended. The city in ruins but the sun temple on the outskirts inviolate.

Five hundred holy women—young acllas at their looms and mamaconas practicing the rites, all of them virgins—and the Spaniards brought them out, enslaved some, raped others, many of them to death.

Soto leads the noble to Pizarro. The noble delivers his embassy, presents Pizarro with ducks, and also with ceramic castles. The ducks have been stuffed and skinned and some Spaniards think this is meant to symbolize what awaits them, the castles standing for the strength of Inca defenses, but they are only gifts, and not particularly precious. The stuffed ducks are meant to be ground into aromatic powder, and each castle is a sort of stein.

The noble wanders the Spanish camp as if it were his own. He inspects the armor and horses, asks to see the swords, takes one man roughly by the beard. The Spaniard beats him until Pizarro steps in. He tells the noble he accepts Atahualpa's invitation to meet in Cajamarca, and sends gifts for the Inca in turn: a handsome Holland shirt and two goblets, Venetian glass.

The noble thanks him and at the far end of the bridge are ghosts or what appear to be, ten or twelve figures dressed in white, glowing under the streetlights. Together they float toward me. The cars on the bridge slow beside them, speed away. The wind brings odd bits of language, not Spanish or Quechua or English and now the figures are close enough to see. They are pale bearded men dressed in white robes and brown leather sandals.

They are arguing angrily in German and it is not the first time I have seen them. According to Günther, they think the world is soon going to be destroyed, that every city on the planet except Piura will be devastated by a rain of sulfur and fire. They have come here to pay twice the market value for fine houses, to stock up on canned tuna and bottled water, to await the end of everywhere else.

No one knows why they think Piura of all places will be saved, and no one much likes these men. They do not bathe, and they do not tip, and they attempt to save pennies by haggling over the price of bread. The Germans are convinced that the truth is something one can know, can be sure of, and this is a beautiful thought however false. They are also convinced that there is precisely one high truth in the world, and that it belongs to them alone.

The Germans reach the apex, and the leader—the tallest of them, the most beautiful—ignores me utterly. Of those who follow, a few do the same, and others look at me, nod gravely, as if they understand why I would choose to sit on a piece of cardboard in the middle of a bridge in the middle of the night, as if we are on the same team in some non-trivial sense. Then Mariángel twists under the blanket, flails, the lattermost men step away, her head comes out and she smiles at me, at them, and they smile too, slow their pace, step closer, reach out and in English I suggest that if they like the number of fingers they currently possess, they had best keep their motherfucking distance.

They perhaps are not familiar with the phrase but recognize the tone, and hurry to catch up with their leader. Mariángel cries and I stand, bring her to my shoulder. I reorganize the blankets, make sure her head is covered. I pace up and back. There are shanties here too in the causeway but not enough light to identify the crops.

A pair of combis pass; another taxi, but the driver is too round in the face. The Germans step down off the bridge. From most distances they seem harmless, but that is proof of nothing. I was fifteen when my friend Joel told me that the truth could be found only twenty miles from Fallash.

Joel, best friend, the only one I told what I had learned about Segovia. He did not mock me, or not cruelly so. Come, he said now, come listen to what Mr. Jones has to say, and the truth will be yours as well. As he spoke it was clear to us both: this diction was not his own, was unconvincing and unconvinced. I did not know how to respond, attempted to commiserate, and he would not have it.

We spoke little after that. The following month he and his family went to live in that community, and so did the brothers and sisters, the aunts and uncles of other people I knew. They were in general friendly and devout and none of them seemed insane. When I told my parents where Joel had gone they said they were sorry but would not elaborate. Years later I learned that there had been rumors of sex slaves and torture, but the newspapers were afraid of Jones' lawyers, and the politicians wanted access to the clout of his flock. Nothing came to light in time, and Jones took his people to live the truth in Guyana.

I remember thinking, If things ever get really bad, I can always move to the jungle. I knew nothing of the jungle then, learned nothing until I went to Iquitos. I went not because of Joel or Jim Jones, but I thought of them as my plane dropped through dense clouds into bright green. Iquitos has 200,000 inhabitants but no roads leading in or out and I wished to know something about what the jungle meant for certain men as they led certain expeditions east: Candia looking for Ambaya, Maldonado looking for Paititi, their failure and thousands dead but also and most importantly Orellana, his absurd and magnificent stretch, the Amazon from the Andes to the Atlantic.

Seventeen hours upriver in pacamari and peque-peque to the edge of Pacaya-Samiria, and then we walked four hours more. I had not understood that the base camp would be so distant. My guide's name was Moisés. I did not believe in portents.

Smaller rivers and creeks encircled us. In Iquitos Moisés had asked me if I wanted him to bring regular food, or if we should let the jungle provide. I did not know what he meant, and guessed wrong.

Out hunting caimans that first night, Moisés walks a few steps ahead with his shotgun in one hand and his machete in the other. I am wearing a borrowed mining helmet to keep both hands free. Dragonflies the size of blackbirds crave the light, strike me in the face again and again, their bodies crackling as I crush them in my hands.

A line of taxis, six in a row, none of them correct. Most snakes also hunt at night, Moisés says, so you must never grab hold of anything as you walk beside the river, not even if you are about to fall: any given vine or root could writhe in your hand, could sink its fangs into you. Antivenins are available in the hospitals of Iquitos, he says, but no one envenomed here ever makes it that far. You might make it back to our base camp, if you are very lucky, but antivenins require refrigeration, and there are no refrigerators at base camp.

On the trails there are also scorpions, and ants, and tarantulas that move like severed hands. One ant leaves a welt on my arm that will last for weeks, yes. These ants wait until someone or something brushes against the thin white trunk of the tree in which they live, and then swarm out. They will even drop from the leaves and twigs above.

It is not easy to keep from slipping off the logs that hunters lay to form paths above the waist-deep mud of low jungle. Or to keep Moisés from cursing you for your clumsiness, your noise, for ruining the hunt again. Or to keep from falling into the water where the caimans wait, and the coral snakes.

The second night we are scheduled to go out in a small canoe, and Moisés does not want to bring me, is sure my weight will sink the craft at some point, and he is right, but it is included in the price of the tour so what can he do? There are torches fore and aft, Moisés in the bow with his three-pronged spear and his club, and me in the stern with my paddle. I ask him why we can't leave the snakes alone and just canoe along, thick frog-song melting around us, the torchlight reflected and rippling in the wake. Moisés points to dark huts along the riverbank. There are children, he says. They come to fetch water, and to bathe, and their mothers bring laundry and soap. Some die each year of snakebite. So we visit when we can, and what we do, it is only a kind of cleaning.

Just then he sees one. The spear flashes. He pulls it back up and I see nothing but a thin twisting darkness held against the bow. The club slams down, the spear-tip flicks and the snake is gone.

Moisés kills four more that night, shows me the colored bands on two of them, and we do not sink until the very end: I reach to catch the edge of the makeshift pier and the canoe slips one way and another and Moisés and I are in the water. I hold to the gunwale until I find my footing. The water is shallow and warm there at the bank, and Moisés says he will never again take anyone so fat on any kind of tour.

My clothes slow to dry. Pneumonia later, Andagoya and I, unless his was bronchitis like Fermín's. Two more taxis, both blue. There are also the mosquitoes that come in waves of thousands. I have repellent designed on behalf of the British Special Forces and even it is useless. Moisés laughs when he sees it. He says that there is no reason to waste so much money, that the jungle itself provides repellent of the highest quality. He leads me to a rotten stump, hacks at it with his machete, brings out a handful of termites. Nature's repellent, he says.

He rubs the termites on his neck and face, his back and chest. He rubs very lightly, as if hoping not even to injure the pale insects. When he is done he smells of eucalyptus, and hands the termites to me. As I rub them up and down my arms, I ask if it truly works. I speak softly and with downward intonation to show that it is not really a question, that I am only making conversation, that I do not doubt his expertise, and he says No, not really, but at least it is free.

Joel never returned from Guyana. Another taxi, a yellow Tico but new. and Orellana leaves the Americas a hero, plans a new expedition, five ships and three hundred men and his new wife. He loses three ships in the course of the crossing, attempts to explore the Amazon upriver from the mouth but loses most of the rest of his crew to malaria and poisoned arrows. He falls ill himself, dies of fever but his wife survives, marries another survivor and there are things that must be seen, the whole of the sunset sky caught across the wide river, and the freshwater dolphins, said to be pink but in fact a fluid collage of purple and silver and orange. There are things that must be smelled, the sweat of the quivering shaman as the ayahuasca takes hold, and things that must be tasted, capybara roasted over wet wood, and the water that pours from the cut vine, it pours and pours from the three-foot length, more water than can be imagined. There are things that must be heard, the red howlers screaming at dawn, and things that must be felt, the cool smooth skin of the fer-de-lance that was waiting beside the path, waiting to be woken by footsteps, and Moisés saw it in time, held me silent, cut and limbed two branches, drove the forked one down across the snake's spine and beat at the head with the other branch, a solid minute of beating, then the clear brown venom dripping from broken fangs into the palm of my hand. And there are things one must know from inside them. The rain, for example. Elsewhere one is told that rain is a temporal thing, that it started at twelve-thirty and ended at twenty past four. This is a sort of lie. Rain is spatial, and this will be known on the river: the rain comes, an opaque curtain, a line on the black water past which the surface roils, the front edge of the storm that is closer now and closer, and I duck as it moves over me, I am inside and it is a living thing, furious around me and beating warm, the great chaotic heart and at times it is hard to breathe, the water or the air is so thick.

# 11.

Tonight Peru plays Chile in Santiago. It is the second-to-last qualifying match for next year's World Cup. If Peru wins they will have earned the last remaining spot. If they tie then nothing will be clear, and if they lose the road steepens sharply.

The match will be shown live on the massive screen at Boby's Disco. The distance is not unwalkable but I am late and so I stop a taxi, observe the license plate and driver, climb in. I tell him where I am going and he nods, says that he wishes he could afford not to work this evening, that the radio will have to suffice, that nothing matters as long as Peru wins and he is quite sure they will.

English names misspelled are common here. I have several students named Jhon, and Boby's is the most popular nightspot in Piura. It is something of a bright beery warehouse. Many of my students go every weekend. They often invite me, and are precisely as disappointed and polite as Dr. Guardiola.

Peru has not qualified for the Cup since 1982: fifteen years of unworthiness. This year however their midfield and defense are often competent or better and many of my colleagues are permitting themselves to have hope. The match does not begin for another hour but Reynaldo insisted that we arrive early and drink well and prepare ourselves. We have been told that beer will cost only one sol per mug, a matter of patriotism and market share.

There is a spring coming up through the seat cover and I shift to the far side of the taxi. The driver asks if there is a problem. I begin to explain, but fail to remember the Spanish word for spring. Words rarely escape me in this way, but when they do they are almost always of this type: not exactly uncommon but rarely thought. I talk instead about a spiraling object that irritates me. The driver does not quite understand. In his place neither would I. He apologizes all the same, and I accept.

I had at first planned to bring Mariángel, but a few days ago I mentioned the event to Casualidad, and she said that Boby's was not an appropriate venue for a baby, not during an important soccer match, not ever. Then she said that she had good news for me. She had spoken with her sister, Socorro, who has four daughters, and it seems that Mariángel's disinclination to use proper words should not be reason for concern for another several months. I have since confirmed this with Eugenia, who has five children, and the manager of the university cafeteria, who has nine, and after saying she hoped I was as relieved as she was, Casualidad offered to work this evening for a certain additional fee.

The taxi pulls onto Ucchuracay, and there is something larger than a playing card hanging from the taxi's rearview mirror. It is as thick as cardboard and sealed in plastic and most likely an image of some saint. One side is covered in illegibly small type, and on the other side is a drawing, a girl framed in pink.

The picture revolves on its string. The driver turns,

sees me watching. He slips the picture off the mirror and hands it back.

- Sarita Colonia, he says.

She is not a saint I know. According to the drawing she had long brown hair parted off-center, large elongated brown eyes, a small nose, a thin mouth. She is someone I have seen a thousand times or never.

Pressed flat at the bottom of the image is a pink carnation. The flower has surely been in its dusty sheath for years, but its color is still bright. It is either miraculous or plastic. I hand the picture back to the driver and he hangs it from the mirror. The slow spinning begins again.

- She was born in Huaraz, the driver says.

I nod but not encouragingly.

- Buried in El Callao, he says.

I nod still less encouragingly: there is no point in trying to keep track of anything as numerous as saints.

- She saved my life, he says. Four years ago I was driving a truck full of mattresses to Cajamarca. I was very tired, and my eyes must have closed, and when I opened them there were two sets of headlights coming toward me. I closed my eyes again and called to Sarita, and she heard me. There was no room on that road for three trucks at once, but I passed between the other two. You understand, yes? There was no room, but I passed between them.

- That is remarkable, I say.

- Thank you, he says.

- So. Cajamarca. Where everything started.

- What do you mean?

- Atahualpa, Pizarro, Valverde.

- Ah. Yes. But Sarita is something different. She was a very good girl, took good care of her brothers and sisters after her parents died.

- And that is sufficient these days?

He looks at me in the mirror.

- Do not mock her, please.

- My apologies.

- Well. She also had a market stand where she sold small things—fruit, clothes. One day three men held her down and tried to rape her, but by the grace of God her vagina disappeared.

- Disappeared.

- Yes. Just disappeared.

We come to Sánchez Cerro, and the taxista shakes his head as he makes the turn.

- It is inconceivable, he says. She has performed thousands of miracles, saved thousands of lives, but the Church will not recognize her.

- Why not?

- Who knows? The Church does as it wishes. Also perhaps because you can ask her for anything, any miracle at all, even if it's wrong, and if you have been faithful she will grant it.

- I don't understand.

- She is a saint for everyone, but especially for criminals. Burglars and prostitutes, kidnappers, even murderers. I could ask her to strike you dead so that I could steal your wallet. Not that I would. But I could. And if I did, you—

He looks again in his mirror, sees my eyes, looks away.

- That probably sounds strange to you.

- A little. It reminds me of Ernil Bernal.

- I don't know who that is.

- The huaquero, the one who discovered the tomb of the Lord of Sipán.

- Perhaps he prayed to Sarita, and she told him where the tomb would be.

- And now people pray to him.

- But that is different, says the taxista. Those people are idiots.

We arrive at Boby's and I pay him for the ride. He pulls the picture again from the mirror, and holds it out.

- Take it, he says.

- I couldn't. You—

- Do you ever drive a car or truck?

- Not here.

- But at some point perhaps you will. And then you will need her.

I accept it and thank him, tuck it away, watch as he drives off. There are many taxis waiting here outside. I take my time checking the face of each driver. Then I stand at the door between two bouncers who collectively weigh less than I do and observe everyone who enters.

Reynaldo arrives very slowly on his motorcycle. The engine dies fifteen feet from the parking lot. He gets off and pushes it, sees me, seems to find it amusing and inscrutable that I do not go running to help. He wheels his motorcycle into a stand. Then he notices me checking faces behind him, and claps me on the back.

- Tonight is not for that, he says. Tonight is for relaxing with beer and soccer.

Inside it is very loud and crowded. We walk up the staircase to the second level. Here one might speak and be heard, and chairs have been saved for us: Günther and Armando and two law professors I've seen often but never met have spaced themselves widely around a table.

Both of the law professors are named Javier and I am surprised not to see more students around us. Perhaps they are filling the many balcony-like spaces above us, or form part of the crowd below. Günther stands, welcomes us, goes for the first round of beer. I sit down beside Armando and he asks if I like the Oquendo book.

I do not yet know if I like it, and wish to read it again before deciding. I remind Armando of the instructions on the first page, that the book is to be opened as if peeling a fruit, and tell him that I have not yet been successful in that regard. He nods as though this were a serious answer. The law professors insult us happily for discussing poetry before a soccer match, and Reynaldo joins in. With equal happiness Armando tells them to go fuck themselves, accuses them of only pretending not to know the poems by heart, is most likely partially right as many Peruvians do.

Günther returns with beer and the evening begins. At the moment the screen is showing the team's trip to Chile. There is a handshake for each player from President Fujimori, and a passenger jet somehow on loan from the Air Force. The players deplane in Santiago, file across the tarmac onto a bus, and now Chileans are casting stones against the windows.

Next come recorded interviews with key players— el Chorri, Maestri, Balerio. None of them has anything of interest to say and we cheer every word. When they are done it is Reynaldo's round and the screen switches to a live broadcast from the Plaza de Armas in Lima. Shamans in jeans and boots and heavy brown ponchos are at work to ensure that Peru will win. They are unshaven and long-haired, look unwashed and either wise or insane. They dance and chant and dance beneath the antique streetlights. The reporter smiles ever wider.

The chanting rises and she steps away, asks the gathered crowds if they believe that the shamans' labor will help the team. The crowds claim to be certain that it will, but laugh as they say so. The shamans pause to rest and the reporter asks where they are from. Huancabamba, they say. I look more carefully, but there are so many shamans in Huancabamba.

The men stand again and the camera comes in close. They bring skulls from old leather bags and set them in strategic arcs on the flagstones. They put necklaces made of teeth around one another's necks. They take crucifixes in each hand and dance again.

It is unclear how much of the dancing is ancient and how much is made up on the spot. The shamans dance, dance and chant, chant and speak of spells and now it is my round. I buy the beer with pocket change, a single sol each, as advertised.

I spill a bit on the stairs, and at the table I am excoriated for arriving with less than full mugs. The shamans wave deer hooves back and forth, set them down and take up condor talons. They stab at a Chilean uniform hung upside-down, and how to explain what sports become?

In terms of Middle Paleolithic tribal warfare, I have heard. And here now there are other concerns added. The War of the Pacific was fought over birdshit and saltpeter. There were millions of tons of each along the respective coasts of Bolivia and southern Peru. Chile wanted it all for fertilizer and gunpowder, waited for an excuse, found one in export taxes, attacked Bolivia in 1879.

It is the round of Javier the Shorter. Students pass by our table from time to time, wave and welcome me. Some pat me on the shoulder, tell me how pleased they are that I have finally come, and of course there was a mutual-defense pact tying Peru to Bolivia.

Peru had two ironclad ships at the beginning of the war. Two months later they had only one, the *Huáscar*, commanded by Grau. He rammed and sank the *Esmeralda*, rescued the survivors and sent condolences to the captain's widow. For six months he and his crew held off the entire Chilean navy: cut their supply lines, burned their ports, recaptured smaller Peruvian vessels. Then Chile brought its six best ships after him, caught him off of Punta Angamos.

Armando's turn at the bar. The *Huáscar* takes seventy-six artillery rounds and founders. Grau is dead on the deck. A month later Chile lands ten thousand troops on the south coast of Peru. After the first few battles, Bolivia withdraws its forces. Peru fights on alone, and more men become martyrs and myths: Bolognesi promising to defend Arica until the last round has been fired, doing so and dying; Ugarte riding his horse off a cliff to keep the flag out of Chilean hands; Cáceres crushing Arteaga's column in Tarapacá and leading three years of guerilla warfare in the mountains.

Chile occupies the rest of the country, loots the cities, pillages universities and medical schools and libraries. Finally Cáceres is trapped at Huamachuco. The treaty is signed. Bolivia loses its only coast. Peru forfeits the province of Tarapacá and the match begins.

Both teams attack sloppily at first. We are hopeful but afraid and shout at the Peruvian players, rage at each missed pass, applaud anything that is not awful. Javier the Taller's turn, and more students back and forth. Our good noise is lessened slightly by a Chilean goal, Marcelo Salas in the thirteenth minute. There is nothing to be done but return to the attack. The ball moves beautifully from time to time but the movement is unsustained.

At halftime there are replays of Maestri bouncing shots off the goalposts. We shake our heads, and the camera cuts to the Plaza de Armas. The shamans there are spitting aguardiente on a picture of the Peruvian team to give the players new strength and virility. I ask if there is any difference between a shaman and a curandero. Everyone at the table agrees that there are many important differences, and no one is sure what they are.

In addition to shamans and curanderos there are warlocks, and until he was caught, Cáceres was called the Warlock of the Andes for his many unlikely escapes. The *Huáscar* is later refloated by Chile, made a trophy, a floating museum, a monument to their victory. My second turn comes as the spitting ends. I attempt to buy the round with a ten-sol bill, am told that for the one-sol mugs only one-sol coins are accepted. I explain to the bartender how perplexingly stupid this is. He says that I should speak to the bouncers. I do though it is pointless, and return to the bar. Beers bought with bills are five soles each and I hiss as I take them up.

The second half begins, Peru pushing hard down both wings. Our noise survives the second Chilean goal, Pedro Reyes on a counterattack, but is staggered by the third, eight minutes from time and Salas again, and beaten senseless by the fourth, again Salas. This is how the game ends and we are silent: another rout, another humiliation. A few Peruvian players are interviewed sadly, and one of the shamans, who apologizes to the country for not casting better spells. Unclear fighting begins and the big screen goes dark.

Armando asks if anyone wants another beer. No one does. He goes nonetheless. Chile's next match is against Bolivia at home. If they win, and they should, it will not matter how Peru does against Paraguay. The air is thick with our bitter breath. I try to remember if there are any Chileans on the university staff, can think of none, and this is fortunate for us all.

The Javiers are no longer present, have apparently been gone for some time. Armando returns, his final beer already half empty. Günther shakes our hands, takes his leave. Reynaldo and I stand as well. He will not look at me. Then over his shoulder I see a face that is familiar. I step around my friend, peer, peer more closely.

The man has not yet seen me. His eyes, yes, and the shape of his face. His age is right, and the fullness of his mouth, his hair a bit long but that is meaningless and now I am to him, have him against the railing, lift him, his hands straining at the balusters but I have him off the ground, am set to throw but then I am wrenched off balance, beer hits me in the face and Reynaldo is pulling at my arm, shouting that he knows this man, this man owns a shoe store, has never driven a taxi and a chair thuds into my back. I turn and many people are screaming at me. I turn back and there is something of a cordon, Armando pushing me along it and down the stairs and out.

The streetlights are far too bright, strike like shrieks. Armando is gone and Reynaldo is with me, leading me by the elbow to his motorcycle. He straddles it, kicks and kicks. It will not start and there is more shouting, Armando's voice, then Armando himself running toward us as the engine fires, the empty mug still in his hand.

It is fortunate that no one gives chase: with the three of us on it, the motorcycle hardly moves at all. A few blocks away we decide to walk instead. As we sober, Reynaldo lectures me on carefulness. I tell him that he is right. He also says that I should not return to Boby's for several months, and this is easy to agree to. I say that it was odd, the number of people who came to the man's defense given the inclination of crowds to instead watch and savor, that while it is certainly possible for a—

- You are the biggest cojudo I have ever met, says Reynaldo.

- Why?

- Most Chileans are as white as you are. You didn't know that?

- Of course. Araucanos on horses, three hundred years, no surrender and the Spaniards finally slaughtered them all. If the Incas had—

- Right. And your accent is good but not perfectly Peruvian, and they were all very drunk, so they thought you were from Chile.

- That does not make much sense.

- When everyone is drunk, not much sense is needed.

We walk for a time, sweat, walk and sweat, come finally to Neuquén and Armando slows. For a moment I believe that he is going to ask again about beer or poetry, and I am not sure how to answer in either case. He points to an apartment above the restaurant, says that he lives there, shakes our hands and my back begins to ache.

Armando will likely later ask Reynaldo for whatever information interests him, and just now this thought irritates me though it certainly should not. Reynaldo tries the motorcycle, and after a moment it starts. He revs the engine to the extent possible, and looks at me.

- Are you sure it is not yet time to give up?

- Of course not.

- You're going to end up killing someone who doesn't deserve it.

I say that I am sorry about how the match turned out. He stares at me, at last shrugs, says that he will visit the shoe store man, pass along my apologies. I thank him. He says that if what happened causes me any trouble at the university, I should call him to testify that I was simply drunk and angry, that it was all a small misunderstanding. I promise that I will. He waves and rides off.

Home. Again tonight the streetlight outside my door shines too brightly. I open the door and there is no writhing but still, all that light. Back out onto the street and I take up a rock and on my very first throw there is a shower of sparks and the light goes dim, a sort of miracle.

Inside, and Casualidad is asleep on the sofa. I wake her, and she asks if Peru won. I tell her, and she nods, stands, rubs her face. I go to Mariángel's room, to her crib, and as always even asleep she rolls away from the stench of beer and smoke and sweat. I go to my room, pull off my shirt, find the picture of Sarita Colonia in the pocket. I hang it from the corner of my headboard. Something must be done.

# 12.

WE ARE ALL HERE, ALL OF US. THE TOMBS ARE OPEN AND THE
bodies laid out as if in state. We wait. Then though there is
no signal we all begin feeding, our faces soon wet with blood
and bile, each of us tearing at the ribcage of the body we have
chosen. The rule is that one can feed only on those one has
lost but I am breaking the rule, have chosen a stranger, eat
deeper in and pull back, my hair caked with gore, look at her
face and something has changed, not a stranger but Pilar and
I cannot stop eating, plunge back in, rip at her intestines, at
the ragged fringe of skin around the hole in her abdomen, her
blood black in the candlelight, and the others in their hundreds now crowd around me—the rest of the dead have been
eaten. I try to fight them off but their great dark wings beat
me down, and there is light and the sound of wind keening
through a thousand wingtips.

# 13.

I stand before the Language Center photocopier. Three of my colleagues are in line behind me. It is almost seven in the evening and we should all be headed home, but these three never leave the office until they have finished preparing for the following day.

I load the copier with a ream of heavy paper in varied colors. I ask the machine for one hundred copies of my flyer, delete the number and ask for two hundred. There is a disheartened release of breath behind me, but I do not turn to see who made the noise. I press the green button. The bar of light slides slowly from one side to the other and quickly back.

The smell of ink densens the air around us. At eighty copies there is more sighing, and again at a hundred and forty. I wait, will my colleagues to criticize me for misappropriating resources, but they never do. As far as I know they have never even told Arantxa, or perhaps they have and she does not care, or does not care enough.

The bar of light slides across a final time. The machine quiets. I take up the flyers, bend for my briefcase and wince:

the bruise across my back is not yet gone. I tuck the flyers away, lift the lid and remove the original. It is somewhat wrinkled, but the information it holds is still valid, and its photograph of Pilar—our first trip to the beach at Yacila—this photograph is perfect and holds her perfectly.

I should thank my colleagues for their patience but do not, walk straight out and down the path and across the parking lot. Long thin clouds, red and orange, the sky's ribcage. Along the white building. The falling light makes the evening feel cooler than it is and there is movement in the branches that intertwine above me, a bending of twigs, a shifting of shadow in the leaves and I jump to one side.

It is only squirrels. They sprint down a trunk, up another, are gone. I step back onto the path, walk faster and faster and out. Past the mural, past the hotel. To the gas station entrance and here I begin: I load my new staple gun, take out a stack of flyers, staple a blue one to the closest telephone pole.

To the corner, and left along the Panamericana, five dust-sick blocks of it. At last the Fourth Bridge. Up onto the bridgehead for a quick look at the riverbed. Back south along the street, stapling again.

For months I used only tape but the flyers fell too quickly. Woody Woodpecker gave me this new idea. I have brought tape as well for windows and other hard or brittle surfaces, but working with this gun, the good jolt up my arm as each staple is driven in, it matters more to me than I would have suspected.

At first hanging flyers took hours. Then I learned the secret of not looking at the photograph any more. Even so it is the least fruitful aspect of the search, is in fact unfruitful or worse. The only telephone calls I have received were from persons hoping I would pay them in advance for information they alleged to possess. When I said that I would happily pay after verifying some portion of the information—half, ten percent, a single fact—they would hang up and not call back.

There was one exception to this, a young man who agreed to meet me in person. His information was deeply detailed and likewise fraudulent. His fingers have perhaps healed by now.

It is not impossible, however, or does not seem so, that someone might someday look at the photograph, might read the description, might recall having seen Pilar on that night in that taxi. This person might remember more of the license plate than I do, or remember the driver as someone they knew or know. And so I continue in concentric circles of decreasing size: walk and staple, walk and tape, yellow and orange and green and blue, pole window payphone wall.

Perhaps it does not make much difference but I am glad to be doing this at night. I like to think of people coming out of their houses early tomorrow morning, these flyers and their colors waiting. I reach up, tape one to a stop sign, and behind me someone speaks:

- Wait, he says.

I bring my arms down. This voice—it is the voice of the taxista. The precise timbre and tone, the slight nasality and slighter rasp.

- Look at me, he says.

I turn quickly and lunge and catch myself: the man is farther away than I had thought, is a fat policeman, is reaching for his pistol. I raise my hands, apologize, say that I am only putting up flyers. His hand stays at his belt. I point at the stop sign.

- Flyers for what?

- My wife. She was killed a year ago.

I hand him one. He reads it, nods. I wait for him to tell me the rules I already know, that I am not allowed to hang them on stop signs or telephone poles, may hang them only on private property, must first ask the owner for permission in each instance, and when he does I will step to him and from a distance of four or five inches I will speak of the rights of the bereaved, will ask why my wife's case was abandoned, will tell him of the man who murdered her, of what it will be like to catch that man, of pliers, tinsnips, of sandpaper and salt.

Instead the policeman wishes me luck, turns and walks away. I staple a flyer to the tamarind in front of which he stood, and continue my walk: around, around, the circles ever smaller. Finally I tape my last copy to the window of a knickknack shop.

According to my reflection, my hair and beard are as long and unkempt as the day I arrived in Piura four years ago. My clothes sweat-drenched. The dust of the bus ride down from Guayaquil. Piura, its station and thieves; Arantxa hiring me, yes, but also asking for me to be cleaner. I did not mind this. I had no reason to mind. Eugenia gave me directions to a near guesthouse and on the way I bought cheap versions of appropriate clothing. I showered, and asked the owner where best to get my hair cut, my beard trimmed. He said that there were five salons on the Óvalo Grau, and that the hairdressers were all large butterflies, by which I later learned he meant homosexuals. He also said that I should avoid the centermost salon as its owner was toad-like, by which I later learned he meant devious.

I chose the southernmost salon. The one unoccupied hairdresser led me to a chair at the back. He draped the plastic apron across me and things went well for a time. He was working on a sideburn when the largest bee I had ever seen flew in and began circling near the ceiling.

The hairdresser did not seem to notice though the bee was the size of a walnut, hairy and shiny black. I shifted beneath the plastic and watched. The bee bumped around in the corner, perhaps confused by the mirrors that met there. The hairdresser left to look for some implement not ready to hand, and the bee dove for my face, entangled itself in my beard.

There were several moments of screaming and jumping and thrashing. Finally I got my arms free and swatted the bee squarely. It bounced off the ground and was airborne again but just barely, and then was gone, out the door, unseen by any of the hairdressers or other clients, all of whom were now staring at me.

I told them that everything was fine, that there had been a sheep caught in my beard, but it hadn't stung me. They began to laugh. I told them the truth: that it had been a very large sheep. I held my fingers two inches apart to show them. It was not easy for the other clients to stay in their seats, they were laughing so hard. I smiled to show that I too found the situation humorous. I sat back down and waited for the hairdresser to continue.

The issue with bee and sheep is nothing like the issue with spring, is closer to the case of womanizer and Batman, and there is movement inside the knickknack shop. I cup my hands over my eyes, peer through my reflection. Something shifts toward me, a vague face, then nothing.

I turn away, should have saved a dozen copies back, would take them as before to the market though there is no clear reason to do so, no reason to think Pilar ever made it that far. The police interviewed all of the fruit vendors at the beginning of the investigation, but none of them recognized Pilar's picture or the partial license plate. None remembered seeing anything untoward the night she was taken. I spoke with each vendor in later months and received the same answers and now a horn, a car swerving toward me and away, gone around the corner.

Back home, and Casualidad carries Mariángel from one room to the next, and Mariángel whimpers against her shoulder. Eight days ago I came home for lunch and found Casualidad struggling to dust the top of the refrigerator. I asked where Mariángel was, and there were sounds from elsewhere:

splashing, gurgling. We found Mariángel upside down and drowning in the toilet. I pulled her out unhurt but surprised. Casualidad toweled her dry and I shouted and we agreed that the bathroom door would be opened only when necessary and always immediately closed. There was nothing for a few days but then bloody pus came from one of Mariángel's ears and it is always the ear, always, unless it is the stomach or something else. I administered drops, held her as she cried all night. The next night also was very long, and the next, but last night we slept well, the infection seemingly receded.

Casualidad hands her to me, says that we are nearly out of drops, that she will bring more in the morning. She gathers her things and goes. I carry Mariángel to the bathroom, find the drops. The bottle is not nearly but wholly empty.

I start to bundle Mariángel for the walk to the nearest pharmacy, but her whimper, it seems not the same as before, not quite as loud or sharp, more spoiled than in pain. For a time we walk and walk, patio to bedroom and back. I sing Carole King and it does not help and no this is not a time for singing. I walk and whisper, and Mariángel quiets, smiles, whispers back.

We go to my bedroom, play games with pocket change, amuse ourselves with the shifting sounds and patterns. This suffices for a time. Then she teaches me to beat on the mattress with my fists to make the coins dance.

When all the coins have fallen behind the bed I propose milk but she is not thirsty; I propose sleep but she will not close her eyes. At her suggestion we move to the floor. She opens the closet and goes inside, puts each foot into each shoe in turn. She loses herself in the hangered shirts and trousers, turns and ruffles them, laughs, a forest of clothing between us.

She pulls at the hangers, pushes her way out. She takes me by the sleeve and leads me back to the bed but will not yet let me lift her. Instead she reaches, grabs the image of Sarita

Colonia in both hands, pulls until the string breaks. She chews on the corner of the plasticized card, reaches one arm around my neck, chews harder. I take her up and again we walk. I hear her gnawing there close to my ear, the click of her teeth on the card, and she slumps.

I wait, certain that she is only pretending. I walk to her crib, and she does not move. I lay her down and yes: asleep, breathing deeply. Mosquito netting, fan, curtains. I pull Sarita from her hands, back out of the bedroom.

It is very late. I sit on the couch, hold the remote control but do not turn the television on. The image of Sarita is undamaged. No tearing, no holes, no indentations or marks of any kind. I set down the remote, walk to my bedroom. I reknot the string and hang the image again from my headboard. I work a sentence back and forth in my mind until it is sufficiently concise: that Sarita find the taxista, and break him. Let lips do what hands do, Sarita, and I do not pray as such but hold the sentence gently in my mind.

# 14.

It is time for Ecuador: my visa expires tomorrow. I feed
Mariángel her bottle, trace her cheeks, set her on my bed. I
pack a few things into my knapsack and Mariángel watches
until watching is insufficient, comes to help, rearranges the
objects until the pattern they form pleases her. Arrangement
and rearrangment are two of her favorite activities.

My trip up the coast to Tumbes and across the border
to Machala at times takes five hours each way, and at times
takes nine. The exact amount of time required depends on
many things: some I do not understand and others I cannot
control. The alternate route—north as always to Sullana
but then northeast into the foothills and across the Macará
River—is faster, more attractive and more interesting. I took it
often for visas and research in early years here, but the border
crossing at the bridge is open only until six in the evening,
closes on and off throughout the day without apparent reason,
and I do not want to risk being away any longer than necessary.

Now Casualidad arrives: she will stay with Mariángel
for an additional day's wage. I thank her, kiss Mariángel, take

up my knapsack. My daughter reaches for me and I kiss her again. As I pull away she grabs at my hand, catches my ring-finger, tugs at my wedding band. I ask her if she would have me go ringless. I walk to the door and she starts to cry. The humid heat swarms around me and there is an old yellow taxi parked at the curb. The license plate is wrong but it is as though the driver were waiting for me. I have not arranged to be picked up. Casualidad would not have called without my asking, and perhaps not even then.

I step slowly to the curb, and look in through the window on the passenger's side. The driver is asleep, and his thin dark face is almost familiar.

- It was you, wasn't it? I say.

The man wakes, rubs his face.

- Mister? he says.

His eyes are muddy green. We come to agreement on a fare to the El Dorado station, and I am silent all the way there. I have ridden with El Dorado many times before. Their buses are not fast or comfortable. Neither are the buses of any other company, and here rather than a single large bus station we have many small ones, each company with its own dark hot room where one goes to buy tickets and wait and wait. El Dorado, the Gilded One. It was a Muisca ritual on Lake Guatavita: the king-elect borne onto a raft of rushes, incense burning in four braziers on the corners and hundreds more on shore, the king-elect stripped naked, coated with resin and covered in gold dust, ornaments of gold and emeralds stacked at his feet, four subject chiefs on the raft as well and they row him to the center of the lake, pour the treasure into the water as offering and sacrifice, row back to shore where the rest of the tribe sings, dances, and now the king-elect is king.

The Spaniards hear of the ritual, conquer the Muisca but find less gold than they had imagined, and slowly El Dorado becomes not a man but a place. Gonzalo Pizarro has it clear in his mind: a city of gold in a forest of cinnamon trees. He gathers hundreds of Spanish soldiers and thousands of native bearers, chooses his nephew Orellana as one of his lieutenants, and Carvajal is taken on as chaplain, will later write the chronicle that fixes them in history. Pizarro leads southeast out of Quito. Through the Andes, then downriver along the Río Coca, the foothill gorges, water surging fast and cold beside them. Machete and ax, storm and flood, seven months of this slow work. Finally they approach the endless furling green of high jungle, the river now navigable, but half the Spaniards and three quarters of the bearers have died of sickness, snakebite, ambush. Pizarro orders camp built on a bluff, puts his carpenters to work on a boat, a twenty-five foot brigantine to carry the sick, the wounded, the heaviest of gear. They eat the last of their horses and dogs. They finish the boat and a van pulls sharply out of an alley, cuts us off, my driver shouts, curses, sees that the other driver is a friend, laughs and waves.

By Christmas the Spaniards are at risk of starving but their guides say a confluence is near, the Coca and Napo joining, and one day's travel up the Napo there is food. Orellana offers to take the brigantine and sixty men, says he will be back in twelve days with supplies, and does he know or suspect the truth? His men no longer have the strength to row upriver or cut trails along the shore. He sends messages, and they never arrive: Pizarro has turned back toward Quito, will accuse Orellana of betrayal, and Orellana will be saved only by Carvajal's record of decisions justified, lands claimed, villages torched.

Onto Sánchez Cerro, the city woken, the haze building. On and on. Orellana orders stops when necessary: to hunt sloths, monkeys, lizards; to steal cassava and sugar cane; to build a more seaworthy boat; to heighten its bulwarks against arrows. Six months, on and on, the men delirious in the heat, and the Napo flows into the widest river they have ever seen. Attacks grow more common, native archers on shore or in canoes. One day Carvajal sees them as tall pale-skinned women with braided hair, and he knows this story already, the story that will give the jungle and river their name, women of the moon, archers of Artemis: the Amazon.

And now the weather changes, the heat lessening, stirred at times by breeze. Now in places the jungle cedes to shallow hills. Now the men sense the tidal surge; eighteen months and four thousand miles from Quito, they spill out into the Atlantic, among the greatest voyages ever accidentally made, El Dorado now elsewhere, still waiting.

Sidewalk stands, hay limas hay piña hay plátanos de seda. It was not only the Spaniards, of course. There were Portuguese explorers, and Germans. Sir Walter Raleigh placed El Dorado well up the Orinoco in Guyana and Jim Jones must have known of this, perhaps saw himself as the Gilded One and Jonestown as his city of gold, his myth of freedom, his point of access to the twisted divine and the taxi stops in front of the station.

Up the walkway, into the dark hot room, standing in line at the counter and all I wish to do is sit down. El Dorado in Milton, in Voltaire, in Poe and Conrad, *El Dorado* with Robert Mitchum and John Wayne. Nothing in this station is gilt but in theory there are buses to Tumbes leaving every fifteen minutes for the next hour and today is like many recent days in that I would rather slouch and detest myself than search. I would like to be less tired. I would like for the cinema to be once again just a cinema. I would like for bars to be only bars, and for the desert to be only sand and rocks and deeply improbable plants.

As penance I walk the room, stare into the faces of thin young men until they look away. When I have seen them all I sit and look at the ticket I bought. Each ticket corresponds to a given seat on a given bus. On buses from Piura to Tumbes the correspondence is ignored and on the same buses back to Piura it is strictly observed.

To the extent that there is a line I am well back in it, so

far back that I will not make it onto the first bus that comes. I put my ticket away and eat a tangerine, spit the seeds into the coil of peel in my hand. Then I drop the peel and seeds on the ground behind my seat. There are few garbage cans anywhere in Peru. Years ago the Shining Path used them as bomb casings, so they were removed, even in cities like Piura where terrorists rarely attacked, and most have not yet been replaced.

A newspaper on the bench beside me, and there is a smiling near-naked woman on the back cover. This newspaper calls them Naughty Ones, and she holds a revolver as if about to execute the photographer. She wears incandescent blue eyeshadow and something of a police uniform made into a bikini, the top sprung open, a small red star covering part of one immense bleached nipple. Her name is listed as Deisi, and this may well be true.

On the inside pages are stock markets crashing across Asia and aliens landing in Ica and a fight between an American company and a Franco-Australian consortium to control Yanacocha, the richest gold mine in the world, thirty miles from Cajamarca and there is no end to these things. Also there are injury reports for the soccer games to be played later today, and Guzmán has been locked in a tiny cell in Callao since he was captured in 1992. Psoriasis eats small pieces of him daily, and terrorists do not appear to be such a problem now. Of course, that also seemed true ten months ago, and then men and women came to the Japanese ambassador's residence dressed as waiters and waitresses, poured champagne and smiled at each of the hundreds of gala guests, pulled out automatic weapons as their colleagues blew a hole in the back of the building.

Nearly everyone at the university knew someone who knew someone related to one of the seventy-two hostages still there four months later. Then music was heard, military marches played through very large speakers, while underground there was digging, Chavín de Huántar, the operation named for a temple complex three thousand years old in Ancash, not far from what once was Yungay. The assault lasted fifteen minutes, and afterwards Fujimori himself walked in, stepping over MRTA cadavers to shake hands with his commandos.

The first bus comes and the people in line behind me mob forward, a marvelous thing to see, viscous and fast and unacceptable: when the shoving is finished, those who would have had to wait for the third or fourth bus are seated at the head of the line. I take up my knapsack and walk, address the women nearest the gate, my voice starting low and rising quickly:

- I wish to sit down.

- Sorry, says one of the women. I am sitting here, so you must sit somewhere else.

- You are sitting in my seat. Please move.

- This is not your seat. I have been sitting here for an hour, waiting for a friend.

- Do not lie to me, madam. You pressed forward with all the others.

The women to either side of her begin to berate me. Both are well dressed and have unsightly moles. A man standing beside me shrugs and shakes his head as if to say, But yes, but yes, the race is to the swift after all, and the battle to the strong. He smiles at me, and at the women, wishing both to commiserate and make peace, but there will be no peace. I lean down to the woman.

- Will you move? Or shall I move you?

The women around her shout and one rises up as if to slap me and the second bus comes. It is now that I notice my right hand, not hand but fist. I smile at the woman in the seat I no longer require. I board the bus, sit halfway back, and wait for the seat-thieves to get on. They do, one by one. All except the woman I threatened. She is still sitting inside the station, scanning the crowd for her friend who has not yet arrived.

~∞~

The desert north of Piura is littered with bright blue plastic bags. This is always the case. They are strewn in the sandy openings and caught in the branches of the thorn-scrub and algarrobos. I suspect they come from the small collections of reed huts that hunch beside the highway. In most contexts the bags would be garbage, but in this wide brown desolate dry death, they are beautiful.

There are rumors that some of the MRTA members were disarmed and executed in the course of the assault. This may be true, but I have not yet met anyone who cares. Perhaps they will care later. Perhaps not. It is also said that this tactic was ordered not by the president or any of his military commanders but by Vladimiro Montesinos, who is the head of the intelligence service and is said to run most aspects of the government. It is thought that he arranged for the massacre in Barrios Altos, fifteen dead; and a year later at La Cantuta, nine students and a professor taken and later found murdered; and for the torture of intelligence officers who leaked information about these and other extra-judicial killings. Everyone cares about these things and yet I have not heard too much dissent. Inflation is down and most people here are less afraid than they have been in some time.

Armando deserves an answer and so for a while I read Oquendo de Amat. So then for you the rain is an intimate apparatus for measuring change, he says. I am not sure how much this matters, but I like how it sounds, and this trip through the desert to Machala, it is the reverse of the last leg of the first time, my arrival.

That trip was planned to make a certain kind of sense— after four months of cash carpentry for an uncle in Orange County, I would visit archives in Managua, in Panama City, in Cajamarca and Lima. Then the trip ripened into something else. Managua, yes, twelve days with the Colección Somoza at the IHNCA, and a single afternoon on the Pacific coast: a beer, two, staring out at the route of Espinosa's expedition in Balboa's ships, Orellana and Francisco Pizarro onboard. Panama City next and the Biblioteca Nacional yes but then a visit to Panama la Vieja. The remains of the cathedral and bell tower and Bishop's House, staring at stones overgrown, pointless on so many levels and there were other days in the archives but more spent chasing: Pizarro's land on the Chagres and his blood trail through the Pearl Islands with Morales; the scattered bricks of Acla and a guide who swings an invisible sword three times, claims that I am standing where Balboa's head lands. Back to Panama City and a taxi not to the airport but to the Muelle Fiscal. From there the long slow green coast: an old cargo boat to Jaqué, dolphins and a whale alongside; a low lancha across the Colombian border to Juradó; cargo boat again to Bahía Solano and from there to Buenaventura, the San Juan delta and Andagoya falls into the water, returns years later to found or refound the city, stows his family and heads east, challenges Benalcázar and is crushed, returns to find his wife and children dead of fever. A bus inland to Cali, fighting freight trucks on each straightaway; another down through Popayán to Pasto, and small quiet roads to the coast. A fisherman takes me to Isla del Gallo. Pizarro here three months and the line in the sand. Gorgona, eight months with Ruiz's interpreters and here is the difference. A twelve-hour ferry across the border to Esmeraldas, the Ecuadorian border guards careful through my bags, then down the coast to Coaque, Pizarro and Orellana taking gold and silver and emeralds, a plague of buboes and inland to Quito, south to Guayaquil, a ferry to Puná, Pizarro plotting but the islanders attack first, kill three Spaniards and Soto arrives, will carry them to Tumbes and the invasion will begin and a ferry to Machala where I will be in four or eight hours.

Talara, and the oil wells here pump so slowly and

never stop. Mariángel would find them dinosaur-like, would tilt her head to either side and smile. Guzmán too once believed he had the one and only truth. I wonder what he believes now. I put the Oquendo book away, lean my head back and hope for sleep.

Sweat is pooled in my navel, is thick in the rolls of fat above and below. The bus has stopped. There are no passengers waiting beside the road, no stores or restaurants nearby. Perhaps the bus has run out of gas.

Running up the stairs now is a bent man who climbs aboard, stands at the head of the aisle and shouts hoarsely about how sorry he is for this disturbance, but he has books to sell, books on plumbing and gardening and the Virgin of Guadalupe, and he is sure such books will interest such well-educated people as ourselves.

We ignore him in unison, as if we had rehearsed it. After a time he falls silent, looks around for an empty seat. The only one on the entire bus is the one next to me. This is often the case. The man comes and sits down, untucks his shirt, smells slightly of vinegar. We look at each other and then we look out the window.

- The desert, says the man.

- Yes, I say.

- Very hot.

- Yes.

- And dry.

I close my eyes.

- But it will not be dry much longer, he says.

I open my eyes.

- El Niño, he says. Today or tomorrow or the next day. The ocean is heating up. Soon Piura will be like the jungle.

- Nothing is like the jungle.
- Were you here in 1983?
- No.
- So you know nothing about El Niño.

The ocean can be seen out the window, which makes the air feel not quite as hot as it truly is. I wish to ask more questions but do not know which. The bus slows, enters a town, and the man stands and walks up the aisle.

This is Máncora, where Pilar and I spent our honeymoon. Máncora is much nicer than the coastal towns closer to Piura. There are cheap bungalows with patios giving on to the beach, and hammocks that will take my weight, and every restaurant knows the secret to enrollado de pescado, a rolled flounder filet stuffed with shrimp or prawns. The sauce is sometimes white and flecked with crabmeat, and sometimes red, now sour, now sweet. I think briefly, stupidly, of stepping off the bus. The beach here, how Pilar swam and loved, her body turning in the water. But Mariángel, the taxista, and we pull away.

A few minutes later the bus stops in a long line of highway traffic. There is something like far-off thunder but the sky is cloudless. We wait. The heat thickens the air like soup. We wait. The driver turns off the engine and goes to sleep.

I follow several other passengers as they debark, and we stand in the shade of the bus, where it is no cooler than anywhere else. One man walks forward up the stalled line of cars. We watch until he disappears. We wait and wait. Then he comes back, and someone asks.

- The army, he says. Artillery practice, he says.
- In case Ecuador invades, I say.

I mean this to be amusing but everyone nods somberly as if I have named the most likely scenario, as if closing the Panamericana in the middle of the day for artillery practice were reasonable, as if there were nowhere else in the desert to do it.

⟶◦⟵

In Tumbes the colectivos are waiting. The driver of the first one in line grows sad as I approach: when other potential passengers notice me sitting in a given car, they often select a different one. Sometimes the drivers ask me to pay a double fare, and I always refuse on principle. This man does not ask, is simply sad, and I slump deep into the seat.

It is only forty minutes to Ecuador now. Pizarro makes land, but Tumbes is not as he remembers it from the second voyage: the civil war has left it in ruins. He continues south, founds the first Spanish city on this side of the continent, San Miguel de Piura and we push north through the last waste of desert, come to the strewn plastic and paper and rags of the market stalls in Aguas Verdes.

My passport is observed and stamped by the Peruvian officials, who do not care how many times I return with a tourist visa only. Then I walk through the heat and across the Zarumilla River, litter-scabbed and brown and almost dry.

In Ecuador my passport is observed again, the years of tourist visas, and the officials here touch their lips and smile. They welcome me to their country and ask how long I plan to stay. They know the answer but this is our game.

- I am not entirely sure, I say.
- Would a month be sufficient?
- A month would be ideal.

They smile again, welcome me again, stamp my passport and direct me to the customs office. I have never in my life had anything to declare. What would it feel like, declaring?

Back out into the screaming sunlight. The market stalls of Huaquillas are precisely the same as those of Aguas Verdes. Underwear and coat hangers and pirated cassettes and unidentifiable plastic objects. Dollars and sucres and soles can all be used, and I watch as two European tourists are pickpocketed: a thief kneels in the dust, pretending to have dropped something at the feet of one of the women.

    - My keys, he says in Spanish, and then in English, as he takes romantic, attentive hold of her pant-leg, and lifts her foot.

    - Your what?

    - My keys, I have lost my keys.

    The woman laughs, off-balance, and calls to her friend, who comes and takes her hand, steadies her. The woman's foot is lifted and set down, lifted and set down. Behind the women are two more men, their hands deep in the matching purple backpacks, so agile, so quick, so deft, but as I step forward I see that this once they have failed—they shake their heads at the kneeling man, who pretends now to find his keys, and says attentive, romantic goodbyes.

    Leaving the border is like throwing a switch: the desert ends, is replaced by banana plantations. Another bus takes me to Machala, and a taxi to the water at Puerto Bolívar. There is no beach here, just pavement and waveless murk, and I must wait for a minimum of six hours. I once tried staying only five, and for an hour the border guards did not let me back through. You have not seen enough of our country, they kept saying. You have not seen anything at all.

    I choose a restaurant, take a seat on the patio. Across the brown of the strait is the Jambelí Archipelago, pleasant enough and green. Hard to the north is an arc of the gulf, bluer water and slivers of polished lead: dolphins, eight or ten of them, headed toward Puná.

    The waiter comes. I ask if he has enrollado de pescado, knowing already that he does not, but hoping, hoping. He does not. He apologizes. He says that there is a fine ceviche today, and I agree to try it, though the ceviche here is for some reason less heartening than what one receives in Piura or Máncora. Perhaps there is a secret to ceviche too, and no one has told the people of Machala.

The last time I saw dolphins was in Colán, two years ago or more. Colán is the closest reasonable beach to Piura. The rich have lined the shore with their fine summer houses, and the restaurants and cafes are built behind. The water cannot be seen from their patios, and the dust from the street settles in your beer.

Of those who wade in the water at Colán, all but the tourists know to scuff their feet until the water is deep enough to dive. If one instead takes normal steps, sooner or later one's foot will land on a stingray, and the barbed spine will plunge in and rip out, taking its plug of flesh. The venom is black and must be sucked from the foot as it is dipped in boiling water.

Reynaldo's aunt had money once, and still has a house in Colán, glass and salt-stained wood. From the deck each night Reynaldo and I watched as the sun set. Piurans believe that the sunset in Colán is the most beautiful in the world, and as far as I know they are correct. They also speak of the moon as seen from Paita across the bay, and they could be right about this as well.

The dolphins we saw that afternoon would not swim with us, and the next morning the beach was thick with eels. The waiter brings the ceviche, and a beer, and a plate of onions in lemon juice. The eels were three and four feet long, white with brown shading. Their mouths were wedges and their teeth were the tips of needles.

Half of the eels were already dead or dying. The others were burrowing into the wet sand. Once in, only six or seven inches of tail stuck out, and by the end of the day they were gone, eaten by dogs and seagulls and vultures. Reynaldo told me that when certain eels are caught by fishermen, they are sold to the Japanese for hundreds of dollars per pound. There is a trick, Reynaldo said. The eels must be skinned, but if this happens after they have died, they secrete a substance of some kind which fouls the meat, so they must be skinned while still alive.

Over time the waiter brings a second beer, a third and a fourth, and the sun goes down, not as in Colán but not unbeautifully. The mosquitoes come out. I am careful to read no more than half a meter per hour. For a bookmark I am using a cancer brochure, its cover a sketch of a woman checking herself in the mirror.

Finally it has been long enough. I call to the waiter, scribble in the air. He brings the bill and I pay. Another taxi, another bus. Huaquillas, like everywhere else in this world, is less ugly by night.

Customs, and then Immigrations.

- But you have been in our country less than a day! says one officer.

I pantomime distress.

- Ecuador cannot be seen in a day, says another.

- Yes, I know. I wish there were something I could do. But I have been called back. What can I do? They have called me back.

- Who has called you back? Your employer?

- No. My friends. They—

- You are lying to me, sir. You have come to Ecuador only for the visa. You care nothing for our country. You will not be allowed to leave.

I bow my head, reach mournfully for my wallet, and ask if there is any way this uncomfortable situation can be rearranged so as to make it more comfortable.

One of the officials takes out a calculator, punches random numbers.

- The fine will be one hundred dollars, he says.

So this is now the starting point.

- I am so sorry, I say, but one hundred dollars is far too much. I could perhaps pay twenty.

- Twenty? Twenty is unreasonable, sir. It is insulting. You must pay the fine, and the fine is one hundred dollars. Though we could also possibly accept ninety.

It takes ten minutes for us to meet at sixty-eight. The men thank me for visiting Ecuador, and ask me to return soon, to stay longer next time, to enjoy their country, for it is a marvelous country, and they are right, and I say so.

Another colectivo, and this one has no windows, and though it is still very hot there is enough wind to make me pleased that I remembered to bring a sweater. It is a fine wool sweater, blue and thick, and living in Piura I have no need of it except for night trips back from Ecuador.

Tumbes, the bus station, the lines. Then the tiny damp dark bathroom, the fetid hole, footprints worn into the cement on either side. I am there much longer than I mean to be, am lightheaded coming out as the motor of the one waiting bus is started. Perhaps the fish in the ceviche was less than fresh. I pull myself on and the bus sways toward me. I push through, and find a small dark man pretending to be asleep in my window seat.

The overhead rack is full of bags. I stuff my knapsack in on top of them, and tap the man on the shoulder as lightly as I am able under the circumstances.

- It was you, wasn't it, I say.

I say this only because it seems a likely means of success—this man's ears protrude sharply from his head.

- What?

- If I'm not mistaken, you're in my seat.

He does not contest this, and I am happy for him. He stands and moves so as not to impede my entrance. His shirt is thin and his sandals are old. One of his ankles is swollen oddly, bulging above the joint.

The lights are dimmed as I sit down; the bus lurches and turns and the man lands mostly in my lap. I pretend this has not happened. He apologizes, lifts and slides and stares out the far window.

We stop briefly in front of the Customs office but are waved through uninspected, and it does not take long for the driver to turn on the music: salsa, fine bus music. If Mariángel were here, she and I would dance in place. On through the dark. Out the window is the Southern Cross, and its lowest star can almost not be seen, but the constellation points in the direction we are heading. Perhaps this will help.

The ocean appears but cannot be heard, not with the music, not with the noise of the motor. Máncora. Perhaps sleep, and now Talara, the oil wells lit a blurry brown. The bus stops wherever people wait, and the aisle fills. At some point the salsa becomes merengue, even better, smoother, kinder— merengue is a sort of love—but in Peru the waxing crescent moon is a malevolent smile. I suspect this is not widely known.

A light cramp begins at the base of my stomach, fades, returns and fades again. My neighbor's head begins to bob. At last he gives in, slumps, his head resting against my shoulder. For a time I attempt again to sleep, my cheek against the top of the man's head, but it does not quite work, bruises my cheekbone and gums. I straighten and watch him as well as one can watch something so close to one's eyes. One magnificent ear. His mouth, slightly open. His face twitches, he smiles and frowns in his sleep. I do not wish to know his dreams.

Again the cramp and fading. My neighbor starts to drool, and I consider waking him. The drooling continues, intensifies, and there is a voice, a woman's voice, from the back of the bus. It is not clear what she is saying. I shrug to wake my neighbor.

- I am not your pillow, I say, but I say this kindly.

The man blinks and nods and shifts away. The cramp is now somewhere between present and not-present, seems to be biding time. The woman's voice is slightly louder. We are not far from Sullana, and Sullana is not far from Piura—I will be home by three in the morning if all goes well, if the bus does not miss a turn and slide off the highway and come to rest not quite at its tipping point, not quite killing all of us.

Unfortunately my neighbor appears to be unnerved by the woman's words or voice. Maybe he knows her, or someone like her. She goes quiet for a time, then starts up again. My neighbor takes out a knife and opens it. It has a fine blade.

The voice silences again. The man puts away his knife. The woman shrieks, he brings the knife back out, and the shrieking lessens to murmuring as if this were a kind of game. There is also something that might be begging, though it is not easy to hear, not with the motor and merengue and cramps that come in series. My neighbor stands, and if he goes there will be blood, and police, and I will not see Mariángel for many, many hours.

- I wouldn't, I say. What if he's got a gun? He could be a policeman, you know. Your knife is a good one, but you'd never get close enough to use it.

He considers, sits back down and fidgets. He checks his watch, fidgets some more. He curses and stands and I catch his arm.

- You'll just get yourself in trouble. A few more minutes and we're in Sullana. Maybe one of them will get off there.

I let go, shake my head, turn to look out the window, clutch at my stomach and am fortunate: the woman has gone quiet. My neighbor sits down and leans back. The knife is still open in his hand.

Dim light filters in: Sullana, its bus station, cement and dust. Passengers exit and enter. My neighbor and I, we wait. He appears to be holding his breath. A woman slides past us and off the bus, a woman with dyed-blonde hair, and she looks like the sort of woman who might become upset late at night on a bus and begin to shriek.

When she is gone the door closes and the bus pulls out of the parking lot.

- You see? I say. It's better this way.

My neighbor closes his eyes. He looks very tired, and somewhat disappointed. Then we are unfortunate, the woman's voice again, murmuring and moaning. My neighbor looks at me. I shrug and look away. And a thought: perhaps this was how it started for Pilar.

A scream, more begging, and I am up and grab for my neighbor's knife but he holds it away from me, pushes at my chest, brings the blade to my throat, thin and cold against my skin.

- What the fuck are you doing? he says.

- I was wrong, I say. If you want him, go and get him. But if you do not, give the knife to me and I will take care of it.

He tells me to sit calmly back, and I do. He stands and limps down the aisle. He stops near the back, and I wait for the glint of metal, the sound of the knife plunging home not real but imagined and it will stay with me for months of bad nights but this is not what happens. The man has turned to the seat on the other side of the aisle. He appears to be chatting, and puts his knife away.

Then there are sirens and lights. The bus pulls off the highway and the motor and music die. The door opens and three customs officers board: apparently they have changed their mind about us. I take my knapsack and follow other passengers off the bus. My passport is checked, my knapsack searched.

I look up at the bus windows, and behind them are shadows, figures moving along the aisle, and now there is a scream. I wait for the officers to pull someone out onto the ground—the man, the woman, someone else. In the end only the officers themselves descend.

The stomach cramps are gone. Back in my seat I wait for my neighbor to reappear, but he does not. I close my eyes. As the motor starts I feel someone sit carefully beside me. I open my eyes. This man is carrying a briefcase, has a beard and glasses, is smiling triumphantly. He could surely tell me the story but I do not want to know. I feel that if I say anything he will start laughing, and I will not be responsible for that.

To escape from him I think of Pilar, that first trip to a beach, the day of the photograph on the flyer. Yacila is not far from Colán, and the water is most often too cold for stingrays but warm enough for swimming. There was an old woman in a long black dress waist-deep in the surf, netting sand lice; there were men digging under their stranded fishing boats, pushing logs beneath, rolling the boats forward into the waves; there were children paddling rafts beyond the break, and there was also a stingray, in spite of all we had been promised there was a stingray, and I learned too late the importance of scuffing one's feet. Someone brought boiling water. Pilar put her mouth to the wound, sucked and spat for twenty minutes. The pain filled and erased me.

At the El Dorado station in Piura I grab my knapsack and push forward. Waiting outside are taxis and mototaxis and constant honking. I take the largest taxi though the driver asks twice the standard fare. He believes I am new to Piura and know nothing of the fares and distances here, and tonight I will let him persist in this belief.

We come to the Virgin, my street, my house. It is still very hot, and there is no wind, and my sweater has become a ridiculous thing. For some reason the dogs are quiet and the streetlight has not yet been repaired and these things are helpful but I think of tomorrow, of the following days, of what is waiting. Perhaps in Machala I should have taken a swim, and headed due west, and kept swimming.

# 15.

I START FOR THE GATE, DO NOT WISH TO BUY CANDY BUT MUST and will and in two of three classes today I had to teach functional language. The sets were for restaurants and business meetings respectively. Many of the phrases involved are irrational and incoherent and I hate them. *Now, then.* Now? Then?

Because today is Criolla Song Day, a wooden platform was raised at the center of campus and filled with musicians. They played tondero and marinera, landó and festejo, all of it marvelous but I do not want it coming through my window as I teach. Because today is also Halloween, I expected my students to be giddy and loud and oddly dressed, to slip through my hands like eels. Instead they were magnificent.

True criolla means only a guitar and a cajón and at least one voice; occasionally there are also spoons and the jaw of a burro. The lyrics are patriotic, nostalgic, enamored, defiant, and what saved me today was my students' overflowing joy at pretending to be what they are not. In my Intermediate class we drilled the hateful phrases chorally and individually, and then I assigned the roles: customer and manager and waiter or waitress. They wrote and memorized their lines, and recited them for me, five minutes scheduled per group but they went to ten and fifteen. They delighted in improvisation and would have continued for hours if I'd let them, serving each other plates of delicious imaginary fried chicken. They laughed at their mistakes and cheered each idiom well used, each cleverness, each deft performance. It was heartrending, yes, and restorative.

To the gate and out and through the robed and bearded Germans standing unhappily in front of the Texaco station. It pleases me to see them unhappy but the sun has set so there is no time to taunt. Across the Panamericana and into a corner store. The closest thing left to candy is individually wrapped Halls throat lozenges. There are half a dozen stores such as this nearby and in all of them this will be the case. I ask the man to load all that he has into plastic bags. He points me to a chair and begins counting.

I slump, and rest my head against the wall. Criolla Song Day, Halloween, the final rounds of the tondero and marinera dance competitions at Club Grau, All Saints' Day, the Day of the Dead, and Mariángel's birthday—all this in three days. One consolation is that each event is an opportunity to renew the search, and the card still hangs from my headboard but now not unproblematically: what if Sarita Colonia located and broke the taxista and I never found out?

What I have been told, and it may very well be true: her father was a carpenter, and she was born in a town called Belén, which is Spanish for Bethlehem. The shopkeeper is still at work counting lozenges and in the dust on his counter I rewrite less simply the prayer I do not pray, that instead Sarita deliver him to me, or that once having broken him she send me signs. There are still the matters of identity and assurance, the questions of how one might know wholly and know that one knows wholly. New and still longer sentences might be required but I am out of counter and dust and my ideas are not yet clear.

The bags of Halls at last ready, I pay and step outside and am assaulted: the streets are now full of unaccompanied children, most of them in unidentifiable costumes, and perhaps there is not a problem here with madmen who slip razors into apples, who dust candy corn with rat poison. Perhaps the insane—and there are many, riding buses, driving taxis, in CREMPT and shouting on the corners—perhaps each year on this day they all go suddenly benign.

I am not the only one under attack. The children demand candy of all passers-by, and all cars stopped at stop signs, and all drunks collapsed in alleys. One must give them the candy they ask for or they will say, Do not be evil.

They will not be smiling as they say this. Also, these children do not shout Trick or Treat! Instead they shout Halloween! I fight through them to my house and promise that their candy will soon be ready and slam the door in their ambiguously painted faces. I take up my daughter and hold her. I thank Casualidad for her good work today and every day, escort her to the entry, wish her a safe trip home.

It occurs to me that she has never told me where in Piura she lives, and I have never asked. Her sister lives in Catacaos, a small town ten minutes to the southwest though it cannot be reached in that amount of time, and I have the sister's phone number written somewhere. I eat the dinner left ready on the table, bite after slow bite until the pounding and screaming can no longer be ignored. Then I put Mariángel in the new and elaborate baby carrier my mother sent early as part of a package for her birthday. It is an improvement on her shrinking sling, though I have not yet learned the purpose of all the straps.

It appears that Mariángel loves Halloween, or perhaps she loves only the spinning each time I turn to the door. In spite of the quantities I purchased it is not long before my Halls are gone, agotado, the same word one uses to express exhaustion, and there are only a few hours of third-round dancing left to be seen at Club Grau. I lock my front door, shift Mariángel around to my chest, fight through the children in the street and flag down a taxi near the park. The streetlights here are unbroken and shine just bright enough to show that the matacojudo trees are at last in bloom.

The taxista is an excessively tall man. He hunches over the steering wheel, his head almost touching the windshield, and it is soon clear that he has only recently arrived in Piura: he has never heard of Club Grau, and asks what I am willing to pay to get there. The night smells of sugar and sweat. At Sánchez Cerro I tell him to continue straight ahead, then remember my plan and direct us first east.

Each year Boby's hosts a Halloween party—black walls, blood-red light, all the draught beer one can drink for fifty soles. As regards that beer there is only one man serving from beside a single keg, and I am not unhappy to be unwelcome though there is a contest as well, with a plane ticket to New York as top prize for best costume. Reynaldo spends weeks designing clothes and appendages that will enable him to impersonate an alien from the year's most popular science fiction movie. The precise alien involved is often a secret. He invests unreasonable sums in his materials, and loses annually to an engineering student from Trujillo who entered the university nine years ago and is at least three years from graduation.

Second prize in the contest is always an electric sandwich maker. Reynaldo has given me two. At some point the student will either graduate or be expelled, will move back to Trujillo, and then, Reynaldo says, the ticket to New York shall be his.

I ask the driver to work slowly up the block and back along it. I watch the costumed revelers that arrive and those that leave and those that are spilled in the parking lot. There is no Almagro in view tonight, no Soto or Orellana or Pizarro, no wooden swords whatsoever. This is surely for the best, and was my costume ever once correctly guessed by anyone holding a bowl of candy and leaning out into the light of his or her own front porch? It was not. Not even the second of the two consecutive years I wore precisely the same costume, with Pizarro's initials written as a hint below the blurring coat of arms on my cardboard shield, not even when I held that shield up to the light and said I'm the same as last year! The men and women nodded and rubbed their chins and said, Sir Galahad? Then they said, King Arthur? Then they said, A robot? and gave up and smiled a little when I told them again and gave me less candy than they otherwise might have, and immediately gave me more, worried I would think they had stinted me because of my size, and immediately wished that for my own good they had stinted me because of my size.

And now I tell the driver that I have made a mistake, that this is not where I wish to be, that I will happily pay twice the fare we agreed upon. He shrugs and we pull away. I wonder what happened to all that armor. I would be unsurprised if my mother threw it out after my father's death, and unsurprised if she did not, and as my father fell he must have landed on one of my old costumes: he had flecks of silver paint on his face when my mother found him. She said that she'd run upstairs to call the ambulance and then back downstairs to hold him and knew there was no point to an ambulance though his body was still warm. She sat on the damp cement floor and cried and took his head in her lap and cried and traced his face with her hands and cried and there were flecks of silver on her fingertips now and she looked, and there they were, tiny points of light scattered across his face, I remember her telling me this, am almost sure I remember.

~⬦⬦~

There are hundreds of other spectators like Mariángel and me, so little right to be here, though we have been invited, we have all been invited. The small coliseum stepped in cement is full, but in Peru there is always room for one more, I have found, even one of my proportions. There are small twinkling lights strung across the open space above us; they are mostly red and green though Christmas is still two months away.

There is also gold and silver bunting, and the spectators have sorted themselves according to the city from which they come: Sullana, Chiclayo, Trujillo, even Lima. They all have cowbells and horns and tambourines. The noise as they cheer for their dancers is a gleeful abyss.

Dozens of vendors make their way through us. I request juice for Mariángel from one, a beer from another, a chicken sandwich from a third. I test the sandwich before paying for it. Elsewhere, uncommon meats are said to taste like chicken. Here, every so often the chicken will taste like fish. It is a question, I believe, of excess fishmeal in the feed, and can likewise affect eggs and anything made from them: once a lemon meringue pie that tasted of lemons and vanilla and sugar and day-old herring.

When we have eaten I begin a slow round. I look as carefully as I am able, and there are a hundred faces that are so nearly right. I also see many of my colleagues, and wave to each.

Mariángel pulls at my beard and the fifteen-to-eighteen-year-old tondero dancers begin as we retake our seats. The youngest dancers danced hours ago, and I am sorry to have missed them. Beside us sits one perhaps five years old, her mascara streaming from her eyes as she screams at her father that she is not at all tired and does not want to go home.

The dress for tondero is simple. Both the boys and the girls are barefoot. The boys are in loose white trousers tied with rope at the waist, loose white shirts and wide straw hats. The girls are also mostly in white, knee-length dresses with bits of color here and there. Some bear clay pots on their heads. I have never seen one fall.

The music begins, minor-toned, a military band filling space with horns and drums. The dancers start onto the floor, one pair after another until all six pairs are weaving a slow circle around the edge of the coliseum. As they draw close their mothers stand and block my view, cameras and cowbells and shouting and the only way to make them sit down is to throw relatively heavy objects.

There are important differences between tondero and marinera, and after four years of student essays and Club Grau competitions I know almost all of them. Mariángel struggles at my chest, and I turn her to face outward. The word tondero is not Spanish or Quechua but Malgache. And the three-part dance, glosa and canto and fuga, it is modeled on the movement of chickens. As Claudia wrote in an essay last semester, "The dance figures the wedding of the cock and hen; he chases and measures her until he is able to catch her by the neck."

The dancers have taken their positions and the dance begins. Like the dress it is simple: all smile and hip, all beseech and coquette. The boys wave vast handkerchiefs and sweep the ground with their hats, inviting the girls to notice. The girls have their own handkerchiefs, equally vast, dipping and twirling. They lift their hemlines ever so slightly, mark the rhythm with their hips, scrape the outside of one foot back and forth across the ground, and this same movement, I have seen it in nearby villages, when a man or woman is embarrassed, or wishes to appear so.

The boys dance bent at the waist, spinning around their partners, hoping to catch their eyes, and the girls flee them, but slowly, slowly. Their gazes meet and fall away. They advance toward one another and retreat, her skirt lifted still higher, her bare ankles blurred in the dance, the handkerchiefs held aloft. A circle is made, him searching for the encounter, her keeping it not quite at bay. Both rasp the ground with their feet too quickly to be seen, and they spin together, spin tighter, gather into one another as the final drumbeat echoes off our sweaty faces.

That is only the first half of the dance. Mariángel holds my thumbs as if flying a plane. A drumroll ripples, rises and falls, and everything happens again, still faster or so it seems. I watch until the music ends and the cheering bears down on me, cuts at my side, takes my breath. When it calms there is a time of waiting. The winner is announced, and mothers rise up to block my view. I buy another chicken sandwich.

It is time now for marinera. Unless I am careful all the women turn into Pilar. She danced every year at this competition and never won or placed. It was here that I saw her for the first time though she was at that moment my student, three months in my classroom day after day and each day I had failed to see her. I watched as she danced, and she was too brusque for marinera, and still I could not look away. She would have been better dancing tondero. Did no one think to tell her? And when she came to class the following Monday—her pronunciation as always indecipherable, her random use of the past and present and future, her insistence on the continuous forms as if there were no other options, her avoidance of modal verbs as if there were something to fear in could and would and should and might and will—now I could see her, because I had seen her dance, and this is unforgivable.

The pacazo shat on my head and my students sat only in the farthest rows, all but Pilar, and yes, marinera is more strictly structured than tondero, more urban, prettier and less joyous. The dancers move straight-backed, smiling but formal. The night Mariángel was born, the nurse took her away to clean her, and the doctor told Pilar to rest; I slept for an hour on a bench in the lobby, woke and went to the viewing room, and Pilar was already there, had dragged herself along the floor from the recovery room, calling to no one, trailing blood, had pulled herself up to the rail to watch Mariángel sleep, and how could I not then have known?

The music progresses minor to major to minor. The women wear vastly colorful dresses, sapphire and teal and fuchsia with gold and silver braiding. The men are in something not quite like tuxedos, and I turn for a scan of those nearest. Nothing. Those slightly farther away, and still nothing. At the edge of the next circle sit the mayor and his wife. The mansion he is building with municipal funds meant for sewer systems and law enforcement is almost finished, or so I have heard. Last year he danced with his wife during the final evening's intermission, and he is a fine dancer, as is she.

I see a young woman sitting thirty yards to my right, and I am uncertain, then sure, then uncertain again. I believe she is the putilla, the woman from the Pórticos Hotel. Brown hair neither long nor short and yes it must be her—the odd posed smile, and the slip.

What the movement of chickens is to tondero, the movement of Peruvian pace horses is to marinera. These are horses that move in ways I have not seen elsewhere: no bounce or surge but pure smooth forward movement. They seem docile until ridden and are then exuberant, and flick their hooves to the side with impossible speed, this motion the result of searing sands and four hundred years of careful breeding.

The dance builds, seduction and love, the smiles never faltering, the bodies held erect, all color all movement all grace, and the final flourish. The putilla—but she is not a putilla now, is wearing tan jeans, a cream-colored shirt, a brown jacket. I close my eyes and have it: she is a chilalo. These are the precise colors, and perhaps in the future she will be something else again. She stands and stretches. Her jacket is scuffed at the elbows, the colors faded in spots. She turns and looks at or near me but does not see me. If she saw me she would remember, and laugh.

She stretches again, longer, the position held. I smell perfume but it cannot be hers at this distance. She threads her way down through the crowd, turns at the gates and is gone.

Chilalos come often to my back yard, alight in my almond tree and sing poorly for hours. They screech, it is a fact, when they think they are singing. And there is a phrase: morir como un chilalo. To die like a chilalo, yes. It is believed that they are so nervous that if you were to catch one, to take it in your hand, its heart would stop from fright.

Mariángel begins to cry, wants simply to be home and I agree. I beg the pardon of everyone on my way down through the stands. I brush their shoulders and they turn but are too surprised to say anything—here my bulk is astonishing, even to people who know me well.

Past the mayor and his wife, the vendors, past dancers still waiting their turn, and these are the oldest ones, beyond the age for such things. Their make-up cannot hide what time has done to them. Perhaps they have been dancing since they could walk and still have never made the winner's podium. I wish them well. They know the odds, and still they hope. How could that be anything but beautiful? I smile as I edge past, a smile for each of them, then out through the gates.

There is no one else at the taxi stand. I wait, watch, finally nod to a driver. It is a fast trip home, the streets nearly empty of children. I see only a skeleton standing on a corner and a ghoul hunched in an alley.

Just inside my front door there are several Halls scattered on the floor. I sing to Mariángel, set her in her crib, gather the lozenges and go to the back patio. The almond tree is nearly barren. There is a lechuza, silent and watching. I eat the lozenges, holding them at the back of my mouth, one after another until my throat is numb.

⟋⟍⟋⟍

Saturday morning is not a comfortable time. Casualidad is disoriented, and bumps into furniture with some regularity. I ask how she is feeling, and she smiles but does not reply. I tell her she is welcome to take the day off. She nods, turns toward the kitchen and walks straight into the doorjamb.

I convince her to lie down for a moment, and have just gotten her comfortable on the couch when Mariángel wakes crying. She does not want her juice, and my singing, four straight splendid Susana Baca songs, has no effect. I put her in the carrier and twirl around the living room until I am dizzy. This also has no effect.

I check, and yes, there is swelling at the back of her gums. I find the necessary cream, daub and rub as indicated, and she bites me, draws blood, quiets slightly. It is time for San Teodoro. Casualidad is still asleep so we write her a note. Then out and past the Virgin in her case, turning and along the warehouse from which the burglars occasionally come, and also the rats that breed and breed. Rats do not see well in bright light or so it seems: more than once they have run from the patio into the house and straight toward where I stood in the kitchen. When this occurs, if I remain still they pass close alongside, and it requires no great effort to kick them against the wall and beat them to death with a skillet. Even when I miss, which is often, they are not hard to track down, as once indoors they most often run along the edge of the closest wall, guided unluckily by their whiskers.

San Teodoro is not Piura's only cemetery but it is its largest and oldest by some measure. Past a chifa and a primary school, past the enthusiastic nuns and sad but willing schizophrenics playing volleyball on the dirt strip in front of CREMPT, past houses that must once have been very fine. At the cemetery gates there are vendors selling candles and shrouds and cardboard images of saints, and others selling flowers of all sizes and colors, flowers from the mountains and jungle, roses and orchids and sunflowers and dozens of species whose names Reynaldo has never told me. There are also people selling pastries and cotton candy, ice cream and snow cones, soft drinks and beer and many varieties of emoliente, a sort of tea made with roots and vines and spices. One kind of emoliente is said to cure liver ailments, and there are others for the kidneys and bowels and heart. Each has its own distinct taste, and they are all equally repulsive.

The cemetery is vast and inside there is nothing like the oaks in Fallash, no grass-covered plots like my father's. Instead of grass there is sand, and most of the dead are buried not in plots of any kind but in niches set in great structures of whitewashed cement. The structures reach ten and twelve stories high, and each niche has a ledge where flowers and candles may be set. At this time of year there are also great lengths of extension cord, so that electric lights may take the place of candles for any who so wish.

Past the small chapel and through the few hundred old graves set in the ground, each with its headstone, many with photographs behind glass. Standing before the nearest whitewashed structure there are a dozen young men with bamboo ladders. For a small fee they will take their ladders to the loved one's niche, will place flowers and candles or lights in whatever pattern is desired.

Pilar's tomb is on the lowest level, just off the ground. It is cleaner than the tombs to either side, is dusted daily, a service I have hired. Mariángel and I sit for a while beside her. The ground is not comfortable, but tonight we will bring blankets. I watch the young men and their ladders, check their faces, smile. I place my hand on the large smooth cameo that bears Pilar's picture, and close my eyes.

Then we go back to the flower vendors and I ask for

three of each species. The vendors laugh when I say this, laugh and nod and say, Very well. When they are done with their gathering I have more flowers than can be carried in one trip, so I pay two small boys to help me. They are too young for ladder-work, and they laugh and joke as they stumble under their loads, but not a single flower falls. When we arrive they ask how I want the flowers arranged, and I tell them that arrangement is not their concern. They are happy to hear this, thank me when I pay them, run back to the vendors.

I choose one flower at a time and Mariángel lays each as she pleases. There is a certain nonlinear logic to her decisions. The mound rises until it has covered the front of the niche, and I redistribute only those that block my view of the picture. It is what we can do for now.

When we return tonight there will be fewer flowers, as some will have been taken by those who lacked the means or inclination to buy them. This is not the problem it might seem to be, not today. There will be fewer flowers, and still enough.

Back home for lunch, and Casualidad is still asleep on the couch. Her hands twitch and her breathing is shallow and quick. Something, sweat or tears or something else, has gathered in her eye patch, dripped down her cheek and dried dark.

I wake her, tell her that she needs to see a doctor, that I will take her, that I will pay. She shakes her head. I repeat the same sentences in different orders at different volumes. Finally she agrees, and goes to get her purse and change into her street clothes.

Fifteen minutes later she has not yet returned. I find her standing in Mariángel's room staring at the floor. I ask if she is ready, and she says that she is but not for the hospital, that instead she will go home early if it is all right with me, that nothing is needed but rest.

She seems steady on her feet. Her breathing comes more easily and she does not look quite as pale. I tell her we will accompany her home. She nods, walks past me and out the front door, is gone by the time I have gathered Mariángel and run to catch her.

We check the closest side streets and do not find her. We stop back by the house to call Fermín, and he promises to call me if she is not home in half an hour. Then Mariángel and I follow the smell of grilled sausages to Neuquén, order lunch and lean back. Armando is not there, and the guachimán does not know where he has gone. I suspect he would not tell me if he knew.

Back home, and Mariángel helps me stir the ingredients for the two cakes we will need. We dance and babble as they bake. In the end one is large and one is not and neither is symmetrical. While they cool we go to the patio. She stands at the edge, squints into the sun, pleased at the things she sees.

Still she has not truly spoken, but she has lost much of her dislike of falling, walks unsteadily in pursuit of most movement: the leaves and flowers swaying, the birds that land, occasional butterflies. She walks toward the birds, and her presence does not seem to bother them. They will not let her touch them, but wait until she is inches away and reaching before flitting up to the wall. They do not screech at her the way they screech at me.

After dinner we frost the cakes as best we are able. When it is dark I dress us both and we return to Club Grau for the finals. The night feels loosely hinged though the noise is no different than before. Twitchy and sad, I watch a round of tondero and a round of marinera. The lights flicker overhead, and the announcer's microphone fades in and out.

I swing Mariángel around to my back and push down the steps, begging the pardon of those whom I bump, ignoring their stares. At the bottom I stop to look at the crowd. There is an oddness in my head as I glance from one face to another. It is a moment before I realize I am searching not for the taxista but for the chilalo and there is a rigid ache now low in my chest. I stop, bend, hope to catch my breath. The mothers in the front row pull away and I feel something slip, Mariángel falling out of the baby carrier, tumbling forward over my shoulder, I catch her in the air and she laughs, thinks it is wonderful, this tumbling, this falling.

There is no question: I must read the manual, must learn the meaning of all the straps, must be more careful in all senses. Another taxi, and back at the house I lay Mariángel down to sleep. I load my backpack with blankets and pillows, with sandwiches and bananas, with juice in cartons, with diapers and plastic bags. I fill a thermos with milk and another with warm oatmeal. I put the smaller of the two cakes into a cardboard box and it is time.

Again I walk, Mariángel in her old sling and asleep on my chest. I check the license plate of each passing taxi, of the dozens parked outside the cemetery gates. Then I buy sixty slim white candles. Joined together four at a time they will not be put out by the wind. If I am lucky they will last the whole night.

Inside the cemetery is something of a solemn circus. The whitewashed structures are lit with electric bulbs. There are clusters of candles, and flowers have been woven into wreaths and hung. The chapel is filled with people, and I check every face. Each Mass said for the dead will play into the following one, a swath that will not end until sunrise.

Couples walk arm in arm, calling to old friends, quietly and with great affection. Along the sides of the structures there are people seated on the ground. They are mostly very old. They pray, pass bottles back and forth, rarely speak.

In places also there are other infants; they cry from time to time, and are quieted. Their older brothers and sisters cannot be made to stay still at the niches, and have sorted themselves by age. The youngest run shrieking from one place to another, gathering melted wax into large gray balls that later will be used for games, the rules invented and argued and hewn mid-play. Other children, slightly older, gather in circles to wish they were elsewhere. Still others, still older, have already met their boyfriends and girlfriends, are gathered in pairs to kiss deeply in the long and flickering shadows.

I spread our blankets on the ground. Fewer flowers are missing than I had thought. Mariángel wakes, and I prop her up on the pillows so that she will be able to see everything. She immediately goes back to sleep.

I nod to those at the niches on either side, and wave to friends from the university as they walk by. Pilar's parents and brothers have not come from Chiclayo, or have not yet arrived. Given what happened after her body was found, I do not know which would surprise me more, to see them here tonight, or not to.

Suddenly Reynaldo stands before me. I smile, stand, dust myself off. We shake hands, and he tells me that he is here for his parents and grandparents and two uncles. I nod. There is a moment of quiet. I ask if he will be attending Mariángel's party tomorrow, and he does not pause before saying that he will.

A Peruvian who pauses before saying Yes is in fact saying No. This took me two years to learn, was a source of much frustration, but does no harm once everyone involved knows the code. Reynaldo pats me on the shoulder, and I must look sadder than I feel, because he says this:

- The first one is the hardest. The rest are not so easy either. But they are easier. A little.

I say that there is nothing about which to worry. He nods. The candles burn slowly down. He rubs his eyes and gestures at those around us, the old men and women drunk or asleep.

- This must be very strange for you.
- Everything in the world is strange.
- Did you hear about the party at Boby's?
- No. Should I try to guess?
- Yes, but you will fail.
- Perhaps you should just tell me.
- Máximo Yerlequé, the engineering student? He went as the phoenix. Weeks ago he told me how the costume would work, as he always does, to make me suffer. His wings were of many colors, and inside them he put fireworks of some kind that would explode and burn away the feathers. Beneath that he had another suit, the color of ashes. And below that was still another layer, the same as the first but even brighter.
- And you?
- I went as an alien from *Men in Black*. It was among the best I have ever done. Beautiful leather work. You should have seen it.
- Which alien? The giant cockroach?
- No. That was the most remarkable alien, yes? But I am not sufficiently tall. So I went as another—a sort of large armadillo. How do you say armadillo in English?
- Ar-ma-dill-o.
- Ah. Very similar. Do you remember this creature?
- No.
- From the beginning of the movie. The one that pretends to be an illegal immigrant from Mexico. It has the immigrant's head on a stick, and when it attacks, Mr. Tommy Lee Jones shoots it with his special gun, and the creature explodes. There was a blue substance all over the border guard.
- I remember now. The armadillo.
- It was a marvelous costume. The eye-stalks of different lengths, they were superb.
- Was it good enough to—
- Not in a fair contest. But the phoenix never made it

to the stage.

    - I don't understand.

    - The fireworks went off too quickly and were too strong. They burned through the suit of ashes and into the new plumage. Máximo is still in the hospital.

    - Is he going to live?

    - Probably, but the scarring will last for all his life.

    - And so you won!

    - Yes. At the semester break in July I will fly to New York, and then take a bus to California. There are buses, yes? And you should come with me. We could start again, together.

    - Start what again?

    - At last the conditions are right. I will not be coming back.

    - Is there a chance that at some point you will say something that I am capable of understanding?

    - It is time for me to do my doctorate. With your help I am going to find a university in California that will give me a fellowship.

    - Ah, I say. An excellent plan. But—

    - There will be women, and basketball. You really should come along.

    - Yes and yes and no. The larger point: you do not have a great deal of time. Your application will be due in a month, perhaps two. In that time you will need to obtain copies of your transcripts, have them translated and legalized. You will need others to write letters of recommendation for you, and you must write a statement of purpose. There is your university application to complete, and another for the department itself. Is your English good enough for the TOEFL score they require? Do you have the—

    - Are you trying to discourage me?

    - Of course not. I—

    - Am I not smart enough for your universities?

Now two economics professors walk by, stop to say hello. When they are gone I try again, but Reynaldo no longer wants to talk. We watch the unsteady light. Without smiling he says goodnight and walks away.

I watch him go. I sit back down, settle into my space. I hold my thoughts steady for a time. Finally I tire. Pilar's family came immediately to Piura when she disappeared. In those first days they were good to Mariángel and me. Then the goatherds found Pilar and the police brought her broken body to us and horrific things were said.

And it was not just those moments. The next day, beginning calmer: they wanted her buried in Chiclayo. I said that she would be buried here. Voices rising, they asked and then demanded to be allowed to take and raise Mariángel. I told them to fuck themselves. Voices louder and louder and blood on my walls by the end, some of it mine but mostly that of Pilar's brothers.

Since that day I have not seen or talked to anyone in her family. Her oldest brother calls every few weeks to ask Casualidad about Mariángel's health and happiness, but if I happen to answer the phone he hangs up without speaking. And six months ago her parents came to Piura, went to the house while I was at work, spent an hour with Mariángel, Casualidad calling and calling to tell me but I was out of the office and not in class and no one could find me.

I was at the deer pen, remembering. When I returned to my desk I saw the messages and called and told Casualidad to tell them that I would be home in five minutes and that if they were still there or ever came back I would hurt them. I went, and they had gone. To my knowledge they have not tried again. Many things about this are wrong, yes. There are still worse things.

It would be nice to sleep like those at the niches to either side, but there are more like me than like them, more who do not sleep but sit and stare or walk. Those who walk come and go in their hundreds. They are generally not outwardly unhappy. They observe the quantity of flowers around me, and nod, and smile. This helps or seems to.

An hour, two. When the bells ring for midnight Mass, I take out the birthday cake, set a candle deep in the frosting, light it, and wake Mariángel in order to sing to her. There is a lovely custom here. The night before a birthday is called the quema, the burn: at midnight one's friends gather in order to sing. They sing "Las Mañanitas," and they sing "Happy Birthday" twice, first slowly and solemnly in English, and then vigorously in Spanish. It is incomprehensible and splendid.

> Éstas son las mañanitas
> que cantaba el Rey David,
> a las muchachas bonitas
> se las cantaba así:
> Despierta, mi bien, despierta,
> mira, que ya amaneció.
> Ya los pajaritos cantan,
> la luna ya se metió.

The words lie: there are no birds singing, and the moon has not yet set, is still razor-like above us, and none of this matters. The first line I sing alone, but as I begin the second I am joined by other voices. Only a few at first, then many, the song gathering strength as those to my left and right wake and join in, and still others come, twenty or thirty people, there are harmonies slipping up and down and it is impossibly beautiful.

When the song ends they draw even closer, a rough circle around the pillows that hold Mariángel. Someone starts in with "Happy Birthday." We plod together through the English version, and sprint through the Spanish.

Mariángel leans to the candle, and I blow lightly past

her. The flame gutters and goes out, and there is applause from all over the cemetery, rippling through the clusters of tombs, echoing in waves around us. Mariángel applauds as well and I lift her. We are both kissed by each woman, patted on the back by each man. I break the cake with my hands, tearing it into smaller and smaller pieces until there are only crumbs in the box, and I give a crumb to each person, and they take it on their tongues like communion.

When this is done they smile, nod, wander off. I sit back down and rearrange the pillows. Soon around me there is snoring, a new sort of chorus. Mariángel and I hunch together to await first light.

II.

# 16.

Vigils end when dawn is unambiguous. Mariángel still sleeps. The night has left me riven. I gather our things and lift her. The walk home through the hot wet air feels slower than it must actually be.

Casualidad is waiting in the kitchen and Fermín is in the back yard watering the almond tree. Their presence confuses me—I did not ask or want them to come so early, did not ask them to come at all except as guests for the party, and even then only if Casualidad was feeling well. My mouth is slow to get words in the correct order, and halfway through my question Casualidad laughs loudly. It is the first time I have heard her laugh, or very nearly so. I ask how she is, and she says that she is feeling much better. She asks how our time at the cemetery went, and her eye is mainly clear.

There is a large cake now on the dining room table. It has nothing to do with the larger of the two cakes I made. This cake is still larger and much more beautiful, with hard smooth white frosting, and yellow rosettes of icing around the upper edge. It is not leaning in any direction, and my first thought is that Casualidad has somehow encased the cake I made within this other, better cake. Of course that cannot be true, and I try to ask how it happened that my cake is gone and this cake is here. She laughs again mid-question and as answer this will have to suffice.

Casualidad takes Mariángel, and I ask her not to let me sleep for more than an hour. When I wake it is almost noon. I shower and dress and walk to the nearest store, return home with what I should have bought days ago: ice cream and plantain chips, beer and varied soft drinks, plastic cups and plates and forks, paper napkins and cardboard birthday hats.

Here plantain chips are called chifles, and while similar to potato chips they are superior in every way. I pour a bag of them into a large bowl, and at the bottom of the bag are two glassine packets, one filled with dried and shredded beef, the other with massive corn nuts. I sprinkle these across the top of the chifles and already Arantxa arrives.

I present her with the largest and finest hat, the kind a cardboard corsair might wear. Her gift is an orange shirt that should fit Mariángel by late in the year after next. I pass Arantxa the bowl of chifles, and as she chews we examine the arguments for and against each English professor erasing the words and drawings and schematics from his or her chalkboard at the end of each class, and I promise to do better in the future.

The doorbell rings again. On the stoop now is a crowd of an unlikely size, and I ask Casualidad to arrange for the delivery of more chifles, more soft drinks, more cardboard hats, and also a good deal of beer. The delivery charges will not be negligible, but there is no other clean option. I had thought that not many of my English Section colleagues would come—only the good-hearted, the best-hearted, and those few with nothing better to do. Instead all seventeen have come, and their gifts for Mariángel involve prominent ribbons and knitting, and there is a shortage of chairs.

After a time the doorbell seems done, and then it rings again. At the door is Reynaldo. Instead of congratulating Mariángel immediately as did all the other guests, he first says that he is sorry for last night. I tell him the truth, that it was nothing, or nearly nothing, and that to the extent it was more than nothing it was at least two-thirds my fault. He smiles and hands me a bottle of good pisco.

I ask how his research is going and he says that the deer are shitting cleaner seeds than ever, but that he doesn't know if he has enough pods in stock to last until harvest. His face appears suddenly fuller than I remember, the flesh of his neck straining at his shirt collar. I ask if he has been putting on weight, and he seems to become afraid or something like it, and punches my arm hard in a friendly manner as though practicing for American citizenship.

Everyone is now present and hatted and I ask Casualidad if she knows where the birthday candles are. She nods, takes up the cake and is gone for some time. I go to the kitchen and find her crying. The cake holds perhaps thirty candles, their layout apparently random. In her hand is an empty matchbox. Dozens of used matches have been stacked like miniscule cordwood on the counter.

- I got confused, she says, and all these matches, I can't remember why I kept them.

I tell her not to move, and after a small amount of searching I find Fermín standing alone in the front yard. I ask what he is looking at, and he says that there is nothing. I say that his mother is ill, and he nods. I say that she needs to see a doctor, not tomorrow but today, and give him a hundred soles.

He takes the bill and hides it in his underpants. Then he follows me into the kitchen, helps me to remove the candles and to convince Casualidad that I want her to rest for a day or two.

- But you will fire me if I don't come to work, she says.

- No. I will fire you only if you do come to work.

- You will fire me?

- Yes. I mean, no.

- So I am fired.

- No, but I want you to see a doctor. I will take care of Mariángel today and tomorrow by myself, and you will visit the doctor and rest. On Tuesday, if you are feeling better, you can come back to work.

- And if I'm not feeling better?

- Then you will rest for another day. You will rest for as many days as you need. And when you feel better you will come back, and we will be waiting to welcome you.

She does not believe me, but when Fermín repeats everything I said word for word, she allows us to walk her to the front door. Fermín runs to the corner for a mototaxi, and they are gone.

I attempt to repair the cake but the hard smooth frosting will not spread in any direction. After a time I desist, place a clean candle at its center, find a new box of matches and light the wick. I bring the cake in, locate Mariángel where she sits on Arantxa's lap, carry the cake to her. Again there is singing, only "Happy Birthday" now but as always in both languages.

I walk Mariángel around the room to kiss and be kissed by all the guests, and she falls asleep halfway through. I take her to her crib and close her door. Back in the dining room, Arantxa is cutting the cake in fancifully shaped and roughly equal portions, and Reynaldo is serving the ice cream. When all of it is gone, humming begins and the cardboard hats come off.

These are two of many ways in which Piurans intimate that it is time for the dancing to start. The music alternates, rock and salsa, as is one possible custom here. I take a turn with each of the female professors, and two turns with Arantxa. Too sweaty to be comfortable close to anyone, I walk out onto the patio, and a moment later Arantxa comes with the bottle of pisco and two shot glasses.

- It's from Aránzazu, she says.

Pisco is made from grapes, is something of a brandy; this bottle is from the region that gave the drink its name and I have no idea what Arantxa means.

- My name, she says. Haven't you ever wondered?

I try to remember whether I have or not. It does not seem likely. She fills the glasses, hands me one, we drink and she pours again.

- Aránzazu, I say, just to try the word in my mouth.

- It's Basque. *You, among thorns.* One of our Virgins.

She moves her chair closer to mine and begins to speak of distance, mentions an article she has read, quotes it on cultural differences as regards personal space: a Brit at arm's-length and a Zambian's breath on one's cheek. The phrasing is familiar. Perhaps I have read the same article.

- I could stay tonight and help you with Mariángel, says Arantxa.

It is a proposition to be considered, and I do. But, Pilar. And something else also, something wrong and vicious in some way: a thought of the chilalo. I thank Arantxa, say that I will spend the evening looking for someone who can take Casualidad's place until she is well. Then I ask if, should worse come to worst, I might take Mariángel to work with me tomorrow. It takes two more shots of pisco and a large amount of conversation, but at last Arantxa agrees that there are certain circumstances under which that would be the best of several bad options.

She stands, walks out onto the lawn, rests her hand on the trunk of the almond tree. From inside the house comes the screech of furniture being moved, surely the table slid to one side to provide more space for dancing. From the stereo comes a song of Rubén Blades. Here he is known as the Intellectual of Salsa. This may well be the same as speaking of the Intellectual of Codfish or Paste, but his music is smartly arranged and his lyrics often tell stories of social and other injustices.

Arantxa circles the tree but her hand never leaves its trunk, her fingers trailing lightly across the bark. Then she flinches, stops, looks at her forearm. She smiles. She looks at me, holds her arm up. I see nothing new, ask if it is an insect bite or allergic reaction of some kind.

- It's started, she says.
- What?

And then I hear the sound.

Oquendo says for example we will make another sky, and here in Cossto the muzak is live. The organist in the balcony sways as though he were blind. The chords come in bunches like berries, like blackbirds, like flies.

Cossto is the only supermarket in Piura. There was another, once, slightly closer to our house, called Éxito, Success. The floors there were unclean and the selection was meager and the vegetables were not appealing. Cossto is small as supermarkets go, but it is among Mariángel's favorite places as there is so much to grab and chew and throw.

Yesterday's sky went dark, yes, and Arantxa and I danced again, and the raindrops chattered and chucked on the roof. The storm did not last long, but that is not the point. The point is that here it has no business raining so early in November, and Fermín came back in the evening to tell me that Casualidad had been to see a doctor, was following his orders carefully and was already feeling better, would rest for a day as suggested and be on time for work Tuesday morning. This did not seem likely but I thanked him for the news and asked if he had bus fare home. He nodded and said that he didn't. Mariángel woke crying just then, and I became confused, told

Fermín that we all looked forward to seeing his mother again soon and closed the door.

The Humboldt Current's upswell gives northern Peru the richest sea in the world. The fish department here at Cossto is accordingly magnificent: sea bass and Conger eel, grouper and shark, flounder and salmon and drum and this morning Mariángel fought against me at first, became entangled, but I worked her free, told her of what was to come, worked her back in more gently and soon had her secure on my back, all straps known and in place. The roads were damp and thinly puddled and smelled of rot, but there was no rain falling. This is fortunate, as the nearest thing I have seen to preparatory action for El Niño is a flyer advertising a conference regarding sewage and dengue and shrimp.

Throughout my morning class Mariángel rode on my back, and each time I turned to write on the board, my students lost concentration and laughed. For my latter two classes she rode on my chest, facing inward when she wished to sleep and outward when not. Because of her many facial expressions my students think that she is a genius and will grow up to be an economist or prophet.

My Pre-Intermediate students filled in their worksheets, bottle diaper booties earache teething heartbreak rash, and there are many fish whose English names I do not know: cabrillón, cachema, lisa, ojo de uva. Every so often a rack is over-filled and fish slide to the floor. They are always cleaned up promptly and with much grace by young men in clean red uniforms.

When the worksheets were full and corrected, we had discussions, in pairs and small groups and large groups, wherein I facilitated and did not intrude, or intruded only rarely, as rarely as possible, sufficiently seldom to have avoided reprimand in the event that anyone was watching, and they, the students, attempted to formulate and defend educated opinions as to the two most important qualities for a parent to have. There was consensus in favor of patience and wealth. We then debated discipline and feeding techniques. I asked them to draw up daily baby schedules, and when they were done I assured them that all such schedules are pointless.

Next to the fish are the trays of shrimp and prawns and lobster, of baby squid and adult squid, of giant squid cut in rondelles so big, so very deep and wide that they are hard to believe, even when as a joke one fits one over one's head. The person who made the joke was a student from the university. He was banned for life from the Cossto premises, his eyes still widened in wonder.

Midway through my Intermediate class I noticed the students ignoring me and conspiring, and my anger rose up, was undercut by their singing: "Happy Birthday" for Mariángel yet again. It was the same words and music as ever but something in the timbre of the loudest voice reminded me of the time that "Happy Verbena" was sung instead. A verbena is an amateur talent show organized by a given university department with the purpose of mocking that department's professorial and administrative staff and as many other people as possible. The entity that sang was the Language Center Choir, a nonexistent thing, and they sang beautifully, a single verse. I was the conductor, and my baton was chalk, and my hair was mussed. That was my second verbena, and my second-to-last.

There is also chicken here, and pork and lamb and kid goat, and a good deal of beef though the cuts are not as fine as one might desire. The pasta and legume aisles are well stocked, and according to the newspapers rice will soon be abundant and nearly free as so many farmers planted it when their cotton crops failed in the heat of April.

My last verbena was two years ago, Communications, a month before Pilar's graduation, and her classmates had at me. The first skit was a fake television news report about a fat foreign archaeologist who had been sentenced to life in prison for attempting to steal a priceless artifact. A photograph flashed onto the big screen: Pilar and I very nearly holding hands. We in the crowd, we laughed, some of us less than others, as the anchor went into deeper and deeper detail regarding precisely how fat and foreign the archaeologist was. For the second skit, the fattest male student in the department dressed as a conquistador—fake beard, cardboard armor, plastic sword—and the second fattest wore mock-aclla vestments, balloon breasts and a wig of smooth black hair that hung almost to his waist. The virgin priestess spoke Spanish with a Chiclayan accent, the conquistador with an American one. He ran fish-eyed and foamed at the mouth, chased and cornered her, gathered her onto his shoulder and staggered off stage.

Pilar looked at me to see how I would take this and other jokes. It was her gaze that kept me from taking the stage, from grabbing the microphone, from shouting, There is no equivalence and it is only this, their hooks in me, their fanged hooks, *their motherfucking fangs.*

Which no one would have understood, and not only her gaze, as she had agreed to teach there the following spring, introductory courses until she finished her Master's and also there is fruit: melons, limes and pineapples and bananas, oranges and lucumas, papayas. And carambolas. And mameys and tamarinds and guavas, and three species of passion fruit, and there are cherimoyas, a dark green fruit shaped like a hand grenade and so sweet that it seems unlikely to be natural at all.

My Upper Intermediate class centered on ten-minute essays. Only a single student referred to El Niño as The Boy Phenomenon. The day was thus successful in spite of its many diaper changings and juice-based interruptions.

Waiting in my office was a package sent from Chiclayo: a birthday gift for Mariángel from Pilar's parents. The gift was three beautiful and dangerous cloth dolls. They came wearing felt hats, bright clothes, shiny bead jewelry; they came bearing wooden bowls full of corn and peas and lentils. Mariángel loved them but the jewelry and bowls and hats can be and were immediately choked upon. I set the dolls on top of the filing cabinet there in my office. Mariángel shrieked and hated me. I stuffed them into my briefcase, and when we are home I will sneak them onto her room's highest shelf, and push them back against the wall where she is unlikely to see or notice them and they might wait beautifully for years.

The dolls came with a letter addressed to Mariángel only, and the thank-you card will be signed by her only as well, and Mariángel and I, we observe and grab and chew and throw, aisle after aisle, mamey to ojo de uva and back again and at last are done. Today's interstices were spent trying and failing to find a replacement for Casualidad, and am I ever disappointed at Cossto? Only from time to time. Peanut butter is not a common commodity. There are few breakfast cereals and fewer cheeses. These are my supermarket disappointments, these and the fact that the sweaty women at the cash registers sometimes wipe their brows with the bills of my change before holding them out to me and it happens again now, this very moment.

I stare at the woman, and do not reach for the bills, and my searching has lately been tepid. This is not to be forgiven. I stare at the stock boys, at my fellow customers, consider climbing up for a better look at the organist, but how to reach him? Where are the stairs? And Mariángel and I are very hungry so instead we gather our bags, walk out into feverish honking, choose a taxi, and this weekend, yes, once again the search.

The ride is splendid and involves mainly tickling, but once home I see that I forgot to buy spaghetti. I check the cupboards. Of course there is none. I boil carrots and strain them, pour Mariángel's milk and unspillable juice. I heat the tomato sauce and splash it across rice left over from some lunch days ago. Mariángel finds it delicious. I push mine around my

plate, draw in it, maps of ancient cities. Mariángel finishes her
juice and smacks her lips and laughs.

Another dozen telephone calls before work, and the
best option thus far is an arthritic-sounding woman who can
begin tomorrow afternoon. I pack the requisite supplies for a
second day with Mariángel on my chest. Then the doorbell
rings. It is Casualidad. She is smiling and appears calm.

I ask how she is feeling. She says that she is fine. I ask
if she remembers what happened at Mariángel's party. She says
that of course she does, that she is so sorry about the cake,
that she is still very embarrassed about forgetting that it was
Mariángel's birthday, not mine. I ask what her doctor said, and
she says that he told her to buy a llama fetus.

- You went to a curandero?
- Yes.
- And did you actually buy the llama?
- Just a fetus. They sell them at the market.
- I know that. I know they do.
- In big glass jars.
- Why didn't you go to the hospital?
- Because the hospital doctors know nothing.

This is when I begin to shout. It is possible that
not all of the things I shout are coherent. As I often tell my
students, it is far more difficult than one might suspect to use
imprecations and vulgarities correctly in a language other than
one's own. When I am done she is crying, and so is Mariángel,
and so am I. I call Arantxa and say that an emergency has
arisen, that I need the morning off. I can hear her shrug down
the phone line, I am sure of it.

We get a taxi, Casualidad and Mariángel and I, and go
to the public hospital. The walls there have not recently been

painted. The equipment has not recently been manufactured. The nurses have not recently been born.

Three hours in the waiting room with several dozen other people, all of them coughing in our direction. Finally the doctor. He examines Casualidad for thirty seconds: pulse respiration temperature. Then for thirty seconds he listens to her remembering out loud how things happened, and when.

- This behavior, he says, it sounds like the result of stress.

I nod and Casualidad stares at the floor.

- Everyone is very stressed, he continues. It is El Niño, I believe. El Niño makes everyone crazy.

- It isn't even here yet, I say.

- It doesn't have to be here to make you crazy. You only have to think of it. Have you been thinking of El Niño, Pilar?

Sweat surges from my face and hands, I lift, and then slump back—of course, Casualidad's real name. She looks at me, back at him, nods and I stare at the floor.

- So this is definitely a case of stress, he says. Relax more when you can, take aspirin for headaches, remember to remove your shoes at night, and come back to see me if the problem persists.

The air grows daily hotter and more humid. My students ask to be excused, one student after another, and if I let them go they do not return. The reason for these departures, and for the staff meeting that will start any moment now, is the University Olympiad.

We are all here, English and German and French and Italian professors, our complete contingent. From her place at the auditorium lectern Arantxa looks proudly at me, as if I am the optimal solution to all current problems. Then she looks the same way at the next person down the row of chairs, and the next, and the next.

She begins with a brief history for the benefit of recent hires, and it appears that the aspirin or llama fetus is working: I dropped by my house at four unexpected moments yesterday afternoon and six thus far today, and Casualidad was acting normally in each case. I no longer allow her to move heavy objects or clean strenuously, and insist that she spend Mariángel's naps not dusting or ironing or washing but likewise napping. Perhaps this will be enough.

- What I'm saying, says Arantxa, is that by joining our strengths, we will also be covering for one another's potential weaknesses.

There is a murmur in the room: sincere but guarded consent. The true Winter Olympiad soon to be conducted in Nagano is, like winter itself, all but meaningless in Piura. Here there is no ice except in drinks, no snow except on television. There are also no ice rinks anywhere in Peru, and no ski resorts, though there is one mountain down which one might ski, one run per day after first spending five hours ascending by jeep and then by horse or mule and then on foot.

- That's exactly it! says Arantxa. That's exactly the right spirit!

The University Olympiad: one team from each of the eight undergraduate programs, and the medal race is always won by Engineering or Business. The Language Center draws students from all departments, but because it was founded by Engineering, we may join their teams if we wish, and at times even if we do not. Points are given for participation regardless of whether one places, and we are most often asked firmly to compete in unpopular sports such as pole vault. We generally agree to do so, generally vault to the best of our abilities.

- So when students bring us notes signed by their Sports Delegate, says Arantxa, we as professors need to understand those notes not as attempts to skip class, but as statements of unity and solidarity. No matter what the student is needed for, whether it be chopping confetti or writing new cheers or practicing discus, university policy is to take that need seriously, to accept the note and register the absence as Excused.

I raise my hand, ask if we are required to be pleasant while doing so.

- Encouraged! says Arantxa. But not required.

She says that while the actual Olympiad doesn't start until next week, sign-ups for the various events have already begun. She says that we are to let her know in person if there is a given sport we wish to play, and that on Monday she will be contacting those of us who have for whatever reason not yet signed up for anything. Then she says that Engineering has already elected its queen, and names the student in question. A certain hubbub ensues as those around me agree that this student gives us a good chance against Business this year.

- The department has also chosen the theme for its float, Arantxa says. The theme is Viaducts!

The silence that follows this announcement thickens briefly. We all become embarrassed on her behalf. Then she smiles and pulls from behind the lectern a beautifully drawn poster of the float as imagined by the dean. Good Christ but Arantxa is an excellent administrator.

She begins asking for volunteers for various roles, has little trouble filling them. Allegorical car: that is how one says float in Spanish. Students dressed and face-painted in their respective department's color will walk alongside their float the entire way from the university to the coliseum, and points will be allotted according to each float's aesthetic qualities, to the quantity of waving and smiling and beauty produced by each queen, to the exuberance of each department's cheers. Once the coliseum is reached and filled, still more points will be allotted as the result of dance squads, indoor fireworks, banners of varying sizes.

- The parade is always the most interesting part! says Arantxa.

The parade is not always the least interesting part. My second year here, the Law float was vaguely Athenian. There were large amounts of red crepe paper and balloons, and the queen in her red evening gown stood in the bed of the truck among students in red togas. There were loose stone columns made of styrofoam, and torches held aloft. The students holding the torches slipped and slid as the truck lurched along the route. The queen was a very attractive young woman and continued to smile and wave even as she was borne off on the shoulders of her pep squad while behind her the float was consumed in flames.

Torches are no longer permitted and the fluorescent lights stutter and glow across the full tan arcs of the tops of Arantxa's breasts, just visible given her not immodest blouse. Then there is silence. Arantxa is staring at me, has obviously seen me look. She shakes her head.

- Anyone else? she says.

The silence recommences.

- I know an hour a day sounds like a lot, she says, but it really is fun, and you'll learn all about sheet metal, how to cut and shape it.

Further silence.

- Really? she says. Please? she says.

- I'll do it, says Günther.

I do not remember Günther ever volunteering for anything before, but he has saved us now, stands to bow at scattered but rising applause, and we cheer for him, how we cheer.

# 17.

Q<small>UICKLY AND SWEATING ACROSS CAMPUS AND OUT THROUGH</small> the gates. My evening class was meant to end early, but a student had questions, good and interesting questions about the future continuous. It is a tense for which he has no need just yet. I tried to keep my impatience less than manifest, come now to the corner, lift my hand as a taxi approaches, but it already has a passenger. I scan beyond for another. The first one is to me and past, the right color the right make the right age and I did not see the driver's face, cannot quite read the license plate at this distance but it began with P and ended with 22 or something like it.

I stand and sweat and stare, hope for brake lights, and there are none. I look in all directions for another taxi. By the time one comes, the first has long since disappeared.

My voice catches as I give the driver an address a block from where I wish to go. He seems confused by the fact that I do not try to talk him down on the fare. I hunch deeply into the seat and it is not a long ride.

I thank him as I pay, but he does not want my thanks.

A breeze rises, dies. Again the two men and their plastic chairs, again the curtains and soft music; again the porcelain puppies on the mantel but briefly this time, and again the eyebrows.

- You remembered to make a reservation! says Ms. Alina. And you were almost on time for it!

There is no sarcasm in her tone: she is genuinely happy for me, unduly happy, so happy it makes me nervous. She takes me by the arm for the walk upstairs. She kisses me on the cheek at the threshold to Jenny's room, gestures deftly to say that I may enter at will.

Jenny, still thinner, still blonder. Her current robe and camisole are decorated with the stylized pelicans and fish of the Chimú ruins at Chan Chan, and I wonder where she buys them. She is likewise surprised at my reservation-making and approximate punctuality. She says that she is pleased to see me so early in the evening, and so sober.

These seem for a time to be good things. I walk the room from corner to corner, something I have never done. Hanging from the corner of the mirror is an image of Sarita Colonia, and perhaps it is new, or perhaps I am capable of seeing it only now that I know who she is.

As I undress, I tell her of Minchacaman and his vast wealth, of the marvelous Chimú artisans, their metallurgical gifts, their ceramics and featherwork. Then comes the Inca army led by the future emperor Túpac Yupanqui. The war is not unbalanced until the Incas are reinforced. Minchacaman sues for terms, is imprisoned and taken to Cuzco for the victory rituals. With him go the riches and artisans that will transform the Inca capital into the extraordinary city of gold that in sixty years the Spaniards will sack.

I begin to contrast Garcilaso's fanciful telling of the war with Rostworoski's rigor, but Jenny is staring out the window.

- I did not mean to bore you, I say.

She smiles and says nothing. The smile, it troubles me.

She removes her robe, comes toward me, the slow roll of her hips yes but that first taxi, the passenger in the front seat, long black hair. Jenny removes her camisole, arches her back, the exclamation point yes but if I had not been distracted there on the corner and what does it mean that I am here with penance already scheduled and suddenly I am incapable. For a time she tries various means. Soon it is clear there is no point.

    - It's all right, Jenny says.

This courtesy appears mainly professional. She sees that I wish to respond but cannot, and keeps talking, and the phrase blossoms slowly or seems to, becomes a moment wholly as she finds new and better ways to say over and over: It's all right. This is a second share of humiliation but also needed. I weep beside her until my time is done.

Across town. Six hundred years ago Chan Chan had fifty thousand inhabitants, was the largest city anywhere in the Americas. Casualidad greets me, smiles, says nothing about what time she will now be getting home. She tells me that Mariángel had a good and active day, walked constantly at her side, ate well and is already asleep. She says that for my dessert there is a covered pan in the refrigerator, an attempt at tres leches, and she believes it turned out well.

A shower, and dinner. The tres leches is superb, perpetually almost too sweet, the soft thin layer of meringue dusted with cinnamon, the cake below so moist it is almost a form of pudding. Ten conjoined citadels each with a thousand adobe structures. Then television. I dab at the new sweat on my chest with a sock as I watch the least funny comedians of any time or place. I watch the goalless first half of a soccer match, doze through the second half of a movie. Then comes the news. It begins with two anchorpersons grinning so widely that I know I will not be able to bear whatever they have to report. I find the remote as quickly as I am able, get the sound turned down just in time.

Already I regret what I have done: bright on the screen is a man I haven't seen in months. Today he is not green but purple. I lift the remote, and waver. It might be best not to know. I set the remote back down.

The purple man is posed on a cliff top, a jag of black rock pushing into the sea, and behind him is a large wooden building, a restaurant or hotel of some kind. He lifts a small ugly confusing piece of sculpture, appraises it and throws it off the cliff. The camera pans down, switching into and out of slow motion. There is a medium-sized splash. The naked man hefts another piece of sculpture.

Now standing beside him is a friar or someone dressed to look like one. He and the purple man have a brief and unamicable discussion. The friar sets down his staff and pushes back his hood. Then he jumps off the cliff, arcs into a dive, slashes into the water.

The purple man throws the second sculpture, and it does not miss the bobbing friar by much. The friar shouts and treads water strongly enough to raise and shake his fist. The purple man smiles and hefts a third sculpture. He throws, hefts and throws, hefts and throws, is shown mainly from the waist up but once the camera slips and his penis dangles like the head of a dead purple bird and how many bad sculptures has he brought?

Now the friar is again on the cliff top, water streaming from his tunic and hair. His sandals look handmade. There is a piece of seaweed caught in the rosary on his waistcord, and he has a cut on his forehead—he dove too deeply, or a bit of sculpture clipped him. He shouts at the purple man, and the purple man shouts back, throws another sculpture, shouts and hefts and throws.

The friar takes up his staff, bears it like a sword and the purple man bares his teeth. The friar drops the staff and tackles the purple man, and the two of them roll around in ovals there on the cliff top, roll and roll until they are scratched and exhausted. They separate, and glare at one another. Each shouts once more and the news turns to something bad or good that is happening to stocks in Brazil.

Seven in the morning and the sky is clouded over. There was a little rain very late last night. It will have erased certain clues, will have washed others clean.

Casualidad has come, will care for Mariángel, and now Reynaldo arrives, asks if I am ready. I kiss Mariángel, and Casualidad promises that the world's finest cherimoya mousse will await our return. I tell her that dessert-oriented compensation is no longer necessary, has in fact never been. Reynaldo tells her to ignore me, to go ahead with the mousse, that if I can't appreciate it properly he certainly can.

Again across the river, again a speck in the sky, again the highway reaching south into the desert. We spend the bus ride discussing the chemistry programs he is considering. In each case he is surprised and disappointed to discover how little I know.

Again debarking at the largest of the three algarrobos. The air moves in hot thick waves around us. Reynaldo has brought plastic bags for the preservation of specimens. He is wearing what he calls his botany helmet, has a magnifying glass in a sheath on his belt, bears a daypack full of other tools and instruments. I discourage him from observing anything for this first mile but he cannot help himself—Look, a gigantón! Do you have any idea how tall they grow? The books say five meters, but I once saw one that was almost eight—and so we advance more slowly than I would prefer.

The dunes, the cabuya, the palo santo. The caracara does not show, is surely off hunting. More dunes. At last the algarrobo grove. We pass the cairn, and it seems smaller than I remember. I count, and yes: almost two months since the last time I came. Before it had never been more than a month. Out of the grove and on slowly. The path is thinner here, harder to follow, and there are other paths splitting off to either side.

I find nothing, and Reynaldo finds many things but none new—guayacán, palo de vaca, higuerón. We walk and look and sweat. If only, if only: an entire school of History. The Arabs defeat Martel at Tours-Poitiers and take Constantinople at the end of the Second Siege, Balboa discovers Peru, no rain falls the night before Waterloo. If only if only, pointless and pointless and pointless.

I watch Reynaldo, watch him search, find, take samples. For a time it is only a distraction but then his way of searching seems the point: I have been wrong all along, have been looking wrongly. Here I should be not historian or detective but botanist. I should be looking not for narrative strands but for specimens, non-native subspecies, plastic or cloth or metal or rubber or clay and devolved from Pilar's moment in and through this space as she walked, dragged herself, died and Reynaldo stops me, points to a fat leafless tree, its trunk covered in spines.

- Have I ever told you about the porotillo?

He has told me two or three times, but it is a relief to hear him talk and I shake my head.

- One of our most valuable trees. You don't normally see them down so low. This one doesn't have any nests, but most do, nests of all kinds, birds and squirrels and termites. Sometimes pericos carve holes in the trunk, and live there, and when they leave for whatever reason the bats move in.

I smile as we walk closer, knowing what is to come.

- Vampire bats, he says.

- Hence Atahualpa's cape. And what are the flowers like? This is his favorite part to tell.

- They are wonderful, he says, and bright red. They cover the tree, and when they fall they cover the ground, a carpet of red, so bright that they stain the soil itself.

We look, and he is right as I knew he would be, the dirt slightly redder here than elsewhere. I consider saving some. There would be no point.

- This kind of tree, it is also where huayruros come from. Surely you have seen them. Bright red seeds with black spots, very shiny and smooth, there are necklaces made of them, and bracelets. The next time we're in the market I'll show you.

I nod, thank him, suggest that we move on. Pilar loved huayruro necklaces. She had half a dozen of varying lengths and weaves—gifts from grandparents and cousins and one from a high school boyfriend. If I asked she would sometimes drape herself in them naked and stand before me. I left campus at lunch to buy her one more, three interwoven strands, bright silver clasp, beautiful. I brought it home that night to give her and she was just heading out and I caught her as she stepped to the curb, smelled the cypress of her, the sage.

Another mile, and another. I find and gather half a dozen scattered pages. They are from a car manual, surely just trash blown here from the highway. I tuck them away all the same to look at more carefully later not in peace but in quiet, and now we may return to Piura whenever we decide it is time.

Slightly farther along we come to a ravine in which Pilar walked for a time. It may or may not be the upper reach of the ravine nearer the algarrobo grove—I have never walked its whole length. Her footprints leading out were found well north of here.

The loam in the bottom is still damp from last night. We walk a few hundred yards along the edge. Reynaldo slides down the side, crouches, stands quickly, stiff-legged.

- Puma, he says, and points.

I join him, and the tracks are familiar, each one an

open pair of petals.

    - They're goat tracks, I say. Look, the spread toes, you can see them clearly.

    He clambers up the far side. I look again at the tracks, and a few feet away I see another, nearly round, five inches across, the wide pad-mark at the base and the four oval toes. Reynaldo looks at me, smiles. I consider, and smile back.

    We continue along the ravine, silent for a time. Then he stops.

    - Shouldn't we have seen the cross by now?

    - A little farther, I think.

    We go a little farther, and a little farther still. I stop. The cross that marks the place where Pilar came out of the ravine is bright orange and five feet tall: it cannot be the case that we have missed it. I look at Reynaldo and he shrugs. A little farther still.

    - You already found something, right? says Reynaldo.

    - Yes. But where is the cross?

    He adjusts his helmet, takes a drink from his canteen. Along and along. A maze of woody plant, low and gray. I ask Reynaldo to remind me of its name, and he says he isn't sure. It takes fifteen minutes for him to get all the samples and data he needs. Along again, and we come to a stunted hualtaco. Reynaldo stops. I circle.

    - Maybe something knocked it down, he says. The rain, for example. We could have walked right by it.

    - I dug the hole three feet deep.

    - So maybe someone stole it.

    - An orange cross?

    - Maybe someone just needed firewood, he says, and maybe it's okay for you to stop doing this.

    I look at him, and he raises his hands.

    - Fine, he says. Come as often as you want.

    He keeps talking and there is something odd about

the hualtaco's trunk. I step closer. Two feet off the ground the trunk is scarred. Reynaldo calls to me as I kneel, asks what I have found, walks over, stands beside me.

The scars are six inches long, thick but shallow, four of them in parallel, as if a hand, as if fingernails. I point to them, and Reynaldo nods, frowns. I bring out my camera, ratchet through half a dozen shots though this sight like others will spiral through me for a month of bad nights and I say it will be time to go home as soon as we have found the cross or what is left of it.

# 18.

THE FINAL MATCHES HAVE BEEN PLAYED AND PERU MANAGED
the unlikely, beating Paraguay one to nothing; in the fighting
afterwards there were several dozen injuries. Chile however
beat Bolivia three goals to none in Santiago, Bolivia down to
nine men by the end. Thus Chile and Peru have tied in the
standings, and Chile will advance on goal difference, and
the Peruvian team will watch the World Cup on television
once again.

As my Upper Intermediate students discuss these
developments, I watch their faces carefully. They seem less sad
than might be imagined. I ask, and Claudia says it is because
they foresaw the result in all but its details. This manner
of losing out on goal difference, she says, it is the history
of modern Peru written in letters that are small but bright.
She says all this in English, and though it is perhaps untrue,
pedagogically I have rarely been so pleased.

Back to my office after class, and this evening the
faculty room whiteboard bears a single word: Yams! By now we
all recognize the handwriting. I look at Eugenia and she looks

at me. Together we look back at the word and nod and shake our heads.

Thanksgiving means little in Peru, and yet there is a phrase: Día de Acción de Gracias. It is as good a phrase as many though less precise than some, can refer to any day on which a Mass of thanks is said, and Pilar would have loved Thanksgiving. Last year I planned to provide for her first full feast. I had already begun making lists of dishes, of ingredients.

I say goodnight to Eugenia, wave to those in line at the photocopier, begin my way home. The most enthusiastic among them have drawn Pilgrims and cornucopiae, have taped them to classroom walls. We generally do not otherwise celebrate the holiday, but last week a guest lecturer came from somewhere cold, Chicago perhaps, or somewhere even colder. She is a friend of the rector's, a not-unknown linguist, and lectured us well on triphthongs. Over coffee afterwards she was surprised or appalled to learn that we had never treated our faculty to a Thanksgiving meal.

I turned to look at Arantxa, expected to see her embarrassed for not having thought of it first. I found her looking at me with what appeared to be the same expectation. The guest lecturer said that while she wouldn't be able to stay until Thanksgiving itself, she could extend her visit by several days, could make all necessary preparations, and we could all dine together a week early.

Arantxa and I decided that we were grateful. The linguist has since spoken with the bakers at the university cafeteria in regard to pumpkins and sugar and crust. She has arranged for canned cranberry sauce to be express-mailed from the U.S. She has discussed stuffing with many of us individually and in small groups, and has made reference to other foodstuffs from her childhood holidays—deviled eggs and jello salad and celery sticks. She has three days left to finish. We are all excited to see if she will make it.

The pages I found in the desert were from the owner's manual of a Tico. I took them to a dealership here and learned nothing else except that they were less new than I had supposed, which means less than it seems. The passenger in the front seat, perhaps it was a long-haired man, and now my house.

Casualidad comes from the kitchen, a dish towel over her shoulder. She says that Mariángel was fussy at dinnertime, wanted each object in the house relocated slightly to the left. Her playpen is in the living room, says Casualidad, and she is napping there or sleeping.

Together we step forward to look. The playpen is empty. On the far side of the room Mariángel is on her tiptoes, her face bright red, the telephone cord around her neck. In two steps I am to her and lifting and she laughs and I almost drop her, am short of air, gasp. A game, of course, only playing, of course: the cord not around her neck but tucked under her chin where she wanted it.

All the same I shout. Casualidad raises her hands, says that the playpen has never failed to hold Mariángel before. She apologizes regardless, promises to watch more carefully from now on, and leaves for home.

The next few hours are quiet and tense. I sit at the kitchen table, and Mariángel removes pots and pans from cabinets, sets them on the ground, puts them back in new places. I nod vigorously at each of her decisions, and pockets of residual adrenaline flame up each time I remember. Rum over ice helps a little.

Finally she sleeps. It seems very late and I decide that I would like a fried egg sandwich but am unable to locate the skillet. I pour another rum, check all the likely places a second time. Then I begin with the unlikely ones.

An hour and three glasses later I still have not found it. Instead, deep in the lowest cupboard I find two enameled ceramic steins—Günther's wedding gift to Pilar and me. I take them up and rinse them, but they have been unused for months, require scrubbing, which at the moment is beyond my capacity.

Another glass and my capacity grows, becomes adequate, is suddenly vast. I bring out the scrubber. One of the steins is whole and the other's pewter lid has broken off. I scrub and rinse and dry. I apply glue to the broken lid, and to the shaft. As I set the pieces together, I see that one edge of the lid is bent. It is a problem and no solution occurs.

There is nothing specifically castle-like about the steins' design, and yet they project a certain defensive strength, part flanking tower and part portcullis. The first bears a scene of two men sitting at a round wooden table—one is a monk and the other is some sort of royalty—and an aproned waiter. All three men have thick mustaches. Along the bottom of the mug are the words Erst Mach' Dein' Sach: Dann Trink' Und Lach.

The other mug shows a man and a woman dancing. This man, too, has a thick mustache. The woman's face is blurred. To one side is a musician playing an instrument that lays flat on his lap. They all wear short pants and high socks and the next time I see the cultists I will suggest this as their new look. The background is cobalt blue. It will now be much harder to straighten the lid. I suspect that at some point I knew what the instrument is called. With luck the glue will fail.

So much of my time and attention has lately been devoted to ping pong. This is not a factor of my wishes or desires but has not been wholly unpleasant. Until this week I had not played ping pong in many years, had never played it competitively or well, but the dean himself called me with the request. I asked why I was needed, and his answer involved scheduling conflicts and shoulder injuries. I did not have to win any matches, he said—the department was hoping only that I might help them log a few participation points. I told him that my reply would be forthcoming in a matter of hours.

Four minutes later Arantxa came to my office to tell me that I could comply or be fired. I stared at her and waited, as though contemplating rebellion. Arantxa was not deceived. She knows that I know that she understands ping pong as a means by which one might be brought back into a given sort of life, and also that she wants very, very badly to beat Business in the medal race. In the end I broke and smiled, and she pretended not to be delighted.

The first two rounds were yesterday morning. I won both matches by default: my Language and Literature opponent allegedly chose instead to sit quietly with his girlfriend on a bench near the cafeteria, and my Art opponent arrived eleven minutes late. My spot in the semifinals ensured, I defaulted my afternoon match against a Law opponent whose serves, it is said, cannot be seen. This morning I played a Business student and scored no points whatsoever. Tonight then is the bronze medal match, and my opponent studies History, and Casualidad has brought Mariángel to watch. The crowd is sparse, as most other students and faculty so inclined are watching basketball across campus or volleyball at the coliseum, and this suits me precisely.

My opponent is thin and quick. He has brought his own paddle, its handle inscribed with what I suspect are his initials. He twice neglects to account for the strength of my wrist, however, and I lose the first game by only nine.

I spend the break looking thoughtfully at the faces of my paddle, as if winning were only a matter of adjustment. We begin again, and though it has occurred to me to use my bulk to disguise my serve, the second game is less fraught than the first. I am three points from medal-less elimination when my opponent jumps to slam a lob and breaks his ankle as he lands.

When he has stopped screaming and been tended to,

I come to the sidelines, and Mariángel applauds. This is not in reference to my victory but to the pattern of sweat on the armpits of my shirt. Applauding is now among her favorite activities, and the things that occasion it are often unexpected but not inappropriate: a surprisingly short telephone pole, a particularly fine cow, an inordinately translucent plastic bag.

As we walk to the basketball courts, I observe Casualidad from many angles. She seems to be doing well. I say this, and she thanks me. The house is less tidy than before and less clean, and this is not an unfair exchange.

We come to the parking lot, and Mariángel decides suddenly that she would like a zapote leaf. I remind her that she did not much care for the last one I brought her. She takes hold of my thumb and bites it. It takes her fifteen minutes to choose one that is precisely as bright and glossy and beautiful as most of the others, and thus we miss the first half of Reynaldo's game.

He too is playing for Engineering, has no interest in medals as such but cares a great deal about winning. He is in fact a good player but does not look like one, not even while playing: he has grown still heavier and lacks grace but rebounds well, bounces Law students left and right out of the key, and twice completely off the court. We cheer each of his achievements, especially the improbable running jump-hook that he hits from just inside the free-throw line with nine seconds left to win.

He celebrates with his teammates for a time, then comes over, drips sweat in Mariángel's face as he kisses her forehead, punches me on the shoulder and asks if the Lakers are having tryouts anytime soon. I say that they called last night, were wondering why he wasn't there already, were worried that he might have lost his way. He smiles, thanks us for coming, and rejoins the celebration he has caused.

My tie is uncooperative. I retie it four times on my walk to work, and still I can feel the knot bulging asymmetrically, and still the long end is too short. A fifth attempt, at last success, and there is a small crowd gathered near the Language Center entrance. I cannot think of any reason why this would be.

As always I do not need to push my way through, instead simply walk, and watch as the crowd parts before me. Halfway in I find Arantxa, Eugenia and the guest lecturer. The guest lecturer is gesticulating unsteadily. Arantxa leads me to one side. The problem is the turkey, she says.

I nod as if that were a reasonable problem, and then realize: today, a week from Thanksgiving, and thus this afternoon our feast unless these gesticulations interfere. Arantxa says that the guest lecturer had assumed that turkeys could be bought dead and plucked and frozen in the supermarket. This is not the case in Piura except at Christmas, as she learned last night. They can however be bought alive and feathered and warm at the outdoor market, as she learned this morning.

Eugenia and the guest lecturer join us, and the crowd has grown: the morning-shift professors listen in as they sort their realia and flashcards, as they count their handouts and chalk. According to the guest lecturer's calculations, the cooking of the turkey must begin immediately. Eugenia has been to the cafeteria, but no qualified butchers will be present before noon. Arantxa looks at me now, and her thoughts are as if written on a whiteboard: any American with forearms as large as mine must by definition have experience pursuant to the death of poultry.

That assumption is not quite incorrect. I ask to see the turkey, am led around the corner and halfway down the side of the building. The crowd follows. The turkey is immense. Its wings and feet are tied with plastic twine. I ask the guest lecturer why she didn't have it killed and dressed there at the market. She blinks, blinks again, and I nod.

I look at the people nearest me. Surely most of them could kill the turkey better than I can. I stare at the bird and wait. Arantxa clears her throat. I nod, wait more. She rubs her temples and crosses her arms and finally asks me outright. It pleases me to be repaying my debt in this way.

First I ask Eugenia to locate and bring Don Teófilo, and those around me nod. Don Teófilo is the senior-most gardener here at the university, and knows the answers to many questions. To judge by his face and posture and gait he is the oldest man I have ever met. It takes a suitably long time for him to arrive.

The crowd has doubled in size, mainly students coming to ask if their professors called in sick. Arantxa shouts for quiet, announces that all language classes will start fifteen minutes late, and that all conversation in our vicinity must take place in the language appropriate to the class being missed. This is so unfeasible that it works perfectly: the students laugh, and become the Crowd of Babel.

I describe the particulars of the situation to Don Teófilo, and ask if suitable implements are available. He promises me that they are and goes to get them. We wait. We wait longer. Finally he comes bearing a machete and a large block of wood.

I attempt to repurpose my tie as a headband but it droops into my eyes, so instead I hand it to Eugenia, and the students press in so close that there is no room to swing. I take up the unreasonably calm turkey, who has perhaps been quieted with pisco. I walk twenty paces from the wall, and the crowd loosens, eases itself around me until I am its very eye. Don Teófilo sets the block of wood on the ground at my feet. I lay the turkey beside it and this is all very close to being finished.

Then the guest lecturer wraps her hands around my elbow. My willingness is inspirational, she says. At first it seemed impossible, she says, but now it doesn't. I begin to suspect that I understand her meaning, hope that I am incorrect and sadly am not: she holds out her hands, requests the machete.

The crowd, still bigger, rippling—assistant gardeners, students from distant buildings, professors from every department. I suggest to the guest lecturer that this is not the moment to begin learning butchery. She looks at me, squeezes my elbow tighter. She reminds me quietly of all her work in preparation for the feast this evening. Then she tells a long anecdote about cousins of hers who live on farms, how as children they used to insult her, and in what terms.

Arantxa elbows me, says something too softly for me to hear. I look up. It is the rector. He is smiling. He nearly always smiles. He says he heard that great and important events were unfolding, and hoped to witness them firsthand. Arantxa explains the dinner and its ramifications. The guest lecturer tells her anecdote again, and details her plan. She adds that I have volunteered to hold the turkey still.

The rector could not be more pleased. He congratulates his friend on her newfound heartiness, and thanks me for my assistance. I say that he is welcome, and hand her the machete. I tell her that she will have to chop with great force so as to kill the turkey cleanly, but also with great precision so as not to hit my fingers. She nods. The circle of professors and students and gardeners and now minor administrators, now housekeepers, now couriers draws tighter around the wooden block.

I ask the guest lecturer to practice first, and she does, striking the block with great force and precision a sufficient number of times in a row. She smiles at me, and wipes away some sweat. I stretch the turkey's neck across the block.

She draws back the machete, the circle leans in, the machete falls with sufficient precision but little force and the turkey seems to explode in place. Blood spurts into my face from the partly severed neck and I hold as tightly as I can and beg her to swing again. One wing comes free and she swings, her eyes closed and the machete landing square between my fists, the turkey's head limp in my left hand and its body wrenching out of my right, both wings free and beating and blood spraying from the neck as the turkey ricochets from rector to student to gardener, blood jetting into our eyes and hair and open mouths, the guest lecturer still swinging, again and again into the wooden block.

It is Don Teófilo who catches the turkey mid-air, pulls it to the ground, holds it until it goes still. Tonight's feast will be subdued, perhaps even vegetarian. The yams, however, will be delicious. The yams here are always delicious. There is an International Potato Center in Lima, and I have heard that it has each of Peru's four thousand indigenous tuber species displayed. One day I shall go and learn them all, and Eugenia drapes my tie around my neck. I nod to her. I hand the turkey's head to the rector. I clap him bloodily on the shoulder, and thank him for his continual support.

# 19.

AND ALREADY IT IS TIME FOR SAN TEODORO AGAIN: THE FIRST anniversary of Pilar's death. It will be a few hours only of flowers and quietness and Mariángel will stay with Casualidad so the preparations are far simpler. Then as I open the door to leave, the telephone rings.

This new telephone, I often appreciate its cordlessness, and it has many types of ring from which to choose, though I have not yet found one I enjoy. Casualidad answers, comes running for me with the receiver. The line pops and crackles. It is Pilar's father, calling from Chiclayo. I cover the mouthpiece, ask Casualidad if she is sure he wants to speak with me. She says that he said my name specifically.

I greet him quietly. He asks how I am, and his voice comes to me low, rich, warm in spite of the crackling, as if this call were something else, something new and larger. He says that he and his wife are well, that their sons are also well. He asks if Mariángel has begun to talk, and I say that she does not yet speak clearly as such but that her walking and applauding have greatly improved.

He laughs, asks if she truly likes her birthday dolls. In fact they are still hidden on her highest shelf but I tell him that there are few things she enjoys more than taking off their felt hats and putting them back on. He says he was unaware that the hats were removable. The phone changes shape and texture, will not rest steady in my hand as I finally understand: there is nothing to match forgiveness for unlikelihood. I go to thank him for calling on such a day, for everything such a call signifies, but he interrupts.

- Do you remember what I told you at the wedding?

His voice has thinned and tightened and a chiclón has appeared in the back yard.

- You told me many things.

A chiclón is a bird the size and color of a crow, but it is not a crow.

- I told you to take care of Pilar.

They have thick black beaks that appear too large for their bodies.

- Yes.

On the ground they move like very small dinosaurs.

- And do you remember what I told you at the funeral?

Whatever this call began as, it is now something else, and I am unsure whether he intended this change from the beginning, whether it matters, and the eyes are massive and only black, pure pupil, or so it seems from this distance.

- You told me many things there as well.

When they copulate, the male stands on the female's wing joints, flapping to maintain his balance.

- Why did you let her go alone to the market at night? What sort of husband does that? What sort of man?

The chiclón leans back on its tail.

- I do not know the answer to any of those questions.

It spreads its wings low.

- Perhaps you do not know, but I do. Pilar loved you

very much, but at times she was unhappy and then she would tell us the truth: how careless you were, how lazy, how selfish with your time. So careless and lazy and selfish that you would let her go alone to the market at night.

This is something I have seen them do on the open grass of the university. I have been told that they do so to warm their bodies in the sun, and I do not answer.

- God punishes us every day with grief, he says.

At the moment the sky is a melding of gray clouds and black.

- Why would God punish you?

It must be something else.

- For letting Pilar marry someone who would not protect her. Do you know why we did not go to her grave on the Day of the Dead?

They are sometimes called guardacaballos, follow horses and cattle through fields, eat the insects raised by the heavy hooves.

- No.

At the university they follow lawnmowers instead.

- Because we knew you would be there, he says. And are you going to the cemetery today?

The noise of the chiclón is not a song of any kind.

- Yes.

The chiclón gathers itself, hops to the base of the almond tree.

- This year, but not any subsequent year, and not on her birthday, not ever. You have all the other days, yes? So those two days, let her be ours again.

I tell him that it will be as he says, and the chiclón stares in through the window, stares and flies away.

◦⟨)⟨)◦

There are far fewer men and women selling flowers and candles and food and cardboard images than there were before, but even so there are several of each. I purchase a spray of sunflowers, a packet of candles, walk in through the gates and past the empty chapel. Today there are no young men with ladders, and not many mourners. A few of them, the oldest, are sitting on lightweight portable chairs of the type I will most likely never remember to buy.

I clean the dust from Pilar's niche with my shirttail, and fan the sunflowers across the ground. Her father's words were and are true but nothing new, nothing I have not already held to myself like coals. I sit down, lean back, close my eyes, work to rid my mind of his voices.

And now I can bring the good pictures, one by one, easy at first. Pilar dancing marinera at the coliseum, her dress garnet and gold, a sheen of sweat on her forehead as she lifts her vast handkerchief and smiles. Pilar swimming in Yacila, teaching a young girl to hold her breath, coming slow out of the water. Pilar walking to where I sit on the terrace of our hotel in Máncora; she is carrying two coconuts, two plastic straws, hands one of each to me, is astounded that I do not find the milk delicious. Pilar at the deer pen, Pilar standing in strings of huayruro beads. Pilar at an ice cream cart in the Plaza de Armas, her hair bright in the sun.

A voice, and I look. Not far away a middle-aged woman is praying her way around a string of rosary beads. I watch her, wish suddenly for beads, as suddenly am glad I do not have them.

Pilar asleep on the bus to Chiclayo. I kiss her cheek, close my eyes, a jolt and now the world at an unlikely angle, the skyline diagonal to us, Pilar leaning into me so strongly that I cannot move and it is a moment before we understand: the bus, a turn taken too wide, we slid off the highway and came to rest not quite at the tipping point. We step carefully toward the door, and walking is both difficult and complex, as if gravity itself has been altered. At the door we each panic, jump and run, convinced that the bus is at this moment falling. An hour waiting for another bus and it never comes. Finally giving up, walking along the highway, hitchhiking. The empty bed of a truck. Not the bus to Chiclayo but the bus coming home from there. The truck bed not quite empty, sacks of something, perhaps rice.

The middle-aged woman walks away, passes a young man who stands at the near edge of the next whitewashed structure over. He is leaning forward, his forehead resting against the stone or so it seems, his lips unmoving and Pilar at a chifa, asking the waiter for an Inca Kola and another tray of dim sum. Pilar. There must be more. Pilar lying on the beach at Colán and her bathing suit is new, I remember that it was new, do not remember the color and something small hits the top of my head, another and another, it is raining, harder and harder.

I do not know what I am meant to do: staying seems stupid and leaving seems wrong. My candles go out. I stand, step into what seems like shelter tight against the niched wall but there is no shelter, the rain filling the air and the oldest mourners stand, fold their chairs, shuffle toward the gates.

If they are going then I will stay. I sit back down in what is now mud. Pilar. Pilar in Cajamarca. Cajamarca, yes, but I cannot hold her clear in my mind, not with the water drilling holes in the ground around me, not with the steam that rises, not in the dense heart of this heat. Pilar in a taxi, and she laughs. Pilar in the desert, the ravine, both of her wrists broken and why did he do that, why did he feel that need and I stand, walk out of the cemetery.

Dusk. I circle, my clothes stuck to me, heavier and heavier. The rain masses, thins. The circle wider, ever wider. A foot of water in the gutters. The rain at last silent and soft but perhaps preparations will begin truly now, preparations for what can only come.

For a time there are high-walled buildings, signless, and I cannot guess their use. Farther along the arc are small grocery stores, chifas, hardware and paint. Then a set of angles that is known to me, and the light is a known light, the colors also known.

I stop at the doorway, look in. There are many coffins displayed: open and closed, painted and varnished, of many materials and many sizes, and in that sea of coffins is a desk, and a boy is sitting at the desk, his hair shaved almost to the skull, no shoes, his shirt and shorts clean, pressed. He is writing on brown paper, and the fluorescent lights tremble above him. His father comes out from the back, sees me where I stand dripping on the sidewalk, recognizes me and beckons me in.

We shake hands, and he presents his son to me, Leoncio, the best grade-school soccer player in Piura, he says, though last week's match did not go well. Leoncio smiles and returns to his homework. The father asks how the cemetery was, if my time there was satisfactory. I ask how he knew, and he says that he never allows himself to forget a date—death, wake, burial, hundreds of them, thousands if he lives long enough. He has not yet forgotten a single one, he says, and this is part of the service he provides.

I lean over Leoncio. The mimeographed sheets are his English homework, and the exercises themselves are rife with typographical errors. I ask how he likes English class. It is fine, he says.

- And the homework, is it hard?
- Not so hard, except for today.

I ask if I can be of help. He says he believes that I can. His father apologizes for the lack of chairs, closes a coffin and pushes it closer to the desk. Leoncio and I work carefully through the last section, irregular verbs in the past, I was and you slept and he drank and she said and it ran and we swam and they fought.

Afterwards the walk is a certain drifting, the streetlights muted by mist. Home is not far away. A shower first, then coffee, I think. Time with Mariángel. Dinner and sleep, sleep, yes.

In through the front door. The house is very quiet. Then suddenly it is not and oh they have failed, both of them, the aspirin and llama fetus have failed, there is screaming and the breaking of plates in the kitchen and Casualidad runs past me tearing at her hair. The birds, she says, the birds, runs past me again and into the wall, bounces off, I catch but cannot hold her and Mariángel is more or less singing out on the patio. Casualidad runs into my bedroom. I chase after her and find her thrashing on the floor, wound in the mosquito netting I had strung around my bed.

My weight on top of her is enough. I lift and she goes to scream and I lower. I wait. When I lift a second time she is barely breathing.

- The hummingbirds, she whispers, in my hair.

I check her hair and promise that no hummingbirds are present. I gather Mariángel, grab at the phone, call Arantxa, and she comes soon enough. She sits with Casualidad on the floor of my bedroom, strips the netting away and smooths her face. Casualidad is quiet now. I find the telephone number for her sister in Catacaos, and twenty minutes later she comes as well.

When Socorro has seen what there is to see, there is a small discussion. Arantxa holds my hand unnecessarily for a time, then says that she and Socorro will take Casualidad to the hospital. She says other things as well, but it is hard to know what any of them mean.

# 20.

THE WALK IS LONG, THE NIGHT AIR IS HOT AND THICK AND wet, and Mariángel moves like a netful of cod on my back. She is not unhappy but unquiet, and I know where we are going but not why: Arantxa called me to her office before my first class, asked if I could be at her house by eight, left the nature of the event opaque. Her voice was ever so slightly higher pitched than usual. I suspect that either I am to be fired or the evening will involve candles, incense, quiet jazz on the veranda though Arantxa hates jazz and her house has no veranda.

It is now Socorro who cleans and cooks and looks after Mariángel each day. She charges me half again what I paid Casualidad. This is not unfair, as Casualidad and Fermín have since moved in with her and her husband and their four daughters in Catacaos.

On Socorro's first morning with us, when I went to leave for work Mariángel cried, wailed, reached for me and screamed. Socorro said that by day's end all would be well, and she was right. The two of them are warily cordial associates and Mariángel pounds on the back of my head, grabs fistfuls of my hair and pulls.

I shift her around to my chest, and she will not have it. I shift her back to my back, and when I am again walking steadily she calms. Parallel now to the river and two blocks away. I listen for its sound, hear only nightbirds and cars.

This morning Socorro reported back as she strained Mariángel's juice: the first doctor had not had any helpful suggestions. She dropped the strainer in the sink, shrugged, said that there were still other doctors to see. I agreed, doctors of all kinds. I told her that Casualidad will see one after another until the problem is solved, that she will take all necessary tests, that I will pay, need only to know whom to pay and how much, and we cross the Old Bridge into Miraflores.

This evening my Upper Intermediate Students began worrying about their final exam. They asked me questions, dozens, many of them less than straightforward and none entirely new. I gave answer after answer. Finally the questions became repetitive, a sign that the students are not yet at ease but can think of no more specific needs. In response I handed out that which I save for each semester's moment of this type: the first page of *Finnegans Wake*.

Miraflores is more pleasant than Castilla, less dry and dusty in normal times, though the tap water here is abysmal, a sulfur stew. I asked my students to begin at the beginning. They read silently for ten or fifteen seconds, then looked up. I told them to continue. They read for another five seconds, leaned back and looked up again—all of them, very nearly simultaneously. I told them that discussion would be an option once they had finished the page, and they pretended to try until Hector stood and announced that he spoke for everyone in saying that my joke was not amusing. I said that it was not a joke. He asked why I was doing this to them. I said that as regarded their future lives, they would need to become accustomed to such bafflement, but that the upcoming exam would be the text's mirrored image.

This helped less than I had hoped, and Arantxa's was not the only invitation I received today. The dean of Communications came to my office in person and asked me to be his guest at their department's verbena on Friday. I paused, and thanked him for thinking of me.

At last Arantxa's house. The front steps are less well lit than they might be. I knock on the door, and the weight of my fist swings it open. The inside of her house is even darker.

I call out, hear nothing, wait. I observe my immediate surroundings, and call out again. I partially crouch, call out once more, charge into the house and the lights come on and thirty people yell.

They do not yell quite in unison and the words are thus indecipherable, but now I see their faces, the faces of so many of my colleagues and friends. All of them are smiling, then cooing as Mariángel begins to cry. I twist to get at her, calm her, and the smells register at last: not incense but once again stuffing and yams.

So it is a surprise post-Thanksgiving party of sorts, and these people, these colleagues, they regard me with great warmth. They lead me to the dining room where there is not jazz but blues. They seat me at the head of a table beautifully laid with candles and flowers and plates but empty of food, and the chair they have chosen is a sturdy one. They all stand back as Arantxa comes from the kitchen.

She is happy and sweating and aproned and holding a hat. At first the hat is a mystery, and then it is not: it is a homemade pilgrim's hat. It fits perfectly, which is another mystery. My colleagues fear that I won't want to wear it, insist that it must stay. I would not take it off for anything, but it is enjoyable to pretend to be barely convinced by their pleading.

When Arantxa comes out again she is bearing a turkey on a platter, and I suspect it is the turkey whose head I once held—with the guest lecturer we had ham. Arantxa looks at me, seems about to speak but then the turkey slips. Günther jumps to her side, rights the platter, helps guide it to the table.

A constant coming and going, Arantxa and Günther and half a dozen others, kitchen to dining room and back until the table is loaded with local approximations of Thanksgiving foodstuffs: tamarind sauce instead of cranberry, white rice instead of mashed potatoes. Arantxa pours wine and raises her glass. No one falls quiet. She raises it higher, taps it with her spoon, finally shouts and there is silence. Günther brings a shrouded whiteboard from behind a door, reveals one colorful point at a time and Arantxa reads:

- Here's to our bronze medalist!

Everyone applauds.

- And to our turkey restrainer!

Louder applause and laughter.

- And to everyone's favorite English professor!

More laughter, less applause, a tiny bit of whistling. Arantxa blushes as I toast her back and thank her, thank them all, bid them drink. Now at last we sit, begin, and Mariángel is passed from lap to lap. She is calm for longer with some people than with others, and it does not depend on age or gender or how long she has known them, is for now an unbreakable code.

The food is excellent except for dessert: dry donuts, plain. Eugenia says that she made them from scratch, and hopes they are similar to the donuts one might eat in California. I tell her they are exactly the same.

At last Mariángel tires, pouts, and I take her to Arantxa's bedroom, sing her to sleep—Sarah Vaughan, in case Arantxa is listening. The objects on the dresser are less perfectly aligned than I would have suspected, and there is a piled foot of clothing on the floor of her half-closed closet. The photographs on the walls are mostly of her family and home in Bilbao, but there are also a few taken here. One shows Arantxa standing between Günther and me, our arms interlocked. It was taken outside the cafeteria perhaps three years ago. We all look younger and thinner and tanner and stronger than I ever remember feeling.

By the time I return the dishes have been cleared and everyone has moved to the living room. The discussion widens: the rain, the river, the Olympiad and its upcoming closing ceremony. We analyze recent encouraging efforts from some of Peru's youngest professional soccer players. We lament the difficulty of finding certain kinds of illustrative realia.

I tell Arantxa that it is inappropriate if not illegal for her to love blues and hate jazz. She says that she doesn't see why given how many of her best friend's siblings she detests. We all then discuss which of the two forms is better and happily reach no consensus.

Of everyone here, only Reynaldo does not seem delighted. I go to sit beside him and ask. He nods and smiles, a sad and tired smile.

- You were right, he says. There is not enough time. Everything in your country must be done excessively in advance.

- Not everything, but most things, yes. I'm sorry.

- It does not matter. I will simply wait another year, will start my preparations early next fall, and all will go well.

- Your ticket will still be good by then?

- No, it is only good for a year, but I am working on a plan for it too, will tell you as soon as I am sure that it is correct.

I nod, pat his back, ask about the new species he discovered in the desert.

- Nothing new about it. *Ziziphus obtusifolia*, very common in Mexico. The only question is what it was doing this far south.

There is a short silence in the room. I lean to Günther, tell him that not long ago I was admiring the steins that he gave Pilar and me for our wedding, and ask where he got them. A far deeper silence now. I look around, smile, tell them that it's all right, tell Günther that I really would like to know. He looks at Arantxa, nods and smiles, says that he isn't sure where they were made, but his mother mailed them from Mainz.

- They are beautiful, I say, and so useful.

- I hoped they would be, Günther says. They are originals.

Dr. Guardiola signals for quiet, coughs, coughs at greater length. We wait, and when he has recovered he asks me to list things for which I am thankful. This moment, I think. If only, I think.

- The sun of Colán and the moon of Paita, I say.

There is much shouting and hooting of support but Reynaldo says that regional clichés are disallowed. I add the flesh of the cherimoya and the juice of the maracuyá. Those around me will now not be restrained, must each name their favorite Piuran foods.

When that is done, the chairs are pushed back, the coffee table is slid to one side, and of course we dance: rock and salsa, salsa and rock. I am asked to demonstrate a typical Thanksgiving dance, and invent one that involves much dipping and waving of the pilgrim hat. Everyone claps, and comments on the similarity of my dance to tondero, and wonders which one came first.

Later I rest in the bathroom. Arantxa's scale has colored markers at a variety of different weights—another code, one best left unbroken. Now a gecko scuttles up the far wall. As I watch it, exhaustion comes for me.

First to the living room, to begin the process of saying goodbye. I thank Arantxa, thank them all, for what they have managed this evening. The men shake my hand and the women kiss my cheek and they each protest that I am leaving too soon. But Mariángel, I say. They nod as if understanding, and perhaps they do. Perhaps they understand perfectly.

Next to Arantxa's room. I gather Mariángel from the bed, and here is another cause for thanks, this pleasure, lifting her warm and smelling faintly of caramel, limp in sleep, then curling into me. I walk back to the living room, expect the light and noise to wake and frighten her, but the lamps have been dimmed, the music quieted. My colleagues are still dancing, but silently or very nearly so, each pair set face to face, undulant parallel lines to the open front door, the dancers' arms arced above us, a tunnel that echoes with whispered fondness, my friends trailing us out and down the steps, dispatching us into the night as if a message.

# 21.

Months. Children, paint on their faces. Cotton candy and a sudden perfect erosion: every mountain, every butte mesa hill worn flat and the canyons and valleys and gullies filling with that selfsame mud and rock and ice. Then quietness. Stasis, yes. Metal hands. A single altitude, everywhere.

# 22.

Dawn, cloudless, silent. There was something, not gold but gold-colored. I wait. Gone. I reach through the new netting, turn off the fan, snuff out the mosquito coils that are now also necessary. Today is the fourth and last day. I think I will not start it just yet.

The rains came again as exams began, fell heavy but incoherent, splintered sunlight and downpour. The doors and windows of my house no longer open easily and its smells too are new, subtly sodden. The university's first leak was not large but also not to be missed: a steady drip in the office where salaries are paid. On my walks that week I saw men carrying bags of concrete, women bearing sheets of corrugated tin, children dragging rolls of plastic sheeting. Fights broke out over canned peaches. No one would sell toilet paper at any price.

The government has also at last become alarmed. The damage done fifteen years ago by the last El Niño has disappeared, the drains rebuilt throughout the city, even in front of my house. Many streets are unusable for the piles of asphalt, the stacks of shovels and picks, the barefoot men pouring tar. Earthmoving equipment has been arrayed along the riverbanks, fresh cement lines the causeway walls, loads of rock have been dumped at the bases of the bridges, and all these things look wrong. The river itself remains thin, almost ridiculous. The shanties and their chickens and crops are all still in place, as if there is no chance of change.

A noise outside my room, Mariángel stirring but not yet awake. Her new hobby is pulling me to my feet so that she might pass back and forth between my legs. She is tall enough now that it is not always undangerous. She still enjoys applauding, clapped with Socorro and the rest of the crowd as I stepped onto the stage to receive my bronze medal. It weighed exactly as much as I suspected, and Arantxa shook my hand with both of hers, once again delighted although the race had gone to Business in the end.

Reynaldo has just come back from Lima. His current plan is to use his ticket to visit the United States as a tourist, to observe firsthand the graduate schools he is considering. He renewed his passport, applied for a visa, was turned down though he had a letter from the university in hand. Familyless working-age men are rarely awarded such visas, he was told, and tickets won in contests are immaterial. He says that he is already planning his next application, that he now understands the vectors in play. The consul assumes that no Peruvian intends to return to Peru unless the contrary can be proven incontrovertibly, and Reynaldo himself must provide the proof.

Another noise—Socorro arriving. I ask her often for news of Casualidad, and each time the news is the same: the name of a hospital, the name of a doctor, the name of a test. The list of conditions, diseases and syndromes for which she can be tested locally is dwindling. The doctors are intrigued, and speak of symposia.

The rain, the exams, my students, I walked among them and loved them and hoped they would succeed. They sweated and wrote and sweated and swiped at mosquitoes. I looked out the window and from time to time saw men moving past, though my exams were all in classrooms on the third floor of the main building, and there are no balconies on the windowed side. These are the ladder-men. They paint walls, clear gutters, wash windows. The slats of their ladders are thin, do not look like comfortable footing, but the men do not complain, and when it is time to alter their position, instead of descending to shift the ladder left or right they straddle the top of it and sidle, the ladder becoming fixed stilts.

Almost time. When my students finished their exams, they handed them in and thanked me, apologized for where their sweat had darkened the paper. They exited the classrooms and glided down the stairs and gathered beneath the first-floor awnings. There they smoked, watched the rain, established betting pools that require a great deal of paperwork and small sums of money.

Much of the gambling centers on which of the four bridges will fall, and which will fall first. The Sánchez Cerro, the Bolognesi, the Old and the Fourth: one named for a dictator, one for a hero, one for its age and one for its place in Piuran bridge-building chronology. I have been told that the betting is strong in favor of the Sánchez Cerro going first, given that it nearly falls every year, even when there is no rain at all. Few are willing to bet that the Old Bridge will fall. It figures on thousands of postcards, in many Peruvian songs, in all Piura-based documentaries and beer commercials. Its lamps are ornate and pleasing. The Old Bridge falling would be a puncture wound to the local soul.

Mariángel shouts, and Socorro goes to her. It will likely not rain today, did not rain yesterday or the day before or the day before that. Canned peaches are once again available in every store and the price of toilet paper has dropped to near-normal. Some of my neighbors contend that this El Niño will be relatively weak, a month or five weeks at most. Other neighbors say that there will be no end, and these are the neighbors who are gathering their belongings in plastic-lined boxes, stacking them in rented pick-ups, driving south. I have even seen cars on the Panamericana, their trunks tied open and filled with children looking back at the damp world of which I am a part.

And it is time. I push through the netting and dress. A quick breakfast, a gathering of pens and grade sheets, then out to the patio. Mariángel is already there. She sits in her playpen, coos to dolls stripped of their bowls, hats, jewelry. I do not know how she could have seen the dolls at the back of her top shelf, but last night she did, and wanted them immediately, and does not seem too distraught at their current poverty.

I position the chairs and table in the shade of the awning. I fetch a calculator, and the three stained manila folders that hold my exams. I arrange the exams in stacks around me, sit, and most of my colleagues hate this time of year more than any other—the extended weekend of Immaculate Conception lost to grading, stack after stack, exam after exam—but it all pleases me immeasurably.

I have spent each long day sweating here with Mariángel, watching birds and listening to Lorenzo Humberto Sotomayor as sung by other people and grading luxuriously: multiple choice and true-or-false, matching and short answer and sentence completion, tasks not found in nature. There is a sort of pleasure in the industrial repetition of that grading, and my questions were overly difficult but my students are so very smart and wise. They are undeserved by anyone.

That which remains to be done is half the essays of each group. These essays present a more thorough kind of pleasure. I begin with Pre-Intermediate work on household pets. First is Natalia writing well on her tarantula. Next is Alberto writing less well but more passionately and at greater length in regard to his Schnauzer, and already Mariángel is bored with the dolls.

We discuss her boredom briefly. Socorro comes, bears her off for milk and other games. Fortunato has written about a species of bird I suspect he has invented and it goes on and on in this way, short breaks each three exams to rest my eyes, and at last the Pre-Intermediate stack is done.

Sitting back for a moment, watching the arrozeros come and go, and the sky is no longer quite cloudless. Then Intermediate. Jhon on an earthquake in Trujillo. Estela on a hurricane hitting Cuba. Milton on a small lake south of Cajamarca, and I wait for his natural disaster to occur, and it does not, but his descriptions of the water's varying shades are splendid.

It is one in the afternoon when I end this second stack. Socorro asks where I would like lunch served, but if I stop now I will not finish in time. Mariángel yells and I go to her, take her, sing briefly and dance. I attempt to explain: any day but today. I suggest to Socorro that she gather blankets and toys and take Mariángel to the park.

More clouds, and Upper Intermediate. Claudia, Hector, Lidia; Norma, Domitila, Ramiro; Gerardo, Wilfredo, Zaira, superb work on generational differences, on and on. And when I have finished grading, have tallied the points from the many exams' many sections, have recorded the totals, have calculated final semester grades and listed them on their respective sheets, have replaced the exams in their stained manila folders, I then walk and run and walk to the university, along and through and across, arrive at the Language Center only nine minutes after final grades were due—my best yet.

I present the folders to Eugenia, and answer her questions as to how well my students have done. I bow as I hand my grade sheets to Arantxa, and thank her for another semester finely administered. I promise the two of them that I will attend the upcoming graduation ceremony, but pause first so that they will know the truth.

I say hello to the other professors present, and we reminisce hurriedly, a sentence or two with each. Then I walk out of the Language Center thinking *On this day* and unsure to what the phrase might best refer, and I am almost quick on my feet, am free, free for weeks, two of them and more, through Christmas and New Year's but only that long, for there is summer school, always summer school, and on this day I stop by the pen to wish the deer pleasant holidays, and find Reynaldo there as well, exchange shoulder punches with him and listen to his worries that if El Niño has truly come, it may well complicate his extraction research in ways he cannot yet foresee. I shake my head and nod and hold grass out to the deer and he punches my shoulder again, much harder now, for corrupting his fodder research, and I apologize and we hug extremely briefly and plan to make plans at some point in the near future, and on this day I salute Dr. Guardiola from across the quad and hurry in the opposite direction to avoid being invited to a retreat, and on this day I wave to Don Teófilo where he kneels among the begonias, and he laughs, all those decades light on his shoulders, he pulls a weed, waves back and wishes me well.

The rain holds off, and the sky is a study in grays and blues, and the poinciana trees are in full rich orange bloom. As of tomorrow the university will be empty or nearly so, will be all but silent, much as it was my first few weeks here. I knew no one, and came daily to the campus to borrow books I hoped could teach me to do the job for which I had been hired. I lived in a boarding house a block from the university gate. All of the furniture was covered in clear plastic. My bed was not quite as large as my body. The owner reminded me daily that I was not to approach the kitchen under any circumstances.

As of my second night there I decided to eat elsewhere

when possible. That was perhaps a week before Christmas. A telephone call to my mother, and then out, circling, walking and walking. At last a restaurant specializing in roast chicken—one of this city's several dozen.

I sit down at a table in the center of the restaurant, and am the only client. The chair is hard plastic. The table is linoleum and the lights are very bright and the music is unpleasantly loud. There is a television mounted in the corner, a soap opera, and all the waiters are watching it.

During a commercial break one of the men comes over. He has a pea-sized mole growing from his eyebrow. We both shout to be heard, and I order a roast chicken, whole. To go? he asks. No, I say. The waiter looks at the ground, at the television, at me, and asks if I would like a bigger table.

I look around the restaurant. All the other tables are of precisely the same dimensions. I shake my head, and tell him that I am from California, and that today happens to be my birthday. I shout this with what I hope will sound like great confidence and joviality, as if eating alone in a chicken restaurant were a California birthday custom.

The waiter is too smart to believe me, smiles sadly and takes his leave, returns abruptly with a beer I have not ordered. He says that it is courtesy of the owner, and points to a small, closed door on the far side of the restaurant. I thank him. Ten minutes later the chicha is extinguished; the soap opera actors shout briefly, and are turned down as well.

All four of the waiters come walking in a line, and behind them is an aproned cook. The cook's face is bright with grease and pleasure. He is holding a platter bearing a large amount of French fries, and a roast chicken from which protrudes a single candle, lit.

The waiters take up positions around me, the four cardinal points. The cook begs my pardon, says that the nearby bakeries have all just closed, that otherwise he would have treated me to a muffin, that the following year I will have to arrive earlier in the evening. I assure him that the chicken and candle and sentiment are more than enough.

The five men sing to me, both birthday songs, and they sing surprisingly well. The cook sets the platter on the table. I blow out the candle, wishing for happiness. The cook applauds. The waiters look at each other, at the cook, at me. I nod. The waiters and the cook nod back. The cook returns to his spits, and the waiters to their soap opera.

Wishes are not normal things, though we make them all the time. In through my front door, and Mariángel is again in her playpen on the patio, and Socorro is slapping at my bookshelves with a rag. I say that I endorse full-heartedly her disciplinary techniques, but that I am curious to know what my books have done this time, that they should deserve such punishment.

She doesn't answer, and now she is weeping. I catch her wrist and take the rag from her hand. She sits at the dining room table. I bring glasses of water for us both, but she will not drink. She sits and looks out the window. There are no birds in the almond tree.

- Casualidad, she says. A tumor, she says.
- Where?
- Her brain.
- Oh no. No, no. I'm so sorry.

She nods. I let my hand rest on her shoulder, then leave her there staring at the tree. I go to my room, call the hospital. Yes, says the doctor who authorized and analyzed the scan. Down below, hard against the brainpan. Inoperable and malignant. She will last a month, perhaps two, and I smash the phone and its cradle.

# 23.

Oquendo says that one's gaze is a waiter. I put Armando's book away until such time as it might be needed again. We will leave in five minutes and these days rain falls often but with little force or volume. The river remains almost ridiculous and the cheaper newspapers roil: El Niño has faded, will not come at all, and money spent on bridges and drains was wasted the way so much is wasted here.

But this is not the view of most scientists. They measure the temperatures of oceans, say that bigger rains are biding their time, and this too is strange, to bide, and time. I call to Mariángel from the door, and she comes. I fit her into the carrier, and draw down the near-canopy I have built of plastic pipes and sheeting.

Out into the drizzle, past the Virgin, along and across and then through a park, not the one closest to our house but another, and in this other park, too, are matacojudo trees. Mariángel's sounds are happy ones. The matacojudo fruit are tiny and green where they hang. The canopy protects us both to a limited extent.

Again we have a new telephone and for a week I phoned the doctor daily to ask him to reconsider Casualidad's scan. He no longer takes my calls. Past San Teodoro and another two blocks. I have spoken with other doctors, sent them copies of the scan, and they concurred: malignant, inoperable. They have referred me to still other doctors, who have ideas regarding ways in which Casualidad's end can be directed, her pain lessened, her comfort augmented in all possible ways.

The woman at the window works her beads as she makes my change. The short fat manager tears our tickets. Inside, the air is as ever slightly cooler and today the cinema is almost empty.

We take our seat, eighth row from the front and Mariángel in my lap. She closes her eyes, sleeps for nine or ten seconds, and then water starts dripping from the ceiling onto the top of my head and spatters down around her. We move five seats to the right, and here there is no leak, but the splatting of water on fabric continues, a preliminary soundtrack.

There are more bats than usual, and far more mosquitoes. It is of course absurd for us to have come. It would have been likewise absurd for us not to. I lift Mariángel higher on my lap and someone calls from just behind us, calls Oye Chino!

And again: the timbre and tone, nasality and rasp. Sweat swells from my pores, runs from my face. I wait. No more words come. I wait, wait, turn slowly as if only to look up the aisle, as if waiting for a friend and the friend will arrive at any moment.

The man sitting behind us is all but albino. He looks at me. I smile, turn back. I wipe my face with my handkerchief. The lights drop and *Mars Attacks!* begins, happens very quickly in my brain: cows on fire, donuts and prostitutes, nitrogen-breathing Martians with cheek wattles and orange eyeballs, kindhearted Muslim ex-World Champion boxer, stuffed cat.

The Martians hate birds, seem invincible, but Slim Whitman yodeling "Indian Love Call" causes their heads to explode, and now Tom Jones appears as himself, sings not for the first time of how not unusual it is to see him cry. The curtain falls. Mariángel and I slide along the row away from the drip, up the aisle and out. I will have to remember to tell Casualidad about the Martians' hatred. Perhaps it will help in some way.

It is drizzling harder than before. We squint through the raucous honks and step to the curb. At the moment there are only mototaxis, and choosing one is difficult as the majority are wrong—misbalanced, weak motor, hairline axle fracture. Then someone chucks my shoulder, and it is Reynaldo.

- How did you like it? I ask.

He tweaks Mariángel's cheek, wins a smile.

- Very much, he says. The effects were very special.

- The projector broke only once.

- And the whistling was minimal, yes.

A pause. We listen to the drizzle.

- Have there been any advances to your plans? I ask.

- The dean offered to help me obtain a fellowship to study in Spain.

- The dean does not know you very well.

- No. But you do. Could you write a letter of reference for me to give to the American consul?

- Of course. When will you need it?

- I will be reapplying in two months—any time before that would be fine. And do you think it will help?

I do not.

- I do.

- Good. Excellent. Thank you.

We say our goodbyes and he walks to his motorcycle, gets on, kicks again and again. Twelve times, sixteen, twenty. He dismounts and shrugs.

- It worked perfectly on the way over here.

I nod and shake my head.

- Why don't you believe me?

- Because you are lying.

- Yes. It died halfway here and I had to push it. But until that moment, perfectly.

I wave and he waves back; he walks his motorcycle away, and I select a mototaxi. The seat is well padded, the bearings smooth, the shock absorbers healthy. It seems outstanding, yes, but there is also something of a noise, a random knocking sound from below, at times sharp, at times soft. When we arrive, not to our house but to the nearest store, as we step out I see what I'd missed before. It is a woman's shoe, its strap caught in the spokes.

I pay and now it comes: at the cinema I failed to search. It is not that I had no time but that I forgot. The mototaxista drives off and the shoe is slammed again and again into the mud and this is the world, this is where we live. I have not searched worthily in weeks, have not searched at all in days, and there is no excuse nor any suitable punishment, no faces around worth scanning and no taxis pass.

The store, its filthy floor, its cobwebbed corners, its flickering light. Also there is a girl. From her eyes I would guess that she is eight, and from her size I would guess that she is five. She is holding a toddler, probably her brother, slightly bigger than Mariángel, and the girl stares not at me but at the counter and the dusty things behind it.

- Your store is beautiful, she says to the old man who waits for me to decide what I need.

He thanks her and brings down the diapers and rum to which I finally point.

- I wish I had a store this beautiful, says the girl.

And this is also the world, this is also where we live.

Mariángel and I sit at the dining room table. Breakfast

noises come from the kitchen, and she bangs her silverware against her high chair's tray. The route I am planning for this evening is as always unsimple. The taxistas here gather at so many different bars, present so many possibilities.

Socorro brings Mariángel a cup of granadilla juice, sees my maps and tracings, asks what they are for. For a game my students will play, I say. She smiles, says that the eggs will soon be ready. I smile back though they will look and taste like scouring pads: Socorro is very good with Mariángel, and cleans even more thoroughly than Casualidad, but her work at the stove is unfortunate.

Halfway through the process of raising the cup to her lips, Mariángel loses concentration and pours a few drops down her cheek. I take a napkin, wipe her dry, help the spout toward her mouth. Socorro comes with the eggs. I ask about Casualidad, and Socorro nods.

- Yesterday she went to the Huaringas to be cured.
- The Huaringas.
- Yes. She will live in Frías with our parents until she has recovered wholly, and then she will come back to work for you.

I am unable to keep my expression neutral.

- Yes, Socorro says, I know. But nothing else has worked either.
- Why didn't you tell me before?
- She asked me not to.
- So why are you telling me now?

Socorro shrugs, returns to the kitchen. The Huaringas. I went, once: three months since Pilar's body had been discovered, and the police had found nothing, caught no one. It was Casualidad herself who told me of the fourteen lakes and their powers. Reynaldo said that going would be ridiculous and stupid but might still be worth trying. Dr. Guardiola begged me not to and I went all the same, eight hours east up into the Andes, Piura to Chulucanas, to Carrasquillo, to Canchaque

232

and Quispampa, to Huancabamba.

An office as if any travel agency, and there I am asked to explain and pay. When this is done a guide takes me beyond to Salalá. The eggs, yes, scouring pads or worse. What I see when I arrive is not what I heard Casualidad describe, but perhaps I did not listen well enough.

The sun begins to set and I am led to a dirt field behind the curandero's house. At the center of the field is a long wooden table, and standing on the far side are the eighteen other clients. They have come from many places—Trujillo and Cajamarca, Lima, Cuzco and Arequipa. There is even one from Argentina.

There is another group as well: tourists who have come to pay less and only watch. They sit on dirty mattresses a short distance away and Mariángel gathers scrambled egg in a spoon, flicks it all the way to the kitchen door. For a moment I cannot decide between scolding and joining her. In the end I do neither, call instead to Socorro and together we clean up the mess.

The curandero arrives with four assistants, receives the bottles of perfume, the bags of sugar and limes that we were all instructed to bring. He bears them away, and for a time we speak among ourselves. Some have come for help with health, others with love, others with luck or work, and now an assistant asks if he might talk privately with me.

He leads me to the edge of the field, says that sadly a miscommunication has occurred. For vengeance, he says, one must visit not a curandero or a shaman but a warlock. The warlocks, he says, live mainly farther out. I am welcome to go and visit one, but curanderos do not give refunds. Alternatively I am welcome to change my request and continue with the ceremony here.

I protest for a time, make accusations of malfeasance, and they are useless; I reconsider, settle on justice, am led back to my place as the curandero returns. When the moon has risen fully he begins his chant. It is mostly in Quechua with occasional bits in Spanish, appears to be part invocation, part history, part love song.

Toast, cold, and reasonable coffee. I tell Socorro she can have the toast for herself. She says that she has already eaten, takes Mariángel for a bath, and the curandero chants for an hour as he arranges and rearranges the bottles and sticks and shells and daggers and stones and herbs on the table. The sugar and limes and perfume are brought, are arranged and rearranged as well. Then he stops, and pours each of us a glass of San Pedro. Some of the other clients waver after drinking. I feel only a slight pleasant dizziness, nothing like the ayahuasca in the jungle.

The curandero drinks too, builds a fire of palo santo, begins his trance. The assistants call us forward one by one so that the curandero might ask us questions. One by one we answer. He fans smoke in our faces, speaks of the means by which our problems will cease to exist. Some clients are asked to ingest a sort of snuff but I am not among them and the curandero sends us one by one away.

My maps and tracing, my route for tonight, and I do not remember the questions he asked me, do not remember my answers or his explanation, had already forgotten all this as I reached my place in the field and now those to either side of me are vomiting and the assistants pass among us, praise those who are sickest. The curandero comes, and we are made to shake our limbs and shout and be purified. He strikes us lightly with metal bars and quince branches. He calls for us to shout more loudly, to shake our limbs more strongly, says that we are flowering, that he can see it, and this goes on for hours in that high thin air. The moon sets, and there are only stars. The tourists at their distance try not to fall asleep and mainly succeed.

At dawn the table is cleared, the implements gathered in cloth bags, and it is time for us to walk four hard cold hours up and along and through to the chosen lake itself. I remember fog, mud, great beauty, I remember fields of wheat and potatoes, oca and olluca. The surrounding peaks rise and rise. We walk, walk, at last arrive.

The curandero says that this is Shimbe, the lake nearest to Salalá, and also the best of the fourteen for the purposes of this group in his opinion. It is larger than I had imagined, and more beautiful, though the shore is thick with abandoned underpants. The reason for this is unclear, then too clear: as epilogue or prologue we are made to strip off our outer clothes, and walk into the lake, and submerge, and remove one item of innerwear, and leave it behind. Underpants, says the curandero, are the item most commonly chosen, and this is as it should be.

He leads us to the edge, arranges his implements on a large flat rock, bids us enter. The water is very, very cold. The mud is velvety underfoot. We come mainly naked out of the lake and are met with towels, are led in more shouting, more shaking of our limbs. There is a warmth rising in my chest that I cannot explain, a fullness of energy and my shouting is happier, purified, flowered, the beauty of those mountains and ridiculous, stupid, pointless, changed nothing and the curanderos do not work cheap—if Casualidad had enough money to pay them, it was barely enough, and all that she had left of what I have given her.

By now she will be on her way to Frías. There she will die, and the only questions are when it will happen and how much she will suffer first. I owe her too much not to say goodbye in person.

I lift Mariángel from her high chair and set her on my lap. Over the years Casualidad spoke of Frías now and again, but always in fragments. I know only that it is very small, and somewhere northeast of Piura, and not easy to reach even under the best of circumstances. I ask Socorro about the roads. She says that they are for the most part safe except when it rains heavily. We look out the window together. It is raining, lightly. I ask her if I might leave Mariángel with her tomorrow and the following day, and she nods.

- Casualidad will be very happy to see you, she says.
- And I may be able to help in some way.
- I am sure that you will.
- Are there hotels?
- Two of them.

I nod. Mariángel has finished her juice. I imagine Casualidad walking down into the freezing water, coming out, her body blurred.

I will have to answer for this, that there was no scan of bars last night. Instead I packed my knapsack. Then Mariángel and I played a series of Peruvian baby-games involving spicy roast chicken which unfortunately has burned, and woodsmen from San Juan to whom no one will give bread or cheese though they will give them chili peppers. Then I reordered my books with the help of rum. Now it is six in the morning and I am standing on an empty street corner in Chulucanas.

If my daughter is awake she has already called for me. Chulucanas is the first and only town of significant size on the way to Frías. I have been here many times, always on Saturday afternoons and in the interest of ceramics. It is an easy eighty minutes from Piura, and the flower pots and owls are gorgeous and mainly a glowing rust-red and come in many sizes. There is also a profusion of perfectly round men and women, sold in pairs and kissing or dancing marinera.

The best known potters work outside of town in a flat dusty space called La Encantada. One is welcome to watch them. Many have won pottery competitions here and on other continents, and the trophies are displayed on shelves in houses with dirt floors and immense televisions. According to Socorro, if I wait long enough on this corner, sooner or later a van will pass by, and the van will probably be going to Frías, and there is no other way to get there.

In Peru it is considered lucky to receive a ceramic owl as a gift. I have received dozens and have noticed no effect. There is the smell of lemons in either the air or my imagination, and I once came to Chulucanas not for pottery but for the Feria del Limón. The quantities of fruit were remarkable.

Mosquitoes bite but not unduly. I wait an hour. I wait another hour. I wait ten more minutes, and three vans come at once, and all three are going to Frías. They will leave one by one as they fill, the drivers say. Each driver tries to convince me that the first van to fill will not be his. I stand off to one side and curse them and sweat and wait.

It takes a third hour for the forward-most van to fill halfway. The drivers do not seem discouraged. I consider walking to the nearest shop for Christmas gifts, but carrying them to Frías and back would guarantee that they be given broken and glued.

A fourth hour, and four more customers take their places in the van. I climb in as well, and it is a long process, this climbing: there is not enough room between the bench seats for me to sit or move easily. I lean forward to the driver, pay three fares, one each for myself and the small empty spaces to either side of me. The other passengers—six men, two women, a small number of small children—they look at me as if such wealth and luxury were mysterious and shameful, and they are surely right.

The road is unpaved but smooth and the orchards appear empty. The road turns and cuts and climbs and the temperature holds, the day warming and the air thinning simultaneously and in equal measure. The sky bears no clouds. There are villages with the usual animals, goats and pigs and chickens and dogs and burros in the streets. Children watch the van pass, but not with undue curiosity, perhaps because I am not clearly visible given the glare off the windows.

The road gets steeper and worse, tightens in switchbacks, and the van strains at the pitch. Creeks are crossed. Sleeping is not easy, but I am occasionally briefly triumphant.

I wake yet again, and now there are egg-shaped rocks three stories high to both sides of the road. Gatherings of houses have been built around them, and the road weaves tighter. Banana trees, cypress and palms, swollen ceibos and their wooly fruit. A river below, and small fields of sugar cane. I had forgotten it could grow at such altitudes.

Early afternoon, a last set of switchbacks, and a town in the lap of the mountains: Frías. There are peaks to all sides but no higher level ground. The plaza is plain, almost treeless.

The town hall is blue, its upper balcony crowded and trembling. The adjacent church is wholly white. The van stops between them, and the other passengers walk quickly away, leaving me to my slow squeezing out.

The driver confirms what Socorro told me, that there is no way back to Chulucanas except in these same vans, and none will be leaving until tomorrow morning. I show him Casualidad's address. He points up the widest street—small cypresses to the left and right, and the roadway strewn with manure.

The street steepens as I walk. Low adobe houses, their mud plaster smoothed and painted. I ask again at a small shop, am told to turn right at the corner. I do, and thirty yards ahead there is a group of people, and even from here I can hear the moans and sobbing.

I walk halfway to the group, then stop. I check the address. I count the number of houses between me and them and yes: I have arrived too late, and Casualidad is gone, and the world is unbearably wrong.

I set down my knapsack, pull out the jacket and tie I brought against the possibility of this moment. Four tries to get the tie tied. I walk and stop again. Those gathered are all men, all stumbling, and there are many unlabeled bottles empty and slumped in the mud. The men wear field-stained ponchos, field-torn pants, sandals. They stare at my clothes. The tie in particular feels like a poor decision.

Casualidad's house has a weathered pink door with a small iron ring in its center. A length of old twine hangs from the ring. Now the door opens. A figure appears. It is Casualidad.

She waves to me. I stand and stare. She beckons. I step back. She beckons again, and I take a seat in the middle of the road. I rest my eyes for a moment.

Now Fermín is standing beside me, is thanking me for coming, is calling to the men. Two of the drunkest come. They try to pull me to my feet, are unsuccessful. I tell them that I am pleased to be precisely where I am, and Casualidad walks toward me. No one else seems to notice her. When she is four or five feet away, she stops and whispers:

- Would you like some coffee?

I attempt to answer, fail.

- You don't feel well. Would you prefer tea? There is also Sprite, and Fanta, not here but at the store.

I look at the mumbling mourners.

- A hundred years, says Casualidad.

- What?

- Our neighbor. Doña Silvana. She lived to be a hundred years old.

I stand, and we smile at each other for a moment. Casualidad is thin and pale and looks not well but better than the last time I saw her. A very old couple joins us, the man leaning lightly on the woman's arm. Casualidad introduces me to them: her parents. Both are short and kind. Their living room is a single step down from the street, and I duck to avoid the doorjamb.

The living room is cold, obliquely dark and pleasant. The walls are a foot thick at their thinnest, set for siege. There is only one chair, and Casualidad's father carries it over to me.

It is barely sufficiently strong.

Two square windows look out onto the street, show passersby from the waist down, and the sills are full of empty bottles. In one corner are an oil lamp and a lantern, neither lit. Casualidad and her parents seat themselves on one of the low wooden benches that line all walls.

Fermín is sent to the store, returns with Fanta, and Casualidad's mother serves me. There is a rosary pegged to a wall, and beside it a roll of toilet paper hung on a nail. A small picture of the Virgin, an unmade bed, a gray blanket hiding an unidentifiable mass. The interior doorways lack doors, and through one there are other rooms that cannot be well discerned, and through the other is the kitchen, roofless.

I tell Casualidad that according to Hollywood, Martians hate small birds even more than she does. She appears to find this neither troubling nor amusing. I ask her about the Huaringas, the curandero, his bottles and herbs, the flowering and shouting, the underpants. She says that they were fine.

Her father asks me if the Fanta is cold enough, and I say that it is the perfect temperature. This makes him very happy. Casualidad's mother gesticulates in circles for a moment, points at two maroon ponchos that hang by the front door. Between them is a plastic bag full of nails, and above is a lasso. I make noises to indicate that I agree with whatever she means.

Casualidad asks about Mariángel, and I say that she is well: walking well, applauding well. She smiles. She moves the blanket-covered mass slowly to one side, lies down, closes her eyes. I look to the kitchen, see cooking pots suspended, stacks of mud bricks, a sleeping cat. Occasional chickens walk into the living room and are kicked back.

The overhead beams are skinned but rough, forking in places. I am asked to describe the trip from Piura, and do so uninterestingly. The ceiling above the beams is bamboo poles and then clay shingles, each layer seen partially. The packed dirt of the floor is nearly even.

When he sees that I am done observing, Casualidad's father says that we should all go to Doña Silvana's house. He looks at Casualidad where she sleeps. I intimate and then suggest and then say and then insist that it would be better if instead I went and arranged for my hotel room, but it seems that I have been named a guest of honor by the drunk men outside and there is no escape.

Doña Silvana's house is much the same as that of Casualidad's parents, though here the doorways are covered partially by empty grain sacks slit and hung. There are several chairs, and one small table. In the middle of the room is a pair of sawhorses, and on the sawhorses is a coffin, and in the coffin is Doña Silvana.

Her blouse is embroidered blue, green, red at the cuffs and breast. She is very thin, and her skin looks lightly oiled. Of course her eyes are closed but they do not always appear to be. Guttering candles burn at each corner of the coffin, and what would it take to live a hundred years?

Something is explained to me about a son who works in the jungle near Jaén and has not arrived. People walk in and out. There is a toddler in fur-lined overalls who wanders top-heavily, grabs at the white handles of the coffin, is pulled away. I ask Casualidad's father about the fur. Rabbit, he says, and I nod with more enthusiasm than is appropriate.

In the kitchen there are bunched plantains and short stacked lengths of cane. The living room benches are covered with knit cloth. There is also a bright painting with shapes evoking landscape. It hangs by its corner, rhomboid. And the flowers: roses, carnations, irises in the coffin, random arrangements leaning against the far wall, and Doña Silvana's daughter asks if I am ready for lunch.

The daughter is surely seventy years old. I thank her and say that there is no need for her or anyone to go to such trouble. She says that the food has already been prepared, that all guests must eat, that everyone but me has already eaten. I thank her again, tell her that I am still feeling a bit rough from the trip, say that under no circumstances would I be capable of eating anything of any kind, and she nods and brings me a fork.

There is a large crucifix resting on Doña Silvana's chest, which makes it hard for me to breathe. The whole of the coffin is covered with nearly transparent netting, though there do not seem to be any insects present. I hold the fork like a weapon.

Old women circle for a time, and when they are done my lunch is ready on the table which now sits two feet from the corpse of Doña Silvana. I am encouraged to sit down. On the plate is boiled white rice, a flank steak, chifles. The toddler brings me a quarter of a glass of lemonade.

The edges of the coffin are scrolled like bits of banister. At its foot are three letters, SPR, most likely Doña Silvana's initials but perhaps something else. The lid leans in the corner, and beside it is a box filled with candle stubs burned down too far to serve. I chew my food carefully, turn each particle to mush, and smile.

Men missing teeth come in. I am hugged an inordinate number of times. The men sit on the benches, lie down, sleep. Children enter on tiptoe, pull at the petals of the flowers, stare briefly at Doña Silvana in precisely the way I stare at books written in languages I do not speak or plan to learn.

After an hour I am made to understand that I may leave. Fermín follows me out and I give him an envelope. The money inside will not buy comfort for Casualidad but might rent something close. Fermín thanks me, says that Doña Silvana's burial will be tomorrow morning. I agree that it will, and say that I hope it goes well.

We stop by his grandparents' house, and Casualidad still sleeps. There is nothing for me to do until she wakes. I tell Fermín that I will see him soon, and walk down to the plaza.

The town's two hotels stand side by side adjacent to the church. One is open and the other is not. The room I eventually choose has three beds. Two have mattresses filled with damp straw, and I nap what is meant to be briefly in the swaybacked third.

When I wake it is dark and getting cold. I return along empty streets to Casualidad's house, and inside there is no sound, no movement, no light. I walk back to the plaza, find a restaurant, eat a breaded chicken fillet and drink five beers. The television program the waiters and I watch is professional wrestling from the United States. The overdubbed translation is flawless but unnecessary: good and evil however feigned are clearer here than anywhere else on earth.

I watch carefully, as if scanning the rabid crowd were useful. Then there is someone standing very close beside me, and I turn to look. The man does not pull away. He appears intent on studying my pores. It is not the first time I have been observed in this way, and always in towns of this size. He is very drunk, wears a muddy poncho, is perhaps from the group of mourners though I do not recognize his face, and now he sweeps his poncho back to show a machete in a scabbard on his belt.

- I know you, he says.
- I doubt that, I say.
- You work for the C.I.A.
- As a matter of fact I do not.

He pulls out the chair opposite me, sits heavily, and on the screen an immense man in blue breaks a chair across the back of an equally immense man in gray.

- Yes, the drunk man says. We're going to have to go.
- Go where?
- The police station.
- Why would we go there?
- Because you are lying. And I am a bounty hunter.

His elbow slips off the table and he slumps, rights himself violently, pulls out his machete and holds it up to me.

I look around. Only two of the waiters are watching us, and neither looks likely to intervene.

- What do you think about this? the man says.

- It is a very nice machete. Please put it away.

- To the police station. Right now.

- I would be happy to go with you to the police station, or perhaps instead to buy you something to drink. First, however, I will need to see your identification.

- Fine. Perfect. I am very proud to show it to you.

He stands, sets the machete on the table, searches his pockets. It is a very slow, very thorough search. With each pocket proved empty he grows slightly sadder. Finally he finds a scrap of paper. He looks at it, stands at attention, holds it out for me to read.

It is an ATM receipt from last June, a Chiclayo branch of the Banco de Crédito. I read it aloud to him, and he nods, tucks it away. We stare at each other for a moment. He sways, says that he forbids me to move, that he will be back immediately.

He sheathes his machete, walks to the door, stands staring at the night, and then stumbles down the stairs. I look at the waiters. They are watching the wrestling again. The immense man in gray throws the immense man in blue out of the ring, lets his head fall back and roars. I call for the bill, pay, and when the waiter brings my change, he says that I was lucky. I tell him he has no idea. He nods, looks over my shoulder, turns abruptly away.

Of course the drunk man is back. He walks over to me, stands very close, stares up into my face.

- I know you, he says. You work for the C.I.A.

- As a matter of fact I do. And I could not be more pleased about the ways in which our two great countries have cooperated and collaborated in recent years.

I call to the waiter for a pair of beers. The drunk man smiles. We drink to both cooperation and collaboration. I tell him how good it is to have made his acquaintance, and say that

I will be right back. I walk to my hotel, and rain beats the roof all night long.

My last waking is later than it should be. I dress, take up my knapsack, stand for a time in the plaza. The roads are wet and bright with sun. It is not clear to me how I am to speak to Casualidad without being obliged to attend the burial, and before I have reached an answer, Fermín arrives on a short thin horse. Walking behind him are his grandparents. They smile and ask what I am doing in the plaza when the burial is scheduled to begin at any moment. Did I have trouble finding the house? They take me by the arms, and are remarkably strong.

I explain that I wish only to speak briefly with their daughter, that if I stay for the burial I will miss the van that must take me back home. But no but no, they say. For a guest of honor to miss the burial would cause the greatest of possible offenses. Also, the vans will not be leaving for some time, as the drivers are all from Frías, all knew Doña Silvana, will all be at the burial as well.

The drunk men are still gathered outside the house, and some are awake. Inside, the candle-stub box is overflowing. We sit and wait for an hour. Then the true wailing begins, forty long and Biblical minutes, screams rising each time a nephew attempts to nail down the lid, falling off slightly each time he desists.

Finally the lid is managed. The coffin is carried, two men on one side and three on the other, and they do not walk straight lines. We work uphill. As we pass storefronts the owners come out to join us, and we grow. All of the women are wearing only black. The cemetery is not far away.

Most of the plots are set in the ground, old and ornate and untended; there is only one whitewashed cluster of niches, recently begun. There is no priest, no reading. The niche intended for Doña Silvana has not yet been cleaned, and we wait as the rocks and dirt and dust are removed. There is more wailing. The coffin is slid into the niche and each bearer touches it, palm flat against the wood. The hole is plugged with bricks and plaster and the women begin to lose consciousness. They are lowered carefully, and water is called for, and they are revived in the order they fell.

People begin to shout at one another in Spanish and Quechua. I search the crowd for Casualidad, and now Fermín runs to me, offers a tour of the cemetery. I tell him that no tour will be necessary, that I need only to speak with his mother, that I must hurry so as not to miss my van. He points out the drivers, who are among the shouters. I ask how long and he says perhaps an hour. I ask if there is any other way. He says yes, horses, a two-day trip, and also his mother just went home to take a nap.

And so we tour the cemetery, Fermín and I and a mute named Teobaldo who cackles and burps. On one side is a brick wall, and the children sitting on it watch us walk. One of the tombs has something like a ten-foot church built above it. I observe it for a time, until Teobaldo comes and stands directly in front of me. He stares at the church. I look at the back of his head. It has a normal shape. I move on to the next tomb, and so does he, again precisely in front of me.

There are palm trees planted in many places and Fermín begins to speak. First he says it is a shame that the son from Jaén did not arrive in time. Then he tells me about the English classes he had before moving to Piura, and the karate classes, and the two American doctors who were here for a day five years ago. At the next tomb we stop to observe, he pushes Teobaldo out of the way.

- The man buried here ran off to Lima with his girlfriend, he says. His wife tracked them down. There was blood all over the floor.

I nod as thoughtfully as I am able. The next tomb too

holds a man killed by his wife for unfaithfulness, and the next as well. Casualidad has never mentioned Fermín's father in any context. All things are possible. At some point I will have to decide whether or not to ask.

Fermín points to the closest peak, tells me of climbing it, of looking for the spot where a tomb full of gold was once found. I ask if he is sure, and he insists. The story is somewhat confused in the telling, has something to do with two brothers and a storm and the Chiclayo police, and now I remember not a fact but a phrase: the Venus of Frías.

- It was not a simple climb, Fermín says. It was a complicated climb.

Casualidad's father comes to us and says the vans will be leaving soon. We stop by the house. Casualidad lies sleeping and her breathing is not easy. Her parents thank me for coming. I say that it was a pleasure, and the old man shakes his head. Fermín says that if he had been the one to find the gold, he would have buried it forever there on the mountain. I say that that would have been a fairly good plan, that there are things I need to tell his mother, things I want her to know. Casualidad's father says that she already knows them. I have no idea what he means and rain starts falling, lightly.

I do not want to stay another day. It is absurd for me to have come all this way only to say goodbye by letter. But there is no third option, and I ask Casualidad's mother for paper, a pen, an envelope.

Teobaldo shuffles up just as I finish, burps, takes my knapsack and turns as if to flee. I grab him by the back of the shirt, and he goes limp and falls. I pull my knapsack away. He stretches for a stick, and draws a picture in the dirt. The picture involves unnecessary curlicues but is clearly of a van leaving a cow or a fat man behind. I lift him, thank him, and he sticks a finger up my nose. Then he runs and everyone waves and I follow.

# 24.

MARIÁNGEL SITTING ON MY SHOULDERS, HER HANDS TIGHT BUT open across my eyes as I veer from one room to the next and there is no longer a question to be asked: El Niño has come. The true rain began a week ago as the van arrived in Chulucanas. My slow climb out and down, the rain so thick that mist rose beneath it, and the far side of the street could not be seen. There were no taxis waiting. I ran to the closest shop, sat on a stool and counted owls, hoped to outwait the worst.

Kitchen to dining room to patio to dining room to bedroom to bathroom and back. When I was done counting I went and stood at the window. I waited, sat and waited, stood and waited. Then I chose and bought Christmas ceramics for Socorro, for Arantxa, for Reynaldo and Günther, for all the other university professors and authorities with whom I am on friendly terms.

The rain fell so hard for so long that I even bought a vase for my mother; the shipping costs make the clerks giddy and the vase will surely break on the way and Mariángel lets her hands slip from my eyes, grabs my ears, steers. There was no one left for whom to buy, and a single taxi passed, the water up to its rims. Slowly away from the shop, slowly and expensively to the bus station, and there another complex of downpour and puddle and unpleasantness. The ride home was much longer than eighty minutes. In a tree beside the highway I saw, I thought I saw, was quite sure but then no, it was only a dead branch five feet long, a small piece of bark rising something like a crest.

There have since been no days without rain. At first it was easily absorbed or ran into drains and away, but this is no longer the case. Water stands, rises, stands. The streets are creeks and my yard is a pond and tonight is Christmas Eve.

Patio to dining room to patio to dining room to living room. At last she tires or appears to and we rest for a moment on the couch. Tinsel hangs from each protrusion on our walls. It does not look particularly festive but seemed necessary as this year we have no tree. Real conifers are not to be found at reasonable prices in Piura, and when yesterday I brought out our plastic pine, I found it dense with mold. Mariángel and I hung ornaments on the almond tree instead and in an hour the rain had felled them all.

Now we hear new dripping. This means it is time for the Game of Leaks. At the birth of each I place a dish to catch the drips, and use the shape and size and texture of other ceiling stains to guess the location of the next leak to appear. I have not yet guessed successfully, but there is always hope.

I put a pot in a corner of the living room, a salad bowl in the center of Mariángel's bedroom, and the clock says it is lunchtime. Socorro is spending Christmas with her family in Catacaos so our lunch is leftovers: broccoli and mashed potatoes and roast beef. We eat at the kitchen table because of its proximity to the refrigerator, and also because the dining room table is full of gifts, some received, some yet to give.

When we are done I stack the dishes, gather wrapping

paper and tape, and it is too humid for tape, I know this already, put it back and bring out a stapler. Mercedes Sosa sings of love and justice intermittently as the electricity comes and goes. I wrap the first present precisely, staple a bow to the top, and give it to Mariángel.

She bangs it on the ground, grows bored, and I help her free the gift from its paper. The rubber pig delights her. She chews on its head, and I wrap the present I have gotten for her to give me: a short monograph by an amateur historian from Chiclayo on the tomb Fermín described. Then I unwrap it and thank her and she chews her pig and smiles.

I read the monograph last night. It is not badly handled. 1956, September, the police stop a nervous stranger in the Plaza de Armas, and in his suitcase there is an unlikely amount of gold. The director of the Brüning Museum traces it to Frías, to the base of a peak called Cedrillo, to a tomb sixteen hundred years old that had been opened by violent rain. The pieces are in some ways stylistically improbable. There are links, perhaps, between the little-known local culture that produced them and the Moche or Vicús. Or perhaps the pieces are not local at all, were carried in from Ecuador or Colombia. Or perhaps the explanation is otherwise, and Frías floats free in history.

In other museums were pieces that had never quite settled into any collection—figurines and goblets, pendants and necklaces—and these were brought and compared. A few were clearly of the same lineage as the crown, the scepter, and the finest piece from this new find. The Venus of Frías is a hollow statuette only six inches tall, but no one who sees it can look away.

A young woman, naked except for the raindrop-shaped flecks of gold hanging from her ears, at her waist, and they flutter at any movement. Her figure built up of layer after layer of laminated gold. Immense eyes of inlaid platinum. Narrow hips, long neck, elongated skull. Her arms at her sides but her wrists bent sharply, her palms perpendicular to her thighs, as if stylized in dance, as if balancing on an unseen beam: beautiful in a wholly disturbing sense.

I did not take any notes as for me the text is of no professional use. It was nonetheless good to feel old muscles stretch, and Mariángel tears at the paper of more gifts recently arrived. I lean to help, and first is a box from my mother. It came inexplicably clean through customs, arrived at the university with no fees due, and in it are animal-oriented books for Mariángel—the bull, the ant and the elephant, the bears, the other elephant, the wild things and the dog who does not like all but one of another dog's hats—and a packet of three fine dress shirts for me, white and beige and pale blue.

Next is a box from Pilar's parents. Inside are shoes for Mariángel in many styles, all perfectly sized. Then box after box from friends at the university, all for Mariángel, mainly clothes and mainly lovely and she ignores them.

Now we are left only with gifts intended for others and meant to have been mailed last month or hand-delivered days ago. Each is already in its box and I wrap, a furious wrapping, paper swaths of no particular dimension around and around until only paper can be seen, and staples at every corner. For this process Mariángel is of precisely as much help as I would have guessed.

Slightly less than halfway done, and our wrapping paper is slightly more than halfway gone. I look for the scissors, and do not see them. I check the far corners of the table, check my back pockets, check the floor. Mariángel turns away, and I call to her; at the sound of my voice she runs, falls as I stand and she screams, I leap and lift her and the scissors fall away, there is blood on the tips, on Mariángel's face, I wipe and wipe and the wounds on her cheeks are not deep, are in fact more scratches than cuts.

In the bathroom there is antiseptic cream, and there are bandages. Five minutes later she looks deformed but is chewing her pig happily again and I am exhausted. Also I am fortunate, in that I decided some time ago that I wished for the two of us to spend tonight alone together, and thus declined the invitations we received.

According to the tradition that will reign in those homes, gifts will not be opened until just after midnight. First will come champagne, and best wishes, and a dinner of turkey and Arabic rice and applesauce and salad with spinach and bacon and croutons. There will also be panetón and hot chocolate. At the moment the clock strikes twelve each person will hug everyone in their vicinity, and I wonder if all this happens in each Peruvian household, or only in that of Pilar's family.

The head comes off of the pig. Mariángel hands it to me, begins work on the legs, and panetón is light airy fruitcake originally from Italy. Toasted and buttered it is a splendid thing. Arabic rice is regular rice mixed with toasted noodles and parmesan cheese, and is likewise very fine. Also, the hot chocolate in Peru is nothing like the drink of the same name in the United States. Instead it is steaming liquid fudge that smells of butter and cinnamon. It is not something one forgets.

Another tradition is the evening-long lighting of firecrackers shipped in from Lima. The most popular variety is a stick of dynamite cut in fourths called white rats. I do not know where fireworks are warehoused here, but in Lima they are stored in ancient houses of bamboo and adobe in dense neighborhoods downtown, are sold from the hundreds of stands set up each December in front of these same houses. Each year there are televised warnings and newspaper exposés— no business licenses or permits, no working fire hydrants, no extinguishers—and each year nothing happens but we all know what is to come. There will be a dropped cigarette or careless demonstration, and the stand next door will catch fire. The explosions will begin, small at first. Whole blocks will burn down and hundreds of people will die.

In Piura we have already heard the sounds and seen the lights though they were unrelated to Christmas. It was May or June, not fireworks but a blaze at the Air Force base outside of town. The wind pushed the flames toward the ammunition depot, and the firefighters were unwilling to close in. The fireball could be seen from anywhere in Piura. The shockwave shattered windows at great distances. I remember, we all remember, the sky suddenly orange, the jolt to our chest, something gone desperately wrong and the column of rising smoke

The pig is now bipedal and Mariángel continues to chew. All the boxes are wrapped and labeled or addressed. I lean back. It is time for the writing and enveloping of Christmas cards and I do not believe I have the strength, though the cards themselves are beautiful, handmade, sold door to door by the men and women of CREMPT, and those men and women, were they therapists or patients or boosters? They came calmly to my door and unlike the many others, the newspaper recyclers and bottle collectors and candy vendors, those from CREMPT rang and rang and rang until I answered. Their patience was not to be questioned.

I take up the stapler, spin it on its end. Hold it to the light. Go to my desk, and yes, a few dozen flyers left over from last time. Outside the rain is light, and there is time, and this will require perhaps more strength than writing Christmas cards, but of an easier sort to access or so I think. I put away the stapler and bring out my staple gun.

It does not go well. The rain stays light and is even so too strong. To keep the flyers from soaking through and tearing I would have to coat them in plastic. Perhaps at some point I will but for now I continue, and the sight, Pilar's torn face, I want to stop but will not, must not. We leave halves of her all over the neighborhood.

~◊~

The sound is wrong. I open my eyes. It is not yet dawn. I wait, and there is the music of water, yes, that dripping into dishes whose sound is correct. There is also another dripping, similarly water into water but less echoed.

I roll over, stand, and my feet are submerged. A moment before I understand. I slosh to Mariángel, carry her in her playpen to the dining room table and sing her back to sleep, Robert Johnson, my voice as rich as ever. I call Socorro, tell her what has happened, say I will pay her triple to come in today. Then I call a number Reynaldo gave me weeks ago, emergency construction supplies, and while waiting for delivery I go from room to room.

Most of what is wet can be cleaned and dried. Pots and dishes, clothes and shoes: I lift them, and set them higher. The boxes from Chulucanas will all need to be replaced, but the ceramics they hold are unruined except for the ones I drop.

Room to room to room. The food can only be thrown away. Some of the books can be dried out but all those on the bottom shelves are unsalvageable—perhaps a third of my library. And my research. All of the lowermost crates. The computer disks, useless now. Some of the work is stored on hard drives at the university or back in Fallash but the notebooks, so much I never typed up, working so hard and so well and so fast but Pilar's death and also ruined are the journals I have kept in regard to my trips into the desert, my evenings on bridges, everything I have done since I realized the police would fail and if I consider any of this carefully I will likewise be ruined. I stack the waterlogged books and crates beside the front door. I gather the rest of what has been made garbage in plastic bags, and Socorro arrives, sloshes in to say that most of the houses on my street are in similar conditions. The river too, she says. I ask what she means. She says that it is no longer a pathetic thing, is a true river now, deep and fast and dark. I say that I believe her, that I cannot wait to see.

Mariángel wakes crying and Socorro goes to her, sees the scratches, asks how they happened. I wait, and it is as I'd hoped, the question meant not for me to answer, meant simply to show concern. She takes Mariángel from the playpen, turns and says that she almost forgot: a truck is waiting out front.

I go, and the truck holds my supplies, lumber and nails and bags of cement at twelve times their pre-rain prices. The work begins, and one by one the makeshift dikes rise. I build those for the outer doors first, a foot high such that no more water can enter. Next I build one half as tall in each inner doorway. It is not a fast thing taken wholly, and there is no rest. Framing and mixing and pouring, again and again.

By early afternoon it is a matter of bailing, Socorro helping when Mariángel lets her, towels soaked and wrung into buckets over and over and over and over and over and over and over. Then the telephone rings. It is my mother. She begins the conversation the way she does every year, saying that she hopes this will be our best Christmas ever.

I look at the mudbanks in the corners of the room, at the scratches on my daughter's face, and say that we are fine. And the rain? she asks. The El Niño? I explain to her the lack of need for any additional definite article in such a construction, and say that surely the press is exaggerating any problem that may or may not have arisen.

This comforts her, I think. She asks how Mariángel and I are enjoying our gifts. I tell her that they are outstanding, particularly the book about dogs and hats. I ask how she is enjoying her gift from us, and she says that the gift has not yet arrived, and I sit beside the vase to rest, and say, How strange, I sent it weeks ago. If my father were still alive, he would make a joke about clerks and burros. Then she says, You'll never guess what I found in the attic!

I give up pre-emptively.

- Your armor! she says. Remember how much fun you used to have wearing all that armor?

- Who moved it to the attic?

- That's where it's always been, honey. We—

- No, it used to be down in the basement.

- I don't think so. With how damp it gets? Anyway, I was going to throw it out, but I thought maybe I should ask you first.

- Yes, please, throw it out.

- Are you sure? All those Halloweens! I looked for the spaceman suit too, but it wasn't there. Did you give it away?

- I never dressed up as an astronaut.

- Of course you did. The year your father told you he'd been joking about that Spanish guy, remember? And you—

- Dad never—

- Johnny, I was there. You were so angry!

A pause, and then she knows I do not believe her and is talking again, more and more details, and I remember none of them. Finally she says that it doesn't matter, that everyone recalls everything differently, that she will leave the armor out on the curb as long as I'm sure. I say that I am. We exchange expressions of love and longing, and hopes that the other will visit soon, and that is our Christmas conversation.

So her memory has shifted, or mine has, or both. Regardless, it can only have occurred for the commonest of reasons, and my mother has not been to Peru since my wedding. I do not expect her to visit again. She reacts to the interior of airplanes the way others react to being thrown off of cliffs and a second call comes as we are finishing the clean-up—Reynaldo. He says that he heard our street was under water, says he would have called sooner but he's been on the coast all week shoring up his aunt's house. We talk of floods and repairs. He asks about my plans for tonight, and I repeat Socorro's words about the river.

He says that it is true, that it is not only the Piura that has risen, that where the Chira meets the ocean near Colán the mouth is wider than he has ever seen it. I ask if he would like to join me for a look at the bridges. He says that he does not have much time, that he needs to finish purchasing supplies for his return to the coast tomorrow. I wait. He mutters. I wait and he says yes, fine, all right, he can meet me at the Mobil station for a beer or two.

The walk, light rain, then slightly heavier, then nothing, and from a distance I hear or else feel it: the Fourth Bridge has begun to hum, the water strong and steady against its piers. Closer, and now a sort of marketplace. It is much the same crowd as gathers outside the cemetery for the Day of the Dead, and others have joined in, palm readers and pickpockets, vendors of hangers and cotton swabs. There are hundreds, and they pack in tightly, pull at the sleeves of my shirt.

I push through and across, and here is the station. There are outdoor tables set up; Reynaldo is sitting at one of them, waves when he sees me. Along the near bank is a new breakwater of boulders the size of houses, and drinking and smoking there are perhaps a hundred people, many of them students from the university.

Some of the students have brought deck chairs, and some are whooping and calling from atop the boulders. I ask and am answered: the game is to spot the corpses swept down from the mountains, to guess the species and hit them with rocks. The ones that look like hippos are horses, say the students, and the ones that look like rhinos are cows. Dogs look like goats and goats look a bit like thin children.

I take a seat beside Reynaldo.

- What happened to the people who lived down there?
- Down where?
- In the riverbed.
- No one lived in the riverbed.

- There were five or six families in shanties along the near wall. They had chickens, and plants.

Reynaldo shrugs, says he never saw them but imagines they moved in time. He buys two beers from a vendor and hands one to me. Taxis pass, the wrong age or the wrong make or the wrong color. I tell him that I would be happy to join him in Colán if there is any need.

- No, he says, but thank you. The workers have all been hired and tomorrow they will have their materials. Even I am there for supervisory purposes only.

- So you think all will be well?

- The ocean has risen and continues to rise. Smaller homes to either side have begun to shift on their foundations. We will be lucky not to lose the house.

He asks how Mariángel is dealing with the weather. I tell him the story of the scissors, and he smiles at our eventual relative good luck. He stares at the water and at me. I nod, watch the bridge, and a line of taxis comes slowly across it. The first two pull into the gas station, stop beside the pumps. The second of the two is the right make and color and age. I stand and Reynaldo stands with me, looks.

The license plate begins with P, and the rest is obscured by mud. I walk and Reynaldo walks with me. I run as the driver stands from his car, a thin dark man and I am reaching but he is so very fast, slips to the side and I lunge and miss and his fist cracks against my cheek. I fall and slide, come to rest in a puddle of rainwater and gasoline and the man is on top of me, pounds at the back of my head and neck and I try to twist but he is so much stronger than he appeared. He forces my face down toward the water, I arch and wrench left and right, down to the water and into it, then a lifting, a release, and I can breathe and turn and see.

Reynaldo pushes the man back. The man yells and points. Reynaldo nods, says that he knows, turns and shouts at me, shouts for me to look, to look at the man's face, to see that he is in no way the man I have so often described.

I look. The man's face is fuller than it seemed, and he is taller, broader, younger. I stand and walk to his taxi, wipe the license plate clean with my hand. It ends with 14. Reynaldo talks to the man about stress, about pisco, about getting me home. The man shakes his head. Reynaldo offers him twenty soles, forty, fifty. Students have begun to gather. There is more pointing, more yelling, but finally the man accepts a hundred, gets into his taxi, drives away.

The students are silent until a shout rises from the riverbank. A cadaver has been spotted, and they run, ready their stones. Someone calls that it looks like a horse, and everyone throws. We hear the sound of stones plunking off distended flesh, and a vast cheer spreads.

Reynaldo takes my elbow, pulls me down the closest street. The streetlights are on but dark with insect clouds. We are walking faster than necessary, and now he speaks quietly but with great urgency.

- Does this happen all the time? Or only when you are with me?

- Not only with you, though lately—

- I am tired of it, John. So tired.

- As tired as I am?

- Of course not. But that's all the more reason.

- For what?

He stops me, turns, faces me.

- John. It's been long enough.

I pat him on the shoulder and tell him to shut the fuck up. He nods and looks away. Then he shakes his head.

- I think that I won't. It has been long enough. You can stop. You need to stop.

I tilt my head, open my mouth and close it. We look at one another. He shakes his head. He wipes the rain and sweat from his face, says that he has no idea, that he is sorry, that he is not sorry. I nod, whatever that might mean. He says that he has to go, that he does not want to go but has to. I say that he should, and he does.

New Year's Day, and Mariángel and I tend to one another lazily: I put new cream and bandages on her face, and she pokes at the bruise on my cheek, kisses the scrape on my nose. We are reasonably rested, as party-going was not out of the question but we never quite left the house. Instead we walked with excitement from room to room, and took the tops off of bottles and put them back on, and became frustrated for no clear reason, and banged our heads against the wall, and listened to fireworks and mosquitoes for hours, and at some point slept.

The mosquitoes are no longer what they once were in terms of number or kind. There is a species that can bite through clothing, and another that can be heard through closed windows. Screens and fans and netting and toxic green coils are no longer sufficient. For each room I have purchased a small electric apparatus into which blue tablets are fitted. These tablets cause the mosquitoes to become disoriented, send them spiraling, and the mosquitoes collapse onto desktops and floors and die.

When there is no electricity, I use the apparati as paperweights and light a green coil in each corner. On television, ditches are being dug and tarps laid to protect Chan Chan from the rain. I think of Jenny and her camisoles, Minchacaman and his riches, Jenny.

While Mariángel and I walked and listened and slept, elsewhere people were throwing scrap paper out of office windows, and walking around blocks carrying empty luggage, and eating twelve grapes or raisins under tables, and burning effigies made from old clothes, and wearing yellow underwear, and these are only the traditions of which I know. There was also a fire in downtown Lima, the result not of fireworks but of oil left on a stove. The weather kept it small, and there were no deaths.

Scratch paper: a phrase that makes no sense and yet that is what I called scrap paper as a child. Chan Chan will melt if not protected, and the news switches to Piura. Hard rain in the mountains, says the newscaster. Coming swells, and all four bridges will close, and Mariángel does not appear to believe him.

Socorro arrives as agreed at lunchtime, asks what happened to me, nods when I say that I fell. Everyone is falling, she says. You must be very careful, she says.

She has brought majado de yuca in tupperware, makes salad and rice and we eat. After lunch she tries to clean but Mariángel is bored with me and I do not blame her. They go together to the kitchen table, and Socorro arranges crayons.

I walk to the entryway, stand for a moment among the stacks of sodden texts and notes. I had not worked with any of it in so long, and thus my anger is a form of nostalgia but nonetheless real and yes my thesis is dead: it would take more work to reconstruct and organize what I have lost than to begin something new. Then I open the front door and look out. The world is built of mounds of garbage, the usual scattering of litter overlaid by what was thrown out last night. Rags and cardboard, calendars and scrap paper. In spite of the rain there are children picking through the piles. I watch them, their sorting, and think of my own. It has been nearly two months. A sudden shiver. I run to the closet, open the padlock and the door.

The boxes holding all these months of evidence have rotted and collapsed. The pile is three feet high, a mass of mold and mud. Everything is covered in a filth of itself.

I dig down in, search for what might be salvaged. There seems to be nothing. I stand and stare, stand and look down, stare. There is no longer any reason to be here, and no reason to be anywhere else. I gather muck in my fists, walk to the front door, throw it as far as I can. Back to the closet, and more gathering. Running now, armfuls when I can, and my hands and chest and face are covered with this sludge of what I thought would lead me to him.

Some small bits toward the bottom are identifiable but pointless all the same, were always pointless, clumps of hair and shards of plastic, broken glass cutting into my hands, for all I know my taxista left Piura the day he murdered Pilar and is now in Iquitos or Arequipa or somewhere still farther away, muddy aluminum foil and chunks of rubber, has moved to Bolivia, to Chile or Argentina, back and forth and back and forth until all of it has been thrown into the street, and even this is not enough, my books, my notebooks, back and forth until they are gone and I rage, wade out into the street, this pointlessness, those hours and that hope, fall and stand and the dense stench has filled me.

A bell, ringing, nearing. Blood and rainwater drip from my fingers. I step back through the piles, and around the corner comes the garbage truck. Slowing, stopping. There are half a dozen men, their mouths and noses covered with handkerchiefs. They lower their shovels and begin to work.

New Year's Day—the symmetry, so precise and absurd. I start to laugh, laugh and gasp, look at the mud on my hands. I spread my fingers, wipe the mud in careful lines beneath my eyes. Ready now. Exquisite. The rain harder and I spin, laugh. The truck, the men and their shovels, I will help but another noise, not the ringing of the bell but a scream.

I turn. Socorro is standing in the doorway. She is holding Mariángel, who fights to get down. I drop my hands to my sides. Mariángel screams again and my breath catches in my chest, cuts its way up through my throat, spills black into the air.

# 25.

THE MAN ON THE BUS TO TUMBES WAS CORRECT. THE WEATHER has gone wholly from desert to jungle. Floors everywhere are lined with pots and pans and cans, a symphony of water into water. Taxi fares have risen above reasonable levels, and as the roads grow less passable, the taxis take more often to the sidewalks. This would bother me a great deal if I still walked back and forth to work.

Mariángel sits in her crib and I stand alongside. The rain is loud and the house is very dark. There has been no electricity since dinner, and we are playing the game where she is the fish and the crib is her pond and I am the night wind. She flutters her hands like fins and puckers her lips. The ripples of froth I blow across the top are particularly convincing tonight, as I have added a new layer of finer mesh.

In addition to mosquitoes there are now tiny black flies—lameojos, eye-lickers. They come in clouds at the hottest times of the day, and waving one's arms about one's face does no good. They return to swarm again and again until one catches and crushes them individually, and their miniscule bodies are harder than one might guess, beetle-like almost.

The repellents available in Piura work well against neither mosquitoes nor lameojos. The electricity comes on, goes immediately back off, and the rain has softened slightly. My mother has promised to alert her sister in Shreveport. I do not know exactly why.

Mariángel lies on her back, flutters less flamboyantly. Also there are many moths, most of them small, others three or four inches across. They stay for a time, live on my walls, leave at moments when rain is not falling. The smaller ones are most often brown. The larger ones are black or appear so.

There are ants as well, several types, some very small and black, some amber and still smaller. And crickets: summer evenings in a cabin by a lake, cheerful chirping as one drifts to sleep, yes, but not here, not now. These crickets come in thousands. They swarm the streetlights, and the fallen soak the sidewalks. In our house I track them down and smash them. More come the following morning, and these crickets, they are cannibals. This is not hearsay. I see them at their work, reach for the nearest shoe and Mariángel's eyes close, open, close, stay closed, then open.

I send wave after wave across the top of the crib, and massive green grasshoppers have cracked two of my windows, yes. Also there are latigazos, which look like long thin black ants with wings, but the tip of their abdomen emits venom of a sort. This venom leaves blisters on your skin, and the blisters hurt for days and last for weeks.

The rain has stopped. I make up a song about the loveliest fish in the lake, "Ventilator Blues" reimagined as reggae. Mariángel and I save certain insects in bottles no longer filled with mustard. Moth, latigazo, cricket, grasshopper, and also small black beetles that look like ants and act like cattle and pop like dry seaweed when stepped upon. They appear to eat nothing, and survive indefinitely regardless of whether we remember to punch air holes in the lid.

Mariángel is asleep or pretending. I whisper that it is time for chocolate. There is no response, and so I may begin.

I step carefully over the dike, pull her door closed, walk from darkness into darkness. The pots and pans and cans in the dining room are more than one sort of solution. I check the level of leakwater in each, ensure that none is more or less than half-full, and there was and is a single sentence of Oquendo's in a box at or near the middle of a poem at or near the middle of the book: Sadness is prohibited. This sentence is magical or dictatorial. I hope soon to decide.

Most of the receptacles have already been rigged with metal hangers twisted to form a loop above. I locate the few that are hangerless, fetch my pliers and bend to the work, and Armando came to my office early this afternoon. He was smiling extremely widely, was sober and yet ever so slightly off balance. I invited him to sit down. He stayed standing, kept smiling, waited for me to ask, finally said that the shipment would arrive tomorrow.

When all of the hangers are emplaced I walk pot to pan to can inserting a candle in each loop, and I very nearly asked Armando to which shipment he referred, then remembered two weeks before, the first time I have seen him in perhaps a month and he is not smiling at all. Before he can even speak I nod, apologize, bring his copy of 5 *Metros de Poemas* out of my bottom drawer and hand it to him. He appears confused. I wait. This is not what he has come for, he says, though he is grateful to have it back and hopes I have enjoyed it. I promise that I did. He says that he had heard about the flood in my house, the loss of so many books, so much research, had wanted to help in some way. The new texts will not be for me to keep, he says, are for the library's permanent collection, but he has chosen only works he thinks I might find interesting, perhaps even useful. Armando has always meant well. I thank him at great length. Tomorrow I will go look and thank him again.

Circling again through the darkness, this time to crease it with light.

When all of the candles are lit, I close each door leading out of the dining room, open the windows that give onto the patio, and remove the screens. I take my seat in the darkest corner. The air grows brighter and warmer as wax melts and wicks lengthen, brighter and warmer and brighter and warmer, sweat runs down my face and arms and chest and I watch as the room fills with insects.

Mosquitoes, crickets, beetles, moths: the candles flare as the insects fly through them, the darkness itself catching fire or so it seems. The insects fall into the pots, pans, cans, fall and drown, hundreds of them, until the surface of the water is so thick with death that the next insect to fall lands as if on solid ground, walks to the rim and escapes to further life.

The room, hotter and hotter. The dense high whir of a thousand transparent wings. The insects do not seek me out but land on me occasionally nonetheless—in my hair, in my beard, on my shoulders, on my thighs. I brush them to the floor and crush them.

As the receptacles fill, I empty them into the toilet. I add new water, return to the dining room and light the candles again, sit back to watch, again. A stench, burnt feathers and dried blood. I watch and I watch and I watch.

There was rain this morning, and there will be more this evening, but at the moment there is sun. I sit in the cafeteria and drink my awful coffee. I swipe at lameojos. Today would be my second wedding anniversary if Pilar were still alive.

A distant bell rings. It is not meant for me. Our summer

courses consist of three straight daily hours per class, and I have Elementary in the morning, Upper Intermediate in the afternoon. The amounts bet on which bridge will fall first have reached appreciable proportions. There are many leaks in the classrooms, and some of the leaks are not small, and we have been instructed to pretend that nothing is wrong.

Pilar. The cypress of her. She smiles, says that if we don't start now we will be late. Dressing then, both of us, and dressing one another—she draws her long black hair forward over one shoulder so that I might zip up the back of her dress, and she turns. Snugs my tie gently to my chin. Kisses me on the cheek. A fine dinner somewhere, anywhere, wine and flowers, and a gift, a necklace or brooch. For the pleasure of it also some manifestation of the traditional gift, whatever it is that one gives on a second anniversary—paper or leather or bronze? Home and yes and then and perhaps I will not go to the library after all.

Another coffee, worse, and this morning as I left for work I asked Socorro about Casualidad. She took up a broom, began sweeping insects into piles, said that all is well except for the birds and the fact that Casualidad refuses to eat. I waited, said that I was sorry. Socorro nodded. Her husband is going to Frías next week, she said, can take anything I might wish to send.

This evening I will thus fill another envelope and rewrap the colorful useless blouses meant for Casualidad for Christmas. I have already given Fermín his bicycle. He is now back in Catacaos. Socorro says that he would rather be there than in Frías, and this does not show in his face.

More probably Casualidad does not wish for him to watch her die. He bicycles to my house weekly, weeds in the rain, and from the patio I ask what life is like for him in Catacaos. He smiles but never answers. It is as if he were free to speak only at certain altitudes.

A third coffee, the worst so far. I have not seen Reynaldo since the evening at the bridge, have heard that he is less often here at the university than at his aunt's house in Colán. The house has survived the ocean's rising thus far, but the job is not yet done. Many other homes are already gone, reduced to foundation and scraps of wall.

Now I see Armando, a hundred feet away and nearing. He sees me as well, waves, stops, waves again, then turns and walks in the opposite direction. This is him giving me the opportunity to be gracious, and so I will.

Out of the cafeteria and into the sun, across the grass, past a bench in thin shade. The smell of decomposing leaves. Along and across, sun and shade and sun, and at last into the library.

The foyer here has always been a pleasant space. It is most often filled with local paintings or sketches and they are generally better than they have any reason to be. Today it is photographs of sand. There are perhaps thirty of them, dune after dune, and as I look they turn abstract, pure line and shade. They are so beautiful that my stomach starts to ache.

To the reception desk, and yes, Armando has reserved a dozen books in my name. They are brought to me in the reading room: a handsome gathering of new Ginzburg essays, a doorstop collection of monographs grouped in Rostworoski's honor, a beautifully managed Justice-and-Power inventory of the Cuzco Departmental Archive; O'Phelan Godoy on the Great Rebellion and Varón Gabai's take on the Pizarros and a critical edition of Pachacuti Yamqui's *Relación de antigüedades deste reyno del Piru* that I've seen before and would like to see again. Two volumes of linguistic enthnography, and two of anthropological linguistics, and the Alianza edition of Cabeza de Vaca's *Naufragios*. At the bottom of the stack is a book by Inge Schjellerup called *Incas and Spaniards in the Conquest of the Chachapoyas*, and how perfect it would have been a decade ago.

Altogether, then, a well and kindly chosen shipment—a few books of personal interest only, a few central to my work, and several just far enough from it that any link could be ignored should I so wish. I take up the O'Phelan Godoy, and Arantxa sits down beside me. She is as sad as I have ever seen her. I close the O'Phelan Godoy. She shakes her head.

- I don't know, she whispers.

- Perhaps I can help, I whisper back.

- You are not the solution. You are the problem.

- And if I solve myself?

- I wish that was amusing. I wish anything was amusing. But I am tired. And Reynaldo is tired. Do you know what he said to me?

- He is here in Piura? I thought—

- I was called to the rector's office to account for you, and was told to wait outside, and waited and waited and waited. The secretary stared at me the entire time. You understand how that might make me feel? And then Reynaldo came out. He did not look up as he walked past, but he spoke to me. And do you know what he said? He said, That was the final time.

Arantxa waits for me to answer, and I do not, and finally she continues.

- It is best for all of us, John, if I am not entirely clear as to his meaning. You are very, very fortunate to have such a good friend.

- I am.

- Yes. And here is something I wish you to know: I no longer care how good your friends are. I no longer care what you did or did not do at the Mobil Station or anywhere else. I just want you to stop causing problems for other people.

- Today is the—

- I know what today is for you. I know. But I'm not sure how much I care about that either. It has been too long for me to care the way I once might have.

She stares at the floor. I wait. Finally she shrugs.

- Okay, she whispers. The rector knows that something is deeply wrong, but doesn't know what. Several students came to tell him about what happened, but their accounts were confused—some said you started a fight, some said a taxista attacked you for no reason, some had no idea. Reynaldo's version was, I suspect, of no help whatsoever in terms of clarification. I told the rector that I knew nothing about it, which was true at the time.

- Thank you.

- Your thanks do not interest me. And I assure you, John, that this is my final time as well.

Arantxa stands, walks away. I am surprised and then unsurprised that she remembers the date of my anniversary. I think about this for a moment. The other professors in the room finish glaring at me and return to their reading.

A month after her graduation, Pilar in her wedding dress, beautiful, yes. My mother, her fear of flight withstood or drugged just long and well enough. The church in Chiclayo, rustic and fine. The ceremony, long and imperfect and true: a dropped ring rolling and rolling and saved at the edge of a grate by an old woman no one recognized, and an accidental vulgarity as I worked through my vow, and a flower-girl cousin who stepped on Pilar's veil-train, snapping her head back as we exited.

Then the reception in Ferreñafe. My mother lovely in a summer dress, beige and gold and tan, unready for the heat but she smiled and smiled and smiled. The extremely wealthy man for whom Pilar's father ploughed and planted, ploughs and plants, had lent us his back yard. There was a massive tent, a cascade of flowers. There was a raised wooden dance floor, and music from somewhere unseen.

Like most Peruvian receptions ours commenced with ten or twelve runs through "The Blue Danube" such that I might dance with Pilar, with my mother, Pilar's mother, Pilar's aunts and nieces. From my family there were no men but me, and this was surmountable: three friends had come from Berkeley and two from Irvine, and after them were Pilar's own brothers and uncles and nephews.

The afternoon sky a rich full blue, the sun bright and not too hot, and pachamanca begins as a large hole in the ground. A base of eucalyptus is laid, covered in stones, and the wood burns alone for hours. When the stones start to glow they are removed. More wood is added, and the stones put back in layers with spices and that which is to be cooked. Stones and potatoes and yams, stones and beef and pork, stones and chicken and plantains, stones and marmaquilla and paico, stones and corn and cheese. The hole is covered with plantain leaves, canvas and soil. In the soil one places a bouquet and a cross and then one waits.

At our reception the results were outstanding. The problem, then, as plates emptied: there is an equally delicious northern variant called copús. It involves vinegar-cured goat heads, lamb and bananas and yucca, is cooked likewise underground but in clay pots and over algarrobo, and when the wealthy man of Ferreñafe came to see that all was as it should be, he noted our choice and announced that eating pachamanca rather than copús showed a lack of regional loyalty.

There are persons like this everywhere, yes, men and women who heighten their sense of worth by sticking shovels up the asses of others. I do not often lack an appropriate response to such people, but this once I was left mute. Perhaps it was the tight tuxedo.

Happily my silence did not matter. Pilar's brothers turned brave and stood. Pachamanca was the older and more authentic form, they said, born of the Incas themselves. The food as prepared was honor and tribute and gratefulness, they said. Eat, they said. Eat and be grateful.

The man of Ferreñafe waved their answer away. He turned, and Pilar's mother led us in a toast to his departure. Then her father toasted the memory of my father. It was an odd moment but I loved him for the act.

The cake was served, the magnificent cake, and the air filled with the scents of vanilla and cinammon and cloves. Afterwards came rock and salsa, salsa and rock, beer in endless pitchers, happiness. My mother danced and danced and how did I not know that she loved to dance? There were cryptic references to honeymoon pleasures, even on the part of Pilar's father. Drunk, Arantxa and Günther danced negroïde, and she was very good, and he was very German. There was laughter, and promises were made and chocolates passed.

I have not seen my mother since then and was it Pilar's father, or one of her uncles? Máncora, yes, the bungalow, yes, and yes. But in the whole of those days I believe I did not think even once about the exchange student who came to my high school from Abancay. I know what this makes me, do not have to be told what this makes me.

Yes, and still. Perhaps there will be a time to visit those beaches again. Currently the highway is broken in all directions, but workers go each day, bear materials and equipment to each gap.

It is late. The slaughter is done, and tonight there is electricity: fan, lights, music. Ginzburg's essays are very good if often far from my field, and he would smile at the use of those words in this context, far and field.

I finish "Idols and Likenesses," glance through "Style," start "Distance and Perspective." It begins with a retelling of Sokal's parody of people like me, and I am unsure how offended to be. Mariángel wakes and whimpers. I go to her, hold her and suddenly remember: chickenpox, her vaccination, scheduled for today and forgotten. There is further whimpering, and my forgetting, unforgivable, but then a quieting, and it may have been only a return to the night-waking of many months ago.

I lay her down, sing her to sleep and return to Ginzburg. He says, Here I shall insist on a different and even opposite theme: the irreducibility of memory to history. I wipe sweat from my hands, my face. In any culture, he says, collective memory conveyed through rituals, ceremonies, and similar events reinforces a link with the past of a kind that involves no explicit reflection on the distance that separates us from it and the power goes out.

I bring five candles from the dining room, set them on the coffee table, light them, can now just barely read. The past, Ginzburg says, must be understood both on its own terms and as a link in the chain that in the last analysis leads up to ourselves. I lower the book, lean back. I stand, walk to my room, and yes, in the drawer of my nightstand: a notebook, empty, clean. There is no reason to take it from the drawer, no reason not to, and finally I do.

A pen from the kitchen and back to the dining room, sitting down on the couch, rebeginning the essay. Slow notes on half a dozen thoughts. Reading further, and there is movement near my head and away: a moth the size of a sparrow has flown into the living room.

It circles the couch where I sit, circles again and lands on the floor. I do not know how it survived the pots and pans and cans. I could easily crush it, perhaps would if we were in the dining room, but we are not, and there has been enough death. I go to the kitchen, return with a glass of lemonade, step too close and it flutters up, lands again a few feet away.

I have no answer to this question, says Ginzburg, and the moth lifts again though I have not moved; it circles and goes for the candles. Three of them are extinguished in various passes. The moth flails against the tabletop, strikes me twice in the mouth. I set down the Ginzburg and watch.

This moth, too, appears black, though flickers of color come from its body each time it catches the light. With time its passes through the candles grow ragged, almost desperate. Then it collapses on top of the stereo.

I watch it a bit longer, unmoving, both of us unmoving. I go to it and look. I touch its abdomen, and the moth flops back into the air. It circles the table and the remaining candles once more, lands again on the floor, very near the wall this time, its head against the base of a ceramic owl, its body heaving tinily.

Its wings are not solid black, I now see, but striated with varying grays. Its body is still segmented like that of the caterpillar it once was, and high on its abdomen are small quadrilaterals of metallic orange-gold that can only be seen like this, the body at rest. A moment later the heaving stops.

The lights blare, Charly García sings suddenly of love and strange new haircuts, the fan spins and blows the last candles out. Again the moth flies, flame-singed wings, invisible striations and quadrilaterals, falls spiraling. In a good world it would find its way out of my house, would fly into the wet night and away, and instead it is dead on my floor.

# 26.

THE FILM HAS ALREADY BEGUN. THE HOUSES, THE FLOWERPOTS, the houses are flowerpots, the countryside bright as lemon rind and Pilar wants to play golf with him. We ring the doorbell. Piura becomes Vilcashuamán. Men and women arrive on bicycles, bring out images and sell them cheaply, ever more cheaply. The view has unfolded. We are dwarves, all of us. The cities must have been built on the tips of umbrellas and now life seems better because it is higher up and the film is half-over, the borrowed film, half-over.

# 27.

Downriver the Piura broke its left bank, flooded a dozen villages, washed most of Chato Chico away. This was ten days ago. Now there are something like refugee camps tucked into small spaces throughout the city. The shelters have walls of straw matting, and plastic tarps for roofs. In some cases livestock was saved and the camps are thus louder than one might expect.

Those same rains continued, and bridges all over the region slumped and closed or fell: Talara, Paita, Tumbes. On most Piuran streets one less walked than waded. Also there was thunder and lightning, rarities here, and the dogs howled for hours.

Lately however there has been a sort of lull. The pools of standing water have grown shallower. The clouds are still battleships, and the humidity and temperature are still appropriate only in jungles, and the epidemics have begun, malaria and cholera, dengue and yellow fever, three cases of bubonic plague confirmed in Cajamarca, but no rain fell the day before yesterday, none fell yesterday, none is scheduled for today and I am suddenly very late.

I cinch my tie, take up my briefcase, and it will be too small so I dump its contents into my daypack. Stumbling over the dike in the doorway, remembering my wallet on my nightstand, turning and stumbling again and there will be scrapes if not bruises. Quickly to the kitchen, and I do not know why it took me so long to decide. I load the three bottles in, zip the daypack barely closed, hurry to the entryway where I thank Socorro for breakfast, kiss Mariángel goodbye, open the front door and very nearly step on the hairless dog curled on the stoop.

I retreat into the house and pull the door closed, then nudge it back open. Broken tail, scarred haunches. The dog has lifted its head half an inch off the cement to look at me. I wait for it to do something, anything, to growl or snarl or leap. It lays its head back down and closes its eyes. I tell it loudly to go away. Its eyes do not open.

Again I wait. Then I call to Socorro, ask her to bring last night's leftovers. She comes, has brought nothing, wants to know what I need them for. I glare at and show her. She says that if I feed the dog it will never leave. I say that it does not look inclined to leave regardless.

She goes to the kitchen, returns not with food but with a mop. I ask her to stop. I tell her that I will deal with the dog, that all I need are the leftovers, that she should not worry herself. She does not believe me but brings a bowl of stiff cold boiled white rice, and when I fling the rice to the far corner of the yard, the dog stands, goes, eats, lies down there on what is left of the grass.

Thus with luck a custom has been formed, an arrangement, bad food at irregular intervals in exchange for sleeping anywhere but my stoop. I run down the walk and to the corner. Today is Friday the Thirteenth, which means nothing in Peru—here it is Tuesday the Thirteenth that is thought to bring bad luck. The first taxi I see is full but the second is available, and whiskey has always seemed to me improbable in regard to the status it confers among my Piuran acquaintances. At Cossto each given bottle costs twice what it should, and whenever offered will be accepted, will be emptied before anything else is touched.

Past the park, and in the center is a group of small children filling water balloons from a spigot. This is a matter of Carnaval, which in Piura is nothing like what occurs elsewhere and on television. We do not have the intricate masks of Venice, do not have the towering feathered floats and full brown breasts of Río. Instead we have these children filling their balloons with water and occasionally much worse.

We also have their older brothers and sisters armed with tins of shoe polish and small sacks of flour and plastic bags filled with paint. Last year there was an evening when a group of adolescents swarmed me. I came so very near to catching one of them, the tallest, but sweat had slickened his wrist. It took an hour to get the shoe polish out of my eyebrows.

In theory Carnaval begins a month before Easter. I do not know why the children have started so early this year. We round the corner and here they are already emplaced. One balloon is thrown too perfectly, enters through my window and exits through the window on the far side, as if a heavy wet thought now forgotten. Another arrives as I am rolling my window up, and it bursts against the frame, drenches one shoulder of my shirt and the top half of my tie.

Thus despite the absence of rain I arrive to work damp and smelling faintly of sewage. Quickly across campus, and Arantxa's bottle is first. I knock, enter without waiting, set it on her desk. She is talking on the telephone. She covers the mouthpiece as if to speak to me but says nothing. I apologize for interrupting, point to the bottle. She looks at it, at me, at my shirt and tie. I nod and shrug. She looks at the bottle again, seems very slightly more tired but less sad, and I wave and back out of her office.

Next is Armando. I go to the library, find him at his cubicle in the research room upstairs. I sneak up behind him to the extent that I am able, but in that still air he hears me coming. He turns, smiles as I set his bottle on top of Suárez's *Comercio y fraude en el Perú colonial,* sits up straight that I might better clap him on the shoulder. I whisper thanks to him for thinking of me in the course of that last order, and he nods. I say that I will soon begin a regular poker night with friends, that he will be invited, that I plan to take all of his money.

Across campus to the chemistry laboratory, and the regular poker night, it is not something I have thought about a great deal, is not something I have ever done, is the sort of thing managed best by persons very little like me but also does not seem impossible now that I have said it out loud. Reynaldo is washing his hands in a vast sink of stainless steel. To judge from his expression as I walk up, he does not want to talk to me but also does not want not to talk to me. I set the bottle beside the soap. He asks if I would mind bringing it to his office instead.

I follow him perhaps too closely. He pulls a chair in front of his desk, adjusts it minutely. He does not seem angry or sad, seems only to be waiting.

- This bottle, I say, is a very small thank you for a very, very large favor.

Reynaldo nods, scratches the back of his neck.

- But it is not the whole thank you, I say. There is also a letter of reference, the most extraordinarily perfect letter of reference that has ever been written for anyone.

He tilts his head to one side, smiles slightly.

- I do not mean to be difficult, he says. You're welcome, of course you are welcome. But that feels wrong, doesn't it.

- You will never have to save me again.

- Your shirt, he says. Carnaval?

- Yes. Better than last year, anyway.

- And how did it go with the rector?

- I did not realize he was capable of that sort of anger.

Reynaldo nods, looks down at the top of his desk.

- So, I say. Soon there will be a weekly poker match taking place at my house. Will you join us?

He pauses and says that he will. I had hoped for but not expected better. I thank him again, trot down and out and along and one might believe that three daily consecutive hours of class would result in greater educational intensity. In fact this is only the case in regard to the games of Hangman that I use to fill each group's final minutes.

In my Elementary class I nearly always win, though I allow my students many extra letters, permit them to put hands, feet, clothes and extravagant facial hair on the man to be hung. When despair is evident I redraw him such that the chair has been kicked away, and his eyes have been replaced with histrionic crosses, and urine spills from his pant-legs. My students sometimes smile and in my Upper Intermediate course the stakes rise ever higher. This is not often to my advantage, but I do not begrudge the hand-drawn certificates for free gum and drinks and lunches that I award. My only regret is that they go so exclusively to the strongest students, the ones now aware of my finest Hangman tactic: myth, lynx, syzygy.

Mariángel and I sit on the patio and watch the thick late sunlight. It feels like a permanent thing though surely it is not. She invents unlikely combinations of vowels and consonants, and I nod and nod and nod.

I was still damp as of my afternoon class, requested volunteers for dialogue and role play, received none, accomplished little, ended ten minutes short. There was another balloon thrown successfully as my taxi pulled out of the university gate. In it was not water but rotten milk.

As compensation, once Socorro had gone I threw the dinner she had prepared into the far corner of the front yard and ordered takeout from a nearby restaurant called El Torno. Magnificent: seco de chabelo, a dish of cooked blood spiced with mint called rachi-rachi, carambola juice and cherimoya mousse and Mariángel lifts the forefinger of my right hand, bites it as hard as she can. She has not forgiven me for the chickenpox vaccination. She screamed, how she screamed, not in pain but in indignation.

She opens her mouth perhaps to imitate that scream and instead the doorbell rings, frightens both of us. When our hearts have settled, we laugh, and I relax back into my chair. Mariángel grabs my wrist and pulls, and then Reynaldo's voice and so we go.

He shakes my hand, kisses Mariángel, strides in as if today were a month ago. He sits at the dining room table, undoes his tie. Mariángel pounds her fists on his knee, reaches for the tie, and he lets her pull it from around his neck.

- I have come to help you celebrate this pause in the rain, he says.

I have no idea what this means, and we look at one another. He opens his briefcase, brings out the bottle I gave him this morning. Much of the whiskey remains. I pour, and he toasts the belt Mariángel has made of his tie, and we drink. He asks if I know what day tomorrow will be.

- Saturday the fourteenth.
- Yes, he says. Of February.
- Oh. Yes.
- I have a special plan.
- Involving me?
- Yes. That does not make you my valentine, however. There is nothing we can do about the date.

- All right.

- The plan is a surprise.

- Okay.

- You will need to be ready at nine o'clock in the morning. If you are not ready I will go alone, and that is something you would regret.

- Nine o'clock in the morning.

- Yes.

- So we are not going to watch the drunk soccer in Catacaos again.

- Of course not. By halftime we were covered with flour and paint.

- Perhaps we were rooting for the wrong team.

- Perhaps. Did you enjoy it?

- From an anthropological persp—

- Neither did I, which is why that is not what we are doing this year. I repeat: our activity will be a surprise.

He waits for me to beg for further details. When I do not, he opens his briefcase again and brings out a small wooden chess set. We have never before discussed chess in any context.

He sets the board up and says that we still have a certain amount of time before poker season. He pours the following round, and we discuss openings. We agree to discuss them again once we have learned something about them. We trade pawns and knights and bishops at nearly random intervals.

By the time I pour the third round we have learned that I am slightly less terrible than he is. Mariángel ignores us, instead answers the telephone, though it has not rung. She paces as she whispers syllables into the receiver, gesticulates as she explains whatever she is explaining to whomever she imagines on the other end of the line.

This is her new favorite activity. I bought a toy phone to encourage it, and she showed no interest though it beeps and buzzes and has something of a dial tone of its own. Now she sighs, tired of the ignorance or stupidity of her pretend interlocutor. She hangs up and comes to watch, steals a rook, puts it in her mouth.

I look at her, and she looks at me. I ask for the rook and she shakes her head. I am just able to continue smiling and breathing as I take hold of her, and she opens her mouth and laughs. There is no rook inside. We check the immediate area, and no rook, no rook. Mariángel is back on the phone. I go to the kitchen, look for something with which to make do, and this is the worst of all phrases.

At nine forty-five Reynaldo arrives in a pick-up truck he does not own. The sky is a bright tense blue. Socorro is playing with Mariángel on the patio and I am ready in the sense that I am open to possibility.

I ask Reynaldo from whom and why he borrowed the truck. He says that it belongs to the university gardening staff but can be rented for a small fee, and that with the roads as they are, his aunt's station wagon is not an option. He asks if I have packed my things. I remind him that last night he said nothing about things.

- Lunch, he says, and beer. Also a bathing suit, and a towel, and old tennis shoes.

- Where are we going swimming?

- Everywhere. We will observe the results of the rains, and we will swim, first in other places and then at my aunt's house in Colán.

- And the stingrays?

- There are no rays, not now.

- What about currents?

- The currents will be strong, yes, and we will stay close to shore. Where is your bathing suit?

This is a question that has not been asked by anyone in a very long time. Reynaldo and Socorro arrange sandwiches while I search. When all things are readied, Socorro tells me to enjoy myself and not drown. I ask her to please smile when saying things like that.

Reynaldo and I chat as we edge through the broken streets. We chat at the Texaco station, chat heading east past a small cemetery, a school, a flooded factory. As we leave the city we fall silent.

The landscape. It is wholly new. We look at one another, look out again. It is as if the known horizon were a painting on cloth, and we have torn through to a place neither of us has ever been. El Niño has restored to us the color green, has filled what was empty desert with thickets of bright bushes grown head-high.

North onto the Panamericana, farther and farther, again new, and still stranger—for the first time in my Piuran years, the Andes can be seen from this highway. Their sharp lines rise and rise and rise, gray and black and white against the sky. I had no idea they were so close though I have driven through them many times, and after a moment I understand: the rain rinsing all dust from the air, giving us fresh vision.

Not quite to Sullana we leave the highway, push west on a paved but unstable road, try for Punta Pitos. The first four turnoffs end in washouts, the smallest twelve feet deep. A dump truck driver gathering gravel tells us that one route is still open, draws a map in the dirt, and when we go that route too is closed. We hit very large holes, and bang our heads on the metal ceiling.

Back to the paved road. Watching the bushes and trees, I imagine new and better ways to teach the present perfect. Five minutes of this and again turning, this time toward Punta Dorada. The trails here are also abysmal, but running ravines and up we arrive at a bluff.

The sunlight bounces off the white rock, hovers in the black, drenches us as we hike around the point. Below us penguins nest. They are an unexpected phenomenon each time I see them.

Farther along, a hundred sea lions on the sand, a flock of pelicans, and Reynaldo leads me to a ledge from which one might fall fifteen feet into the ocean if the wave below is cresting, or thirty if it gutters. He looks at me and jumps. For a moment I think I will be unable to follow but then I do. The surf drives us against mussel beds, pulls us away and drives us against them again. Our skin opens on the shells and for a time it seems there is no way out of the water, but at last we are lifted on the largest of waves, a savage and desperate happiness.

A second jump, a third, and that is sufficient. On our walk back to the bluff I pick a new path, lead us into a rising cloud of mosquitoes with bites like bee stings. We run to the truck, drive to the paved road and then southwest toward Colán. Along the way we eat our sandwiches and drink our beers and sing with Aterciopelados, toasting Miss Panela and Chica Difícil.

The toasts and singing end when we arrive at the crest. Reynaldo pulls the truck off the road, and points though there is no need: the ocean has broken through to either side of the town below, has formed an inner barrier of water, a moat, and Colán is the crumbling castle.

As always the massive cross is to our right, and to our left is San Lucas, an old church claimed to be far older. We edge down through the bluffs, come to the edge of the water. Reynaldo smiles and guns the engine. Two young boys wade in the channels alongside the roadbed, draw away from our splashing as we pass. We arc toward the town, and to our left is a broken-toothed smile: house intact, house destroyed, house inexistent.

At Reynaldo's aunt's house, crazed waves smash at the breakwater he has built, at what is left to either side. The surf pounds twelve feet deep up the walkway, and the water is thick with lumber. We watch. We count half an hour from the moment of our last bite of sandwich. Then we jump from the upper deck. The sea is feverish and fast and we swim for a very long time.

As we come out, Reynaldo invents a sport, running from one property to the next between waves, holding fast to whatever still stands as the water slams in. One house has benches set in concrete, and we sit on the benches and lock our arms and feet as the thick wild waves break over us. At one point I am dragged from the bench, wrenched and staggered and thrown back toward the house, see a rail-end rushing at me but ripple blindly past it, untouched.

Back to the house, and another beer, and then abrupt darkness. The rain begins as we run to the truck. It thickens as Reynaldo starts the engine, roars as we race out through the ruins of town.

Now Reynaldo points. A young woman is standing in the water off to one side, the rain cutting furrows around her, and she waves at me or us. Reynaldo stops the truck. She runs toward us, walks, runs, water rising at each footfall, rivulets down her arms. I open my window as she nears. She is of medium height, her hair is of medium length and she, yes, neither dark-skinned nor light, she half-smiles and it is her, the girl from the Pórticos Hotel, putilla, chilalo, though now she is a waterbird, an avocet or egret.

- Hello, she says.
- Hello, says Reynaldo.
- You are going to Piura?
- Yes, I say. Let me just—
- I would rather ride in back. May I?
Reynaldo punches me in the arm.

- No, I say. You ride in here and I'll ride in back.

Reynaldo punches me again.

- Or the three of us could fit here inside if the seat is sufficiently—

Reynaldo punches me a third time, and I punch him back as hard as I am able given the spatial arrangements. He shakes his head and whispers:

- Jackass. In your lap.

- No thank you, she says. I would much rather ride in back.

She climbs up over the sidewall. I look at Reynaldo. He balls his fist.

- If you hit me again, I say, I will push you from the vehicle and drive back and forth over your body.

- Absolutely terrible, he says. The worst I've ever seen.

- Sorry to disappoint you.

- You should come to my house and practice with my aunt. She is free on Tuesdays. Also on Thursdays. Also on every other day.

He laughs, and we drive. Water thickens the windows. The woman stands in the bed of the truck, leans forward into the wall of wind and rain, and a different smile, complete.

We enter Piura and the woman stretches to Reynaldo's window, directs him toward the river. She has us turn one block short of the malecón and head up Calle Lima. She says the next house is hers, and jumps before we have stopped.

She runs, knocks, turns and waves. An old and worried-looking woman opens the door. I try to see past her and fail. The woman turns again, mouths her thanks, enters.

- On Valentine's Day! says Reynaldo.

I say nothing.

- You should have asked for her name, he says.

- I am not in a position to be asking for anything.

- But I think that you are, he says. I believe and think

that you are.

Home, I thank Socorro, swing Mariángel in violent circles and she vomits mashed banana. This does not appear to bother her. I clean both of us as well as I can, and carry her to my room. She walks in rough ellipses, takes my wallet from the nightstand and throws it across the room, turns to see if I am pleased.

I say that her velocity is adequate, that we will need to work on her aim. We briefly discuss objects and their places. I set her on my bed, stare for a moment at my headboard. It is entirely bare.

I pick up my wallet and set it on my desk. Then I lie down flat on the floor to look under my bed. Mariángel slides to the ground, lies beside me, understands this as some kind of game and there against the far wall, dust-covered and surely damp, is the image of Sarita Colonia.

I pull the bed away from the wall, bring up the picture, clean its plastic cover with my shirttail. The image appears unhurt. Mariángel reaches for the string, and I hold it up and away, try to consider. Mariángel grabs at the fat of my neck. I hang Sarita again from the headboard, take up Mariángel, and how we dance.

# 28.

Gray halflight, outside and in. I correct the last Elementary quiz, and it is all but perfect: nineteen weather words out of twenty and the spelling consistently close. I record the grade, and slip the stack of quizzes into its envelope. I slide the envelope between the coursebook and the workbook so as not to forget and have nothing pressing for the rest of the day.

I wipe the sweat from my forehead, face, forearms. The electricity is less on than off both here and at home, and thus for most of each day lights and computers and fans are remembered luxuries. Up from my desk, stretching, out of my darkening office and onto the landing. There I lean against the railing and stare.

The rain returned a week ago, has not ceased since. Scattered around the Language Center are puddles in places previously considered high ground, and ponds where before there were puddles. This looks as though it should be worrisome, but the Engineering department is half the university, and its professors seem unconcerned.

Fermín came early this morning to collect Casualidad's

salary. He did not look at me as he took the envelope, did not stay to water or weed. The almond tree is budding, and the blooms will have no chance, and our insect collection now fills two shelves.

The cockroaches have grown immense, and faster in the air. When I am fortunate and smack one to the ground, new ants, medium-sized, black and with visible pincers, are waiting below to dismember and run with it in pieces to their holes. Wasps have built small mud houses in each of my bookshelves. Elsewhere are dragonflies as if from the jungle, and spiders that jump surprising distances. Also there are new water-beetles three inches long, brown becoming black, long hind legs with protuberances of a sort. When the puddles drain they survive on land, and they fly, despite their great bulk they fly, and bully the crickets beneath the streetlights.

The streets too have somehow worsened. Yesterday a car disappeared. I did not believe it when told by my students but then it was on the news: a hole larger than the car had formed in the roadway, had filled with water, and the surface of the water reflected perfectly. The man and his infant son escaped, the newsreader said, were helped out through windows by passersby.

Other children have discovered in the rain and ruined roads a source of income. They carry large rocks from the riverbanks, pile these rocks at the corners of major intersections, charge fifty céntimos to place the rocks as stepping stones for anyone who wishes to cross the street without going knee-deep in rainwater and sewage. Then come cars, and again the children charge, fifty céntimos to remove the rocks recently emplaced.

It is far too early to go home, but there are other options. Back into my office for my coat and umbrella and rubber boots. I try the lights, and they come on, go off, return. Out now, up the path and to the deer pen.

The deer are uninterested in the rotting pods I toss toward them, uninterested in my fistfuls of grass, uninterested in anything but lying still beneath the algarrobos and harder things happen elsewhere, have happened and are happening, in the mountains and farther up the coast. There are stories of landslides erasing parts of villages, of hillside cemeteries newly opened by rain, of men who charge a great deal to carry goods and persons on their backs across rivers beneath what is left of bridges, and the men and their loads are sometimes taken by the current. All this, and what has happened in still farther places: hurricanes in Mexico, drought and famine in Indonesia, marooned villagers attacked by hyenas come to dispute what high ground remains in Somalia.

I congratulate myself often on having stocked up, rice and candles in sufficient quantities to survive through April at least. I gather zapote leaves, and again the deer are uninterested, and in the evenings when there is electricity Mariángel and I watch the geckos. There are many more now than before, in part because Socorro is slower and less fanatical than Casualidad, and in part because of the insect surplus.

As before, the gnats and mosquitoes and moths flit around the naked bulbs, and the geckos edge closer, their movement too slow to be seen. Then they are close enough, and their movement is too quick to be seen as the rain-loosened paint gives away and they drop from the ceiling to the floor. Sometimes they land well and scurry off. Sometimes they land badly and twitch until I step on their heads. Sometimes, after I have stepped on their heads, they continue to twitch; sometimes they go still. I toss the bodies out onto the front lawn, and in the morning they are gone, eaten by the hairless dog or something worse.

I accuse the deer individually of shiftlessness and sloth, walk back to my office, and there is a new leak in my ceiling, a beaded line of water that half-circles the base of the light fixture and drips loudly onto my desk. I move all threatened paperwork to a shelf in the foyer. Then I run to Eugenia, come back with a plastic flowerpot.

Arantxa is waiting at my office door. She smells of chorizo and whiskey. We say polite hellos. I set the pot to catch the drips, and she hands me a notice. It is from the Postal Service. A package has arrived for me from Shreveport. Arantxa pats my shoulder and wishes me luck.

As she does so the light above us fails. We both look up. Blue strings of electricity arc beautifully to either side. There is a sharp white flash, and when we look again the ceiling is on fire.

Arantxa jumps to the extinguisher and I take up the phone and already the fire is out. The office stinks of melted plastic but at last we know how it is that rain starts fires. Our colleagues come from the Teachers Room, hear the story, put their arms around our shoulders and treat us as gladiators triumphant. Arantxa and I congratulate one another on not having panicked. She calls the housekeeping staff. It will be hours before my office is habitable. I wave the postal notice back and forth, tell Arantxa I will see her tomorrow, gather papers and walk for the gate.

I am grateful to my aunt for the package regardless of what it might contain, and do not hold her responsible for potential complications. I take a taxi to the post office, step quickly through the rain. The stairs leading to the basement office are steeper than they have any reason to be.

The line is long, and there is half an inch of water on the floor. A very short man has a broom and a bucket and makes no headway: additional water seeps through the walls continually. I take my place. I shuffle with the others and sweat. I listen as the clerk at the counter calls tracking numbers to the clerk in the back room. I stand, shuffle, sweat and the counter clerk smiles when he sees me in line. It is not a beneficent smile.

A thick man comes slowly down the stairs, hesitates behind me, walks directly to the counter and holds out his notice. It is the same as my notice. I go, stand very close beside him, stare at the side of his face.

- What? he says.

I smile. He shakes his head, looks at the clerk, holds his notice out a little farther. Those in line make ambiguous noises behind us.

- You need to stand farther away, says the thick man.

I lean slightly closer in. I ask the man if he can smell the smoke. The counter clerk clears his throat, tells the thick man to take his place in line.

We three turn to look at the line, and at the security guard standing at the bottom of the stairs. The guard looks down at the water, swishes one foot back and forth. The thick man holds his notice out again, says Please. He does not mean it as a request. The clerk shakes his head, and I return to my spot. The thick man stays at the counter and is ignored.

Stand, sweat, shuffle, sweat, stand. At last it is my turn, and the thick man glares at the countertop, and the clerk stares not quite into my eyes. I give him the notice. He calls the tracking number to the other clerk and returns to his staring.

The other clerk brings the package, sets it damply on the counter. It is small and bears my address in my aunt's handwriting. The counter clerk looks at the customs form pasted to the top, reads it out loud, nods.

- We will open the package, he says, to assess the true value.

- The true value, yes. This is not my first time here. I am aware of your procedures.

He slits through the tape and opens the flaps.

- Four bottles, he says, of the very best repellent.

- It is of average quality, I believe.

He opens one of the bottles, sniffs, and his eyes water

over. He closes the bottle and sets it back in place. He wipes his eyes, roots through the rest of the package. He consults a plasticized chart and works his calculator for a time.

- The taxes and fees come to a total of thirty-two dollars. You may also pay in soles.

- Sir, the entire value is only—

- The entire value as listed on the customs sheet, yes. But these bottles are new merchandise and there is no purchase receipt. If this is not in fact your first time here, if you are in fact aware of our procedures, then you know that in certain cases we require a purchase receipt to corroborate the stated value.

- What I know is that in this and all cases you and your—

- Sir, you may pay the thirty-two dollars and take your repellent home, or you may keep your thirty-two dollars and leave the repellent here. It is as you wish.

I glance back, and the crowd tenses. I look at the thick man beside me, and he leans forward and laughs. I allow my head to droop, and the crowd sighs in disappointment or pity as I hand over a fifty-dollar bill.

It is not uncommon, here, to come across counterfeit bills, and in general it makes no difference as long as the quality is high. The clerk notices nothing, hands me my change. I walk up and out, stop a taxi, and the back label of each bottle reads, "Do not apply on or near plastic, leather, or painted surfaces."

Perhaps it will be strong enough, and this amount should last me until autumn. Home, Mariángel, Socorro. A long shower and fresh clothes. Dinner and geckos and dancing. The repellent came with a letter from Aunt Claire, nine pages of Shreveport news. I read it aloud to Mariángel and by the middle of the elegy to a recently deceased Methodist pastor that occupies pages four through seven she is asleep.

David Leroy Dykes, Jr.: my aunt writes out his entire name in each instance and I am unsure why. He was a good and decent man or so it appears from her description but any more will put me to sleep as well so I switch to the essays gathered in homage to Rostworoski and perhaps at some point a new topic will present itself. I spend time with Soldi on fragments from Mejía Xesspe, and with Meggers on pre-Conquest populations in the Amazon. Then I settle into a short piece by Pease on the writing of Inca history by early Spanish chroniclers. It is nearly wholly familiar but the arrangement is deft: little work of any use until Cieza de León and Juan Díez de Betanzos in the 1550s, and all of it pre-formed by the chroniclers' need for contextual verisimilitude, their descriptions given credence only insofar as they map to Bible stories, to myths of Greece and Rome, to medieval bestiaries, to rumors of the Almoravids. The resultant limitations are implied if not explored, and Pease's ending is gem-like, Spanish historians converting the ritual memories of the Incas into historical memories of the world, and yes and yes.

It is very late. I move to Ballesteros Gaibrois on Martínez Compañón, and from there to Pereyra on a rare form of quipu. At some later point there is a man on the back of an elephant. Two elephants. Now a telephone rings. For a moment I am unsure whether it rang in my house or on one of the elephants. The one in my house rings again.

- And the letter? says Reynaldo.

- From my aunt?

- Your what?

- Claire.

- Let us begin this conversation again. Hello. My name is Reynaldo. Not long ago you promised to—

- The letter! I just need to give it one last polish and print it out. Do you want me to bring it over tonight?

- I don't leave until Monday evening. Anytime before that is fine. But it's finished?

- Finished, and very strong. I suspect you will have no trouble this time.

- Excellent. Thank you.

- My pleasure.

We say our goodbyes, and I run for a notepad and pen.

Saturday, and a late waking. I read through the morning, scattered but sharp—Curatola on guano in Chincha, Rowe on the Inca's estates, Szeminski on ethnic transformation. I am visited regularly by Mariángel wearing shoes on her hands. The rain is less heavy today, and it is time for something I wish and do not wish to try, something that cannot be put off any longer if I am going to do it at all.

I put it off until after lunch. When Socorro has gathered the plates, I look at Mariángel and she looks at me. I gather her up, and together we track down the baby carrier. We wipe away dust and stretch the canopy to its fullest extension.

Out the door, and we walk, and search for an available taxi. We walk and search, walk and search and walk. We pay our way across each intersection, and by the time a free taxi is found we are most of the way to our destination and so instead keep walking.

Along the river, and at the Sánchez Cerro Bridge the pilings buzz and blur. I have already made enquiries at the vegetarian restaurant across the street from the young woman's house. Her name is Karina Giovanetti, and she dreams of Italy, works part-time at a store specializing in knickknacks. Away from the river now, left and up the road, to her door. I swing the carrier around, and Mariángel stares at me, smiles, and the rain gathers in her hair.

I knock. There is no answer. I knock again, and can't stop knocking. The door opens. It is the old worried woman. I ask if Karina is home. The worried woman slams the door. I wait. Mariángel bites my shoulder. I wait and she bites me again. This is a code I have not yet broken, and the thing is done, tried, and we can go home.

We turn away and the door opens and inside is Karina. She is humming a song of some kind, and the humming is not in tune. She stands nervously, and the worried woman hunches behind her.

- Hello, says Karina.
- Hello.
- You are the one from Colán.
- Yes.
- And last year at the Pórticos Hotel.
- Yes.
- And one evening a few months ago you looked in through the window of my shop.

I agree to this as well though I have no idea. Karina looks at Mariángel, smiles and invites us in. The house is narrow in all directions, as though pure hallway. Karina leads us to a sitting room. I take Mariángel out of the carrier and seat her beside me on the couch. Karina stands to one side, the worried woman to the other. The facing wall is three feet away, and I gaze as though it were adorned.

- I wondered when you would come, says Karina. I thought it would be sooner.

- I am not rapid in most regards.

Mariángel climbs into my lap, turns her head as though hiding from Karina, and then laughs, a game, only a game.

- Would you or your daughter like something to drink? asks Karina. Some lemonade? Inca Kola?

- We are fine, but thank you for asking.

The worried woman nods, leaves the room, returns thirty seconds later with a glass of Inca Kola and a towel. She watches as I dry Mariángel and the baby carrier. She frowns, and leaves the room again.

Karina says that her aunt is always like this. I attempt

to smile. She takes the towel, folds it unevenly.

- That night in the Pórticos Hotel, you were telling stories about me.

- Yes. Not exactly. Partially, yes.

- Why not about one of the other women?

- Because they were all the same.

She squints, leaves, comes back with more Inca Kola. The armrest is unsteady and I set the glass on the ground. Mariángel climbs down and immediately wants back up.

- Do you like my house?

- It's very nice. Very narrow.

- Yes. When dogs come to visit they have to wag their tails up and down.

I laugh to show that her joke has been successful, that she might feel confident using it again in other company. Mariángel laughs too, laughs again as Karina laughs, a pleasant chain. Somewhere nearby a television is turned on, the news, loudly.

I look at Karina and at the floor and at Mariángel. When I enquired at the vegetarian restaurant, there was apparently more information available, but the waitress was not disposed to share it unless I ordered from the full dinner menu. I wonder if I should tell Karina that I have been snooping.

- So you have been snooping, says Karina.

My foot twitches and there is the sound and I know but look anyway: the glass overturned but not broken, the spilled Inca Kola gold against the hardwood floor.

- Don't worry, she says.

She towels up the spill. Mariángel climbs down again, squats to watch Karina work, then walks to the wall, runs her fingers along the molding, shows me happily how dirty it is.

- I have made a few inquiries, I say. But I would never snoop.

- And did you find out everything you wished to know?

- Almost.

Mariángel wanders out of the room, turns toward the noise of the news. I stand and follow and Karina's aunt calls to us from the same direction. We follow her voice up the hall and into another sitting room. This one is slightly less narrow. There is another couch, and on a table facing it is the television, and the program is not news but a documentary about Cajamarca.

I nod and turn as if there were no reason to stay but Karina sits down, takes Mariángel onto her knee. I wait for the struggle and scream but neither comes. Cajamarca, its hills ever green or nearly so. The cathedral, and the Plaza de Armas. Santa Apolonia and its throne, butter and cream and cheese at a market stand, and I ask if anyone knows how the Peruvian teams are doing in the Copa de Libertadores.

- Their first match is against each other on Wednesday, says the aunt.

Karina looks at me and winks. Mariángel struggles again to the ground, walks around to the aunt, pulls at the woman's bracelets. I know perhaps a thousand historical anecdotes involving Cajamarca and cannot remember any of them and now a farm is shown, a farm on the outskirts of the city. This farm is called La Colpa, says the documentarian, and it is famous for the fact that its cows come when called by name.

We nod in unison, Karina and the aunt and I: it is the sort of place one hears of but never visits. Austrian tourists are shown sitting on a split-rail fence. A farmer calls names one by one, and one by one cows trot into sight. Each cow crosses the paddock, passes through a gate in the fence on which the tourists sit, and enters a stall. Each stall is labeled, and no cow is ever wrong.

Mariángel draws close to the television, reaches up to touch the cows on the screen. The tourists are allowed to try, call names from a list the farmer has provided. Their pronunciation is not sufficiently precise and no more cows come. This does not sadden the tourists, and hearing them speak among themselves reminds me of the German cultists, makes me wonder if there is a way for them to be responsible for El Niño without God existing.

The tourists attempt to milk the cows already present, and are again unsuccessful. They take pictures of one another, and thank the farmer, and there is a commercial break. Karina says that she hasn't been to Cajamarca in years. I nod and frown unclearly, take Mariángel onto my lap.

The aunt clicks off the television and informs me that it is time for her and Karina to go. She does not indicate a destination. I smile, and Mariángel is whimpering. Perhaps I have squeezed her too tightly.

I thank the aunt for the Inca Kola, and she says that I am very welcome. Then Karina leads us back to the first sitting room, helps me work Mariángel's feet through the straps of the carrier.

- There is a bar called La Carroza, she says. Do you know it?

- My students have spoken of it.

- I'll be there next Friday night.

- They spoke of it as a place to avoid.

She nods, kisses me on the cheek, and no conclusion whatsoever can be drawn from this: it is simply how Peruvian women take leave of anyone at all. She opens the door and rain blows in. I push out into the street and the door closes quietly behind us.

# 29.

Out my front door and no taxis visible and walking
through light drizzle. My shoulders dampen, my hair and
beard. I near the park, and its greens are so bright, the air itself
tinged with green. I am in the midst of an unnecessary happiness when balloons begin to strike around me.

I am very ready for Easter and the end of all this but
because I am already damp I feel no great need to chase the
children and catch and crush them. One balloon moreover does
not break when thrown, skitters across the grass behind me. It
is small and dense and substantially less than full. I retrieve it
and throw it back as hard as I am able, which is very, very hard.
It hits the boy on the forehead. He wavers, tumbles, and the
other children cheer and then are furious.

A taxi now, and I climb in quickly, expect the children
to follow but they are already tracking new victims on the far
side of the park. The taxi lurches into and out of each hole. At
the speeds that are possible, stop signs are unnecessary. The
rain strengthens and the window thickens and blurs.

Around the corner and to the light. The morass of final

exams has been traversed and even the worst of my students passed, all but two who chose to cheat, wrote lexical sets on their wrists. By the time the exam began the lists were useless, smeared by sweat and rain, and the students surely would have passed without them.

To and into the parking lot and something has happened. Something large, it seems. There are students gathered in many groups. I walk toward them, and look down the slope at the lower ground beyond, and understand: they have gathered to see the flood.

Already in certain places scaffolding has been assembled and planks have been laid to form interlinked walkways. I walk slowly along them toward the Language Center, and from any distance they appear to rest on the surface of the water, make Jesus of us all in one respect. Everywhere things float, chairs and lecterns and wastepaper baskets, and on each floating object is an insect resting or drifting to safety: cockroach, dragonfly, uncollected species.

Many trees have fallen, and men in boots slosh in all directions. It is the water table, say the hydraulic engineers when they stop to rest from their sloshing. The water table has been rising, they say, and with last night's rain it rose above the level of the ground.

I ask how it is that this area and my neighborhood flooded months apart. They look at me as if such a question were too stupid to bear consideration. I nod and laugh and smile and say that I hold them responsible for this flood at least, that I expect them to clean my classrooms personally. They have been here since four in the morning organizing the rental or purchase of large pieces of equipment, the removal of earth and the digging of ditches, the installment of scaffolding and planks and pumps and pipes and thus do not smile back.

In the Language Center the water stands at our knees. My office now smells less like melted plastic than like Venice in late summer. Back by the photocopier Arantxa is screaming out a window. It is unclear at whom she is screaming and why and I wish my smile were less obvious. I go to Eugenia, and confirm that we are only responsible for local salvage: course books, resource materials, administrative records, whatever is not waterlogged or coated with filth. We must move it all to higher ground where the sun, Eugenia says, will dry it.

At the moment there is no sun. I return to Arantxa, who has begun to calm, has sent Günther to Groundskeeping for rubber boots. I remove my tie, and she tells me to put it back on. I hang it around her neck, and when Günther arrives with the boots, she calls for Eugenia and the four of us begin ferrying stacks to the balconies above.

It is thought that we will soon be joined by other language professors who hear of what has happened, who come to see and help; we assure one another that at the very least the other coordinators will arrive to assist at some point. Arantxa carries well, Günther and Eugenia are acceptable, but I am the outstanding ferryman. Stack after stack of soaked documents, and even dry the paper will only be worth recycling. Sweat runs. Insects of varied size and color skate along the surface, cling to the legs of our trousers, are crushed and brushed away.

Sign-ups for the fall term were to begin today, so we arrange a temporary space for Eugenia in a classroom on the third floor, and post notices. I ask Arantxa if the semester's starting date will be postponed. She says that of course it will not.

Workers rush past us bearing sandbags. They are exhausted, filthy, pleased at the thought of more overtime. The sun occasionally shines, and in those moments there are rainbows, and we sometimes pause to look. When we are finished spreading the books, there are damp special request forms to be sorted from dry ones. There are also people with cameras—university historians and local photojournalists. I smile at most of them when asked.

Altogether seven hours of this. At no point do any other Language Center employees appear. We concur that they came and saw and snuck home. Arantxa thanks the three of us for our good work, says that tomorrow we are welcome to arrive up to twenty minutes late, and details several phrases the other coordinators will soon hear.

I take up the briefcase I have not needed all day. The letter in its envelope is somehow still nearly dry. I ask Eugenia for a large ziplock bag, seal the letter inside, and wade for the chemistry laboratory as here there are no walkways.

Halfway to the lab I stop. I had forgotten or never realized that the deer pen sits in a sort of natural basin. The deer swim in circles, their tongues out. They do not have much longer.

Wading on as quickly as possible. Reynaldo is standing outside the chemistry laboratory, holds an armful of wet files and stares at an algarrobo, his favorite algarrobo, uprooted and fallen. He looks at me, and I look back.

- I'm sorry.

- Yes, he says.

- And your other trees?

- Every single one grown from treated seeds has fallen. And it was our own fault. We loved them too much.

- I don't understand.

- We watered them constantly. Their tap roots had no reason to reach deep enough to hold through something like this. So much work wasted.

- Yes. And there's something else.

- What?

- The deer pen is flooded.

- They'll be fine.

- I don't think so.

We walk to the pen, and he shakes his head, watches

the deer swim.

- What should we do?

- Release them, he says. I have no pods with which to feed them anyway.

He takes out a ring of keys, but the lock on the gate has rusted, and he leaves, comes back with Don Teófilo and two pairs of wire cutters. Together they slice through the fencing, a strand at a time, a perfect square opening. Don Teófilo wades in, the water up to his armpits. He herds the deer slowly out. They stagger to higher ground and head for the bright green desert.

Don Teófilo wipes his face with a handkerchief, and I ask how it is that rain causes the water in our homes to be cut off. He says that he is not sure, but perhaps it has something to do with sediment and the filters in the dam. I look at Reynaldo and nod. He stares at me. I tell him again that I am sorry and he shrugs.

- Yes. But tonight I fly to Lima and with any luck—

- Speaking of which.

I bring out the letter in its bag.

- Thank you, he says.

- You're welcome. What else are you taking?

- This, and a letter from my bank, and a new letter from the university. I think it will be enough.

- You've checked to make sure the airport will be open?

- They have special machines, I believe.

Reynaldo shakes my hand, turns and walks back toward the laboratory. There are still dozens of workers moving sandbags, and I see the rector, glassy-eyed. I ask if he is feeling well, and he says something about tractors. I say that the Language Center situation is under control, and ask if there is any other way in which I might serve, and realize halfway through the sentence that I want nothing but to be home.

He says that more sandbags need to be filled, that my strength would be a welcome asset. I agree that it would. When he has walked away I wade toward the front gate. There are no taxis and so it is the old walk but now longer and slower. Corner, light, Panamericana, across and along. Corner, light, corner. Park, corner, Virgin, hairless dog and quickly inside.

Mariángel, shrieking with pleasure. Again there is no electricity but Socorro has prepared an adequate causa. The telephone line is intact, and after dinner for a time Mariángel explains excessively complicated things to excessively foolish imaginary people. After that I bring out the two books about elephants and read to her by candlelight. Then we dance to my singing, and when she is bored with my voice I lay her down to sleep to the chattering rain.

Following this I prepare the dining room and open the windows and watch insects drown once again. The repellent my aunt sent functions well against none of the local species, and we now face the next great plagues. Socorro is slightly sickened by our growing collection, has asked me to keep it somewhere other than the kitchen.

There is a moth-shaped insect with wasp eyes and a long black nose and a tail that flexes and expands something like a horsehair brush and something like a mace. Its wings are white and reedy, unscaled, a purple iridescence with brown along the ridges. There are also small black bugs with the forearms of weightlifters, and multicolored bugs with backs like shields. They are equally slow, easily caught, and die quickly.

Finally there are cucambas, a type of beetle, large and black with an oily green sheen on their backs. They emit an acidic stink that lasts for days and clings to all surfaces and survives through many washings. They do not appear to fly and cannot walk up steep surfaces, do not move in groups but at each conjunction of walls there are dozens that have arrived individually, and one by one they starve to death, stinking, unable to find their way out.

# 30.

I HAVE SPENT MUCH OF THE PAST FEW DAYS MAKING AND
unmaking the decision. In the end Reynaldo agreed to come as
well. This does not change the fact that it will be my first date
since Pilar died.

Socorro has agreed to stay late. I sing Mariángel to
sleep, and choose clothes that will camouflage the worst of my
bulk. Reynaldo will be here in an hour. I stub my toe on a dike,
gasp obscenities, will not let this be an omen.

I turn on the news, and a new thought now. I send
Socorro to the store and when she returns I run the basin full
of hot water and take off my shirt. It takes forty-five minutes
and three dulled razors and half a dozen cuts but is at last
done: I am beardless the way I have not been since high school.

My jaw is not as prominent as I remember it being and
Reynaldo arrives, sees my face, smiles but does not laugh and
thus I do not have to ask whether or not he was given a tourist
visa. Instead I ask what was wrong with the paperwork, what
was lacking, and he says that the consul did not even peruse it.
So it is at times, he says. I offer to help in any way he sees fit.

He thanks me, says that all he wants is to drink, that he will think the process through and wait three more months and try one final time.

Into the rain, and he asks if I have complained to the proper authorities in regard to the broken streetlight. I say that I have, and shrug as if resigned to municipal incompetence. Reynaldo apologizes to me on their behalf as we reach the corner.

The first nine taxis to pass are all taken. Then comes a mototaxi, and Reynaldo and I together barely fit. The driver checks the suspension and shock absorbers, checks them again, shrugs.

The cuts on my face sting sharply and this is for the best. Our mototaxi weaves among the potholes, proceeds at the same speed as the pedestrians who walk alongside. The driver chats with us about weather, and about insects, and the rear axle snaps.

I am tumbled into a puddle. Reynaldo lands beside me. We stand as quickly as we are able and for a time move back and forth between indignation and shame. The mototaxista is more sad than angry. Then he is more angry than sad, but not at us, and kicks at various parts of his vehicle.

Reynaldo says that we are happy to pay for the successful first half of the trip. The driver accepts. He gathers his belongings from under the seat, begins removing the mirrors so that they will not be stolen, ignores us and so we thank him and say that we are sorry and walk away.

The rain thins slightly but the far side of the Plaza de Armas is badly flooded, more river than street, and we prepare to wade. Someone calls from under an awning. It is Karina. We all say hello and I scratch my naked chin. Karina nods, says that she likes my new face, that she liked the old one as well, that she likes them exactly the same.

The three of us have a short logistical discussion after

which she climbs onto my back and points the way. It is not an unmanageable distance to La Carroza. My shoulders are still sore from the ferrying of wet books but she is a lovely burden and at the door are men with automatic weapons. Karina kisses and introduces them, and we push through.

The hallway is wet and dark and crowded. Beyond is a patio mainly open to the sky; there are a few palm-leaf canopies, and all the tables under them are taken. To one side is a long bamboo bar, and more men with automatic weapons. To the other side are sofas and overstuffed chairs, their surfaces bright with rain.

Karina finds us a free portion of unprotected table. The air is dense with scents: perfume and sweat, rum and sweat, mildew and mudflap and steel. We drink a pitcher of Cuba libre and shout occasional sentences that are beaten down by the rock and salsa. Karina takes my hand and Reynaldo's and leads us to the sheltered dance floor, but there is not sufficient room, not for Reynaldo and I as we are. He nods at the closest tables, and the relocation does not take us very long—the tables, the people and their drinks, the chairs.

Karina is angular and coherent in her movements. Reynaldo is more agile than those whose tables we have moved would have guessed. Many patrons watch me, expect that I will be unable to hear any rhythm however clearly beaten, that I will dance as if to some other song entirely, but in my years here I have learned, and the patrons look away, bemused.

Water streams from our hair and faces. The music is thick in our blood, bats knock mosquitoes from the air, and weak lights weave on the pooled rain. Half an hour passes this way, but then an odd song is played, some wrong mixture of heavy-footed things, and we return to our part of the far table.

More drinks are ordered and we watch others dance. Most are sinuous as if this were television. The very drunkest spread their arms and hop. There is also an older couple dancing like they might die on the way home, and in all corners the young men's hands trace down the bodies of their partners but always stop at the waist, even here, even now.

On the walls are peeling pictures of nearly naked women dancing with dolphins. There are also Victorian images of many kinds hung higher and lower than one would expect. In a break between songs Karina tells us that anything we might wish to buy can be found here. Reynaldo and I cannot think of anything but thank her for the information. She laughs and leaves for the restroom as the music rises again, and in her absence Reynaldo wags his eyebrows and shouts things that I cannot make out but are surely vulgar and amusing.

He leans back as the drinks come. It is hard for me to believe how beautiful mine is: the beads of condensation, the jeweled slice of lemon, the straw. I drain my glass, close my eyes, and in my head is a thought of old time, of previous dancing in other spaces and how it is that I learned. Karina returns and I thank and kiss her. I shake Reynaldo's hand. I walk unsteadily to the door and flooded streets.

Monday and half an hour late to work. In my estimation this will not be a problem as there is so little to do. The fall semester begins the day after tomorrow and almost no one has signed up for English classes.

Most students at this university spend summers with their families in Sullana or Chiclayo or Trujillo. This year few have returned. The rector has assured us personally that it is only a matter of El Niño, that our classrooms will eventually be full. We suspect that he is wrong, but perhaps he is not and hundreds of students will indeed come to sign up immediately after sign-ups have ended.

Flooding has begun in other cities as well, even Lima itself—several of its outskirts went underwater when the Seco spread past its banks. The police had announced the flood three hours in advance, and it appears that no one listened. The mayor showed up half a day later with the National Guard, who spent their time preventing pillaging rather than filling sandbags. We in Piura find this amusing though we know that we should not.

Yesterday morning Mariángel called early from her crib. I went, and she screamed as I entered her bedroom, screamed and beat at my beardless face as I took her up, screamed in fear and then in anger as I began to sing. It was four complete Woody Guthrie songs before she was calm. I will never again shave my beard unless she is present.

My ceiling has been repainted a perfect white and the water table is again below the level of the ground and still there are open ditches cut through lawn, and many pumps at work. A lake has been created in unused acreage beyond the chemistry lab, and pipes run to it from the vicinities of most buildings. The scaffolding but not the planking remains in many places.

Here in the Language Center, the cleaning staff have done extraordinary work: there is still a waterline on the wall but the furniture has all been cleaned and the floor is tidy and dry. Arantxa comes in, pretends to notice nothing new about my face, hands me my preliminary student lists—Elementary, Intermediate, Advanced. All three are very short lists.

She asks if I will be attending the Commencement Address on Friday, says the rector has been working on his speech for weeks and it promises to be particularly good. I smile and say that it sounds as if it will be. I ask if my classrooms are ready. She shakes her head, says that they are, says that I should check them all the same.

When she is gone I read quickly through my lists. It appears that I have an Elementary student named Madeinusa.

311

There is a movie by that name but I have not seen it. Broken into three parts it is an easy name to understand and makes me squint.

I stop by each of my classrooms to see that the chalkboards are clean, that the lights function, that the proper number of chairs has been emplaced. In fact none of this is the case in any of the rooms. One room is on the ground floor, and not even the wads of dead insects have been removed. I argue for ten minutes over the phone and an hour in person with the Director of Housekeeping, who says that all arrangements have been made except those that were unfeasible, and that classes do not begin for another sixty-four hours so there is still plenty of time, and that I as a professor have nothing about which to worry.

When all complaints have been registered I eat lunch alone in the cafeteria, return to my office and pretend to prepare. In fact my preparations were finished a week ago. When I am too bored to pretend any longer I promise Arantxa that tomorrow I will arrive an hour early, and ask if I might leave a corresponding hour early today. She assents but barely.

I have already called Karina: I am many inexcusable things but not a cad. I apologized and attempted to explain and she said that she already knew, which is not likely but her saying so was sufficient. I walk for the gate, and walking is much simpler, one foot and the other, again and again, and walking is only walking.

Then it is more than walking, then less than walking, then much harder. I will not have it. I scan a car that passes. Nothing. Over, finished, and I attempt to let this settle in my mind. It will not and is thus perhaps false. Now walking is almost impossible and I will fall if I do not think through each step.

A taxi instead from the gate to the house. Gathering Mariángel, and remembering: Reynaldo has invited us for dinner. A clean shirt, a bottle of wine, the baby carrier and its canopy. No taxis, and it would have been so easy to pay the previous one extra to wait.

Light rain lightens further, becomes mist. We walk to the Fourth Bridge, push through the crowds and hear the hum: the surface of the river skims only a few feet below the bottom of the deck. We step onto the bridgehead and start across. Now there is a swaying, the bridge or my brain or both. I cling for an instant to the rail and yes, the bridge itself, ten thousand tons of concrete swaying.

As quickly across as is practicable given how many are walking with and against us, sweat thick down my chest, Mariángel laughing as I jog but then angry, and even in the mototaxi angry. I talk to her and she cries and hits me. I talk more, and the crying becomes screaming, and I too raise my voice. There could be nothing stupider.

To Reynaldo's house, a handshake and in, his aunt observing me from many angles before she decides that beardless is an improvement. A beer and another while he helps her load the table. The food is excellent, papa a la Huancaína and lomo saltado and crema volteada, but the aunt is ill with bronchitis or pneumonia, can barely speak without coughing. Also, Mariángel bites everything but her food and throws everything she can lift.

I apologize every few minutes, say to the room that she is never like this. The aunt shakes her head, coughs and shrugs and coughs. Reynaldo's whiskers are too long to be a matter of laziness. I ask, and he says that he is growing a beard to replace mine.

- Mine was irreplaceable. How could you not know that?
- And why shave it off now after so many years?
- No reason.
- Is that what you plan to tell the Immigrations officials when they look at your passport and see a different face altogether?

Yet another element I had not considered. I ask

Reynaldo about his plans for a third attempt at the visa. He looks down and his aunt glares and this was not the right question to ask. Mariángel screams, overturns the soup, starts to cry. I apologize once more. Reynaldo's aunt nods and coughs and coughs and coughs.

When dessert is done Reynaldo and I attempt to sit and talk but neither Mariángel nor the aunt is interested or willing. Instead Reynaldo walks with us for a time. The mist has vanished, and something of a moon is visible. A hundred yards along Mariángel stops crying, and fifty yards farther on she is asleep.

- I want you to know, Reynaldo says, that nothing happened between me and Karina. Nothing untoward. Drinking and dancing and talking. I know of your feelings.

- You have no idea.

- Of course I do. And I told her.

- What?

- About you and Pilar, about what happened and how it affects other things.

- There are no other things.

- You are wrong. There are many. Karina said that she likes you, that you are a better dancer than you appear, that she hopes you will soon visit her house again.

- If this is a joke I will put out your eyes.

Reynaldo laughs.

- All right, I say. Thank you. And what about you? Have you tried again with the Swiss hydrologist?

- There is a tall blonde woman on a beach in California, and she wishes to meet me, wishes to know my name.

- Of course she does.

We are almost to the river. The bridge keens to us. Reynaldo rubs his arms though the night is still very warm. I thank him for dinner, and he nods, backs away, wishes us a pleasant walk home.

Eight in the morning and the taxi comes to a stop. I tell the driver that I will only be a moment, step out, push through to the edge. Shadows of a dinosaur skeleton can just be seen beneath the surface of the fast tarry water and thus the rumor is true and we know which bets have been lost and won: rain came hard in the mountains last night, and three hours ago the Old Bridge fell.

It was Socorro who told me, weeping as she came in through the front door. She begged me not to tell her sister, as the Old Bridge was Casualidad's favorite of the four. I agreed, and would have even if it had been a difficult promise to keep. Pilar loved the bridge too, and so did I.

I stand, watch the water run, am jostled, jostle others in turn. There are dozens of folk songs that tell of Piura: its tondero, its seco de cabrito, the sun of Colán and the moon of Paita, and always the Old Bridge. The skeleton writhes in the current.

I turn and walk, find my taxi, thank the driver for stopping and tell him that there is another destination. He nods, waits for me to close the door. He turns on the radio as we pull into traffic, a local station, and they are discussing the very event.

One of the guests is an engineer who says that in previous years the river has on average run at only two cubic meters per second. I know what a cubic meter is, can picture two of them spread thin and passing in the space of a second: the turgid creek I have always known. Larger numbers are more difficult. When the runoff from last night's rain hit Piura, says the engineer, the river peaked at four thousand cubic meters per second.

The Sánchez Cerro is closed. The Bolognesi is open, and the engineer is unconvinced that this is the best of our options. The Fourth will close to vehicles at every surge and rumor of surge, he says, and there are ropes laid from one end to the other for pedestrians to clutch as they walk.

The police are still looking for a corpse, says the host. There was a car on the Old Bridge when it fell, a husband and wife headed for the airport, and only the woman made it to the surface. Now the program cuts to what sounds like a live interview. There is confusion at first, shouting and static, and a reporter talking to the widow herself. Her anger is vast. There were people watching, she says. She wants to know why none of them dove in to save her husband, and why his body hasn't been recovered, and why she was the one to live.

More shouting and static and if I were to guess I would say that the reporter is being dragged from the woman's room in the hospital. Next there are advertisements—Inca Kola, Kirma Instant Coffee, Bimbo Bread. The program resumes but the taxi stops as already we are to the gate.

My stomach tightens as I pay the driver. Walking and rain and walking. A moment in my office to gather materials, and then to the classroom. Ground floor. Insects gone. Room swept clean. Twenty chairs set in rows. The bell rings and the semester has begun.

I look out across the students in this, my Elementary group. There are only four, and Madeinusa is not among them. I employ key methodologies all the same, speak only English, gesture generously. The first handout is a sheet of corrective annotations for written work. I illustrate each annotation with a chalkboard example: a flawed sentence and the corresponding correction. Though my students all show signs of being false beginners, the limited breadth of their passive vocabulary does not permit examples of sufficient clarity.

Three more students arrive, none of them on my list, and I restart. Still my examples of fragments and run-ons are unsuccessful; the students appear disposed to disbelieve that anything correctly formed in Spanish could be wrong when translated word for word, and their voices, are they inflected with disdain? It seems that they are, seems that they have seen into me and know that I have failed, have found me worthless and wanting.

We abandon corrections and proceed to rules. Again and again I ask whether my policies regarding attendance and plagiarism are sufficiently clear. My students stare out the window at the rain.

A final attempt, blank spaces in which they are to detail their major, hobbies, and previous English-learning experiences. I hand the sheets out, allow five minutes, permit mutterings in Spanish as they work. Two more unlisted students enter in the midst of the process, deforming it. When I collect the sheets I am met with excessive doodling.

I explain the sense in which lines exist to be drawn, and which individual line is involved in this case, and to which side of that line excessive doodling lies. The air is dense with indifference. Sweat gathers in my neck-folds.

I close my eyes, open them again, and a student raises her hand. She is short and has very long hair, works at the sentence she has in her head, and it comes out so slowly, a word, a pause, a correction, a pause, another word. I tell her that just this once she may speak in Spanish, but she shakes her head, perseveres. Finally she reaches the end of the sentence, a question, and it is only this: she wants to know if I am feeling all right.

I look at her, at the other faces, and they hold no indifference, I know that now, and it was a matter not of disdain but of confusion. I thank her. I tell her that I am fine, and thank her again. I thank all of them, and tell them that they may go, that today was fine, a fine start, and tomorrow we will begin again.

Eugenia has left a note in my office. I walk to hers and she sits me down.

- You looked better with the beard, she says. Also, the

processes for your work visa and residency card are nearing completion. It will soon be time for you to present the final set of paperwork.

- Ah.

- Is your current visa valid?

- It is.

This is false but can be remedied with twenty dollars per month in fines plus something extra for the chief immigrations officer, who is incorrupt but enjoys his fineries.

- I'll let you know when everything is perfectly ready. You'll have to go to the consulate in either Loja or Guayaquil. Unfortunately the roads to both are closed due to landslides and collapsed bridges, but they will re-open at some point.

- I can't just go to Machala?

- The consul there does not accept this sort of preparatory paperwork, and neither does the one in Macará. Your two best options are Loja and Guayaquil. Loja is slightly closer and more attractive.

- Loja, then.

- Good. I'll make the arrangements.

Eugenia and I have had this conversation or something similar many times, and the almond tree in my yard should be in full bloom but the rain has killed all the blossoms, so there will be no almonds, green and then yellow and falling, rattling down the roof like rats, and later no seedlings to transplant unsuccessfully, and I remember something from a letter my mother wrote to me perhaps eighteen months ago: she had decided to collect ambiguous farming utensils. I suspect that she will hang them on the walls of her kitchen, and when visitors come they will be made to guess at names and usages. I saw utensils of that nature the last time I was in Loja, or something like them. I will have to make a note to remember.

# 31.

THERE IS MOVEMENT IN THE BRANCHES OF A SMALL CHARÁN just off the path. I tense, focus on not breathing. Here there is almost no light. The movement stops and recommences. Now it rushes and I see the head, for a tenth of a second I see it, the gray crest erect, then the great thick body falling, landing, scrambling forward into bracken and silence.

I push down and in and the rain ceases. I thrash at vines and creepers and the only movement anywhere is my own. It is not easy to sneak through brush so thick given my size and umbrella. The pacazo is gone. But I saw it. That is surely some kind of sign.

To the fork, the parking lot, the back of Administration. Here at last is the stage, the floodlights and their circling moth hordes, the hundreds of chairs in neat rows: the rector's speech is almost over, his audience rapt. I slide up along the outer edge until I see Arantxa in silhouette. She is sitting with others of her rank and I step one row farther forward, clasp my hands at my back, fix my gaze on the rector and nod at each well-made phrase.

He ends on a call for bolder action and clearer thought. The applause runs for almost a minute. I join in: a fine speech, or at least a fine ending. The ceremony is brought to a close and there is still more applause. The audience rises to go.

Without looking at any faces I count the number of persons who slip by behind me. At fourteen I turn to go, feel what can only be Arantxa's hand on my shoulder, and yes, have guessed correctly.

- I didn't think you would come, she says.
- And yet.
- Exactly, she says, and yet.

She smiles, seems about to say something more. She smiles again, turns to the woman behind her and I am free. I head for the gate, pushing gently through groups of students as necessary and why why why do they walk so slowly here?

The rector, a strong public speaker, and also correct as regards those who would return: our attendance lists grew and then stabilized. My students are all aware of one another's names and commercial preferences. Madeinusa is a pleasant young woman and an entirely average student. She keeps a list of first names she considers odder than her own. Her favorite is Jhonfkenedi.

Almost to the gate, and someone calls to me—Reynaldo, jogging to catch up. He asks if I have time for a quick trip to see what is left of the Old Bridge. I nearly tell him that I have already been, but there are half a dozen expressions on his face, none of them peaceful, none of them related to any bridge.

I stop a taxi, and he says he would rather walk, and so we do: slow through the thickening dusk, the rain starting again, steady but untorrential. Reynaldo works his face into a smile, tells me that last week Boby's was shuttered for a night due to a batch of bad beer. I laugh as he knew I would. I ask about his aunt's health, and he says that she is recovering slowly. We both flinch as the streetlights come on.

- There is something else, he says. Do you remember how angry she became?

- When I asked about your visa.

- Yes. It was because that morning I had asked her to sell the house to me.

- I don't understand.

- Not for its true price. For ten soles, or a hundred, or a thousand—simply to have it in my name. I have heard that this is among the most effective ways to convince the Consul.

- And she said no?

- She said no. I think she believed that I was trying to trick her in some way. And then she understood that I would never trick her, and felt guilty for believing that I would, and was still afraid that I was.

- Have you considered actually purchasing some other house?

- I could afford a small one, if I took a large loan from the bank. But I do not want a small house or a large loan. Especially not right before leaving to study. And besides—

He stops, looks down, away, back down, and this ends his sentence for him: And besides, he means, at some point she will die and leave this house to me anyway.

- Perhaps she will change her mind, I say.

- Yes, he says. Perhaps.

The air densens with the smell of wet loam and there are clouds of insects spiraling under streetlights all along this block—water beetle, cockroach, cricket. Beneath each cloud is an unstable surface of staccato movement: hundreds of fist-sized toads. They climb up and down one another to get at that which has flown too low or fallen.

We skirt the cones of light, come to the waterfront. Along it, and we are not the only ones to have had this idea, but the crowd thins to either side of the bridgehead. The river has risen still further or so it seems, the skeleton of metal and cement slightly harder to make out. We stand and watch, stand and listen to the rabid rush of water. Reynaldo shakes his head, starts to speak and stops, starts again:

- Have you talked to Karina recently?

- Well. I—

- Are you planning to call her?

- Why? Are you?

He stops and stands and stares at me, says, True or false: it is all right for misery to end and happiness to begin.

I stand and stare back.

- True or false?

- There is no reason for—

- Superb. And what you must now do is convert the potential energy of your reservoir of knowledge into the kinetic energy of the spinning turbines of action, much as the rector suggested just before you arrived.

I waver between hugging Reynaldo and punching him in the face. Before I have decided, he asks which bridge I bet on to fall first, and how much. He howls at my answers—the Fourth, a hundred soles. He says that I am the biggest cojudo he has ever met, and that he will see me in an hour at Günther's. He pats me on the back and walks away still laughing.

I had forgotten about the birthday party. A taxi, and on my stoop Fermín is petting the hairless dog. As I approach they both run away. I would like more time to consider this but things must be organized first, and Socorro is unable to stay late.

I call Karina, invite her to join me at Günther's party, and she says that she is very sorry but she is busy all weekend. I ask if we might meet at some point next week, and she says that she is busy then too. I say that I am very sorry for not calling again sooner. There is a silence. I repeat the apology. I say that I would like to dance again, to dance longer, and also to walk with her, just to walk. Another silence, and Karina says that perhaps she will have time Monday evening.

I shower and eat, gather what is necessary, stuff Mariángel into her carrier. We stop at a corner store for a gift of whiskey. Günther's house is a five-minute walk from the far side of the Panamericana.

Up to his door, and assaulted by music as it opens—some subspecies of techno, and there is a very small chance I would like it if I understood it. Through crowds to the living room. Günther is thrilled to see us and the whiskey. I thank him for the invitation, nod at Mariángel, and he points up the stairs. I find a bare guest bedroom, pull the door closed behind us, sing César Miró against the synthetic bass thrusting up between the floorboards, and finally Mariángel falls asleep.

Back downstairs, and here complications look likely. Günther has invited young friends, who have brought along still younger friends, some of them students, even mine. This is not a problem when everyone agrees to drink reasonably, which is not the case this evening.

I have shouted conversations with Arantxa and Reynaldo and Eugenia and Armando and others, some of them too long, some not long enough. The youngest of the guests gather to dance in the front yard, where there are toads and unseemly contests. Furniture is broken in several rooms, and as the breakage intensifies, Günther asks me to do him the birthday favor of escorting the loudest of the breakers to the street.

In general they are indignant, but I am persuasive. When the work is done, we who remain have a great amount of beer to ourselves, and the youngest guests are dancing in the kitchen for reasons that are unclear to the rest of us. I check to make sure that Mariángel is still asleep, and coming back down I meet Armando going up. I tell him that as far as I know the only bathroom is off the living room. He agrees that it is, and stares at me for a moment. He turns and staggers down the stairs.

It has become very hot inside, but in the yard there is

a breeze. I gather the dead toads and arrange them lengthwise along the side wall, have just finished when Armando comes to join me. He has brought three beers, and gives two of them to me.

- A crazy birthday party! he says. Like something out of Foucault!

This makes no sense whatsoever. I drink from my left beer, and then from my right. Armando is smiling far too broadly, and now I understand.

- I was under the impression that our kind was unwelcome here. How did you get hired?

- By not telling anyone, he says.

We laugh and laugh and laugh. Armando stumbles, rights himself, wipes at the beer on his shirtfront. He comes still closer, puts his arm most of the way around my shoulders and whispers to me. It is a very loud whisper. The content is unintelligible. The tone would be appropriate if we carried concealed weapons.

- Is that so? I say.

- Exactly, he says.

He raises his finger to his lips. I wholeheartedly agree, and now Günther and Arantxa come to join us. Günther thanks me in English for my assistance with the miscreants. An excellent word, and I tell him so, and along the sidewalk come the German cultists. Their robes are mud-stained, their sandals rotting off their feet, and the tallest, the most beautiful, he is screaming at the others. The others do not respond. They look too exhausted to speak.

Günther shouts at them in German, a single long and angry sentence, then sputters and falls silent. None of them look up. A moment later they have rounded the far corner. He laughs, looks at us, nods and switches to Spanish.

- I told them they caused all ten of the plagues, and tried to start the list but couldn't remember.

- Toads instead of frogs, says Armando. That should still count.

- Yes! says Günther. And mosquitoes and lameojos instead of flies and gnats!

- Many livestock diseases though I do not know their names, says Arantxa. Thunder, and rain for hail. Darkness whenever it is cloudy. No locusts as such, but the grasshoppers will take their place.

- There have been no boils, I say, but many bruises. What does that leave?

We all count on our fingers.

- Only two more to come! says Arantxa. Water into blood, and the death of all the firstborn children!

Slowly our laughter fails us. We nod and look at the ground. I set down my beers, congratulate Günther on another year well-completed. I push my way up to Mariángel, bear her down and obliquely toward the door.

My final class ends, and none of my students need to discuss anything with me, and this is a sort of gift. The slow walk back to my office. There are days of little or no rain but the heat is still with us, and the humidity, and most of the insects.

I return my realia to the realia box, go to my office, find Reynaldo sitting in my chair. I set my books on my desk. Instead of standing up he leans back, squints at me, nods.

- It is time for you to teach me English, he says.

- All right.

- This time I mean it, he says.

- I believe you.

- No, he says. I really mean it. I must be fluent by the time my visa comes through.

He says this more quickly than necessary or normal,

and is sweating heavily. What I see on his face is not quite hope. I tell him to remove himself from my chair, and he says that he has decided to pay me in beer. I say that I do not need beer and he says that that is not the point. I say that I do not want beer and he says that that is also not the point. I ask how often he wants to meet, and he says daily, here at the university when feasible, at his house after dinner when not. I ask when he wants to start. He says tomorrow, stands, nods, thanks me for the use of my chair and goes.

Requests like this are common here: few professors wish to be students alongside those whom they teach. In the past I have always refused. Now I must find a way to prevent Reynaldo from forming any sort of precedent.

I gather my things, am reaching for the light switch when my phone rings. There is no reason for me to answer at this hour but I do in case it is Karina. In fact it is Armando. He asks if he said anything strange at Günther's party. I say that he absolutely did not. He thanks me, says that he was afraid he had had too much to drink and become ridiculous. I say that he was anything but. He thanks me again, and I say that he is welcome. He laughs as if that were a joke, and is silent for another, longer moment. I tell him not to worry and we say our goodbyes.

As I hang up the phone rings again and answering is a simple and unfortunate reflex. This time the caller is Arantxa. She asks me to come to her office. She does not imply that the visit is optional.

She asks me to close the door behind me and I do. Instead of sitting as always at her desk, she takes one of the two chairs placed together near the window, and beckons me to the other. This is perhaps some sort of management technique. I sit down, and she asks me how I am.

I say that I am fine.

- No, she says. I want to know how you truly are.

- Yes. I understand, yes. And I am fine. I am wholly truly fine.

She leans forward, says that if there is anything I want to talk about, she is more than willing. I thank her. I nod. We stare at one another for a time and then hear screams.

We run, and are the first two of many to arrive. The person screaming is a student stranded in a shallow sea of toads come to feed beneath a lamp post in the parking lot. It does not take long for Arantxa and me to clear a path. The student thanks us less than one might imagine, and Arantxa goes to the bathroom to wash her hands.

Quickly to the gate, and how is it that the student failed to notice the toads until amidst them? A taxi home, its radio on, rumors of growing problems with Ecuador, and the present sharpens its knife on the whetstone of the past. These problems are fascinating and cease to interest me the moment I walk in through my door: Mariángel reaches for me, laughs, pulls me from one room to the next, hops over each dike for no reason except the pleasure of movement.

Dinner, and food is occasionally thrown but good-naturedly. Afterwards it is still not yet time so we go to the patio. Mariángel stands beneath the edge of the awning, reaches out to catch drops on her palms, laughs and laughs and turns to make sure I have seen. And I have. Each time I have.

Finally it is no longer too early to prepare: extra diapers, cologne, our finest waterproof windbreakers, bottles of milk and juice. We make our way to Karina's house. She is happy and not surprised that I have brought Mariángel though I had not told her I would. She introduces us to her brother, who is in his third year at a technical institute on the far side of the river, and to her non-identical twin sisters, still in junior high.

All of them seem normal. The brother ignores us as he does his programming homework, and the sisters rearrange Mariángel's barrettes. No father is present or mentioned, and the mother is in Lima working on unexplainable projects.

- She has trouble with distances, says Karina.

- I think all people do.

- I mean that she sees things too late—furniture, walls, stairs—and is always falling.

- Walls?

- Yes. The doctor says it is her vision or inner ear.

The aunt is no less worried than before, comes and goes with Inca Kola. I do not ask why she is so worried as I already have an idea. I do however ask Karina whether she and her aunt are related, as that is not necessarily the case in Peru, where all of one's parents' friends are also called aunt or uncle, and can be treated as such, asked for small favors and loans.

Karina says that her aunt is her mother's sister, and all of us nod. I answer Karina's questions about my mother and father, her life and his death, about my lack of brothers or sisters. I assure them that my mother loved Peru on her one visit, that we are even now in discussions as regards her next trip down, and this is partly true: her last two letters contained references to touristic sites she missed when she came for the wedding and hopes to live long enough to see.

Next there are questions from Karina's aunt about Daly City and Fallash and Berkeley and Irvine, and I answer them as well. Finally there are questions about Cristóbal de Mena and Francisco de Xérez and Juan Ruíz de Arce and Alonso Enríquez de Guzmán. These are perhaps less questions as such than a vaguely expressed interest and I do what I can not to bore. We stay until Mariángel falls asleep, and a while longer, longer than I mean to, not nearly long enough.

Reynaldo's aunt and I are friends again though neither of us has made any reference to the past or future. She comes to my side, removes the empty bowl from in front of me. I tell her how delicious the mazamorra morada was, and she smiles, nods, asks me for specifics.

- How flawlessly creamy the purple corn gelatin! How subtle the hints of cinnamon and quince!

- Yes, she says, it did turn out well tonight.

Reynaldo laughs, stands from the table, leads to the living room where our third English session will occur. Because we are starting late, he says, he will not oblige me to admire his motorcycle before we start, will not refuse to speak in English until I have nodded approvingly at its motor.

I thank him, and we review yesterday's vocabulary: double dribble and luciferase, You have the most captivating smile I've ever seen! and Do you often come to places such as this? Reynaldo is a dedicated student but it may well be too late for his pronunciation. This is unfortunately a common circumstance among adults.

We shift to work on prepositions of place, and this pleases him: all structural work is immediately accessible to his mind, as if syntax were cousin to chemistry. Stand beside, stand near, stand in front of—he moves around the living room to give me good examples of each. Stand in, stand on, stand below and now I feel slightly nauseous. Perhaps that third bowl of mazamorra was unwisely eaten but no that is not quite it. I wave Reynaldo to a stop. I look out the window, see nothing, see only my reflection and it quivers, trembles, cracks and yes an earthquake.

I jump to the nearest doorway, brace myself in the frame. There is a series of soft jolts, then one that is much stronger, and one again softer. I wait, and there is nothing more. I laugh, look around for Reynaldo. He is lying on the floor surrounded by broken puppy figurines. He stands slowly, sadly. I look away very quickly, but not quickly enough not to see that he has wet himself.

He stands behind the couch, shouts to his aunt in her bedroom, and she shouts back that she is fine. I say that I need to call my home to make sure that Mariángel is all right. Staring at the ground, Reynaldo says that I might as well go, that he has had enough English for one day. I gather my books, make a note to discuss the prevalence of earthquakes in California at our next session, how they seem a constant threat though in fact here they are more common and do more damage, and immediately scratch the note out. In the event Reynaldo gets his visa, he will find out soon enough.

The Fourth Bridge is still open and so I am quickly home. Mariángel appears not to have noticed that the ground was ever shaking, is pleased to see me but perhaps more subdued than usual. I bring out the Cabeza de Vaca, take my daughter to the couch and arrange her on my lap, open the book and begin. She fidgets throughout the strange address to the king, calms briefly for the beginning of the hurricane. The two ships go down, and in the very midst of the roaring wind and rain there are voices and bells and flutes and tambourines and Mariángel grabs the book from my hand, runs to the extent she can.

I catch her in the kitchen and she throws herself to the ground, starts to wail. She laughs as I release her, stands and runs again. I return to the living room and take out a book I know will bring her to me: the Immortality-Jinotega volume of the 1973 *Encyclopædia Britannica*.

It is not the whole volume she likes, but the pictures in the entry on insects. It does not matter to her that most of our collection has been eaten by invisible mites. I read aloud of sexual dimorphism in twisted-wing insects, of parthenogenesis and mycetomes, and she comes slowly to the doorway. I read silently of oöthecas and Malphigian tubules, think aloud about what it means to know that there are four million insects living in any given moist acre, and now she is at the edge of the couch, holds *Naufragios* behind her back.

I read to her of polyembryony. The encyclopedia says that a single egg "will spit up in the course of development and give rise to hundreds of larvae." Spit up? This is what it says, and I ask Mariángel which would be more disheartening, eggs spitting up larvae, or a typographical error in the *Encyclopædia Britannica*.

She nods and laughs, slides *Naufragios* under the couch and comes to sit beside me. Paedogenesis is not something she needs to know about just yet, though it occurs in all species to some extent, and we are in the process of skipping that part altogether when the doorbell rings. We determine not to answer it. Then we hear Karina's voice.

After greeting us Karina says that her mother would hate my house given the dikes between each room and the next. I promise to remove them if the rain ever stops and her mother plans to visit. Karina and Mariángel play with the telephone while I make coffee. When I return, Mariángel is draped asleep across Karina's lap. She wakes as I lift her, and Karina comes to sit beside me as I sing in the darkness of Mariángel's bedroom.

Back out to the living room, and I learn more of what is easily learned. Karina studied accounting at the university, graduated the year I arrived, stayed in Piura because this is where her sisters and brother might best live for reasons she does not make clear. She works at the knickknack store hustling, and that is her word, one of her few words in English, all of them not quite expected, hustling only the best of their goods: ceramic pots and statuettes, parrots and dancers and helicopters in silver filigree, carved hardwood boxes. She knows that the moonlight jobs—Gillette Girl, Pilsen Girl, Marlboro Girl—will not be available to her for much longer. Her dream of Italy is vague and touching as are her plans to open a bookstore.

- Here in Piura?

- I would have no competition.

- Perhaps there's a reason.

- Yes. But people might begin to read, if the books were good and cheap.

- They might. How could you sell them cheap?

- I'm going to smuggle them in to avoid the book tax.

- And I will be ever and always your best customer.

An hour, two. Then, on the patio, a very light, yes a very delicate, yes and oh good christ it has been so long. And rain falls. We do not move from my loveseat, and the name jolts in my brain but this is what it must be called, I realize this only now, designed as it is for precisely two persons at once. With me there is little room for her and she fits all the same, and we could move, could leave here, but we don't, and the rain stops and she says she has to go.

Sunday morning, Mariángel cries and my face is stuck to the pillow with dried pus. It feels as though someone has ground salty sand into my eyes. I peel my cheek away, stand and stumble to my daughter. As far as I can tell she is only hungry: unearned, a bit of grace.

I call Socorro's house in Catacaos, and no one answers. I wash my hands and eyes, stumble to the kitchen, put on rubber gloves and strain granadilla for juice, mix creamed wheat, attempt not to whimper each time my eyes refocus. While Mariángel eats I call Karina. Exactly, she says. Conjunctivitis, she says. My eyes are the same as yours, she says, and she will come as soon as she can.

I turn the television on to what sounds like cartoons, feel Mariángel settle on the couch beside me. I lay back and wince perpetually and yesterday was magnificent. No rain, few clouds, and Karina had a surprise for us: the swimming pool at the Río Azul Hotel. Mariángel delighted on my back, we passed through the lobby without looking to either side, took a table out on the terrace. We ordered carambola juice, watched four young Swedish or Norwegian women swim, agreed that they were splendid.

When Karina pulled off her top and shorts, the Scandinavians slipped out of the water, dried themselves and left. It was just as well, as my eyes have only a given capacity. I removed my shirt, applied sunscreen, and waited for Karina to react to the sight, this quantity of me, these colors. She only smiled, even when my entry drove waves up over the edge of the pool.

Standing now, inching along the wall to the bathroom, a shower that lasts thirty seconds. With this rinsing I can see slightly but the pain has not lessened and in fact Karina did not intend to swim as such. She does not much like swimming, prefers instead to dive a single time and then sit in or beside the water. I mainly waded with Mariángel on my shoulders. It was her first time in a swimming pool of any size, and the bright blue of the water astounded her.

Later there was a dragonfly, its colors more vivid than could be expected, orange and green like enamel. It came to rest on the edge of the pool inches from my arm. I tried but could not see its eyes, could not focus on them precisely even at that distance, and remembered reading of this, the thousands of facets breaking up the light, a gridded blurring on the surface of the eye past which cannot be seen.

To my bedroom, clean clothes, lying down on the couch again. Exiting the pool did not please Mariángel, but I have come to know this sun, the way it has of burning me even through sunscreen and palm umbrellas, and if I had stayed out any longer all the skin would now be gone from my body. We ate a lunch of shrimp and avocado. Karina kissed us and left with unnamed plans.

Commercials come. Mariángel climbs on top of me and

coos. Back at our house, soccer was watched and dolls were carried and sung to. In the evening I called Günther, and we complained to one another about the amount of noise in Peru. It was not that yesterday was any louder than any other day, but I have often read of the importance of regular complaining to the mental health and balance of all expatriates.

On and on, the two of us trying to remember still louder things, the loudest. My eyes began to itch, then to burn. I rubbed them, and my fingertips came away smeared with yellow. I told Günther that we had complained sufficiently, hung up and went to the bathroom, looked in the mirror. My eyes were a surprising red and finally Karina arrives.

She is wearing sunglasses, is led by Alejandra, the elder twin by a minute. They have brought eye drops and ointment. The eye drops stop the infection, Alejandra says, and the ointment kills the pain.

Killing as such is not the word, but the pain lessens, and the itching. Alejandra takes Mariángel to the yard to look at grass. Karina and I soak washcloths in cold tea and lay down on my bed and place the washcloths over our eyes. It is a further comfort, and lasts until one of us is needed—a diaper to be changed, vegetables to be boiled and mashed. We take turns. I have not taken turns like this at anything with anyone since Pilar died. It is disconcerting and the only possible option.

Clouds come, elide, and rain starts, grows, and there is thunder, lightning, and Alejandra trembles. We turn on the television and listen to what it says: hard rain in the foothills, predictions of a peak, the Fourth Bridge to be closed even to pedestrians. They both want to leave, and I help by saying that I do not want them to but they should, and Alejandra looks at Karina and says they won't.

Karina accuses Alejandra of being unsuitably nice to me as a form of revenge against Karina herself for not having invited Alejandra to join the rest of us at the pool. Alejandra denies this and looks to me for support. I look from one to the other and say that in retrospect missing the pool was a blessing, and this angers both of them.

The rain thins. Mariángel is angry as well, and it is not clear why. She begins tearing pages from the first book she finds, a guide to Argentina. The rest of us watch her tear and tear. With luck I will never need to visit Argentina. The rain stops, and there is a sudden rift in the clouds, sunlight spilling into my yard. Alejandra takes Mariángel up and says the two of them are going to the park.

Karina and I repeat the cycle, eye drops and ointment and washcloths soaked in tea. For a time we play at being blind. It is more difficult than I might have anticipated: I have lived years in this house and do not know its distances at all. Inanimate things move darkly. The dikes are all higher than I built them. Brushing against a doorframe levers me twice to the floor. Embarrassment too has a smell, almost the smell of copper.

Karina has a thought of music, and so we listen, classical in deference to her idea of Italy. Blindness helps or that is my impression. Even so it is four or five times through each movement in each piece before things clarify: at last the different lines of harmony can be heard, and each individual instrument, or this is what we pretend. The play between lines is what I have always missed, the way the keeping of time shifts from one instrument to another, and a note played at octaves in sequence or echo is more than simple doubling, and Karina and I, yes, the music and blindness, a finding, until Alejandra arrives with Mariángel asleep on her shoulder and we pull our clothes back on as quickly as we can.

I carry my daughter to her crib, come back to the living room, and here it is very quiet. Alejandra is looking at Karina. Karina's shirt is inside out. Alejandra blushes, turns and walks to the front door. Karina asks if I would like her to stay, and the answer is that she can't, and must, and can't.

# III.

# 32.

Late or very early, Mariángel asleep, rain falling but lightly now. A third glass of rum. Back to my bed and stretching out again: no electricity since nightfall but my eyes have healed enough to read by candlelight and far fewer insects and *Naufragios* at last. I had forgotten what a good and strange book it is. If only Cabeza de Vaca had come to Peru instead.

The Spaniards who survive the hurricane spend the winter in Cuba, then sail for Florida, make land near Sarasota. Narváez leads three hundred inland and north before the ships have found safe harbor. They are aided by some local tribes, attacked by others. By the time they reach the mouth of the Apalachicola they are starving, have little idea where they are, and a third are malarial, too sick to walk any more. They decide to continue by water, though they have no boats. They also have no tools, and no boat-building experience, and no navigational skills.

They steal a hundred bushels of corn from the nearest tribe and kill a horse every third day to feed the workers. They construct bellows out of saplings and deerskin, melt down armor and stirrups and crossbows. They make oakum and rigging from palmettos, and pitch from pine resin, and canteens from horsehide. They make sails from their shirts and oars from juniper trunks.

By this point forty are gone from disease and starvation and arrows. They have eaten all of their horses. The five barges they have built can barely hold those still alive, the water less than a foot below the gunwales.

Another glass of rum, and for a month they sail west along the shoreline. Their food runs out and their canteens rot. Another hurricane, and they run to land, are welcomed and then ambushed by natives. An escape and further attacks and further escapes and the current of the Mississippi drives them into the gulf. One morning Cabeza de Vaca wakes to find two of the five barges disappeared. A third, Narváez's, stocked with the strongest men, rows away and will not be seen again. The fourth is lost in yet another storm.

Cabeza de Vaca and his men row for the shore, row and row but the current is too strong. At last only he and his navigator have the strength to stand. At dawn he hears breakers. Waves throw the barge onto shore. The Spaniards rest, find pockets of rainwater, parch corn. A scout is sent out, returns with the news that they are on an inhabited island.

He is sent out again, and this time is trailed back. Half an hour later the Spaniards are surrounded, a hundred bowmen or more, lengths of cane through the dark men's ears and just now I heard a sound. It was a soft sound, or very far away—something like the sound of cloth tearing. I stand and listen, hear nothing, not even rain. I wait. Still nothing, then the quietest of grunts.

As quietly as I am able through the dark, to the dining room and looking out the window at the back yard: a crack in the clouds, the moon halved but bright, the almond tree, the wall. I hunch down, watch the man extend his legs and drop to the grass. It is not easy to keep my smile from becoming laughter.

There is what appears to be a torn rice sack draped over the shards of glass that pointlessly line my wall. The man is short and stout. There is a faint glimmer about his face, perhaps whiskers gone white. It is only a matter of waiting for him to come.

A moment more, both of us listening. He walks to my patio and opens my door. He waits, steps inside, another step and I stand and flip on the light. His hands rise and he turns, blinded, feels his way along the wall as if guided by his whiskers and I catch the back of his shirt, slam him against the wall, sling him around and lift and now he sees.

It will require no great effort to beat him to death. He swings at me and I crush him and lift him again and he begs and tries to turn, says a half-sentence prayer to the Virgin and I crush him again and lift. He begs. I shake my head and he is holding something up, says that he will give it back if I let him go, throws a handful of bills into the air, and this money, from where could it have come? It falls to the floor and he twists and lunges, his shirt rips off in my hand and he runs, he jumps and clambers and there is a moment when I can follow and have him again but this money, I understand nothing, and he is at the top of the wall, squeals as he scrapes across and is gone.

I feel lucky that he prayed to the Virgin rather than to Sarita Colonia, then foolish for having felt lucky. I gather the bills from the floor, look closely, laugh. They are not soles but intis, the previous Peruvian currency—worthless, but a sound tool for escape and a particularly fine souvenir.

I look in on Mariángel, and she has slept through it all. Out to the yard, and I realize I am still carrying the man's shirt. It reeks of onions stewed in sweat. I toss it and the torn rice sack into the garbage, look again at the garden wall. The glass is not pointless after all. I hose the man's blood away.

I take the bills to my bedroom and arrange them on the nightstand. Another rum. Cabeza de Vaca once again, and the bowmen have not attacked. Instead they have given the Spaniards an arrow as a token of friendship, have promised to come soon with food, and this is the sort of thing that gives one hope even when one knows what must come next.

The river began to fall, then rose once more when rains came again in the foothills, and none of the roads leading out of Piura have yet been wholly repaired. This would be a larger problem if I had immediate reason to leave and somewhere to go. As it is, my only urgent trip is a month away, or will be once I am done here.

The regional director and I greet one another elaborately. I present the tejas and TOEFL materials that he loves, and he claps me slowly on the shoulder. We speak of Russia and other places that he has been and I have not. He asks me questions about the Middle East that I have trouble imagining ever being able to answer, and I respond with knowing nods, with the joke about the frog and the scorpion, and I am sure he has heard it before.

Tejas were first made in Ica: a fig or lemon or prune stuffed with pecans and manjar blanco. The ones I have brought are chocotejas from Arequipa, pecans and manjar blanco wrapped in chocolate, a marvelous thing. He offers me one, takes one himself, and we eat slowly. Now it is time to begin.

We speak in euphemisms and look up at the ceiling as if there were something to see: he is willing to pretend not to know that I am working without a work visa, but is uncomfortable doing so. He takes my passport and the requisite number of twenty-dollar bills to clear three months' worth of visa extensions and fines. He calls his secretary in, gives them to her, whispers with great gentleness. She leaves, and he asks to which country my extended travels are likely to take me next.

- Ecuador, I say. I have heard that Loja is very nice.

- A wonderful place. But there is of course the problem.

There are so many problems that in response I squint. He nods and unwraps another teja.

- With luck the peace treaty will be signed as planned, but, well, were you here when they came over the border in 1995?

- Right in the middle of Fujimori's first re-election bid, as I remember.

- And dozens were killed, hundreds wounded—you remember that too, I trust. Three of the four main issues have been settled, and yet there have been movements of troops. The focus is well inland—Tiwinza, the Cordillera del Condor—but all the same you will need to be careful. If shooting begins anywhere along the border, stay where you are until it stops.

I nod, and wish that he would offer me another teja: manjar blanco is something like caramel but softer and sweeter still. When the fighting was done and the Ecuadorian troops had retreated back across the border, we were made to march happily in the streets and hold large heavy banners. The secretary enters with my passport and hands me forms to sign. I thank her, thank him, wish them both a pleasant afternoon, wish them only the best in any and all future endeavors.

Almost daylight. Karina, naked beside me in bed. I have been awake and unmoving for almost an hour. She is lying on her side along the edge and if I move she will spill to the floor.

If I could move I would run my fingertips the length of her arm. Last night, the cinema, now three instead of two, Mariángel and Karina and me. At the counter I learned that Mariángel will not count as a paying customer for seven more months. All this time we could have gone to the cinema on any day we wished.

If I could move I would draw Karina's hair back from her face. It was not raining outside, but it was raining inside, water trapped between ceiling and roof dripping through. We waited for the dripping to lessen and it did not. I told her a minimal version of the burglar, and she was minimally impressed. When it became clear that the projector was not going to function, that *The Devil's Own* was not going to be seen, we stood, sidled, walked out. Other moviegoers had preceded us, and several were gathered at the door to the manager's office. I suspect it was not long before they understood that refunds are under no circumstances ever given.

If I could move I would kiss the back of Karina's neck and she accompanied us home, and stayed, and Mariángel slept, and Karina stayed. The rain came briefly, kindly. Karina asked again, and somehow the answer had changed, had become that she must, couldn't, must.

If I could move and she turns onto her back and I shift tight against the wall to let her. Her lips parted. One breast loose above the sheet. At last and I reach but there is a far shriek and Karina flinches awake, the shrieking louder and of course: Mariángel.

Karina says that she will go to get her if I want. I say that she will not, that I will, please. I say this much louder than necessary.

- Sorry I asked, she says.
- It is not that, I say. But please stay here until I call you.
- What?

It is faster to act than to explain and so I go, take Mariángel up, lock her door with both of us inside. Then I call to Karina. I address her as Socorro, ask her to go home at her earliest convenience. She comes to the door, asks what I am doing. I do not answer. She knocks, tries the doorknob, asks again. I stay silent, and now there is the noise of her footsteps, and nothing for a time, and the slamming of my front door.

By the time the echo has died I know how preposterous I have been but do not know what form amends should take and Mariángel pulls at my ears. To the kitchen. For her there is a bottle of milk but for me there is nothing. When she is done drinking I load her into the carrier and the telephone rings. I spin in slow circles as I talk to keep her entertained, and it is my mother calling.

- What time is it there? she asks. Did I wake you up? I couldn't sleep but I think I counted wrong again.

- Don't worry, Mom, we were awake.

- You're sure?

- Very.

- So what do you think about June? Or else July?

- I like them both. What are you talking about?

- It's been two years, Johnny. I could come with your Aunt Claire.

- Walking or driving?

- Smart mouth you have. I did it once, I can do it again.

This is the sort of thing we all believe about ourselves in the face of all evidence to the contrary.

- That sounds terrific. And how is Aunt Claire?

- Not so great. But she's thinking of moving out.

- Out where?

- Fallash. We'd do the trip before then just to see.

- To see what?

- So many questions! She has no one there since your Uncle Mickey died, I have no one here since your father, so she would maybe move into the house. Your old room? Okay?

- Wow.

- I know! So. What about late June for a visit? Or early July if that's better. And Claire doesn't have to come if you don't want her.

- No, bring her. And June or July, they're both fine. That's the middle of winter here, but—

- I always forget that! You'd think I wouldn't, but every single time I do.

The conversation could go on hours like this but Mariángel is ripping hair out of the sides of my neck. I tell my mother what she surely called to hear: that we love and miss her, and that if for whatever reason her trip down is cancelled I will start working on our next trip up. At last we walk out to buy eggs, sausage, whatever the nearest store has in stock.

In the street there is a crowd: my neighbors, gathered around the Virgin. It looks to be a debate about overgrowth, but their expressions are wrong for that or anything similar. I ask, and am told that the statue is crying.

People part to allow us closer, and we peer. Tears spring from her sculpted eyes. It is either miraculous or condensation.

- As if the First Rebellion had succeeded, I say. As if Sunturhuasi were burning even now, and El Triunfo would never be built.

My neighbors nod and squint. To the store, and home as Socorro walks up. I ask how Casualidad is doing, and she smiles and does not answer. Mariángel and I eat toast and listen to Brahms. I wonder if there is any chance my mother will actually come to visit. I wonder how long it will take for Karina to forgive me.

There is a quiver in the ground or air, something like an explosion but distant, muffled, unlike the night of the ammunition depot though in the same direction. It is a strange enough sensation that I turn on the television to see. There is no news there so I turn on the radio as well. For a moment the talk is only of rain and the river, the crests coming toward Piura, but then the bulletin interrupts: an accident at the Air Force base, a plane that overshot the runway and no one yet knows why. There are a few dozen dead. The passengers were flood victims rescued an hour before from the roofs of houses somewhere to the northeast.

The radio speaks of those who have gathered to look, and there is no reason for them to have done so, as everything is easily seen from anywhere, even here, this very room. The smoke, thinner and bluer than expected. The great black furrow. The smells of charcoal and oil and sweat. The twisted black metal scraps, the screams of those still alive and Mariángel comes to me with a plastic shovel. It is a magnificent yellow. She uses it to dig into my stomach, and yes, I say, and yes.

Socorro redirects her into the kitchen and I take up the telephone, call Karina, tell her that I am so very sorry and ask if she will please come. She will not, she says. I will not act anything like that ever again, I say. She says not to make promises. I wait for her to add, That you can't keep. She adds nothing and there is a shirring noise: the rain once again, thicker and thicker now.

I ask Karina if it is raining at her house as well. She asks if I am damaged and the doorbell rings and Reynaldo shouts for me to open. I ask Karina how long I should leave him outside. She says to go, that she will call me tonight, that perhaps she will visit tomorrow.

Reynaldo, drenched, and I have no idea why he is here, then remember our lesson. He says that he forgot it too, that he came across the river only to buy paint for his aunt's dresser and then remembered and regardless now is stuck. Stuck how, I ask. He looks at me. The bridges are closed, he says, all of them, even to pedestrians.

I ask if he wants to stay with us for a few days. He says that he gladly would, but his aunt is alone in the house, and he is in fact less stuck than he seems. There is a bridge still open twenty minutes south of Piura though it cannot be reached in that amount of time.

We have a quick hour of class all the same. I teach him

to say pawn and rook and several times I nearly begin jokes involving earthquakes and urine. I teach him to say, May I have your telephone number? His hair is cut in the same style as mine though he denies this when I point it out, and his vocabulary has grown quickly but I am not sure anyone will ever understand the words.

A knock at my window and I turn and hope, it can only be Karina, and it is. Almost daylight again. This was my idea. I did not think she would agree or come but here she is.

I run to the door, lead her in by the hand, tell her that I will go start coffee. She does not want coffee, she says. She leads me back to my bed. We lie down. I wait. Together we are waiting. Then I start. I apologize again. I speak of Mariángel and psychological scars, stop speaking when Karina lifts her arm, points at something I failed to notice yesterday: a livid trapezoid.

Her father threw an iron just unplugged, she says. I nod. There is more to discuss, she says, and soon we will. I nod again. She tells me to roll over on my stomach, traces a shape on my back and tells me to guess. I have no idea, and guess a dolphin. She tells me not to be so ridiculous and sentimental, asks me to pay greater attention, draws again, again, again.

When Mariángel wakes, Karina goes to get her. I go to the kitchen, start breakfast, sweat and tremble. Karina carries Mariángel in. There is no shrieking and there are no tears. She holds Mariángel out so that she can kiss me on the cheek, a full loud slobbery smack, and as far as I can tell, my daughter has noticed nothing new whatsoever.

The long slow beautiful morning slows further when for the first time Mariángel manages to turn on the television. In celebration we all sit on the couch and watch. The rains in the foothills have calmed and the crests have passed and the bridges are open again, but the pilings cannot be properly reinforced until the river is a fifth its current size. Two hanging walkways are to be built, one where the Old Bridge was, another between the Fourth and Sánchez Cerro.

After the news the day's soccer coverage begins and Mariángel brings us pebbles from the yard. The first match is minutes away—Alianza Lima versus Unión Minas. Karina still does not want coffee and I make some nonetheless. By the time I return the match has started. I suggest that we watch with the sound turned off, because nearly all of what is said during soccer matches here is as tragically stupid as nearly all of what is said during sporting events of every kind everywhere else in this world, and Karina barely agrees.

For a time there are mainly exchanges of fouls and mud. Karina says that she has been an Alianza fan since birth. I have spent the past four years rooting for Unión Minas, but only out of pity, as they are obliged to live in Cerro de Pasco, a place that is not easy to believe even when one is there. I passed through it once on a trip I took to visit archives in the central Andes. The high plains were magnificent: vast gold grasslands, endless unmarked sky. But Cerro de Pasco sits at fourteen thousand feet, and the surrounding peaks are of naked stone and snow, and the air is too cold and thin to breathe. It is the site of the world's highest open-pit mine, and also the world's highest golf course. These are not reasons to go.

Huánuco, Pasco, Junín, Huancavelica: four departmental archives that may well be rich beyond measure but as they have no catalogues and produce no bulletins it is impossible to know. I found very little of use, hope nonetheless to make the trip again, and Karina reaches for her purse. She brings out a new rubber pig. She hands it to Mariángel, who laughs, bangs it against the floor, attacks it with her teeth—a matter of molars, perhaps, or of primordial rage.

I bring the proper cream from the bathroom cabinet.

Mariángel bites my finger with more force than can be imagined given her size. In Cerro de Pasco the children play in the tailings and look unwell, their eyes never quite focusing at any given distance. There are daily detonations at eleven in the morning and three in the afternoon. The air fills with the stench of rubber burning and all the houses tremble.

Unión Minas generally win or tie their home games because they alone are accustomed to the altitude, and generally lose or tie their away games because they are ungifted. Today they are playing in Lima. In the stands are ten or fifteen thousand Alianza fans and ten or fifteen Unión Minas fans. As long as Alianza wins there will likely be no violence and finally a flurry, four touch passes and a break down the sideline, a cross, a sharp header beating the goalkeeper to the upper-right corner and Alianza Lima is ahead.

This causes Karina to scream, and I do not blame her—it was a lovely goal. Halftime comes, and Karina says that because her team is winning, she will be the one to make the sandwiches. She goes to the kitchen, and I check Mariángel's diaper. I flip through the other channels, stop short: it is the Green Man, orange now and naked except for a necktie, also orange, very long and placed strategically. It appears that he is a guest on some sort of talk or variety program.

I call to Karina, and she comes. I point, and she nods.
- This man, I say.
- Yes?
- Today he's orange, but the last time I saw him he was purple, and before that he was green.
- He has been many colors.
- Why?
- Because he's insane, perhaps, or wishes us to think so.
- Who is he?
- I don't remember the whole story, but he used to be a psychiatrist. Then something happened in his brain and he

killed one of his patients.

- Why isn't he in jail?

- I don't know. I think he was, for a time.

- We should turn the sound up—he might be discussing the event even now.

- The world is not strange enough already? Also, you don't have any bread or cheese or meat. The match will be on at El Torno as well. Where are your shoes?

She turns off the television, takes Mariángel up, walks to the door. I follow them out and down and right and left and down and along. The restaurant seems to have suffered less than the rest of Piura, the paint holding well to the outside walls, dark red. Inside is a wide sheltered patio giving onto a children's playground, and beyond the playground is a zoo. The zoo is larger than it appears and many of the playground structures are sufficiently secure and standing up from their table are two young women. One I don't recognize. The other is Jenny.

I look from her to Karina far too obviously. Karina looks at Jenny, and I look at Jenny, and Jenny looks at both of us. She is wearing white cotton trousers so thin and tight the exclamation point is I believe visible and a tight white blouse knotted above her bare midriff and far too much makeup for this time of day and is walking toward us. I look around as if searching for a free table when in fact all of the tables are now free. Jenny and her friend are almost to us and I open my mouth but there are no right words and she says a quiet but friendly hello to me, another to Karina, tweaks Mariángel's cheek and is gone. I look down, and Karina laughs.

- You professors, she says. You are all the same.

I choose a table and signal the waiter for a menu and have no interest whatsoever in knowing what she means. The conversation is crippled for a time but heals when the food is brought, magnificent anticuchos and tacu-tacu. We eat and watch the scoreless second half. Karina celebrates and

I mourn and Mariángel chews her plastic pig. This pig is of higher quality than the previous one or so it appears: it has not yet lost any limbs, may well last until we lose it. The waiter changes the channel, and the match between Universitario and Sporting Cristal is just beginning, and I call for the check.

I once saw these teams play live—two years ago, another research trip, a Sunday in Lima before my flight on to Arequipa. I had not intended to watch that match or any other, had had no particular plans, the archives and institutes all closed and so I asked the taxista to take me to whatever he considered the site of the city's most significant historical event. The traffic grew thicker and thicker. Tens and then hundreds of pedestrians streamed past us in the streets. Finally the driver stopped the meter and said that I should follow everyone else as they shared my interest in history. I asked for the name of the site. He pointed at his shirt. It was a Sporting Cristal jersey. Champions! he shouted. Two years in a row we are the champions and this year will be the third!

The check is brought. Karina and Mariángel go to play and I wait for my change. My seat was on the center line, and the fans around me were excitable and sweating and normal, but the fans at both ends of the stadium were insane, a mass of light blue to the north, a mass of pale yellow to the south, both held in by cyclone fencing and riot police. The match went well until nearly the end, Cristal up three to two with a minute left. There was vicious play back and forth, and a Cristal player went down. Glass bottles were broken and flung at the field; the two teams charged, and the two sets of fans, the fencing collapsed and the police were overwhelmed. I fought up toward the exit. A man beside me was stabbed in the arm, his blood sprayed across my shirt and the man and his attacker were swept away.

The change comes and I walk to where Karina and Mariángel play. Slide, then trampoline, then racetrack for plastic cars. Mariángel narrates or discusses these activities with sounds that are surely proto-words of some sort, which pleases me until I count. Eighteen months. Time for a specialist, perhaps.

Anticuchos, grilled slabs of marinated cow heart, one of many things that should be but are not eaten everywhere, and now the zoo. There is a cage holding several monkeys that swing and jump and masturbate. There are squirrels, and a pen with tortoises. One of the tortoises stands in the corner of the pen, takes a first step toward the center.

Further in is the bird area, and a snake area adjoined, and what appears to be an area for old home appliances. The boas are immobile, and parrots peck at them through the wire walls. I look back, and the tortoise takes a second step.

In among the parrots and doves and chirocas is a bird I have never seen before. It is the shape of an ostrich though much shorter, with a few thin feathers stretching back from its skull. Those feathers bear something like eyes, and the eyes seem significant.

Karina lifts Mariángel and runs, and Mariángel spreads her arms, believes in flight. I walk to the restaurant as the tortoise takes a third step. The waiter has no idea, but says the old man who tends the appliance area might know.

The old man is fighting a stove, stops when I ask, says the bird is a pavo real. I translate or possibly transliterate: royal turkey. I had hoped for a better name. I walk back to the bird area, grab Karina when she and Mariángel run by. I point at the royal turkey, tell Karina what I have learned, and she nods.

- In English you say peacock.
- How on earth do you know that word?
- It is just one of the ones that I know.
- All right. But that bird is not a peacock.
- Yes it is.
- Peacocks have big colorful tails.
- The male. This is a female.

I disagree forcefully but not for any reason—I have never knowingly seen a female peacock. The tortoise has taken a fourth step. The old man has followed, asks if I would like to buy a secondhand blender. The smallest of the boas strikes at the largest parrot, a fat papagayo, gold-chested, blue wings and back, some slight sky-green in its tail. The blow bends but does not break the wire mesh.

The papagayo flies to a plastic perch, wipes its bill. Its pupils are round and black, its irises white or nonexistent. A raindrop, and another. I tell the old man that we will soon return to see his wares. Steady rain now, stronger and louder. I pick Mariángel up, take Karina's hand and pull toward home.

I have my dictionaries, and Karina was and is correct. She smiles, takes my daughter from me, sings Juan Luis Guerra badly and lays Mariángel down to nap. Then she asks why the peacock was so important. I tell her that probably it was not. I ask why she chose Juan Luis Guerra, and she says that he is a result of happiness, that I would do well to relax just a bit, that she has something in mind.

I raise my eyebrows and she laughs, wags her finger. She goes to her purse, removes a small plastic bag, joins me on the patio. The smell from the bag is not to be mistaken, not when one is from northern California. She rolls one tight, lights it, holds the smoke in, offers the joint to me.

- No thank you. It puts me straight to sleep.
- Perhaps you do it wrong.
- In what possible sense?
She shrugs.
- You should try ayahuasca, she says.
- I have.
- And?
I tell her. She nods, falls asleep, and I sit beside her, watch her sleep, watch the rain in the almond tree, watch the low gray light caught in the broken glass on top of the wall.

# 33.

THIS WILL BE MY FIFTH HOLY WEEK HERE. LAST YEAR I SPENT it walking in the desert: tracing, retracing. The year before, soccer and stabbings, yes, and I found little information of use on my trip to Arequipa but I remember the Maiden of Ampato, a thirteen-year-old Inca girl led to a peak twenty thousand feet high, dressed in ritual fineries, blessed and then executed, a sacrifice meant to calm a nearby volcano. She was bundled with further offerings and buried, encased in ice for five hundred years, and I stood before her there in the museum, put my hands to the glass, her thick braid still well woven, her lips drawn back from her teeth, her flesh still frozen, her hand clutching her side as if to calm that cold. I drank well that night, walked and walked. At dawn I stood at the Yanahuara overlook, watched the light spread into the sky above El Misti, and on the ground thick strings of firecrackers were laid like tracks. An effigy of Fujimori was strung up near the edge of the cliff, and everyone called it Judas and laughed. There were hours of speeches and processions. The firecrackers were lit and the square filled with noise and sparks and smoke. Dozens of drunks stumbled, and we all turned. Music was played and we watched the effigy explode, though burn was the word they used, quema, as if it were the night before his birthday when in fact they had stuffed him with gunpowder and lit the fuse of his necktie.

The year before that I spent Holy Week at Pilar's family's house in Chiclayo. The first day we went to the beach at Pimentel, and I ate I believe a single bad prawn. That night I asked her parents for her hand—a formality, they had promised, and it was as they said. The dysentery made itself known the next day, simultaneous vomiting and shitting blood for hours, fevers during which I would hear lines from songs I had never intended to remember. Through it all Pilar and her mother watched over me. And my first Holy Week was mainly research in Lima—the Archivo General was closed to the public, or should have been, but one of the guards was Armando's grandmother's godson. In the early mornings and late evenings I walked the streets, visited the Seven Churches for no reason I could name, bought a small crucifix of palm leaves and straw at each, and thousands walked with and against me, carried candles and flowers and boughs.

This year the holiday will be spent much closer at hand: Reynaldo wishes to celebrate the survival of his aunt's summer house in Colán, has invited me and Mariángel and Karina and the Swiss hydrologist to spend our four free days with him there. Last night we all agreed to meet at my house today at nine. Mireille arrived at eight-forty, and Reynaldo in his aunt's station wagon at ten, and now comes Karina, eleven twenty-six.

There are not many clouds. We stop at a gas station, at Cossto, are on the road by noon. Again the varied greens, again the Andes if slightly less clearly than before. Mireille is very tall even sitting down, and during the drive she speaks of Byron and a castle. The road is not whole but neither is it impassible if taken slowly.

The massive cross, the ancient church. Down through the bluffs, and still there is water in the fields to both sides. Parked along the road are trucks bearing rebar and concrete. Most of the houses destroyed by El Niño have been demolished and removed, their foundations as if scrubbed clean.

We come to Reynaldo's aunt's house, arrange groceries and sheets and playpen that will also serve as crib. Reynaldo leads us out onto the balcony to admire the breakwater he built. Mireille says that he is a hero, a Dutch boy with a swollen finger. Reynaldo laughs, begins a sentence about other types of swelling, chokes it off in time.

Karina and Mireille take possession of deck chairs, and I hold Mariángel on the railing. Above us are varieties of albatross. Some are all black; others have white throats or breasts or heads. Their wingspans are as vast as in all legends and their lines are as if drawn by children.

Someone shouts up from below, and it is Armando, sand-speckled and bright with sweat, jogging or something like it. We wave back, invite him to join us. He says that he can't stop now, is staying at his sister's house three blocks up, will come to see us this evening. More waving as he jogs off, and from the opposite direction comes a woman who calls that she has three flounders and an octopus for sale. Reynaldo buys it all and prepares the grill. The rest of us pour beer into tall glasses and gather as if we will be of help. Mireille wishes to teach Karina to snow ski, explains this wish at length. The albatrosses fly higher and higher, and there are gulls in the middle sky, and there is a low wedge of pelicans.

I give the word to Mariángel in English and then in Spanish, pelican, alcatraz, and until this instant I had never made the connection: the island prison in the bay. Karina sees that without her there will be no rice, and leaves for the kitchen. I have been to Alcatraz twice. The first time I was guided in to see the cells of Capone and Kelly and Stroud. I was shown the shrapnel scars in the concrete and the spoons used for escape, the placards regarding the Hopi and Modoc and Sioux, the sad poppies and nasturtiums. I was led into solitary confinement, and was astounded: the deep sudden dark, the strangled wait that would not end.

The second time I went, there were no guides. Instead there were portable tape recorders, and cassettes in all languages. There were lines on the floor telling me which direction to go and where to stop. One receives more information this way, and steps may be retraced, and there are innumerable chances to start again, to do it right, to understand, but still I prefer the old way. Guiding oneself is not easy, even with a cassette that speaks one's language.

Lunch is now ready. Karina has prepared salad as well, and I pour more beer. Mireille speaks of schaf reblochon. Peru also has an island prison that has been closed for many years—El Frontón, just off the coast of Lima. In addition to the standard cells there were others. Siberia was a cement hole twelve feet deep. The Parada was a massive stone vise. The Lobera was a cell that faced the open sea, the waves filling the cell and receding, filling and receding.

I have never known wholly the story of its closure, ask, and Reynaldo and Karina look at one another. Karina begins and Reynaldo fills in certain gaps. Many of the prisoners were Shining Path, and they drilled and marched and one day captured three guards, took control of the Pabellón Azul. Marines came in gunboats and the first two through the wall were shot and killed. The marines attacked and pulled back and shelled, attacked and pulled back and shelled until the prisoners surrendered and released the two hostages still alive.

What happened next is unclear, says Karina. The marines were ordered to stand down, were replaced by another organization, something between secret police and special forces, answering only to President García. It was reported that all the other prisoners on the island had been killed in the course of the assault, but there are rumors: prisoners found wounded and executed there or elsewhere, or evacuated and hidden in other prisons. Most of the Pabellón Azul was still standing when the marines regained control of the island. None of it was standing two hours later when journalists and government officials arrived.

Frontón is also a sport, a sort of squash played with wooden paddles against a single wall, and there is likely no connection. The island is barren now, says Reynaldo—even the ruins were bulldozed. Mireille passes the flounder, and Karina interlocks our legs below the table.

After lunch we sleep as long as Mariángel's nap allows, which today is nearly two hours. Then we walk, scuffing our feet studiously in the surf. The only other people on the beach are three boys. They are walking the same direction as us at nearly the same speed and hitting each other with driftwood.

Sand is something new for Mariángel and she wishes to stop constantly, to hunch down and observe, to taste. The water is blue and green in patches, the result of depths and shadows. As we reach the gullied cliffs, Reynaldo tells us that we will need to hurry back, that only an hour remains until high tide takes the beach.

It is hard to hurry, however. At one point Mariángel and I feel the need to corner a crab. The three boys are nearby, and they are throwing rocks at pelicans. I tell them to stop, and they throw again. I shout and they run to a nearby beach house and come back with their father. He walks up to me, stands too close, speaks too loudly about respect.

- I may never corner a crab, I say, but if I wished, I could place my hands on your hips and snap your pelvis.

- John, says Reynaldo.

- What? I could.

- Enough.

I smile at the man, turn and lead the others away. Reynaldo and Mireille quicken their pace, are soon well ahead. Karina takes not my hand but the skin on the back of my arm:

- What the hell was that?

- Happiness.

- That is not how a normal person is happy.

I do not argue, and the rest of the walk loosens slowly, and we are back just in time to beat the tide. Hours of moving shells and pebbles on the balcony. Early in the evening Armando joins us, and together we walk up to the cross to watch the sunset. It is the commonest pastime here. The others find places to sit at the edge of the bluffs. Mariángel and I make our way in and out of small gullies. There is a long thick scarf of cloud near the horizon. The cove curves out toward Paita. Bushes, clumps of grass, trees, all vivid green, even in this odd sloppy light.

I lift Mariángel and point at the vultures. There are perhaps twenty of them circling slowly upward. I have heard that they shit purposefully on their own legs to avoid overheating, that they defend themselves first and best with projectile vomit. It is not hard to believe these things when the vultures can be seen up close, but from a distance they are beautiful.

A cloud passes between us and the sun. Below us are all other things. San Lucas, now weakened by rain, plastic sheeting over holes in the roof. The houses nearest to it are not the beach homes of the rich but the true homes of fishermen: clusters of painted adobe and flat tin roofs. A square of taut algarrobos encloses the cemetery and its graves, and animals are heard: goats, a donkey, a dog.

The sun sets splendidly, of course. We watch for a time. There is a loud pop, and a waterfall of sparks from the hill to our right, and the town's streetlights fade. Reynaldo says it is only that the transformer has blown again. The mosquitoes begin and Mariángel shouts and we walk back down into the black.

Late morning, a single fighter jet arcs silently through the upper sky, and Karina and I teach seaweed to Mariángel. The woman returns, and she has brought gooseneck barnacles; Reynaldo buys them for ceviche. Arantxa once told me that gooseneck barnacles are rare and vastly expensive in Spain. Here they are common, cheap, look like tiny penises and have no particular taste.

Mireille joins us, and she has brought a frisbee. She assumes that I can throw it great distances. When she learns that I cannot, she believes I wish to learn and is equally wrong, but Reynaldo is watching from the balcony, and Karina and Mariángel are underneath, watching from the shade among the wooden beams.

There is too much wind, this is evident. I state the fact, and still Mireille wishes to play. The distance between us lessens and the distance we must run to attempt catches grows. All the same at some point there is a transformation, a need to make one catch, a single catch with some measure of grace or style. At last there is a throw that I might perhaps reach, and I run, the wind dies and the frisbee floats and I run, great sprays of sand and the frisbee hangs and I run and it drifts and I run and reach and hit something very solid very hard.

It takes longer than I would have expected for faces to appear above me. It takes even longer for my breath to return, and still longer for the faces to stop laughing and Mariángel to stop applauding. When I can speak I ask Reynaldo for something to drink, and he nods and jogs.

Others have gathered, neighbors and construction

workers. I am helped to a sitting position. What I hit, it was a cement piling from a house El Niño took away. The piling no longer stands straight, and this is my doing, which is some consolation.

Armando arrives, receives the story, tries not to laugh. He takes Mariángel up, tells me that he and Karina will babysit so that I might rest. This is what I had planned to do today even before hitting the cement piling, and I thank him for making it easier and more thorough.

I sleep on and off and in the evening there is another idea: Mireille wishes to see the service that replaces Mass this one day each year. Everyone else agrees. I had forgotten that today was Good Friday, but am feeling substantially better, have no objections or other suggestions.

Again the walk up, branching right, to the rise on which the church rests. There is a single bell tower that would be white if not for the past months of rain. The rest of the building is sand-colored, squat and deeply worn, all but windowless. The main doors face straight out to sea and a plaque in front declares the church a national monument. The declaration is dated Janary 20, 1983—the very heart not of this El Niño but of the last one.

Dogs are gathering, perhaps a dozen, but they do not have the energy to bark in this heat. As we enter Mireille points at a carving of a double-headed eagle. She whispers something about royal crests and Hapsburgs, and Karina nods and shakes her head.

The service has already begun and the church is full: people from the town dressed in black and weeping, people from summer homes dressed not in black and watching, and several more dogs. The only light is that of candles, and this is an ancient custom or a result of the blown transformer. There is also a band, four aged men with aged wind instruments, and at times they play mutually compatible notes. The muscles of my stomach ache but there is not enough bruising to justify any complaint.

Along the walls are many objects, carvings and paintings and metalwork, and I have studied each before, would welcome the chance to see them again, but they have all been covered with loose burlap. The service proceeds for some time, communion but no consecration. The dogs wander. Wind moves through the church and extinguishes large numbers of candles, but preparations have been made, men are ready, they relight each candle gone dark.

At last the service nears completion. Christ is removed from the cross, and a statue of Mary with movable arms is lifted, and they work through the church, are carried out the doors. Those around us follow, a procession that will circle the town, Reynaldo says, will end only at dawn.

We return to the house, Mariángel asleep and carried by Karina, but she wakes as Karina lays her in the playpen, is furious for reasons I cannot determine. Again and again she demands to be lifted out, to be allowed to walk unassisted. Each time she is freed she begins a search for breakables. It is half an hour and a shattered coffee mug and the rubber pig thrown off the balcony into the surf before she is quiet again.

I join the others gathered on the balcony. There is a round of beer, and another, and several more. We talk of nothing and then as Mireille fills my glass she asks how it is that I do not believe in God.

I toast her question, and say that I do not remember ever saying anything of that kind to her. She says that I did not have to. I look to Karina and Reynaldo and Armando for assistance with a simple exit. They smile and have no interest in helping.

- I am the same as you, I say.
- That is not an answer, she says.
- It is. We all do what we can to beat death back.

- That is interesting but macabre and also not an answer.

- We beat death back with narrative.

- Oh dear.

- Yours was religious but there are many kinds, and you and I make use of some of the same: genealogical, regional, national.

- This is truly your answer, isn't it.

- Look. Biologically each of us is pointless. And we cannot bear being pointless. So we create a point by placing ourselves in stories that grow ever longer.

- John, I surrender.

- You are not allowed to surrender, not yet, and death is the anti-narrative. It is the story not even ending but simply stopping. If the story never ends, death loses. Now you may surrender.

There is a silence. Then laughter. Mireille thanks me for accompanying her to the church. I say that I am glad to have gone. She smiles at everyone, stands and goes to her room. I breathe deeply, catch myself mid-exhalation when she returns. She holds up a deck of cards, asks if anyone is interested in poker.

It is the perfect question, but no one quite remembers the rules. Karina brings out a pen and paper, and we come to slow consensus on the relative order of strength of hands and suits. There is still more beer, and more. We use wooden matches as poker chips, ten céntimos per match. At first there is conversation, but it fades, and we play as if millions or lives were at stake.

It is the sudden absence of beer that in some sense wakes us. Hours have passed. Armando and Karina are out of matches and no one else any longer cares. We shake our heads, cash out our winnings, dump the matches back into the box.

We promise one another that tomorrow there will be adventure, but I know already that we will sleep poorly, the chants of mourning brought to us now and again on the wind. Karina ruffles my hair, says that she liked my little speech, kisses me on the cheek and walks away. Reynaldo and Mireille say goodnight and are gone. I am gathering strength to stand and then Armando's hand is on my thigh.

I look at him. A moment later he withdraws his hand, looks down.

- I'm sorry, he says. From what you said, I thought we—
- What did I say?
- *Our kind.*
- I don't—
- At Günther's party. You said you hadn't thought our kind was welcome at the university.
- Our kind as in constructivists, Armando. As in tropologists. Not as in gay.
- Oh.
- It doesn't matter.
- It does, he says.

I pat him on the shoulder. He stands, starts to say something, walks to the door.

- It really doesn't, I call after him. You do not have to worry. Things will be fine in the morning.

In the morning the beach is covered with dead fish. Chula, says Reynaldo, a trash fish, most likely unwanted catch, thousands of them simply dead, a foot long, more, silver with white bellies, large opaque scales. The smell makes the beach uninhabitable and so we begin: we fill garbage bags, one after another, first from in front of his aunt's house, then working up and down the beach. It is our only adventure.

At night the wind bears away the smell, and we try to build a bonfire. We collect driftwood, spend an hour coaxing with newspaper and cardboard. The flames will not take hold in the wood.

I run to Armando's sister's house, and she says that he is reading on the balcony, has asked not to be disturbed. I walk around the house and down to the beach, take position beneath his balcony, tap repeatedly on a wooden beam with a mussel shell until he leans over the railing and asks me to stop. I say that everyone is waiting. He says that they are not. I say that at the very least he could lend us some floor wax or kerosene to help us with the bonfire. There is silence, and the flat slap of a book dropped on a table.

We walk together back to Reynaldo's aunt's house, unspeaking but not ill at ease. He goes to induce fire with the others, and I lead Mariángel to her room. I sing Los Rodriguez, and she dances, a flopping hopping dance, and at last she tires and sleeps.

Outside there is fire and rum and charades. In turn we step too close to the flames. As the first bottle of rum is emptied the charades become harder, though it helps that Mireille's often involve mountains, and Karina's often involve Italy, and Reynaldo's often involve extraterrestrials.

Another bottle is brought out, and another. None of my charades are successfully guessed though I too have a theme and do not mean my movements to be mysterious. Time after time. It comes to seem unfair, even cruel. Another rum and no one guesses Diego de Almagro, and another rum and no one guesses Friar Valverde, and when it is my turn again I tell them it is a film and act out beating Pilar's murderer to death with a flat stone.

No one attempts to guess. I perform the charade again. I wait, breathing heavily, sweating. Again no one guesses. I tell them to try. I tell them it is easy. I tell them they had better fucking guess it and they try and no one is even close and I all but tell them but then Karina. I had somehow forgotten she was here. They are all waiting.

- My father, I say.

I look at their faces, wave my hands.

- Telling me that I have conqueror blood in my veins. Juan de Segovia, my ancestor. What a load of shit. But helpful shit, yes? The very best kind. Made me strong. Made me angry and so very strong.

Karina comes and stands beside me, pulls my arm and I do not move.

- My father, I say. Can you believe that?

- So you are or you aren't? says Mircille.

- Exactly, I say. For years I was and suddenly I wasn't any more. All lies. The best kind of lies.

I look at Armando, and his eyes are blazing. I look at Reynaldo, Karina, Mireille, and they love me, all of them love me. Karina pulls on my arm again, and this time of course, and so we go.

# 34.

Out through the dark trees and I do not know why but this week my classes have been fluid and deft, my students working cleanly through prepositions of time and adverbs of manner, through the schwa and defining relative clauses, through reporting verbs and false friends. During office hours they come to me in pairs and small groups, sometimes with problems and sometimes only to chat. When there are problems I try to help. When I cannot help I invent geometric proofs to show the students that their problems are slightly smaller than they thought. Then I take the students to the empty deer pen, show them the perfect square opening, request that they ponder it.

The faint shriek of fighter jets, three or perhaps four. Again to the fork in the path. To the parking lot, again the stage and floodlights. There are far fewer moths than before. There are also far fewer spectators though just as many chairs. The verbena has already begun and I search for Armando, find him, take the empty seat beside him and he smiles.

He invited me, I believe, only to have invited me, expected me to pause before giving any answer. Instead I said that I would happily go if he would accept that there were no issues between us. He agreed, and still did not think I would come or so I suspect.

A few of the jokes this evening are at my expense—my bulk, my gait, the size and colors of my underwear—but my likeness is jovial, is often allowed a last laugh. Less kindness is shown to the head librarian and her single eyebrow, to the dean and his limp, to Armando himself: there are puns on his alcoholism and effeminacy. All the same we laugh, the dean and the librarian and Armando and me, we laugh as is required.

From time to time I glance at the rector, and it seems that his laughter wanes sooner than that of those around him. There are many reasons why this might be, and when the verbena ends, students come running to talk to Armando and me, to assure us that no harm was meant, that in fact we are well loved, that laughter had been the only objective. Some of the students are sincere when they say this. Some only believe that they are. I tell them the truth, that I always attempt not to care. Armando says that he found each and every joke extremely amusing, claps the students on the shoulders and laughs, pretending to remember.

His posture is as always ever so slightly off center, his gait minimally unbalanced, not as if he were about to fall but as if at any moment he might bend to pick up something he has dropped. I thank him for having invited me, and he thanks me for having accepted. I shake his hand, shake the hands of the dean and rector, walk for home.

A hundred yards still from the gate, and there is a group of students gathered on the sidewalk beneath an algarrobo. They are staring, and I go to stand and stare with them. There is a fox stretched out dead at the base of the trunk. It is cat-sized and twilight-colored. Its skull has been crushed.

A car or truck, surely, and someone tossed the body to the side. I leave the students there staring. Some things cannot be helped.

Out and along. A few of the old smells are returning,

plumeria and jasmine, and of course the smell of sweat never left. There is standing water only in the deepest of holes. Along and along. I catch myself scanning license plates, stop and look upward instead. There are fewer stars visible than one might perhaps guess, the desert haze building again.

Turning, the park and its trees, the Virgin under glass. She is no longer crying, has not cried in days, and my neighbors discuss the meaning of this more loudly than is necessary. Karina finds them preposterous. I wonder what Pilar would have thought of them. She was often open to this sort of possibility but did not speak of it with me, was unwilling in this and other respects to provoke my derision.

It is not that Pilar feared it, but that she hoped to save me from it. Also it angered her, and she enjoyed the sudden flush of her own anger less than most people I have known. In other moments what seemed to be anger came unprovoked and in fact was something else, a wildness, and Pilar laughed, pinned me down, magnificent. Karina is a spinning something, a knowing something, and she fits me differently: her edges are sharper, hip and wrist and jawline. Her arms are thinner, her smile slower, her eyes less easily read, and holding both women in my mind at one time like this is unjust, is a certain evil, is something for which a bill will at some point come due.

To the corner, the darkened stretch beneath the streetlight I broke, sudden movement toward me and I jump to my stoop and turn. A growl—the hairless dog. It waits, then limps away. In through my front door, Mariángel in Karina's arms and I kiss them both, thank Karina, take Mariángel and she laughs and pokes my forehead.

- Gallum gallum? she says.

Karina kisses me again, tells me that she cannot stay tonight, that she stopped by only for the pleasure of welcoming me into my own home, that she will come find me as soon as she is able. I thank her again, ask if Socorro has already gone home, and hear Socorro clear her throat behind me. Karina smiles, waves, is gone.

I thank Socorro for her loyalty and consistency and care. She frowns. I tell her that there is no need to frown. She says that she does not need advice as regards her facial expressions, and she is right, and I say so. She nods, gathers her belongings, closes the door behind her.

- Gallum, says Mariángel.
- Precisely, I say.

She and I spent most of Tuesday and part of Wednesday visiting a series of doctors. They and their tests found nothing wrong with Mariángel's hearing. She is physically capable of making all relevant sounds. Each facet of her intelligence was judged satisfactory. Be patient, the final doctor said, and she will form words that please you whenever she is ready to do so.

Brief singing, dancing with her light on my chest, but she is already tired, whines and cries, then sleeps. I continue to dance for a time, tango, ever more slowly. I dance my way to her crib, and lay her down.

To the living room, and I settle in with Howar-Malverde's anthology on anthropological linguistics. There is little wrong with it but between essays and on occasion between paragraphs I am instead with Cabeza de Vaca, and the tribe says that Mala Cosa first came fifteen or sixteen years ago, wandered through the countryside, was small and bearded and hard to see clearly. A lit torch would appear in a doorway and he would charge in and take whomever he wished, slash them three times in the side and pull out their intestines, cut a bit off and toss it into the flames of the torch. Then he would slash three times at the victim's arm, sever it at the elbow, reattach the limb and heal all wounds with a touch. And when the tribe was dancing again he would appear, sometimes as a man and sometimes as a woman, would lift their huts and fly into the air with them and come crashing down. He never ate anything he was offered, and when asked where he lived would point deep into the earth, and the Spaniards laugh at these stories, laugh until they are shown the scars on the people's arms and sides.

# 35.

A CLEARING BEHIND THE VILLAGE. A LOW FIRE. THE SHAMAN
tells me that as I drink I must have an intention in my mind,
must ask to see or understand someone or something, anything
or anyone, and he promises my request will be met. I ask to
see God, just in case. Thick bitter liquid from a green glass
bottle—the ayahuasca. Cane alcohol and rough black tobacco.
I vomit several times and the jungle goes still, a wall of deep
green, a deep wall of green.

Then movement. Figures extend from the wall, figures
from Chancay tapestries, from Wari ceramics, geometric fish
and birds and mammals and I know them, have known them
and needed them. They move for minutes or hours. Later there
is a young woman, perhaps a perfect young woman, of and not of
the figures. She is not in love with me. She is not present long.

The figures dissolve into the wall and the wall resolves
into jungle. I am wet with sweat and rain. Somewhere nearby
the shaman is vomiting, singing, vomiting again and Reynaldo
waves from a distance, turns and walks into the chemistry lab.

I do not know why he is here on a Saturday, and he is

likely thinking the same of me. He has dyed his hair medium brown, nearly my color, says that Mireille loves it. He has gotten still larger though not yet as large as me, and at our sporadic English classes we are careful never to speak of happiness, but pat each other on the shoulder and smile.

Quickly into the auditorium. The staff meeting was scheduled to begin twelve minutes ago, and I appear to be the last to arrive. Arantxa smiles at me from the lectern. She waits for me to squeeze along the row to an empty seat. She waits for me to receive a copy of the agenda.

We have never had a printed agenda before. As far as I was aware today's meeting was to have nothing to do with me, but its penultimate element will apparently consist of my explanation of the new class observation framework I developed last week. Informing me of this only now is surely Arantxa's revenge: the observations as framed will result in more work for her than for anyone else.

I settle lower in my seat and apologize to the professors adjoining me. They shrug and smile. In the United States my bulk angered people. I did not blame them. They sought only fairness as understood by their lights, each person contained within an arithmetically averaged volume, allowances made for mild but not extreme deviation. It is not so hard to be fat here, where nothing is fair or expected to be. Karina says that this is changing, but so slowly that one could live one's whole life and not notice.

Arantxa begins with an apology for having forced us to come in on a Saturday, proceeds to an exegesis of the complications that made it necessary, and from there to new rules for the photocopier. Until yesterday no rain had fallen in perhaps ten days. Then there were four hours of thunder and lightning, but the rain itself fell moderately, so instead of death by drowning we had only overworked pipes and therefore sewage in the streets. The thunder made Karina nervous but she hid it as best she could, and this morning on television was a different thing: flamingos in the Bay of Paracas. Karina and I held one another and watched them stand and stalk and preen, and we loved them, because coming down from the highland lakes to the coast is what they do each year when the rainy season ends.

It is said that the Peruvian flag was inspired by flamingos. This seems possible: white down the breast and red on both wings. A meteorologist stood on a bluff above the bay, and spoke directly into the camera. He promised us that the ocean is sufficiently cold, that the Humboldt Current is sufficiently restored, that in spite of yesterday's rain El Niño is dying or dead. Then my mother called to say that Aunt Claire had fallen, had broken her hip, that their trip to Peru would have to be postponed for several months if not more.

- Point Three, says Arantxa, is staplers!

It is possible that my aunt truly has broken her hip, and if so she has saved my mother the trouble of thinking up some less likely excuse. I told my mother how sorry I was, and said that Mariángel and I would travel to Fallash next Christmas if not sooner. Most of the insect species that came with the rains, the latigazos and water beetles and cucambas, they have gone back to wherever they normally live, but mosquitoes are still profuse. Also there are still many toads. Mariángel remains fascinated by them, loves to pet and stomp on them though I beg her to do neither.

Repairs are being made in most places: men patching roadways, rebuilding sidewalks, hammering frames for new drains. Also the matacojudos are falling. I am careful never to pass directly beneath the trees, and how is it that the rains did not kill the blossoms? Are they that much more resilient than algarrobo blossoms, that much stronger or luckier?

- Which brings me to our most recent resource bank acquisitions, says Arantxa.

There is a town south of Piura called Jequetepeque. The river there shares its name, and the valley as well. The region is thick with Moche sites, some quite rich—a headdress made from a single embossed sheet of gold, a sea deity, eight tentacles extending from a face that is half human, half feline, extraordinary piece, stolen by huaqeros from a site called La Mina but years later Scotland Yard recovered it and perhaps there is still hope.

Also at La Mina a cave, wall paintings, polychrome, the blue of great interest though just now I do not remember why and Reynaldo once told me that there is a bacteria that eats highways. It was true. He showed me the newspaper clippings, and the new Viceroy sends two messengers to the citadel at Vilcabamba. It is all that is left of the Inca empire. Cayo Topa and Don Martín are received by Sayri Túpac, the new Inca, a nine-year-old boy. Gasca has sent wine and silk and preserves. Sayri Túpac reciprocates—parrots and ocelots, flutes and cumbi cloth, gold and silver. Don Martín, Martinillo, interpreter for Pizarro throughout the Conquest, the only native to receive a share of Atahualpa's ransom in Cajamarca, the first to receive an encomienda, to marry a Spanish woman, to be granted a knighthood and coat of arms and Arantxa says my name, beckons, smiles in a way that does not at all seem vengeful.

Squeezing out and along, down to the lectern. When Don Martín returns from Vilcabamba, Gasca will confiscate his encomienda; Don Martín will sail to Spain to protest, will die waiting for resolution. Arantxa turns on the overhead projector and hands me a folder. Inside are numbered transparencies. I hold one to the light. It is a perfected version of the first page of the framework proposal I sent her, and there has never been a better administrator.

The professors nod as I describe the past observational failures they all know well: peer-based, student-based, me-based, assessor-from-Lima-based. They nod again and persistently as I move from transparency to transparency, analysis to parameter to aim. Pre-planning, I say. Strengths and weaknesses, I say. Self-evaluation, I say, and this, I have come to believe, is the key.

When I am done I step to the side. Arantxa concludes the meeting, smiles at the scattered applause, leads me to her office. She seats me in front of her desk. She leans across toward me, her blouse agape, and lays her hand on my forearm.

- That was exactly what I'd hoped for, she says. You came through beautifully.

To come. Through. Odd, but there are odder things.

- I think you are ready for greater responsibility, she says. Of course it would be accompanied by greater remuneration. And did you see the sky after the rain?

The clouds stretched feathered and were lit in all possible ways: lavender and rose, purple, orange, even strips of green. Perhaps the green was a reflection of some kind.

- No, I say, I'm afraid I did not.

I lean away. Arantxa's chin gnarls.

- Who is it? she asks.

- What?

- The woman, who is she?

Her phone rings. She closes her eyes. I nod and stand and leave.

-◦◡◦-

Mariángel and I sit perfectly still in the loveseat on the patio. This morning it is the choquecos who have come to fight in the almond tree: small and fasciated, white and black. Their call is a sharp loud hack and they move in groups of nine. Mariángel forgets how still we must remain, reaches for her doll, the birds fly away and Karina loves me backwards in a sense. For her, eye color is meaningless and bulk is of great importance. She wishes always to be uppermost. There is no difficulty in understanding this.

She says that the photos of Pilar on my walls do not bother her, has thus freed me to take them down as I see fit, and she has, I suspect, other men. This is what I understand by moments when she is called to the phone and says nothing upon returning, by moments when I ask if she wants, and before I can finish the sentence she says she won't be able. I have been careful not to force her to choose.

She will be arriving soon and together we will go to Catacaos. She is tired, she says, of being hated by Socorro, and believes that treating Socorro and her family to a Sunday lunch will be beneficial. I have no idea whether or not to agree, but Fermín has not come to water in several weeks, and when recently I asked about Casualidad, Socorro answered inaudibly, and perhaps this also can be addressed.

I have just finished fighting sunblock onto Mariángel's cheeks when the doorbell rings. Long kisses hello and then out, and a mototaxi from the corner. The ten-minute combi ride southwest lasts twenty-five. There are dozens of white egrets hunting in the fields to either side of the road, and Mariángel likes them all.

The combi leaves us at the Plaza de Armas. There Fermín is waiting on a bench beneath tamarinds. Sitting beside him is a man with many thick shell necklaces, and curly black hair down his back.

Fermín nods when we say hello. His sadness is terrifying and there is no need to ask about Casualidad: it must only be a matter of days. The man with the hair and necklaces is friendly, and does not seem insane even when he says that he is Oscar the Prophet. He predicts that I will have ceviche for lunch. I say that I would prefer cabrito, and he nods.

- If I were any good, Catacaos would not be so poor and muddy, he says.

I agree, and ask which restaurant is his favorite, and if he would like to join us. He suggests La Gansita, then says that he has art to make, but that he will join us for chicha afterwards. I smile and shake his hand and there are two types of drink by this name. If the chicha to which he refers were chicha morada, the purple juice made from boiled corn and lemons and sugar, I would happily drink with him, but Oscar means chicha de jora, the drink of the Incas, hours and days of corn soaked and boiled and strained repeatedly and then chewed by very old women and spat out and left in clay bowls to ferment in its stew of saliva.

I have heard that the chewing and spitting have long since been replaced by grating boards and sugar, and that the taste has not changed at all. Fermín leads us to Socorro's house. The dirt street is narrow but the house is whitewashed and clean. Socorro introduces us to her daughters: Elsa, Ema, Eva and Marucha. She watches as Karina asks them questions involving braids. I ask her if La Gansita is a worthy place for a special lunch, and she says she suspects that it is.

Her husband Mauricio comes from the back of the house. His hands are grease-blackened so I shake his elbow instead. He has another hour of work, he says, and it is still too early for lunch. He asks his daughters to take us to the tourist market, and this is a common misconception, that as a rule I would enjoy such a place.

The market consists of three blocks of a narrow street off the plaza. There is pottery from Chulucanas, more pieces involving cunnilingus and fellatio than one might expect, and also many globular men and women, some of them waving white ceramic handkerchiefs as if dancing. Karina says that as a child she danced tondero. She tells us that in fact she was not very good, would surely have been better at marinera, and I do not know what to do with this information.

Next there is work in silver filigree—earrings, musical

instruments, horses and helicopters. There is also jewelry involving shells and semiprecious stones. Chaquira necklaces are the most common, carved bits of spondylus rarely stolen from ancient tombs though the vendors promise that all of them are and I tell Socorro's daughters about the second voyage, Bartolomé Ruiz dropping Pizarro off to camp at the mouth of the San Juan, then pushing south along the Ecuadorian coast. The massive balsa is spotted, pursued, gaffed and drawn close, its bright cotton sails gone limp. Eleven of the twenty Huancavilca sailors dive into the open sea. Ruiz captures the rest, sets free all but the three he intends to train as interpreters for the third voyage—the invasion, the Conquest proper—but for now they are only captured sailors and the Spaniards paw through the raft's baled supplies. Threaded strings of crimson shells precisely like those from which these necklaces came, I say. Gold diadems and silver mirrors, I say. Embroidered mantles. Emeralds and quartz in beaded bags. Gold tweezers, gold rattles, Ruiz stows it all and Xerez takes up his pen if it was in fact Xerez and not Oviedo or Sámano who wrote that infamous and giddy Relación; if the native merchants were in fact Huancavilca rather than Inca; if the crystals were in fact quartz and not amethyst, and Karina is laughing. So are Elsa and Ema. Marucha asks me if I always talk like that, or only on Sundays. Always, I say, always always, and Eva says that she approves, that it is a perfectly fine way to talk.

Farther down the street there is woodwork, cups and platters and serving spoons, and slabs bearing sayings meant to be hung in one's kitchen. And there is leatherwork, saddles and purses and keychains. And there are straw sombreros, some of them expensive and very well made, the weave so tight and the straw so pliable that even when the hats are folded and stuffed into one's back pocket and left there for hours, they spring immediately back to true size and shape.

Scattered through the ceramics and jewelry and hats

are mounted animals for sale, all of them whole-body and bared teeth: squirrel, cat, lop-sided German Shepherd. Staring at these animals are tourists. Almost all of the tourists sound Piuran, but walking parallel to us on the far side of the street is a French family. The boy wants a stuffed squirrel. The mother and sister are repulsed. The father does not opine.

Elsa and Eva are surprised to learn that I do not already know the French family personally. They are more surprised still that I do not want to meet them now. Ema says that at times there are also stuffed pacazos, that perhaps I would be interested in obtaining one, and seems embarrassed by the volume of my reply.

As we turn to head back up the street, Marucha says that in her opinion I should buy three of the best sombreros. Therefore I do. Karina's makes her look as though she were another person entirely—someone quiet in her heart. Mine spreads wide enough to shade Mariángel in the carrier as well, and the one I have bought for Mariángel, the smallest size sold, will not fit her for five or six years, so it becomes a gift for Marucha.

Karina declares that it is late enough for lunch. I buy assorted earrings for the other girls, and we walk back to Socorro's house, then out again with her and Mauricio. Catacaos is famed as a good town for lunch, and its many small dusty dirt-floored restaurants are the reason. The food: seco de chavelo, rachi-rachi, tamales and humitas, majado de yuca, cabrito. Also there is fish and seafood, and I consider making Oscar successful and happy, but cabrito is so very good.

Socorro sits beside Karina and in the corner are two thin men, one playing a cajón and the other playing a guitar, both singing, criolla. They sing and play with great skill and love, Quinteras and Pinglo Alva and Polo Campos, and we applaud, also with love, and sunlight sidles in through the bamboo shades. Dust rises and they play, dust hangs and they sing, dust falls and we listen with a slow sort of desperation.

We are nearly done eating when Oscar arrives. He rattles, sits down, calls to the waiter: chicha de jora. Refusing a local delicacy can of course cause untold offense. I once cared in all contexts, and still care in some.

Oscar recovers quickly from his disappointment, and drains the large gourd from which chicha de jora is poured into the small gourd from which it is drunk. He is careful to toss the last ounce of each small gourdful to the dirt in accordance with a custom I have always liked no matter how sentimental: a sip for Pachamama. Then he suggests a walk to the ruins of Narihualá.

It is a longer walk than would interest me most days and Karina says it is the perfect idea. I ask Fermín if he wants to ride his bike alongside. He shakes his head, says that the bike was stolen a month ago, that he went to my house to tell me and decided to run away instead.

I ask if the bike had been properly locked up. Fermín looks at me and Karina pinches me hard on the back of the arm. I tell Fermín that it doesn't matter, that I will get him another for his birthday. He frowns. I look at Karina. She asks him when his birthday is. Last week, he says. Karina pinches me harder. I pinch her back and tell him that any day now a new bicycle will be arriving at his front door.

The walk is long and very bright, and I thank Marucha: the tube of sunblock I brought is almost empty, and without my new hat, Mariángel and I would soon be peeling thick dead skin from our necks and faces. We pass half a dozen picanterías with the white flag at full mast to show that fermentation is complete, and at each flag Oscar looks at me as if to say that there is still time. Finally we are out of town, and he leads us along a dirt road between empty fields, then into a grove of coconut palms.

Karina holds my hand and Oscar tells us of the grove

owners and their plan to train monkeys for the harvest as seen in some film or documentary. The monkeys were brought from the jungle and refused to do the work. In the end they were made into uncomfortable hats.

The story is clearly intended to entertain Fermín. He breaks sticks into smaller sticks. We rest, and the dense shaded space reaches uncommon heights, and wind moves the fronds and shadows. Narihualá can just be seen, but from this distance it looks like nothing more than another slumped hill.

More walking along dirt roads and another grove and more walking, and at last we arrive. The gate is locked but the guard is a friend of Oscar's and the cousin of Ema's godmother and so the key is brought. Inside there is a small museum. It is closed, and the guard asks if I would like it opened, but I have seen its skulls and pots before, do not need to see them again.

Behind the museum are huge rolls of muddy plastic. Yes, says the guard, we removed it all last week—we thought the rains had ended for good. I nod, say that I had thought the same, and a pack of hairless dogs is running toward us, and a boy, and the boy is shouting.

I lift Mariángel and push Karina behind me. Karina slaps the back of my neck and asks me to please be less ridiculous and she is right: the dogs came hoping for food, and when they see that there is none they wander briefly in circles, then lie down in the dusty shade beside the museum. The boy has not stopped shouting. You need a guide, he yells. I would like to be that guide, he yells. I am a good guide, he yells, the very best.

We establish that his name is Walter, that he is ten years old, that he is a classmate of Elsa's, and that he needs to stop shouting. It is difficult for him not to shout but finally he manages. Elsa tells him that we do not need a guide because I am a historian and already know what there is to know about Narihualá. I thank her and say that all the same I would like to hear Walter's telling, which in the end is very good—a Tallán religious and administrative center for two hundred years, forty thousand square meters of adobe pyramids and ramps and storehouses, but then came the Chimú, he says. And then the Incas. And then the Spaniards. And then the rain.

We thank Walter and pay him, and he waits. We pay him a little more though Socorro tells us not to. He shouts his thanks, tells Elsa that he will see her tomorrow in school, and runs away.

There does not appear to be any active excavation. Oscar asks Mariángel if she will join him for a moment, and finally she reaches out. He puts her on his shoulders, calls to the other girls, and when they come to walk alongside he tells them stories of the gods of the Tallán returning to earth and being astounded by microwave ovens. Mariángel loves his hair above all things. She winds her hands in the thick black curls and pulls, and Oscar pretends to be wounded, mortally, on the very verge of death.

We circle through the ruins for perhaps an hour, then climb to a Catholic church built on top of the main pyramid. The church is pale green and dirty white and pocked with what look like bullet holes. Also it seems to be vibrating. We stop walking. I ask Oscar why the church is vibrating. He hands Mariángel to me and walks to the door, then turns and runs back toward us. We watch a brown cloud seep from the outer walls and the vibration is now clearly sound, the cloud pours toward us and we run downhill as well.

We stop at the bottom and ask one another urgently. No one has been stung. We find this remarkable and pat one another's backs. We rest. Oscar rearranges his necklaces. Then Marucha starts crying. She has lost her sombrero. I look at Mauricio. He looks at Oscar. Oscar looks at me. Karina says we are cowardly cojudos and Socorro agrees. The two of them head back up the hill, get the sombrero and return, each stung only once.

We return to Socorro's home, and she and Karina hug. Fermín turns, walks away. Oscar watches him go, says we cannot leave just yet because he has a gift, some art for Mariángel. We wait and he runs, and I am not convinced my house has room for the art of Oscar, but then he arrives with a very small painting on wood, and it is beautiful, black and cobalt and gold, shards of mirror embedded, a stylized deity, part woman and part bird standing simply, sadly, a waning crescent moon at her feet.

- She is extraordinary, I say.

- Thank you.

- A Tallán goddess, yes? But I don't remember her name.

- They called her Shi. This isn't quite how they represented her, of course. This is just my thought of her.

I tell Oscar that I like her best this way. I clasp his shoulders and thank him. He says that I am welcome, and that if we ever need a prophet we now know whom to call.

The reason I am late is that there was a march along the Panamericana, several hundred people, and what they were marching for or against was not wholly clear though many held signs bearing mosquitoes drawn in crayon. I go to Arantxa's office and stand at the door. Without looking up she frowns, so instead of issuing my excuse I go to my office, drop my belongings on my desk.

Yesterday I failed and Mariángel is burned badly though only in small areas, irregular shapes down her legs. Classes begin in four minutes. There is a great deal of noise and movement in the lounge back beside the photocopier: other professors chatting, describing their weekends, recounting. I prepared today's classwork last night, a final day of review before midterms, but there is always exactly one element which escapes one's notice until this very moment. I put my fingers to my temples. Which element have I missed?

I walk toward the photocopier in case that is it, and no, I need no copies. I turn. At the center of the table in the lounge is yesterday's *El Tiempo*. Time and tense, weather, period and era, quarter and movement. I set down my briefcase and sit, pull the paper toward me to learn the latest euphemisms.

The headline is about a young woman who has been raped and killed: Daniela Rocío Espinoza Farfán. The police found her body yesterday near the highway north of Piura. In the middle of the page is a picture of her with her arms around her two brothers. She is no one I have seen before, was quite pretty, dark eyes and long black hair.

I check to see if anyone has noticed me reading. It appears that no one has. I empty my briefcase, and put everything back in. I stand and sit and stand. There is another picture farther down, a confrontation, policemen, other people. The article is undetailed but apparently the family does not trust the police, has had problems with them before, seized Daniela's body before the autopsy was complete, refuses to give it back. I have thoughts of daggers, of a fer-de-lance brought from the jungle. Then at last I remember: colored chalk.

# 36.

THE MANILA ENVELOPES SIT FAT ON THE TABLE BESIDE ME. Giving perfect scores to all of my students: that would be one way to address the deadline Arantxa has set. I stare at the envelopes, then opt to leave the exams ungraded for now, inviolate, to go instead for my new goggles and gloves and chisel and three-pound sledge—there is no longer any reason for stubbed toes and cut shins.

I swing and swing at the dike in my bedroom doorway, and the shards of concrete that skitter across the floor, the clouds of cement dust that rise, these are celebrations of the river's slow steady fall though that is not how they feel. I swing, and grit sprays across my face, rattles off my goggles. I swing again, harder and harder.

I will not finish the whole house tonight and this does not matter. Tomorrow begins my penultimate visa trip if Eugenia is to be believed, and now Karina comes, Mariángel hanging from one of her legs. Karina too is holding a hammer, small and clawed and blue-handled, has taken it from my toolbox and I have no idea why. Together they mock me for a time, mimic my sloppy broomwork. Then Karina invites me to come see their accomplishment.

They lead to the living room. There they have hung Oscar's bird god above the couch. She looks lovely there though small for such a space. Also she is not quite centered and not quite square and I tell them that she is perfect. We look at her, smile, look and listen to the chittering of my neighbors.

It would seem that they have been drinking heavily for some time. One by one they complain each in new ways that no one now comes to see and pray to the Virgin Who Wept. Their sadness sounds sincere and theological but their disappointment appears to be financial: they speak of plans that have been rendered useless, plans involving kiosks and t-shirts and plaster statuettes.

Then their complaints shift. It appears that Karina and I make irregular amounts of noise. No child should have to hear such things, they say. They are of a mind to contact the university, they say.

Karina laughs loudly into the brief silence that follows. I quietly pretend to agree, and it is Mariángel's bedtime but she demands that Karina and I first sing "Row, Row, Row Your Boat." She communicates this desire by humming something like the proper tune, and rowing feverishly, as if chased. Last night it was nineteen rounds.

Socorro comes from the kitchen, asks if there is anything else I would like her to do, or if she might leave early. I say that there is nothing, and remind her that someone must be at their house tomorrow morning to sign for Fermín's new bicycle. Then I give her an envelope with Casualidad's name written on the front. She takes but does not open it.

- It should be enough, I say.
- Her real name is not Casualidad.
- I know. I'm sorry, Socorro.

She nods. She puts the envelope in her purse. She

frowns at the floor and I go to the bedroom where Mariángel hums and rows and Karina sings.

Half a dozen fighter jets roar past, just above the trees at the near horizon. Every few hundred yards the bus slows as though for more passengers, but it is only the roadway narrowed by washouts, the asphalt ragged in many places. Mariángel sleeps in my lap, Karina against my shoulder.

When I invited Karina to join me on this trip, I had thought it would be something like the old travels with Pilar. I explained the extent to which the library of the National University of Loja and the archives of the Monasterio de la Concepción and the Cabildo Eclesiástico in Cuenca would be of use. Karina asked if I would thus be paying her to babysit. I said that arrangements had already been made for Socorro to come as well. Karina said that there was no need, but that if she were to go on vacation with me, it would have to be both a vacation and with me. In the end we agreed to alternate as principal planners. We flipped a coin to see who would plan first. We will be visiting a national park and a scenic village instead.

In past years one could take a single bus from Piura to Loja. At the chosen bus station we were promised that this will again be the case at some point in the future, but just now, for reasons no one at the counter could explain, the trip must be done in bits. A very old shoeless man bent under canvas nearby nodded his head at each thing said by everyone. Mariángel and I had a brief disagreement about papaya juice. The chosen bus is old and slow and so were all the others and the greenery on the road to Sullana is dusty once again.

From Sullana we take a taxi to Bella Vista, and from there a colectivo, an Impala with no windows, a smoothened morning sky, and the bushes and trees go thicker; some of the trees are enmeshed in vines, and on the vines are small blue flowers. We paid for half the colectivo, and the three other passengers stare but not at me. I think of Tiwinza, of the Cordillera del Condor, and wonder where they are.

Arantxa does not know that Karina is traveling with me. I waited until she and Eugenia were well into the maze of next term's scheduling, interrupted and alleged to be embarrassed to have done so, reminded them of my necessary long weekend across the border, and asked for Monday off as well to conclude my research on the early phases of Benalcázar's Quitan campaign. I informed Arantxa that Benalcázar was originally from the province of Córdoba, much like her own father. If Eugenia had not been present Arantxa would not have pretended to be amused, and would not have given me the fourth day.

The first bridge we come to is half-collapsed and slanting, shored up on the near side, the breach filled with gravel that shirs beneath the wheels. Off to the right is a dump truck sunk in mud. Beyond are goats tied to trees, and hills of harvested lemons, and a slumped grove of houses: Tambo Grande. In this as in all towns the colectivo stops so that young children might come running to sell us things we do not want but often buy anyway—today it is a box of stale popcorn and a plastic bag filled with frozen lemonade.

Past Las Lomas and at last the first rise of the Andes. More flowers, yellow this time. Another bridge, this one mainly whole, and below are fifty soldiers washing underwear. Now in the road a single burro motionless and dead center, facing away and unflinching as we pass. Suyo, and still we rise, and slow at a long downhill pitch, and come to rest last in the line of waiting cars.

We gather our backpacks, fit things in places. We walk down the line to the bridge, and the Macará River is wide and fast and punctured by surges of stone. Soldiers line both banks.

There is a shack for Customs and another for Immigrations, and the officers in them are very bored.

Then there is a rifle shot, and we duck; another shot from farther off, and we duck again. The officers smile as though ducking were dumb. Across the bridge, the Ecuadorian shacks, their paperwork. There are small trucks waiting beyond. We load into one, the bed slants to my side, and the driver asks me to sit closer to the middle.

Others load in as well. The truck pulls out with surprising quickness, and a man sitting on the tailgate is pitched off. The driver sees, smiles, waves and does not stop.

There is a sort of plant massed in places on the telephone lines, globed spores with something like tentacles extending. Small sharp green peaks surround us and it is seven minutes to Macará. We walk to the plaza and exchange small amounts of soles for large amounts of sucres. To a concrete building, Immigrations, and here is the look I know, the smile, the stamping of passports, the unnecessary additional smiles.

At the bus station we buy tickets to Loja. We walk again to the plaza, find a restaurant and address our needs: sandwiches, a clean diaper, the stretching of legs. Karina and I discuss many topics not including that of her aunt's opinion of our taking this trip together, or that of the university's response should they ever find out. Children come, ask where we are from and if they might buy coins from our home countries. They are disappointed by our answers, their collections of U.S. and Peruvian coins already complete, but stay regardless to smile at Mariángel, to take her hand, to wave goodbye as we walk away.

Six hours, the bus driver says. This is an hour more than we were told at the counter, and I have brought many bottles of milk and water for Mariángel, many baggies of raisins and croutons and chifles, and even dispensed at intervals they will be insufficient. There is a small sign instructing us not to smoke or spit, and a television showing a karate film as is nearly always the case. The seats are acceptable even for my size and the roads have in some places been repaired.

Solidly into the Andes now, treed ridges rising, moss and ferns. A series of switchbacks. Raisins for Mariángel. A police checkpoint, and slight politeness as our names are recorded in ledgers. A fallen boulder blocks half the road but we slip past, enter fog, and five minutes later we have climbed up and through to a sign calling a town Cariamanga.

It is less clean here than in Macará but near the bus stop is a view: ridge after ridge rising, and sunlight spilling up and over each. We buy water and visit bathrooms. Back onto the bus, croutons, and for a time Mariángel and I applaud the livestock we pass. Chifles, and the squirming commences. I let her walk up and down the aisle, falling often and heavily and always immediately standing, scowling at the foot over which she has tripped, and at the foot's owner.

Finally she tires, comes to sleep on my chest. On and off Karina also sleeps. I nibble at the last crouton and read Inge Schjellerup and the murder cannot have had anything to do with Pilar, simply cannot.

Mariángel wakes at the second checkpoint and cries all fifty minutes to the third and this trip is no longer feasible. Then there is a woman standing on a dirt patio beneath an awning, and from the awning hangs a hook bearing a carcass, a hog skinned and split lengthwise, hind hooves touching the ground. The woman leans against the carcass, waves, and Mariángel waves back, delighted.

Half an hour later we arrive. Loja is hot and humid and the hotel room costs ten dollars or seventy thousand sucres per person per night. We all smell of urine and sweat and diesel and Karina and I want only to shower and sleep but the consulate closes in sixteen minutes. Karina offers to wait with Mariángel and the few remaining chifles. She says she knows what to do and this cannot be wholly true but there is no other reasonable choice so I take another taxi, and there is a strange thing, a quietness: drivers here do not honk their horns, not even taxistas, not even at intersections, not even at pedestrians standing in the street.

The consul is old and bearded and not pleased to see me, five minutes to four on a Friday afternoon, unhappy to have been caught in this manner, a manner befitting clerks. Also he is clearly disturbed by my odors, and does not understand the purpose of any of the documents I have brought. He asks me difficult questions, and after a time I lose track of my lies, and we end like this:

- You have been working in Peru for four years without a work visa.

- But I was a visiting expert. It was a special case.

- A special case that allows you to work for two years only.

- There are many things of which I am unaware.

- But you are aware, surely, that for the past two years you have been working, and that during that time your visa status was that of a tourist.

- I was informed that the process would take a very long time.

- Yes. And you want to pay a hundred and ten dollars for what?

- For you to validate my signature.

- That can be done anywhere.

- I was told I have to do it here.

- You don't.

- But that's what I was told.

It is now well after non-clerk diplomatic business hours. The consul rearranges paperweights, waits for me to give up and go away. When I do not he takes the money, validates my signatures, says that many telephone calls will have to be made, many details clarified. I say that I understand, and am grateful. He removes his glasses and cleans them, tells me that I should be far more grateful than I appear, that he will be contacting the university, that he doubts any progress will be made, and that he hopes I will enjoy my stay in Loja.

Outside, the sunlight richens, the air still warm, still wet. In the hotel Mariángel chews newspaper and Karina arranges clothes. I kiss my daughter and thank Karina, begin the story of the consul but Karina interrupts:

- Didn't you say that the weather here is cold and dry this time of year?

It is possible that I said such a thing, so I pretend not to have heard the question.

- It's not cold, she says. And not dry. You have noticed, yes?

- Yes. I must have read it somewhere.

- And do you think that at some point it will be cold? Or dry? Or should I repack the coats and hats and gloves and scarves at the bottom of the suitcase?

- I don't know. Somewhere in the middle, perhaps.

- Also there's no hot water.

- The woman said—

- I know. If you ask an hour in advance, they bring it in buckets.

- Tomorrow we'll be at the lodge. Lodges have hot water, yes?

- I have no idea, and neither do you.

I nod and accept gifts of soggy newsprint from Mariángel until it is late enough for a very early dinner. The surrounding hills color the streets and the late light softens. Everything is clean and tree-lined. There are trash receptacles on the corners, four bookstores on the plaza, and cars continue not to honk. We agree on roast chicken for dinner and it is an easy find though the neon is unpleasantly bright.

Mariángel now requires that all on-lookers applaud each bite she takes. It is charming the first time. The other patrons tire of it quickly and I do not blame them but at their refusal to clap she refuses to eat and sharp words are heard in all corners.

Afterwards we walk slightly more. It seems that unlike in Piura no one sleeps in doorways here. We find a quiet bar, and one wall is covered with pictures of Queen Elizabeth II, and another with pictures of Zeppo Marx. The owner's collection of jazz is remarkable. A row of cushioned chairs is set facing the wall as a bed for Mariángel, and Karina asks the bartender for cards. I remind her that in Colán she ended up bankrupt. She says that she has not forgotten, runs through the rules, and apparently she has been studying. Twenty minutes later she has nearly all of my money.

She agrees to a last hand, the loser paying the tab of juice and bourbon. Seven-card stud, and my final card is the queen I need to plug a straight to the ace. Karina flips a flush, smiles, and I ask her for a loan to pay the bill. Then to the hotel, and Mariángel between us on the bed. I would not have thought it possible but she curls into Karina and sleeps.

A late waking, and time for Podocarpus. I am not convinced that we need information as such in order to arrive, but Karina insists and so we walk to the tourist bureau. Some of the people we pass in the streets are dressed in fineries as if working in tourist shows, but that is not how they act, these men and women: they act as if living their very lives.

I stop a young man and ask. He says he is from Saraguro, where such clothes are worn every day. His hair is very straight and long beneath a pressed wool hat. His shirt is a perfect white, his vest a perfect black, his trousers also black and ending just below the knee. From a store comes a woman, and the man calls to her, introduces her, his wife. She is short and round and her clothes are intricate: embroidered fuchsia blouse, black skirt, and a dozen bead necklaces or one of a dozen strings. Her earrings are webs of filigree, connected by a silver chain across the back of her neck. A silver pin is fixed on the poncho across her breast, a parrot-blue stone in the center.

It is confirmed that we are tourists and they are cattle farmers in town to shop for feed. I ask again, and yes, the woman says, in these very clothes she tends cattle. She asks me the same question about my clothes and tourism, and seems equally surprised.

We thank them, walk again, find the bureau off the plaza and are welcomed. Maps are handed to us and spots are indicated. Then a ranger comes, says he is leaving for the park in five minutes, headed for the lodge and can take us.

We load ourselves into the bed of his truck, and the road again, south. Karina holds Mariángel and for a time we half-close our eyes. We pass the same halved hog, and still the woman leans. East into the park, and the country is big and sharp and bright. To one side, smoke from a clearance fire. Up switchbacks through highland conifers, a twisting and to the lodge.

We are for now the only guests. The nightly rate is ten dollars or seventy thousand sucres per person. To show that I too have been studying, I ask the ranger where we might most likely see a spectacled bear. He scratches his face, asks for my map, circles the three areas farthest from the lodge.

- From here, a two-day walk to each, he says. And even then you won't see the bears.

- Why not?

- You would have to be silent. Can the three of you be silent? But there are other animals to see.

I ask which ones, and he says words that I have never heard before, and I write them down. He fixes the spelling and still I do not know what the animals are. He tweaks Mariángel's cheek, nods to Karina and leaves for his post at the gate.

The lodge is clean and well organized though here too there is no hot water. I wait for Karina to comment and she does not. The beds are firmer than at the hotel. I look again at the map, and there is a loop we can walk, three hours hard or four easily according to the distance indicated.

We set off and the wind grows distantly, a thick white sound above our heads. The path up the closest ridge is at times steep and at other times muddy. There are fungi and bromeliads in the trees. Karina walks well and Mariángel revels in the green.

We pass the treeline, reach the ridge, and here the wind hits. The trail thins and we step carefully, only air to either side. Twice the wind lifts Karina from the trail, sets her down well below us.

Higher still through sage, and in spite of wind and the fog that now drops there is a bird, blue and black with an orange topknot, and I have to hold Mariángel to keep her from chasing it. We shelter and eat though it is not yet time for lunch: sandwiches and water, and for Mariángel a beige mixture that the label calls peas and turkey. The wind moves the fog in whipping swells around us.

We walk for some time. Mariángel shivers and I switch her to my chest. The fog deepens and we walk and are silent in silence as if capable of seeing bears. A step, a step, another. Once I slip, and the sound of the rockslide extends invisible miles beneath us.

Karina asks if perhaps we have missed the cutback for the return trail. I assure her that we have missed nothing. We push up through thicker brush. Half an hour later she asks again and I squint and do not answer. More walking, and as she gathers her breath to ask again we break through the fog, are standing on a crest. Half a dozen ridges stretch back to the west in blues, and below us are lakes: small, slate, glacial.

Mariángel points, and we agree, yes, wonderful. We sit and look, drink from the canteen, lean back. I check the map, and the cutback is well behind us.

Back down into the fog, and from this direction the fork is clearly marked. The return trail is longer and drier and less steep. Then the fog ends and ahead are two men, hunched. They have binoculars and are watching a brown bird that is neither far away nor beautiful. It is exactly the size of a breadbox. The men turn as we approach, nod and smile, and one whispers Britishly:

- Bearded Guan!
- What?
- Yes! Look there, the throat!

And he is correct: at the bird's throat is something bright red, skin or a bit of bandana.

- Your first one? the other asks me.
- I believe it is.

Karina reaches as if to fondle and pinches the back of my neck, but there is no way past these men without disturbing their bird, and they whisper among themselves:

- Very rare.
- Endangered!
- Marvelous.
- Marvelous, yes.

The bird slips into the foliage, and the birders let us pass. An hour of easy walk to the lodge, and no one is present but a fire has been started in the wood stove. I attend to Mariángel and Karina warms food. The bathroom faucet must be pushed and turned simultaneously, making my head hurt nearly as much as my legs.

The birders arrive, decline warm ham, drive away, and

coming in now is a Dutch couple with fair Spanish. I do not wish to converse but Karina invites them to sit with us. The woman is blonde and teaches, and the man is bearded and paints. Unfortunately they are both very nice. Their food is also much better than ours, and because they share their wine and ravioli I suggest Hearts. I explain the rules poorly to everyone, shoot the moon three times running and feel somewhat better.

In the morning the ranger comes, is sufficiently impressed by our bird sightings, agrees to give us a ride to the main road: today is for Vilcabamba, not the final refuge of the Incas but the Ecuadorian town of the same name. The first bus to come along stops when Karina waves. The ride is brief and we debark above the plaza.

A girl perhaps four years old rides by on a donkey. She wipes at the mud on her face, climbs down, leads the donkey in circles, climbs back on. From somewhere come the smells of laurel and damp earth and fresh paint. The saddle looks to have been built to fit her, and she whips at the donkey, wanting speed.

Karina has information, and as we walk through the brief town and over a small bridge and another small bridge and up a long hill she tells me: the locals live to be a hundred and twenty due to the air and the altitude and minerals in the water. The people we pass look to be normal ages, young and averagely old and in between.

Near the top of the hill is the resort where Karina has reserved a room. There are many activities, says the lady behind the desk, including ping pong and billiards, and also there are hammocks. We pay our ten dollars or seventy thousand sucres per person. She mentions other possible diversions—horses, bicycles, beauty treatments—and leads us to our room.

The beds are large and well-netted. Karina lies down and I wish to join her but Mariángel's diaper is ready to be changed, and there is something else, something worse: her bottom, red as the throat of a Bearded Guan. This is something which untreated worsens quickly, but I have the proper cream, and Karina helps, tapping Mariángel on the head with an empty plastic bottle as I apply.

There is an outdoor cafeteria, wooden tables and benches, and guests are waiting for the latest of breakfasts: Argentines, Australians, Danes, Israelis. There is also a small monkey who comes to take papaya chunks from our fruit salads. Mariángel is unsure whether or not to be terrified, cries when the cafeteria manager shouts at the monkey, trembles when he promises us that Erasmo is about to learn an important lesson.

The manager leaves, returns with a bucket of water. Erasmo chatters, a clear and present dare, and the manager drenches him. Erasmo vaults, swings, screams almost as loudly as Mariángel. The manager goes back to the kitchen, and Erasmo returns for more papaya. It is vaudeville, I realize, this fruit and water and screaming. I say so to Karina and Mariángel, and neither of them believes me.

When we have finished eating, Karina says that she wishes to ride a horse. She says this as if it were a natural thing to do. I have never ridden a horse and do not see how it could go well, but she is looking at me earnestly and so I nod and smile as if she had suggested sex or a nap. Back in our room she looks for her boots and talks about stirrups. What will occur with Mariángel is unclear.

The desk lady is very sorry. Horseback tours begin at eight o'clock in the morning she says: four hours around the valley and back, eight to noon. Karina grips the loose skin of my elbow and asks if we can ride tomorrow morning. I say that if we do, we will most likely not make it to Macará before the border closes. Karina looks at me as if I have not yet spoken, and yes, of course, and perhaps it will all work out.

For a time we dither. We begin with half a game of billiards, and continue through a third of a game of backgammon, the swimming pool, and lunch. We walk back into the five square blocks of town, and Karina buys handmade paper with petals arranged in the weave. Then she remembers that in Loja I had meant to search for ambiguous farming utensils for my mother. She suggests that Vilcabamba might also serve, and each store we check looks likely, and no store has what we seek.

We sit down at a café to observe still more people who do not look unusually old but possibly are. Karina reminds me that the weather is neither cold nor dry, is in fact warm, is in fact humid, is in fact clouding up at this moment. On a side street, children on bicycles run into one another. We drink our coffee and admire the handmade paper, repeat short words in the hope that Mariángel will like them but she does not. She prefers instead to pretend to run into the street, watching each time to make sure that I disapprove, and the sky is a solid metal sheet.

I call for the bill and rain begins to fall. The bill arrives and rain is falling harder. I pay, and the rain is torrential, and a boy locks his brakes, flips over the handlebars, is helped up by his friends. The rain will not be stopping soon. We run, a paper placemat covering Mariángel's head badly, down and over and over and up, drenched and laughing, into the room and pulling off clothes, Mariángel's first, then mine, then deliciously Karina's.

Dinner is salad and hummus and bread, and fried fish, perhaps trout. Dessert is more fruit salad, and Erasmo, the manager, the bucket of water and screaming. After this there is ping pong but Mariángel cannot simply watch, must grasp at our legs, and so we switch to Scrabble. Mariángel circles the table, pretends to wish to chew each piece. Karina plays in

Spanish and I play in English, and we both cheat as well as we are able.

When she has won we take Mariángel to a patch of grass and scuttle around her like geckos, nip at the backs of her legs until she tires. Then we return to the room. Soon she is asleep. Hours of traced birds, flowers, mammals on my back. I invent name after name and Karina says I am never mistaken.

It is now clear: this bus will not make the border in time. I would have called Arantxa from the last rest stop if I thought advance warning would make her any less angry. We will stay the night in Macará, and with luck tomorrow I will miss only my morning class.

I would like to blame Karina for this situation, would like to be angry, but she sleeps against my shoulder and Mariángel sleeps across our laps and the sunlight lies bright in the leaves of each branch of each tree on each crest. Also our time with the horses did not end disastrously. I was the last to arrive as my bootlaces were problematic, and my horse was not a great deal larger than me. When Karina saw how I sat, she suggested that she carry Mariángel instead, and Mariángel could not believe their distance from the ground.

The land was rife with hillsides. I wished briefly for a lance, fourteen feet long but light in the hand. Karina's horse bit an Australian's horse, and the Australian's horse kicked at Karina's. There was confusion and fear, then something like merriment as the guide circled back.

Through groves of pine and eucalyptus, and the land opened into high fields of corn and sugar cane. The guide goaded his horse to a trot, and most of the other horses trotted too. Some only walked. Mine stopped to eat a bit of bracken. When he was full he cantered until we caught up at a shallow river. There was splashing and sharp cold, and birds singing, wild canaries bright as spattered paint.

Again the river, and this time a wooden bridge. On the far side we climbed a sharp pitch up through something like jungle but friendlier. Over the top and out onto a flat open ridge where Karina took her horse to a gallop and my lungs seized and she laughed, free, circled back to me, Mariángel's arms outstretched, impossible happiness.

Just then my horse tried to buck me off. The thought would have terrified me, the slow falling and landing and breakage, but it had been clear for some time that this horse would not be capable. I leaned to his ear, said that he was correct, that at first the Incas were terrified of horses, a squadron famously trembling and receding as Soto wheeled in front of them outside the Royal Baths in Cajamarca, and yes, Atahualpa had them executed for showing such fear. But soon the Incas learned. They killed their first horse before the Spaniards even got to Cuzco, the counterattack at Vilcashuamán, a beautiful white stallion, and they made banners of its mane and tail.

Perhaps horses like babies understand the tone. Mine lurched once more, lost wind midway. The buck took the form of a hiccough and the brakes squeal as we come to Cariamanga.

We step off the bus, walk to a restaurant on the plaza, sit and order and slump. Even after the food arrives, the nature of the dishes is hard to ascertain, and we no longer remember what we ordered. I chew gristle from a bone and help Mariángel with her soup. Karina lowers her fork.

- Isn't that our bus?
- It can't be. The driver said twenty minutes.
- It looks like our bus.
- No. Ours is more—

Then I see our backpacks strapped to the roof. I throw money on the table, an approximate amount, and Karina has Mariángel and I have our knapsacks and we run but not quickly enough.

We watch the bus disappear. It does this slowly. I turn in abrupt circles, hoping for a taxi. Karina stops my spinning and flags down the next car to pass, a small white pick-up. She asks the driver how much he would charge to catch up to the bus, and he says he'll let us know when we have.

We load in, and the man wishes to practice his English, his French, his German. All of them seem fine to me and I ask him to please drive more quickly. It is fifteen minutes of this before the bus is sighted, and of course: ten dollars, or seventy thousand sucres.

It is the fault of the rainstorm or horse ride or bus or last night's drafty room: Mariángel woke crying every hour, choking on the phlegm in her nose and throat. Now, eight-fifteen in the morning, and we stare at the immigration officers. The officers observe us, and each other. We have been in Ecuador too long for bribes to be reasonably requested. They stamp our passports and do not smile and hope that we will come again soon.

Again the matched lines of soldiers. We cross the bridge, and this time no shots are fired. We ignore the first colectivo, a half-full sedan, and take the second, an empty station wagon. I believe that we have reached an understanding, the driver and I, but five minutes down the road he stops, and waits, and a man comes running. In the man's arms are a goat and two ducks. I wait to see what exactly I must protest. It turns out that the man is the driver's brother, and the brother will not be joining us. The animals are properly bound, fit neatly beside our backpacks and Mariángel loves them.

Sleep comes again for Karina. Mariángel stands in my lap, rests her head on the back of the seat and chats with her new friends. I watch out the window. Suyo. The air, warmer now. I close my eyes. High jungle, a thin path, and it is unclear, we are pursuing or pursued. Soon it will be night. We run faster, ever faster, but the trees are so thick that the others cannot be seen and the snakes and the spiders and the path turns to mud, ends at the bank of a river.

My head snaps forward and Mariángel is screaming in my ear but it is that she is delighted: a duck has worked itself free. We stop, and the driver reties the twine tighter. The jungle, flotsam, yes. Vilcabamba, not the Ecuadorian town but the final refuge of the Incas, and the Spaniards have come, and the battles have been lost. Túpac Amaru lifts his torch, sets fire to the temple, watches its thatched roof become a scurling sheet of flame. He sets fire to the aviaries, the hundreds of parrots and doves and curassows rising up through the opened doors. He sets fire to the storehouses and granaries, the stacks of maize and sugar cane, peanuts and pecans, cassava and cotton, everything that they cannot carry with them.

And they run. It has worked twice before: the Spaniards seeing what has been burned, pursuing for a time, relenting. This time they do not relent. Túpac Amaru and his retinue run and the Punchao is lost, run and his brothers are lost, his children, the mummified bodies of past Incas and still he runs, he and his wife, they run, last breath of an empire of millions and the Spaniards, a handpicked corps of forty under García de Loyola, guided by the Manarí and still following.

Túpac Amaru and Juana Quispe Sisa, they run and run. But she is pregnant. The birth is near. She cannot run any more, and so they walk. The jungle grows denser. It is almost dark. They reach the bank of the Urubamba and here canoes are waiting but Juana is afraid to cross the water at night. She cannot walk any farther. They stop and build a fire.

Las Lomas, and again the children running to our car. The first two soldiers to walk into the firelight are of mixed

blood, half Inca and half Spanish, the sons of scriveners.
They too sit down beside the fire and this is how it ends: in
the course of three days Túpac Amaru will be instructed and
catechized and baptized, will be tried and found guilty, will
denounce his native religion and the power of the Punchao
from the scaffold, will be beheaded. The executioner will not
be Spanish but Cañari. Túpac Amaru's head will be placed on a
pole as an example but tens of thousands will come to worship
it and so it will be buried with his body and the empire is done.

Sullana, the bus station, Mariángel waving goodbye to
the goat and ducks. We run to board our bus and then sit and
wait. I stare out the window. I remember other trips. Now it
is as if this one has been wrong. We pull onto the road. My
heart clutches. Karina looks at me, smiles. Yes, and I smile
back nonetheless.

Piura at last, and a mob of mototaxistas rushes forward
as we enter the station. I hand Mariángel to Karina, take our
packs and proceed first off the bus to clear a path. We get to
the curb, and Karina chucks my shoulder.

- Something is happening, she says.

Something is always happening.

- Something bad.

- Precisely.

- Those two tourists, the Canadians, they aren't getting
off the bus.

- I do not remember any Canadians.

- Will you look?

I will not, until Karina takes hold of my ear. The
mototaxistas at the bus doors are still shoving one another.
The few figures inside the bus cannot be clearly seen.

- I think they're being robbed, says Karina.

- They could just be making friends. Canadians make
friends easily.

- Help them, says Karina.

- Why?

Her face tenses, slackens, and it is as though she has struck me. It no longer matters how late or tired one might be. I drop our backpacks, turn and push through the clotted mototaxistas. Someone punches me in the kidneys. I throw an elbow back with great force. It strikes a young man in the face and he collapses—perhaps the man who hit me, perhaps not.

From the top of the bus stairs I see the two tourists and three thieves. One of the Canadians is holding a kitten in a way that suggests kittens are something she does not often hold, and saying that she would love to buy it but does not know how she could possibly take care of it in the course of their travels. One of the thieves is insisting, insisting, insisting; the other Canadian is watching the discussion, entranced, and behind him the other two thieves are cutting slits in his backpack.

- What the fuck is going on? I ask.

The two farthest thieves drop their hands to their sides, and the third says, Our friends wish to buy a kitten.

- Is there a problem? asks the boyfriend.

- Precede me off the bus, I say to the Canadians, and as soon as you are on the ground, take the first taxi that comes by, not from the parking lot but on the avenue itself.

- What's wrong? asks the girlfriend.

- Once you are in the taxi, you will look at your backpacks, and you will know.

They are smart, these Canadians. They leave, and I follow. The thieves have the smallest of moments in which to come for me. They do not take advantage and now it is gone, and the Canadians are in their taxi, and Karina and Mariángel and I are in ours.

I look back at the bus, at the three thieves as they sadly step down, the kitten gently held. My second class starts in twenty minutes. I will have time only to rinse my face and hands, to change my clothes and race for the university. It will not be a pleasant day, but this is a reasonable price.

Waiting on the front steps is Fermín. His new bicycle is spilled on the lawn, a darker blue than the model they showed me in the store. He is wearing his school uniform, his clothes perfectly pressed, but he is sweating and looks dazed. He is holding the envelope bearing his mother's name. It has been torn open and appears empty.

So this, too, is over. Karina sees, takes Mariángel from me, stands a small distance away. I put my hand on his shoulder. He opens his mouth, and nothing comes out.

- I am so sorry, I say.
- You don't understand.
- That is correct. I can never understand. But—
- The tumor—
- I know.
- The tumor is gone. It fell into her mouth.
- I do not understand.
- That is exactly what I first said.
- The tumor fell into her mouth.
- Yes.
- And now it is gone.
- Yes. She spit it into the garbage.

Socorro comes now to the door, and Karina steps forward, and between them a coherent version is obtained. The tumor grew down through the roof of Casualidad's mouth. It was the size of an apricot but came out in pieces, says Fermín. We all nod, an apricot, pieces, yes. And it felt like the eraser of a pencil, says Fermín. He digs in his school bag, pulls out a pencil, points to the eraser.

Then he hugs me. This is not a known thing, and it lasts several seconds. He pulls away, says that Casualidad will return to work in two or three months, as soon as she is strong enough. He asks if they might use the burial money for her convalescence, and of course. Then he asks if I can provide him with bus fare back to Frías, and I can, or could if I had any money, and instead I borrow from Karina.

Socorro hugs me as well, hugs Karina, takes Mariángel and spins her. On my first try the tie snugs perfectly at the clean collar around my filthy neck. Karina kisses me and I run to the avenue, stop a taxi and climb in, to the university gates, out and running again, stopping only a moment to catch my breath and now I hear it: a thick rustling in the branches overhead. I jump to the side, trip and fall, land on a sprinkler.

Once I can breathe, I stand and check the branches. Nothing can be seen. Onward again, but more slowly. By the time I reach my classroom fewer than half of my students are still waiting. I apologize, and they pretend barely to accept.

It is only a coincidence and nonetheless remarkable: according to my syllabus, today we are to study the lexical set of theft: steal and rob and burgle and mug and pickpocket. The discussion topics are criminals and punishment. The students role-play crime after crime, laugh and strut and lean away if I stand too near.

When class ends I go straight to Arantxa.

- So, she says. Have you finished grading your exams?

- Nearly.

- Nearly! Wonderful. I can't wait to see the results. And where were you this morning?

- Still on my way home from Loja. We made it to the border last night, but—

- We?

- Mariángel and I.

- Ah. And what happened at the border?

- We arrived just as it closed.

- Why didn't you leave Loja earlier?

- Well. Yes. There was a problem with the paperwork for my visa. I had to return to the consulate several times, and there were—

- The consul called an hour ago. We discussed your visit with him on Friday. I asked specifically whether he met with you yesterday as well, and he said that he did not.

- Perhaps he forgot.

This is something I have learned from my students: the importance of sticking to one's story no matter how preposterous.

Arantxa stares at me. I stare as well but at the floor. When no one has spoken in some time I begin to whistle. I whistle until Arantxa throws a bronze paperweight at my head. It is in the shape of a toad and does not miss by much and dents the wall.

- Also, one of your neighbors called yesterday to complain about the noises.

- What noises?

- Inappropriate noises. The kind for which an unmarried person would be fired from his job at this university.

I wait, and nothing happens, and I ask:

- Am I fired?

- So it is true.

I ask again.

- The woman who called was apparently drunk. The vice-rector did not believe her, but asked me to check all the same.

- And what is your decision?

- If I had anyone available to replace you, I would already have called them. And if I hear another word about noises, or if you are a single second late for another class, I will fire you and teach your classes myself.

- Thank you. Thank you very much, Arantxa.

- Go away.

- All right. And thank you. And I am so very sorry.

# 37.

An issue not of sloth but of distraction: my final set of midterms remains less than fully graded. The students are disappointed in me, it is clear in their faces, but the urgency of their desire to know has diminished. I promise to conclude in the course of the weekend and they nod as if believing.

The bell rings but the students do not leave. This happens often at the higher levels. I ask, and they have additional questions about the discourse markers of consequence presented in this evening's lesson. The answers come easily to me, are mostly matters of register. At last the students file out and in truth my promise will not be difficult to keep as I now have time unspoken for: no more rain is coming, this is an obvious thing, and so I have worked late with chisel and sledge, removed the last dike last night.

I gather my texts and materials, drop them off in my office. I stop by Arantxa's office as well, remind her that the first hand will be dealt at nine o'clock sharp. I say that she need bring nothing at all, and she thanks me for the information without altering the expression on her face or the angle of inclination of her head, provides me with no information whatsoever as to whether or not she truly plans to come.

Out and down the path, and a suggestion from my bowels. I detour to the closest restroom and put in the requisite time. As I step to the sink some small black long-winged thing blurs between me and the mirror, has skimmed the very skin of my face, circles and circles again, faster and faster: a bat of some sort. Still it circles, a tightening gyre, then a brusque landing on the back of a hand towel.

I come closer, turn the towel slightly. The thin polished leather of its wings, the upturned nose, the spiked ears and teeth—a vile, delicate animal. I turn the towel slightly more and the bat takes off, circles and circles. I retreat to the center of the room and it lands again on the towel. I wait. The window above the door is surely open but to get there one must round a sharp corner and the bat is confused, I suspect, by all this tile and mirror, its sonar signals bouncing endlessly, its messages and knowing coming too quickly and from all directions, echoes of echoes of echoes.

Also the bat is exhausted or so I believe. I step silently to the towel. I lift it and walk slowly to the door. Out onto a lit circle of grass. I shake the towel softly, and the bat flickers and disappears.

From here the straightest path to the main gate runs past the university chapel. Halfway along its side wall is a painted statue, Christ the Shepherd, beautiful and bearded, his long wooden staff and the Germans are dead. It happened while Karina and Mariángel and I were in Ecuador. All those men likewise bearded and beautiful who came to Piura to be safe, to seem harmless and not bathe, to argue over the price of bread and survive destruction by sulfur and fire, they gathered one morning in the garage of their largest house, sealed the windows and doors, and turned on the engines of their two trucks.

It is thought that they killed themselves because they

could not bear to have been so precisely wrong: destruction not by fire but by water, and principally Piura rather than everywhere else. It is also thought that most of their neighbors saw and heard, but foreigners behaving oddly is what is expected here. The police were not notified until hours too late. The men all died calmly in their seats except the youngest, whose hands and feet were bound for reasons no one yet knows but one might guess.

I called Günther as soon as I found out. He thanked me for my concern, said that there was no reason to be sorry, that the world was not worse for their absence. Then he asked me what I thought of Arantxa. I did not immediately understand his tone, said that she and I were not on the best of terms, and that he knew her as well as I did. He insisted: How did I see her? Here I began to understand. I said that she was smart and highly competent. And his final question: Did I find her attractive?

I told him the truth, that I do, in a smart, competent, large, sad sort of way. This made Günther very happy. To the main gate and out, across the Panamericana and to the store. It took several days for me to come clearly to the fact that more than one issue could be addressed at once but tonight the relevant strands will be joined: Günther, Arantxa, Karina, poker.

I ask the old man behind the counter for rum and soft drinks and lemons and ice and chifles in large quantities. I also invited Reynaldo and Mireille, but they have plans that do not, I believe, involve other persons. Additionally I called Armando, and he answered oddly, paused for lengths of time inappropriate for both the questions and the answers, said he would join us for a late drink if not for cards as such.

I hoist the bags and thank the old man and his store is indeed beautiful. I tell him so and he thanks me, unsurprised. Out and along and classes with Reynaldo continue. His beard is as long as mine was when I first arrived here. He regularly looks at me as though he has asked a question and I am about to answer though the reverse is more often the case.

We conclude each class by watching the news and discussing it briefly in English. This is not easy given his pronunciation. Also, most of the news is in no sense news, as the network owners have long since been bought off or exiled by Fujimori and Montesinos. Many of the newspapers, too, have been corrupted, and the radio stations as well. There are still moments of integrity and good courage, but they have not yet made any substantial difference: it is clear that Fujimori will run for a third term regardless of what the Constitution might say, and that he will win regardless of how actual votes are cast. He and Montesinos are adept at controlling the present. Five years into the future we will see how well they control the past.

Along the edge of the park and almost to the corner when there is a sudden dull jolt to the top of my left shoulder, not strong enough to knock me down but enough to make me drop the bags in that hand and how lucky that the rum was in my right. This is what happens when one ceases to be vigilant. If the pain is an adequate guide I would guess that the matacojudo fell from the top of the tree and the bruise will last for days.

I kick the matacojudo to the far side of the street and feel very slightly better. The soft drinks can be salvaged with careful work around the caps. Even broken chifles are delicious and it took nine calls to the one store on the Plaza de Armas in Frías, but at last it was confirmed: the tumor dropping through and spat out in pieces, Casualidad beginning very slowly to gain weight, her breath coming easier with each passing day and here now is the Dry-eyed Virgin.

I look at her in passing, stop and look closer. She is as she ever was if slightly darker, perhaps from some species of mold. I set down my bags, pull a flowered strand of bougainvillea from a neighbor's wall, wind it into a violet

413

wreath, hang it from a corner of the glass case and feel ridiculous but not entirely wrong.

The hairless dog watches from the sidewalk as I fight with the doorknob. Finally into my house and Mariángel and Karina and such delicate delight. Karina believes that tonight will go poorly but has pledged her best attempt. She and Mariángel bring bowls for the chifles and tall glasses for drinks and two large boxes of wooden matches to use as poker chips. Then there is singing, and some small amount of dancing, and Mariángel is asleep before the doorbell rings.

Correct positioning is crucial and with luck the transparency of my manipulations will work in their favor. I seat Arantxa across from me, place Karina to her left and Günther to her right. I deal and encourage banter. The early cards are unfriendly to Günther and hateful to me which makes Karina and Arantxa very pleased.

We are unable to argue about the relative strength of hands as Karina has posted a list, so instead we argue about the correct plural form of Cuba libre, and drink several pitchers' worth. Arantxa and Karina do not immediately become friends but are more civil to one another than might have been the case. Arantxa and Günther do not immediately fall in love but there is something that might possibly be a species of flirtation exhibited from time to time.

I had thought that the later hours would bring a seriousness of purpose to the game and instead everyone but me stops caring and the discussion turns to politics. Here Karina and Arantxa have common ground. Together they bait me with talk of the United States and its imperialistic abuses. They wait for me to rise up in anger, and instead I agree neither happily nor unhappily, and tell them what they surely already know, that in the teeming cage of simians that is the world there is generally one gorilla per epoch, and this gorilla does whatever it pleases but never imagines itself as evil, in fact imagines itself as benevolent, even helpful, even a shining light, and sometimes actually is benevolent, and occasionally actually is helpful, and once in a great while actually is a shining light, but always the main concern: enough bananas for the gorilla itself.

Another pitcher, the sixth or eighth. I attempt to bring attention back to the cards. Günther wins three straight hands and initiates a second pause, this one consisting of anecdotes involving monkeys in zoos in Germany and Spain and Peru. A pot for Karina, a pot for Arantxa. I gather the cards to deal the next hand, but as I shuffle, reminiscences begin as regards El Niño: the storms and flooding and insects and mess and our small occasional triumphs.

- Also there is La Niña! says Günther.

This is the name of many things, and one is a sort of resort that exists for a year each few decades. Where before there were two ponds far apart with only desert between, the rains have created a lake that covers a hundred square miles and is several feet deep. Karina says that a few of her friends have been to this temporary shore, that it is beautiful, that we should all go together tomorrow. Günther and I nod and look at Arantxa. She says she will call the university first thing in the morning, that she is quite sure a van can be borrowed. Günther says he would be happy to drive it. Karina hands me the phone, says that Reynaldo and Mireille should come too. I call, and Reynaldo sounds no more or less sober than anyone here and agrees on the spot: my house, ten o'clock tomorrow morning.

Once this is settled I suggest that we return our focus to the game, and ask Arantxa to cut the deck. Instead she pushes her matches over into my pile. Günther does the same, and Karina, and there will I suspect be no more poker tonight or ever.

Arantxa says she had best leave, and Günther stretches and nods. We all say our goodbyes, and they are warm, kind, drunk goodbyes, perhaps my favorite kind. Karina and I walk them to the door. As they enter the darkness they take one another's hand and laugh.

I am pulling the door shut when I hear a shout from the opposite direction: Armando, walking lines less than straight. Karina kisses him hello and goodbye and goes to sleep. I serve us the remains of the current pitcher. He lifts his glass to me and brings it forward, clinks too strongly against mine, both break and Cuba libre rains down.

He apologizes, tries and fails to help me sweep up the shards, says he has news I will not believe. I tell him that in the interest of time I have already begun to doubt it, that in a few seconds I hope to reach complete aporia. He puts his hands on my shoulders. Then very loudly he says:

- Juan de Segovia!

- Yes?

- Not you! Not John Segovia. Juan de Segovia!

- Armando—

- No no no! You have no idea. Junín? Junín!

- The department or the province or the district or the city?

- City of Jauja, district of Jauja, province of Jauja.

- Department of Junín.

- Yes. We need to talk.

- We are talking at this very moment.

- Alexis Ñaupara?

- I remember him well.

- To the best of my vast and ever-increasing knowledge you have never met him. My student back at the Católica, years ago. If he ever tells you he found Hayden White on his own, you call him a liar to his face.

- Nothing would please me more.

Armando takes a deep breath, seems to sober suddenly if incompletely.

- So Alexis is in Jauja, the cathedral archives, patterns of criminality in the 1740s. And he knows that right now I'm working on inheritance structures in the same region from more or less the same time frame. When he runs into something that might interest me, he gives a call.

- Very kind.

- Very. And last night he calls again. We talk for half an hour about a mason from Yauyos. Then right at the end he asks if I've ever heard of a Conquest-era Spaniard named Juan de Segovia. I say that in fact I have. He says that he's just run across a copy of Segovia's will, and he's only mentioning it because of how odd it is to find—

- Impossible. There aren't any wills that old still here.

- Or so we thought.

- Seriously, Armando. Impossible. Not even the AG in Lima—

- Originals, maybe. But there he was paging through a notarial register looking for a set of judicial proceedings, and he finds a couple of smaller registers bound up inside. Most are from the same period but one is from the 1530s. And one of the protocols is a will. Juan de Segovia.

I hold up a hand. I prepare another pitcher—the last of the lemons, the last of the ice. I bring new glasses and pour.

- Armando, this was very good of your friend and very good of you, and I thank you both. But he must have misread. The date, the name, the—

- Alexis does not misread. I trained him myself. May I proceed to the even stranger part?

I shrug and raise my glass. Armando nods, tilts his glass softly against mine, drains his drink and wipes his mouth and smiles.

- Segovia left everything to an Inca woman and their baby twins.

- Okay look. Every new thing you say makes the whole story less plausible. There's no evidence that he ever married, ever had children, ever left a will.

- There is now.

- Armando! And to leave everything to—

- I know, all right? I know. But Alexis told me he'll copy out the will as soon as he finishes what he's working on. A week or two, three at the most. And he'll mail it to me. And you'll see. And you'll be sorry. And you'll owe me.

- Armando, I'm grateful. I truly am. I just don't believe it's possible. And even if it's true, I haven't worked on anything along those lines, so—

- Along which lines have you worked, then?

- What?

- Since Pilar died, what work have you done? And even before that! What have you published, and where? You don't go to conferences any more, you don't—

- It's time for you to leave.

- Didn't you just go to Ecuador? Five days? Almost a week in the field and you did no work. Are you a historian or a tourist?

And I move him to the door. His feet touch the floor occasionally and already I am regretting this but I cannot have him here any longer. We reach the threshold and I set him down and he keeps walking. I call to him. He does not turn around. I thank him again. He does not respond. I call out that we are going to La Niña tomorrow, that he is welcome to join us, and already he cannot be seen.

We sit on the patio, Mariángel and Karina and I. It is ten minutes past ten and no one has yet come. They have until eleven, Karina says, and then we will hire a taxi on our own.

She goes inside for more coffee and Mariángel chases a grasshopper across the yard. The grasshopper seems small but is in fact precisely the size it should be. Our insect populations and variety are also normal for this part of the world. Most of the toads are gone, mainly flattened and swept into gutters. And each morning's newspaper informs us of other things changing for the better: today's front page is primarily concerned with a lack of new cases of malaria.

There are also however articles about the Ecuadorian border, and there have never been more fighter jets ripping through the sky than this morning. Another comes just now, its shriek rattling my windows. Like many of the others it is low enough for the pilot to see that I am giving him the finger though I doubt he is looking in the necessary direction.

Mariángel catches and immediately releases the grasshopper, and it flies up and over the wall. I take the phone, call Armando and apologize. He pretends not to know why. I thank him, apologize again, say that I look forward to seeing the copy of the will. I reiterate that he is welcome to join us this morning, and he thanks me but says that today must be reserved for recovery.

Karina comes back to the patio, sets down her mug and takes up the newspaper. I have tried to tell her about Pilar, but each time I start Karina says that she already knows. She fits differently against my mind than Pilar, again with sharper if not uncomfortable angles and during sex with Karina I have called Pilar's name only once. I did not know that I had done it until Karina pushed me away. I said that I was sorry. She said that being sorry was insufficient and I agreed. From other discussions I know that her father often said and says that he is sorry. He lives in Lima but not with her mother, and wrote a book but it was apparently an insane book published in purple ink and did not help at all.

I have not been able to determine if the other men Karina loves are as large as I am. I do however have reason to believe that they are slowly diminishing in number, if such a thing may be measured in terms of the strength and variety of unfamiliar colognes. At some point I hope to be the only one left.

I fetch the six remaining Advanced exams, a red pen, a calculator. Forty-five minutes later two of them are done. Like the rest I have graded they were fine, somewhat better than fine, not quite as good as I expected and I do not know why and the doorbell rings.

Karina goes to answer, brings Arantxa out onto the patio. She is wearing a Werder Bremen jersey that I am quite sure she does not own. I hold up the four ungraded midterms and tell her that they are the last. She shrugs, kisses me hello as if the two of us have come to some sort of peace.

Ten minutes later Reynaldo and Mireille arrive looking dehydrated and dizzy and very pleased with themselves. We insult their hair for a time. Then Günther comes with the van, which smells of cilantro and bad brakes but is otherwise perfect.

Groceries and gasoline and across the Fourth Bridge, the water quiet and well down the banks. Through Castilla and out along the Panamericana. Günther handles the many detours with focused ease. At each fording I wonder if I will be asked to step from the vehicle so that it might pass more easily, but I never am, which is in itself a sort of love, and perhaps the undercarriage will not be unrepairable.

Mariángel starts to whine and so I invent a game. I pull a pretend needle bloodlessly but painfully through each of my fingers, then plunge it through my palm and pull it out the back of my hand. By tugging on the imaginary thread I can make my hand move amusingly. This terrifies Mariángel, and Karina shudders, and so do I: the back porch of my house in Daly City, my father's hand moving identically. I have invented nothing whatsoever. The feeling in my chest is half warmth and half disquiet.

I attempt to explain this to Reynaldo as we edge out of the deepest ravine thus far. We pull back onto the highway and I have a sudden sense of where we are—the desert is still rich and often green but even so I know this stretch of road too well. I sit up, crane forward. Half a mile ahead are the three algarrobos. Karina leans back against me and I look at her but she has done it for no reason, is chatting with Mireille about cherimoyas.

Mariángel lifts my chin, wants me to thread through my fingers again and so I do. She loves the terror of it, the fake pain, squeals and I watch out the window. We slow as we near the three trees, and I cannot look away.

My shoulder is squeezed, Reynaldo, and he has seen me see. Just past the algarrobos we turn west onto a dirt road, and I look back, knowing that it would be stupid and pointless to go, that I cannot possibly go. I say nothing, and Reynaldo says nothing, and Karina is staring at nothing ahead of us and probably knows as well.

Günther calls and points, but it is not La Niña, not yet. Instead it is a porotillo in full flower, the spines unseen at this distance, the long slender blooms so bright, as if the tree were growing its own putillas. We stop to look more closely, and the tips of the blossoms are still closed. When they open the huayruros will be plucked, turned into jewelry and Pilar, how she stood, letting me see, but now Reynaldo is talking, points to a hole halfway up the trunk, talks of what might live in that hole until Mireille makes him stop.

There is an abundance of wild mustard, goats and their goatherds, and suddenly the lake, bluish silver, impossible here, too vast to see across. There are a dozen children splashing in the shallows. Farther out there are windsurfers and a pair of catamarans. We park, and Arantxa and Karina are overly kind to one another as we unpack. When I take off my shirt the bruise on my shoulder is noted and explained and mocked heartily. We walk to the edge, step down into the water, except for Karina who instead stretches out, and the things Mariángel says are so very nearly words.

Scurling now around us are freshwater prawns. This too seems impossible, the lake itself only three months old and how could they have found their way here? Mireille says they were born from eggs laid not during this El Niño but the last one: fifteen years of dry silence, and then life at last. They have already laid their own eggs to hatch in the next El Niño, she says. And tomorrow or the next day the prawns will be netted and eaten.

Arantxa dislikes this so Günther offers another scenario: the prawns survive for a year, and the lake has all but vanished, and the seagulls come to feast, and the caracaras. At least they had their year, says Arantxa. Mireille leans down to the water, rinses her face, says that she will be leaving at the end of the semester. This it would seem is news to all of us but Reynaldo. She adds that we will always be welcome to visit her in Bern, and we tell her how much we hope we will be able.

Out of the water, and in addition to the snacks we bought, Arantxa has arranged proper food in tupperware. Stuffed tomatoes, stuffed potatoes, rice. Afterwards Mariángel and I walk to the dunes. We explore and roll down them. There are wildflowers, and dragonflies, and at one point the quickest of glimpses, something long and gray moving in the thick grass, the whipping tip of its tail.

A rest, and a last long swim. Arantxa holds Günther underwater, brings him up only to kiss. As we walk back to the van there are thorns in places along the trail but no tearing of skin or cloth, no pain, not now, just the colors of sunset reflected in the unlikely water, and the colors, the colors, they are a sudden slow surprise each time we look.

We climb in, and I close my eyes, keep them closed all along the dirt road. Mariángel pries at my eyelids and shouts for milk. When I can feel that we are back on the highway and well and safely past, I join in the shouting and drinking. There is even some singing, Los Morochucos, and I sing quietly, wishing no one to feel inferior.

Mariángel starts to cry when the singing ends, does not stop when it recommences, and there is general agreement that I should be dropped off first. As we pull in past the Virgin, Karina proposes a group trip to Cajamarca for next weekend. The others all have plans. It is too far away for a weekend trip but I promise her that yes we will go, and she smiles, says she will make arrangements, says she has ideas.

I bounce Mariángel up and down, create a sort of Doppler effect within her wails, and remind Karina that it will be my turn to plan. She shrugs, looks at me, and I wait, and wait, finally realize, ask if she would like to come over for a bit. She climbs down, takes up her knapsack. I look at Arantxa, who is staring out the windshield and does not look back.

Karina's annoyance fades in the course of her shower, disappears when I offer her a t-shirt to serve as pajamas and it reaches her knees. I give Mariángel a quick bath, and she falls asleep halfway through her yams. Karina too is asleep in her chair, her head down on the table. I rouse them as little as possible, only enough to get them into bed. I turn on the fans and turn off the lights, lie down beside Karina and secure the netting around us.

I trace a pacazo across Karina's back, ask her to name the species, and already she is back asleep. I trace the department of Junín, and invent outlines for the province and district and city limits of Jauja. Let us say that the will is real, is that of Juan de Segovia, was copied truly by the notary who took it down in the small register he happened to have at hand. Relations, relations: say the notary moves from job to job, carries his registers with him, is obligated to hand all protocols over to the Crown but for whatever reason the small register is never sent. Then the notary dies. Son also a notary, now owns the small register. Son dies. Grandson a priest, carries the register from one parish assignation to another. Final post is Jauja. Small register ownerless when he dies, bound with other orphans into the next available large register to keep them from being lost for good.

All right, perhaps just barely possible. But the contents! Segovia's share of the largest ransom in history, his entire fortune to an Inca woman and their children: unprecedented, spectacularly improbable for the epoch. The original will lost, and how? Destroyed or hidden by someone who thought the money wasted? Who wanted it for himself? Who wanted it to go to the Crown, as it eventually did?

Less and less plausible the more it is considered and I edge into and out of sleep. A moment later hours have passed and I am awake to the sound of news. It is an uncomfortable thing. Blue light shivers obliquely on the walls. I have been brought from a dream where there were white beetles the size of dinner plates flying faster and faster, shattering against tile walls and there were others in the dream but I don't remember whom or what they were doing, don't remember having turned the television on, and perhaps Karina did at some point. I would ask but she is sleeping, one hand curled under her chin.

The sky has only begun to lighten. The newscaster's voice insists. I have another hour at least before Mariángel wakes, but will not be able to sleep through the sounds of this man. I stand and walk and stop.

Another young woman has been raped, murdered, tossed into the desert. Isabel Teresa Otero Manrique, says the newscaster. She was found last night, a hundred yards from the road leading west to Paita. There is footage of her bruised and naked body as the police draw the tarp across.

She was last seen getting into a taxi yesterday evening, says the onsite reporter, though no one knows where she was headed. Eyewitnesses have been interviewed, and their stories conflict: one says the taxi was yellow and one says it was orange. Then another image fills the screen, a snapshot of the young woman at a party of some sort, her undiluted happiness, her hair long and black and straight and it is oh god it is Jenny, Jenny with black hair, Jenny before she dyed her hair blonde and she looks so very much and how am I seeing this only now impossible and oh very much like Pilar.

There is a sound, and I step to the television, turn it off. Karina asks me why I am awake. I say that I wanted juice, and ask if she turned the television on at some point. She looks at me as if she has not understood the question. She asks me what I was watching and I tell her the only possible truth:

- Nothing. It was nothing. The news. Nothing at all.

She rubs her eyes. I tell her to go back to bed and she nods again, asks me to bring her something to drink as well, turns and goes. In the refrigerator I find mango juice. I take her a glass, set it on the nightstand. I turn the television back on but the news has changed, something about Malaysia. There is nothing on the other channels and I walk, living room to dining room to living room to dining room, out into the back yard, the almond tree, around and around. Pilar and then Jenny: it is someone who knows and hates me, wishes to punish me, wishes to render me insane. I think place by place, Daly City Fallash Berkeley Irvine Piura. Around and around and surely I am disliked by many people but this makes no sense. Around. Around, around, stopping. Pilar then Jenny then Karina, and I run into the house up the hallway to my room and Karina is there in my bed, asleep.

I wait, listen to her breathing. I shut and lock the window, make sure the front door is locked, close and lock the rest of the doors and windows. The house, stifling, and the young woman killed last month, who was she?

Back out, around, back in. Nothing. To Mariángel's room and she is sleeping and to my room and Karina is sleeping and something is missing: the headboard, Sarita Colonia, gone.

I look under the bed, and there is nothing. I run my hand between the wall and the side of the bed, and nothing. I place my palm flat on Karina's chest softly enough not to wake her. The clock says six a.m.

To the telephone. Marucha answers, does not sound tired, says that her mother is getting dressed to come to my house. I say that I know, that I need to speak with her nonetheless.

- Yes? says Socorro.
- The picture of Sarita Colonia. Where is it?
- What?
- It was on my bed. Hanging from my headboard. A plastic card with Sarita Colonia's face. It is important and now it is gone.

Silence. Then a sigh, or something rubbing against something else.

- It was under the bed, she says. It was covered with dirt and dust. And there were teeth-marks, as though—
- What did you do with it?
- I'm sorry. I threw it out.
- When?
- Last week. Wednesday? Maybe Tuesday.

I thank her, hang up, go to the trashcan out by the lavadero. If it was Wednesday, the picture might still be here. The can is close to overflowing. I breathe through my mouth and root through rotten fruit, dead geckos, used toilet paper.

Nothing. I stand back, breathe deeply. I carry the can to the center of the yard. I empty it, spread the trash evenly across the grass and work the lawn as if it were a grid, imaginary square to imaginary square.

Still nothing. I start through the trash again, diagonally this time. Then Mariángel cries from her crib. I wait. The crying does not end. I begin gathering, refilling the can. A new picture is only a matter of returning to the market and this is all only superstition, preposterous thing, mummified father carried into the jungle but the old prayer comes to me entire, known somehow by heart.

426

# 38.

Out of the trees, into the sun, across the grass to a bench in sifting shade. I let my weight settle and place my briefcase beside me. My next class does not begin for twenty minutes. I take out a handkerchief, daub at the sweat on my face, have no business sitting, stand instead and walk.

Along the Administration building, and the river continues to fall: the wreckage of the Old Bridge is stark. In a week or two the water will be low enough to remove it and reinforce the other bridges. Vultures land on the banks, and there is greenery around them, and a trip to the Huaringas and skulls, gasoline or dagger or black bees, and how many stings would it take?

To the cafeteria, and turning toward the chapel. Zapote, charán, their leaves quivering in the light wind. Behind the chapel a trellis and bougainvillea blossoms falling around me, bright red, and the blossoms hiss as they slide along the cement.

Of course I walk back and forth to work now once again, checking the license plate of each car and other facets too are needed: we returned to the cinema last night, Karina and Mariángel and I. There were few mosquitoes and many fleas and the film we saw was *The Fifth Element*. I scanned all but ceaselessly and Karina pretended poorly not to notice.

Back toward Administration. It was claimed that Evil requires forty-eight hours to acclimate to conditions on Earth, and this is surely demonstrably false. There was a perfect being and for a moment she was naked and the cinema filled with camera flashes. There was blue bile and entrails but the curtain dropped before any credits were shown so I will never know the disemboweled diva's true name.

As we left the cinema Karina asked what plans I had made for Cajamarca. I said that the trip would have to be postponed, that I wanted her to spend all nights at my house from then on and refrain from taking taxis. She agreed but paused first to let me know she was lying and it is time. Across the parking lot. Right at the fork and she kissed me, said that her sisters needed help with their homework, walked away.

Office, materials, classroom. My students chat. I stand at the lectern and wait. They continue. Something has been lost. I rap sharply on the lectern. Still they chat. I pull a handful of coins from my pocket, sling them into the corner. Now the students look at me, all but two in the very back. I climb onto the lectern, and attempt to keep my balance as it splinters beneath me.

I stand, and stanch my bleeding thumb with an eraser. I will try again with Karina tonight and at last my students are silent. I tell them that something has come up, and explain what a useful phrasal verb that is, to come, and up. They look at one another. I say that some things have gone wrong. They agree. I ask if they have done their homework, and they nod, and I tell them I hope they are not lying. In fact they are not and the lexical preparation goes well and I send them off into a text on relaxing vacations.

Reynaldo has not yet seen *The Fifth Element* and looked unwell the last time we spoke—his hair dyed still lighter, his extra weight full in all directions. He was hours from leaving for his final try at a tourist visa. I asked what documents he was taking to present to the consul. His breathing rasped and guttered beneath the words: in addition to the old letters, he had paperwork showing that he has founded an agricultural consultancy, but he is its only employee and as yet has no clients.

Discussion extension consolidation and I let the students go as early as would be permissible if I had asked. Reynaldo should be back tomorrow with the news. Materials, office. Then the walk home for lunch, and as I pass through the university gate there is a glint in the far low sky. It grows slowly larger, brighter, closer, is nothing but a passenger jet drifting toward the airport.

The only flight that arrives at this time of day is from Iquitos, and I know what the passengers have seen: as the plane rose from the jungle the clouds below were not cotton-like or oceanic, but Arizona covered in snow, buttes and mesas and bluffs, unlimnable desert plain, all of it perfectly white. Half an hour later the clouds were replaced by the Andes flown not over but through, the peaks to either side, the masses of snow and rock edged translucently. Another half an hour and the desert is perhaps still threaded with green, or perhaps scabrous again, sick with mange.

In through my front door to find Mariángel lying on the couch, her head in Socorro's lap, Socorro working with tweezers deep in my daughter's nose, working gently, massaging to either side, my daughter frightened but quiet and at last it comes out: a small dead cockroach. Socorro drops it in a wastepaper basket, says that lunch is almost ready. I sit down at the table unable to imagine being hungry and suddenly am.

Mariángel and I are finishing our crema volteada when the telephone rings. Socorro answers, nods, says that it is for me, has said it tensely. I look at her. She shrugs, sets the receiver on the table beside me. I wait, and finally take it up. It is Pilar's mother. She says she is calling to thank me for not having interfered.

I say that I would never interfere, wonder what she means, and there is a short silence.

- Our trip went very smoothly, she says.

- Did it? I am very pleased.

- I was happy to see that you have been taking good care of the tomb.

Another silence, and two realizations, one mine and one hers, simultaneous: she saw Pilar's tomb when they traveled up yesterday to lay flowers, and it was not that I chose not to interfere at the cemetery but that I forgot Pilar's birthday altogether.

I call Socorro to take Mariángel to her room. The next few minutes are mainly screaming and static. I agree with everything Pilar's mother says, even when it is not words coming out of the phone but rage made sound. Then her voice is muffled and there is further shrieking but not at me and now it is Pilar's father on the line screaming, screaming, Pilar's death, and these other murders, I have done nothing to resolve anything and he is right and as penance I keep listening, keep listening, keep listening until he slams down the telephone, and even after, listening, the silence until it ends.

I wash my face and hands. Re-bandaging my thumb feels like ritual. There are three hours before my next class. I can do nothing for Jenny but perhaps Ms. Alina saw something the night she was killed, perhaps a taxi waiting, perhaps a driver, and perhaps she has seen his face before.

My shoes, my briefcase. Out, and at the corner of the house the hairless dog lies curled in a scrim of shade. Along, and the Virgin in her case on the corner, and I turn toward the river. Five short blocks, walking slowly but never stopping, then south and south and south.

At last the old green house. The plastic chairs are empty and one has been overturned. I knock, hear nothing, knock again and there are noises inside. I wait, knock yet again. The door opens. This man is neither of the two I have seen before. He is chewing something, and I wait for him to finish, and finally he does.

- I am here about Jenny, I say. I am so sorry for what happened, so very sorry. But there are things I need to know. Is the owner here?

The man says nothing, and closes the door. I try the handle but it is locked. I knock again, and still again, louder and louder each time. I speak quietly, less so, and the door swings open sharply and I step forward and would speak but standing in front of me is Jenny herself.

- Mr. Segovia, she says. We talked about reservations, yes?

I try again to speak and again fail.

- Also we are in the middle of lunch, she says. And I have appointments all afternoon. So could you come back this evening, calling first so as to make a reservation?

- Jenny.

- Yes?

- What's your real name?

- That is not information I share with my clients, Mr. Segovia.

- Isabel?

She looks at me, shakes her head.

- Teresa then. Is it Teresa?

- No, Mr. Segovia, it is not. And why is this of such sudden and great importance?

- I do not understand.

- Do not understand what? Why are you here, Mr. Segovia? If it's not—

- I wanted to apologize, I say. Do you remember? The

431

last time we—

- Of course I remember, and it does not matter. I told you that when it happened, and it was true, and again, why have you come?

- But also at El Torno that one afternoon. You—

- That is part of what happens when one has the job I have. It was unpleasant but not unexpected or uncommon.

- Well. Unpleasant, yes. And that is why I am here: to apologize.

- Thank you, Mr. Segovia. I accept, and I hope you will come again this evening, calling first so as to make a reservation.

I promise that I will. She thanks me and closes the door and I turn and walk and understand nothing. North and north. Someone else. Yes. Someone having nothing to do with me, yes. North and north and north, the sweat thick in my hair and clothes and nothing to do with me yes but perhaps still the same man who killed Pilar. Nothing to do with me, and Karina as safe or at risk as anyone else, but perhaps the same man, perhaps.

North, and two hours still before class. I slow my pace and check license plates more carefully. I scan the faces of men eating at an open lunch counter, men sitting on raised wooden chairs as their shoes are shined, men in line at a hardware store and Karina is suddenly beside me, sees me flinch, smiles too widely.

- Hello! she says.

I recover badly but lean forward to kiss her.

- Such a coincidence, she says.

- Where were you? I say.

- Can you believe it? she says.

- I cannot.

She laughs, says that she has been thinking about Cajamarca. She has decided, she says, that it can be next weekend rather than this one, but that we must not let it slide any further. Then she asks why I am letting my beard grow. I scratch at the stubble and say it is more that I am failing to shave.

- So, she says. Cajamarca, not this weekend but next?

There is a thick desperate normalcy in her voice and so I agree.

- Wonderful, she says. Also, do not feel like you ever need to lie to me about the things you see on the news very early in the morning. There are many things in this world to lie about but that is not one of them.

I agree to this too and she smiles. She says that she has an idea for tomorrow night, a fun but quiet idea, that she will call me as soon as she knows if it is feasible. I thank her, and thank her again.

North and north and to the Panamericana but not across it, not yet. Instead I circle back to my house. I have half an hour still, will change into clean clothes, will take Mariángel up and swing her as I always should and must and failed to today.

The park, the Virgin. The hairless dog has moved with the shade closer to my front door. It stands and stretches as I near, then growls and coils, leaps for my face and I swing my briefcase, catch the dog midair and it spins, lands badly, coils and leaps again but I am waiting, knock it against the side of my house, grab its back legs and swing, beat the dog against my doorframe again and again and again.

When I told Karina that I would not be able to join her and her sisters for Parcheesi she did not argue. When I told Socorro that she would be staying late she also did not argue. So: dark clothes and shoes. Mariángel is already asleep and Socorro sits at the kitchen table. I tell her that I will be back at some point and she nods without looking up.

First to the outdoor market. Many of the stalls are closed, those that copy keys and repair shoes, and others are closing, the men and women gathering their unsold fruit in crates, the smells of iron and mango and sewage thick around us. Still other stands have not yet begun to close. Their owners sit very still on small plastic chairs. I find a picture of Sarita Colonia in a plastic sheath, the same drawing I had before though this image is slightly smaller and lacks the pink carnation. Then I find a knife that sits well in my palm.

There are hundreds of bars in Piura and taxistas congregate at many of them. Fortunately most are small and over-lit and thus quickly searched. I start at the Plaza de Armas and work south. La Gaviota, El Castillo, The Yellow: these all can be scanned from the doorway, and nothing.

El Maremoto, El Palo, nothing. Karina keeps no images of saints and believes that her luck is good. I am careful never to ask for evidence. La Cuerda and nothing but then at Steben's Bar there appears to be something: a man the right age, the right size, his face not unfamiliar. He sits alone and watches others. I watch him watch and wait. He drinks slowly. When he goes to the restroom I take a table not far from his. He returns, sees me, and there is no recognition.

I stand and sit again, take out my knife, hold it under the table. Another man comes in the door, short and fat and amused at something he has seen. He goes to the thin man, shakes his hand, says something I do not catch, and both men laugh. He asks if the CREMPT job is finished, and of course, the thin man, I have seen him twice or three times, painting the outer walls of the asylum.

Back out to the street, and La Carroza is not far away but there are others to check first. Milenario, and nothing. Arantxa and Günther are not functioning as well as many might wish, and this morning I saw something else that has changed: the bird god's eyes. A matter of the paint as it cures perhaps but as if she knows something she did not know before.

Sol y Arena, nothing. Nothing at Tiene Cancha but the

smells of beer and cooking oil. At Mandinga I hear the taxista's voice again and it can only be his voice is precisely his voice the knife again out and lifted but the man is too young and has many friends and I end up walking quickly and then running, out and up and across and up and back. Now to La Carroza. The men at the door recognize me. They look at one another, part to allow me through.

I push up through the hallway to the patio. The lighting is bad and the dance floor is full and this will be half an hour of scanning at least. I buy a beer and begin the circle, along the bar and in front of the speakers. There are many faces that are close but none that are right.

Back to the bar and across toward the sofas and overstuffed chairs and I stop. Karina is sitting on a black loveseat, leaning against a man I do not know. Her eyes are closed. If I had to guess from his clothes and bearing I would say he owns houses on more than one continent.

I take a step, stop again as he stands to receive a pair of whiskeys from a waitress. He is taller than I am, broad at the shoulders and narrow elsewhere. He sits back down, hands a glass to Karina. Another step, the knife out. Karina takes his arm, says something and he smiles and I stop, turn, walk away. There will be other times and means and I must never confuse the two, never let them become confused. There are still hundreds of bars to check and the men at the door part again, nod as if they had known all along, show me to the street, the nightcloud sky.

# 39.

I BRING MY BACKPACK DOWN FROM THE TOP OF THE CABINET. It is covered with dust thick as flannel. I take up a wet rag, scrub the surfaces, swab the inner compartments. Then a hand towel, and this trip, unnecessary in all senses until I arrived home from walking the bars: it was not Socorro waiting but Karina.

Socks now, shirts. I accused her of having seen me as I turned to leave La Carroza. The confusion in her answer was genuine or seemed so. Pants and a belt and I asked about the tall rich man. A friend, she said. Of course, I said. A friend who gives good advice, she said, and she accused me of following her to the bar and I told her the truth.

She was silent, looking at me. Finally she shrugged. She had come to my house, she said, because she knew that I had been lying when I promised to go to Cajamarca, and she had wanted to turn that lie into truth. I asked if that was still what she desired. She hesitated, nodded, nodded again, and it was clear that I would lose her if I did not go.

So: Varón Gabai, bandana, and I do not know how it is that Karina believes a three-day trip will clean my mind of the murders, or by what means she believes it will do so. Perhaps she is less than hopeful but can think of no better option. The last thing she said before we fell asleep still dressed and stinking of alcohol and cigarettes and sweat was that she looked forward to taking care of Mariángel while I was in the archives and could the tall rich man also be a friend of Armando's?

The university today, unsteady, my examples splintering, cassettes uncued, the students astonished and angry at one point though I do not remember why and Mariángel walks in. She points at me, points at the window and laughs. She sits down in the middle of the floor, starts to hum, and in the afternoon Arantxa came, asked me to gather students for the final lecture of a visiting Slovenian anthropologist to whom no one wished to listen. Mariángel rolls back and forth from wall to wall. I told Arantxa that I sided with the students: potentially interesting but untidy thoughts expressed unintelligibly. She reminded me that she was giving me tomorrow off though I did not deserve it, and that I would therefore go gather.

Camera, tripod, collapsible lightbox. Half a dozen empty notebooks. Sunglasses, and for the first hour the man spoke on neurocognitive deficits in bonobos. Then for an hour he spoke on the opening bars of the second movement of Beethoven's Third, beating them out against the lectern with what looked to be a soup spoon. Then for an hour he possibly related the two and I am surely forgetting as many things as I am remembering.

Hat, sunblock. To the best of my knowledge Reynaldo has not been seen since he left for Lima. I called his aunt, and she too did not know where he was. The rich man, friend or not, and Karina calls from the kitchen, asks about relative densities of oatmeal. I turn and Socorro is standing at my bedroom door. She is simply watching, does not offer to help me pack, believes that I am wrong to take Mariángel on overnight buses and is surely correct.

- They actually do know their names!

Karina has been talking for twenty minutes with great ebullience. I have at times been listening, and look at her now. I nod, encourage her to continue, wonder who she is talking about and why knowing their own names is so surprising.

- It was Mariángel's favorite part of the day, she says.

She turns to my daughter, makes cattle noises, and of course: the cows from the documentary. Mariángel looks at me, and so I smile. Karina creates horns with her fingers, gores Mariángel, and Mariángel laughs and laughs.

- How was your time at the archive?

- Outstanding.

Abysmal. I had no business there. I read and reread and misread, hour after hour. I shot two rolls of documents I cannot imagine ever needing and this hotel is large and old and strange, half the hallways ending with false doors mounted on limestone walls.

Karina says she is very glad, suggests guinea pig for dinner. I am too hungry for so little meat but say nothing and we walk out into the night. Karina slips her arm through mine. Above us is a single cloud, its edges so bright that the moon must be hidden behind.

- Tomorrow morning we are going to see the hanging tombs, she says. In the afternoon I think I'll take her for a hike up around the petroglyphs, and those rock formations that look different each time you see them.

- Cumbemayo, beautiful, yes.

- When was the last time you were there?

- With Pilar.

- That is not what I meant.

I wait, but no clarification is offered.

- It's all right, Karina says.

But it is not and all I wish to do is sleep.

Another wasted day in the stacks but I stopped sooner and the sun is not yet down and we are walking: cobbled street, Mariángel on my shoulders, Karina holding my hand. They are both sunburned and tired and happy. A turn, and uphill to the Plaza de Armas. Karina and I both wheeze, light-headed in the thin air.

I set Mariángel on the ground and she walks carefully toward the fountain in the center. Karina sits on a bench, stares at the Cathedral, asks me who Amalia Puga was. I still do not know, and say so. She nods, says she is all but certain that Cajamarca has stores with utensils perfect for my mother's collection. Yes, I say, utensils with flanges and gears. Karina says she will be happy to buy one if I can give her a better idea of what is needed.

I tell her that I cannot. She shrugs, says I can search on my own. The light grays. We wait. There are several hundred topics on which we should be able to converse without effort. Still we wait. Clouds have gathered and are thickening.

Around the fountain there is a ring of small plants covered with tiny gold flowers and Mariángel bends, pulls one out by the roots. She shows it to us and I nod. She bends again, pulls out another. I should tell her to stop. We sit and wait and stare. She pulls out a third. I will crush the joints of his fingers first.

- What's wrong? says Karina.

- What?

- You flinched and made a face.

- Yes. I flinch at times, and every so often I make faces. It is nothing.

- I have never seen it before.

- Perhaps you have and do not remember.

- But why do you do it?

- If there was a reasonable answer to that question I would give it to you now.

Karina stands and walks to Mariángel. She kneels down, brushes the dirt from my daughter's hands. She replants the flowers and our bus to Piura leaves tomorrow afternoon. An early breakfast then, and the Belén complex: while I work Karina will show Mariángel the medical museum, the four-breasted women carved into the facade across the street, the polychrome—

Mariángel reaches up and rubs at Karina's eyes. Karina is crying, I see this now. Mariángel's hands leave thin streaks of mud down Karina's face and a sound comes, soft but rising, a sound I had thought I would not hear again for a time.

Twenty minutes more. The bus jolts across another pothole. The rains that began last night have not yet stopped. Mariángel screamed herself to sleep an hour ago, lies draped across my lap. I look at Karina. She stares out the mottled window.

- I'm sorry, I say.

- Yes, she says.

The rain grows harder, thrashes at the bus for a moment, relents. Karina continues not to look at me. I close my eyes. Quito still untaken. Alvarado commandeers ships in Nicaragua, sails south, lands on the coast of Ecuador and flows into the jungle: five hundred Spanish veterans and four thousand porters in chains.

He hangs two curacas, tortures hundreds of natives for information, bids his dogs disembowel them. Four months are lost before he even reaches the Andes—heat, rain, insects, disease. Armor rusting. Food all but gone and at last up into the mountains and now a monstrous earthquake. Climbs and climbs. Nears the final pass as winter brings snow and high winds.

By the time he has made his way down the far side to the Royal Road, he has lost eighty-six Spaniards, almost all of the horses, hundreds of porters. He turns north for Quito, then learns that he is too late: Benalcázar has already conquered it. Alvarado stands, wavers, still seven years from death and Piura at last.

Karina carries her knapsack to a taxi. I carry mine to another. She walks to me, the rain heavy in her hair. She puts her arms around my neck, says she hopes that soon, and I squeeze her tightly to keep her from finishing the sentence.

A slow ride through the flooded streets. Mariángel wakes as I push in through our front door. She struggles against me, strikes me in the face with her fists. I set her down, and she clutches at my knees and shrieks. I lift and hold her, dance, but the shrieking does not stop. To the kitchen for milk. An hour of singing and swaying. Not an earthquake, perhaps, and now she sleeps.

Midnight, and I would eat, would undress and shower, am too tired, to bed and cannot sleep. For hours the rain falls. Not an earthquake at all but a volcano: Mount Cotopaxi erupting above them, vast clouds of ash sweeping down. Voices at times threaded through the storm. Bells and flutes, voices, bells and tambourines, bells.

The doorbell. Still rain but a sense of morning. Knocking and I go. The door deadbolted. I do not remember locking it this way but must have and Socorro. She says that I do not look well. She asks if Mariángel is sick, says that she surely is. I say that she is not and hope to be telling the truth and Socorro stares at me, will not blink.

I turn, shower, dress. Look at the clock. Just past six— no reason for Socorro already to be here and I would ask why but do not care and have not yet planned my classes for today. If I stay here Socorro will stare and stare. I put apples and cheese and half a loaf of bread in a plastic bag, kiss Mariángel softly enough not to wake her, take my umbrella from the closet and slip out of the house.

The corner, the Virgin, soft rain. I stand for a moment. The drain is clogged with debris and reeks. The sound of the rain and a new sound, metallic, a grinding. I turn. Coming up is an old yellow taxi. The driver rolls down his window, brings the taxi to a stop beside me, smiles and lifts his eyebrows.

- Mister? he says.

I shake my head, and he shrugs and pulls away. I think of his eyes. They were known eyes, I believe. I think about his hair and the shape of his face. I look and the car is a Tico and I read the receding license plate, read it again, the first part covered by something dark but it ends with 22.

The taxi passes beneath the matacojudo trees, the remaining fruit ready too for him and I start to walk, more quickly, more quickly still and then running. The rain heavier and I drop my umbrella, my lungs and legs ache and I run, he slows at the corner, stops, waits, the rain still harder and the license plate now clean, the leaf or mud or litter washed away, closer, close enough to see and yes and yes, P and 22.

I call out but too late and he is making the turn, disappears. I arrive at the corner, slip on the pavement and fall hard, my face sharp against the curb. Back to my feet and he is waiting at the stoplight and I run, children and dogs moving out of my path, the light turns and he slides into the intersection and I will lose him unless, and he will, he does, he pulls into the Texaco station and stops at the pump.

Blood streams from my nose and I run, watch his brake lights, hope they will darken, hope he will want a full tank, reach the stoplight red again and I run out into the road, cars swerve and screech and already he is gliding oh motherfucker pulling away from the pump, swinging around and back onto the Panamericana. I watch him go. Another car just misses me.

It is a taxi as well, large and white and it slows, stops, backs toward me.

I enter and point. There is pain drilling in my head, my shoulder, my ankle. The other taxi reaches the river and turns along the malecón. We follow, and my nosebleed ceases. I ask the taxista to close in, tell him that I rode in the other taxi just moments ago, left an important book behind.

The driver nods, straightens his back and leans forward, accelerates. The rain has thinned. My shirt and pants are soaked with rain and sweat and blood. We parallel the river rising now again. A red light at Sánchez Cerro for both our taxi and his, but we slow too late for me to reach him. Green, a distance, and the current tears at what is left of the Old Bridge, the twisted beams, an ornate lamp sticking up from the surface.

Four more blocks, the Bolognesi Bridge, and here traffic sits thick. The other taxista is stopped several cars ahead, has his signal on, intends to cross the river. I pay, step out, push forward through the rain, and there is a policeman on the bridgehead. He holds up his hand to the cross-traffic, waves the cars on the malecón forward.

I begin to run and the old yellow taxi advances slowly and if there is any pause I will make it to his door, will open it and enter, will be only a passenger, will direct us out into the desert but there is no pause, the taxi swings onto the bridge and I stop, the light green at the far end of the bridge and I will not reach him in time. I jump through traffic to the curb and the white taxi nears again. He nods when he sees me, slows and there is a roar, a roar that fills my mind or the world, a scream and the policeman stumbles toward me, rolls and crawls and the bridge shudders, twists, an eruption of steel and cement and great white plumes of water and the bridge is gone.

Men and women stumble as they run. I am on the ground, do not remember falling. Blood pours again from my nose but there is no force now like that which lifts me. I walk onto the bridgehead. There are ten or twelve cars in the water. Within seconds they have disappeared beneath the surface.

A few of those who ran have returned. The policeman stands beside me, pulls off his boots and strips off his uniform, grabs my arm as though we are both to dive. I shake free, watch him fall flailing and right himself midair, watch him swim, strong firm strokes toward the river's center.

And I look across at the far bank. An old yellow Tico is stopped by the side of the road. Its emergency lights flash on and off. Its driver stands at his edge. I kneel, work through the policeman's clothes, find his holster, and it is empty.

# 40.

To the cafeteria, coffee, a table and its tablecloth, a week now and little clarity. I called the police to tell them what I saw and suspect. The officer thanked me and hung up. I called again two days later. The officer who answered this time sounded younger, believed that I was who I claimed to be, confirmed that Pilar's case is again open. I asked if the evidence gathered had survived El Niño. He paused, then said that I would be contacted as appropriate given the circumstances and the manner in which they evolved.

The pacazo cannot be seen and mocks me from the nearest tree. I sip and wait. The rain ended that evening, has not returned. The coffee is no more pleasant than usual and no one joins me. Instead the other professors come bearing their trays and look at me, look away and sit elsewhere. Surely they know, see it on me like stains or the scabs on my face, maintain a minimum distance and thus also from that of which I am a part though perhaps this is not what is happening and perhaps also this is how it always was or nearly so, coffee at a table alone.

Karina and I see one another most days and it is as

though something were suspended, particulate. A thousand Ecuadorian troops have been moved to the border. There was likely a Peruvian response but none has been reported and Fermín has come from Frías to visit his cousins in Catacaos. He spent yesterday afternoon with me and Mariángel, gave us the news: Casualidad strengthens each day. She is able to speak, and is eating well. She cannot yet walk but it will not be long.

Fermín asked if I had any work he might do. The tree is thick with leaves but none are falling, so we trimmed and weeded and watched the birds and geckos. I gave him two hundred soles for whatever might be needed, and wondered if he could tell just by looking.

I still have not seen Reynaldo, have not heard the news that is surely bad. I spoke this morning with Mireille and she could not tell me anything, called his aunt and she is no longer coherent: he was here and then was not and now is or possibly vice versa. I have ten minutes still until class starts. I walk out through the parking lot, left at the fork, the empty deer pen and now the lab.

Reynaldo will be back in a month or two, says a man I have never seen before. He hands me his card. It says he is a botanical chemist. I ask, and yes, he says, brought in from Arequipa on an emergency basis to teach my friend's courses for the rest of the semester and can tell me nothing more. I thank him, shake his hand, walk or jog to the department secretary.

- He was here two days ago but had to go right back down to Lima, she says.

- I don't understand.

- His sister is very sick. He asked for a leave of absence, but he'll be back after the break.

She seems very sad. I thank her and make my way out. Reynaldo never mentioned a sibling to me. Perhaps his visa came through but his trip was planned for the break and I understand nothing and my last students are waiting. They look exhausted.

I tell them that there are occasions when it is all right to be exhausted, when exhaustion is the only appropriate sensation. They do not even have the strength to agree or so it appears.

I put away my notes and ask if anyone has a story to tell. No one does. I ask if they would like to talk about imperialism and truth. This has often worked in the past but fails now. I say that in the future things will be clearer no matter how improbable that sounds. They nod exhaustedly. I say that today can be a free-writing day, any topic, any length, as long as their writing circles toward whatever matters most, and they nod again.

For ninety minutes I walk from desk to desk and answer occasional queries on tense and agreement. I murmur encouragingly at least once to each student. At the end I gather what they have written, and say that I will return the essays corrected on Friday, and we all know that this is a lie.

A young man sitting in back raises his hand. His name escapes me and I signal him while clearing my throat. He says that while he does not presume to speak for anyone else, he personally would prefer that just this once I not grade his writing at all, that today if only today his heart be known but not judged.

Under most other circumstances this would be a trick meant to hide a lack of preparation. I look around the room, ask if anyone else shares the proffered opinion. All do, and I agree but reserve the right to change my mind.

Out onto the path, its patches of deep darkness and lamplight interspersed. The Language Center, my office, my desk. The line at the photocopier is neither long nor short. I wait, and read Pachacuti Yamqui. Arantxa stops by, smiles at me from my doorway, appears on the verge of asking a question but then Günther arrives, kisses her on the cheek, throws his books in his locker and leads her out by the hand.

The machine is free, and still I wait. Puns and

pedagogical advice drift to me from the lounge. I read, wait, read. Two professors wave as they walk by, and two more, and a group of six.

Silence. A moment more to be certain, and yes, they have all gone home. I turn out the lights, walk back to the photocopier, lift the lid and bring the original flyer from its envelope. Months since I have held it. Pilar. Her wet hair glistening black. Her eyebrows, her mouth, and movement outside the far door.

I do not remember intending to leave the door open. I wait, watch. There is no further movement, nothing but the glow of the nearest lamp. I add paper, goldenrod, stolen from the resource bank. The green button, the bar of light sliding up and back, the smell of ink.

Back through the dark. I set the copies on my desk, bring a pack of thin transparent folders from my bottom drawer, slide a flyer into each; there will likely be no more rain but I have thought that before, must not be wrong again and Pilar. That afternoon at Yacila. The old woman walking up out of the waves, the men on their hands and knees, my carelessness and the stingray and that pain. Pilar holds my leg in her lap. She puts her mouth to my calf. She draws the poison from me and again the flicker at the door: someone or something is passing back and forth, silent but known by the shadow cast.

I bring the knife from my briefcase, open the blade, crouch and move quickly along the wall, closer and closer. A quiet sound from outside, as if something pulled slowly through sand. Three quick breaths and I jump through the doorway but my foot catches on the threshold and I fall out into the soft yellow light, slide on the concrete, grab up my knife, push to my feet and spin.

There is nothing. No person, no animal, no movement. I check around the near corner, and again nothing. I have scraped my palms and torn a hole in the knee of my pants and am fortunate not to have stabbed myself. I walk back into the Language Center, close the door behind me, turn on the lights.

I set the knife down on my desk. One gold sheet after another into its plastic folder, and I will not cannot will not look at the picture. My shirt is dense with sweat, and the night smells of jasmine, and then a sound, a scratching, a clawing at the door. I lift the knife and run and fling the door open.

It is Armando, standing on the stoop, laughing. There is no smell of alcohol but he stands at a slant. He shakes his head and walks past me, lists slightly to the right, enters my office and I follow.

- You are a clown, he says. A cojudo and a clown.

- You came to tell me this?

- I didn't come to tell you anything. I came to give you something. Something you do not deserve.

I agree and wonder what he means. He holds up a manila envelope, pulls out a thin sheaf of paper, slaps it down on top of the flyers.

- Alexis never misreads.

It is a single document, twelve pages long: a photocopy of a handwritten transcription of the notarial protocol of the will of Juan de Segovia.

- He only just now had time, says Armando. Several passages in the protocol were rather hard to make out. Others, as you will see, were very easy. They are also quite important to people like you and me.

I nod, scan quickly through. A wife, Magdalena Clara Coya, and the twins, Martín and Inés. The entirety of a vast fortune, or very nearly so. If the protocol is genuine, Armando's assessment of its worth is correct, and there is no reason for it not to be genuine aside from the fact that it is wholly and laughably implausible.

- Do you hear that sound, John? It is the sound of the paradigm shifting like tectonic plates, of your career rising like some new volcano.

- What I hear is some bastard scratching at the door and scaring me all but to death.

- What was the will doing in Jauja instead of Seville or Lima or at the very least Huancayo?

- That is what I tried to ask you the first time you mentioned it.

- Precisely. And why wasn't it found sooner? And in whose interest was it to prevent its execution?

I nod, take out my staple gun, make sure that it is loaded. For a moment Armando stares at me, and at the gun.

- I forgot, he says. These questions no longer interest you.

- That is not the case.

- Shall I take the will back? I know plenty of people who can make proper use of it.

He picks up the document, and sees the flyers beneath. He looks at Pilar's picture, reads the text. He sets the document back down, and puts the envelope beside it.

- We haven't talked since I got back from Cajamarca, I say. Lots of good work there. I meant to tell you.

- When did you go?

- The weekend before last.

He nods. Straightens. Leans across my desk to clap me on the shoulder, says that he is late and walks out into the lamplight. I call to him, ask what he is late for. He does not answer, is gone.

If it is possible for the body to expel a brain tumor and for a vast lake to appear in a desert then perhaps it is possible also for this will to read as it seems to. I put the copy of the protocol in one compartment of my briefcase, and load the flyers into another. I lock my office, turn out the lights.

-◦◦-

- We do not believe you, says Jhon.

- And yet is true, I say. I haven't been to Machu Picchu.

- It is impossible, says Jhon. You who love history and live in Peru. It is staying at a beach house but never going to the beach.

I stand by my lie and the class will not have it, their voices rising against me. At last the bell rings. With luck they will not now forget the present perfect simple in its negative form.

To my office, the walk to the gate, out and across the Panamericana. One license plate after another and nothing close. Along and along and a siren to the north, distant but closing. The smells of sweat and plumeria. Another siren, this time from the south. A third and now a fourth, all screaming toward me.

I check the low sky, see no smoke, walk more quickly all the same. At the corner I turn, and traffic is stopped all along the narrow street. I jog up the line of cars toward the park, the four sirens louder and ever louder and now I see them: dozens of blood-spattered bodies laid out on the grass.

There are perhaps fifteen people giving first aid, half of them doctors or nurses and half civilians, blood on their faces too as they move from victim to victim. I run, and an ambulance appears on the far side of the park, and behind it another. A third comes from the direction of Virgin and the fourth is caught behind me, cannot get past the stopped cars and as I reach the edge of the grass I hear someone laughing.

Closer. It is one of the victims: laughter spilling up through the layer of gauze stretched tightly across her face. I stop, and her nurse too is laughing, and I am close enough to see that the blood is too bright, is not real blood, and the injuries also are feigned.

I walk to the laughing nurse, ask what is happening, and this makes her laugh still harder. I ask the victim, who crosses her arms to show me that she is dead, then points to the next victim over, a young boy.

- Earthquake Simulation Day, he says.

And of course: Yungay, its consequences.

- But you are late, I say.

- What?

- The anniversary of Yungay was two days ago.

The boy knows nothing about that. I look at the nurse, and she shrugs. The cadaver is still laughing and I leave them there, the happy dead and happy living, the three successful ambulance crews and beyond them the crew that has failed.

At home Socorro is waiting at the door. Mariángel runs out past her, wishes for me to smell a raw potato. I take her up, smell it carefully and declare it approved, ask Socorro what is wrong.

- He came an hour ago, she says.

- Who?

- Mister Reynaldo.

- Reynaldo is in Lima.

- I do not know where he is now, but three hours ago he was here. He asked if you were home, and when I said that you were not he asked if he could go into your room. I thought that perhaps it would be a problem, but he is such a good friend of yours, and he asked again and again, and in the end I let him.

Socorro kneads the front of her apron, will not look at me.

- He said that you would understand.

- Would understand what?

- I don't know. He was looking though your desk. And he left you a note, I believe.

To my room and desk, and the top drawer is open. Socorro goes to my bed and brings me the note. It is written in English, and my classes with Reynaldo appear not to have been useless:

> They rejected me again and so I would lose the only thing I have won in my life. You offered to help me and this is what I ask you for: I hope you can give two weeks to me. That will be sufficient to see the universities. Please look in on my aunt if possible for you. I will see you in two weeks.

Look in on, an excellent phrasal verb, and the search is simple: he has taken my passport. Anger surges and fades. This is obviously what was to come, ragingly absurd and foolish, the two-week visit a miniscule reward for such a risk but there is no danger to me—even if the police were to stop me and ask for my papers, forty or fifty soles would work just as well.

Mariángel takes the note from my hand. She watches my expression as she chews at the corner, as she tears the paper into pieces, as she laughs and the telephone rings. Karina. Not this evening, she says, but tomorrow. And something new: the twins would like to play board games.

I hesitate, and Karina says, I know. But it is what they would like. It is what I would like too, she says. And I ask her what if anything we should bring.

I stand on the bank, stare out at what is left of the Bolognesi. Mariángel twists on my back, wishes also to see. I turn partway. The bridge could have been saved if reasonable measures had been taken. The water has dropped several feet since that final storm. A hundred yards downriver there is a pulsing square of green: the roof of a car that was on the bridge when it fell. Each day a bit more of the car comes into view. It is caught in a web of rebar, perhaps from the bridge, perhaps from a warehouse that slid into the river last month.

I stare, and there is no longer any reason to be here, and thus we circle, widely and then less so. License plate after license plate. A bar and no one similar, a sandwich stand and nothing, another bar and license plates and today my students became brilliant once again. Together we flowed through lessons on noun collocation and superlative adjectives, on phobias and diphthongs, on perfect infinitives and ways to request clarification and Mariángel holds my sideburns one in each fist, pulls left and right and left.

Another bar, and nothing. Last night the government announced the creation of a new fund, two billion soles to help the country recover from El Niño. Piura's portion will arrive in August, said the spokesman, and even the few people who believe this know that they shouldn't.

This morning Socorro said that she was no longer willing to work in a house whose walls are losing their paint in great ragged swaths. I suggested that she take charge of arranging for the house to be repainted, expected her to decline, but an hour later she called me at the office. The men had come, she said, had brought the highest quality paint available in Piura, ranges of whites and blues, and did I trust her to choose each tone?

A growl at my ear: Mariángel playing jaguars. I growl in return and she hisses and if the original will was not simply lost, new questions rise. Juan de Segovia's children, yes, Martín and Inés. Inés—a common name now, but in Peru in 1533 there are only two. One is Inés Muñoz, the wife of Martín de Alcántara—half-brother of Francisco Pizarro. Her two young children had died on the voyage over. She arrived in Cajamarca while Atahualpa was still alive, ran the Pizarro compound alone at first, and then with Quispe Sisa, an Inca princess in her middle teens, sister of Atahualpa, given to Pizarro as a gift and baptized into the Christian name Inés Huaylas Yupanqui—the other Inés.

Pizarro never took her as his legal wife and ignored her in his will but gave fortunes to the daughter and son she bore him. I am clawed down the side of the face, claw back and if the date on the will is correct, Juan de Segovia's twins were born before either of Pizarro's children. They were named after Pizarro's half-brother and his wife. And in a matter of months Segovia was dead, his fortune was confiscated, and his wife and children disappeared from history, perhaps dead as well.

Or Pizarro had nothing to do with it, and instead it was some other veteran likewise in love with Magdalena Clara Coya. Or some royal secretary or accountant looking for a percentage of the fortune seized. Or some soldier too recently arrived to have shared in the wealth of Cajamarca and Cuzco, who thought he would be putting the fortune back into play.

And in whichever case, was Segovia murdered or was his will simply destroyed? Was the protocol purposefully hidden, and if so by whom, and did they wish to suppress or to save it? Each possible answer seeds a dozen new questions and we have arrived only ten minutes earlier than invited.

Karina's aunt opens the door. I draw the two bottles of Inca Kola we have brought from the sides of the baby carrier, hand them to her and she nods. She knows of the trips to Ecuador and Cajamarca, surely disapproves and yet smiles. She touches the top of Mariángel's head, and the top of my head too, reaching well up to do so.

Things have altered for the better between her and me, though not as a result of communication: she is not a person to whom one speaks as such. Perhaps her earlier worry was a function of Karina's past men, or of her father. Perhaps the aunt believes that unlike them I am a good man, or might one day grow to be.

There are three rounds of Inca Kola as we discuss the surviving toads. Then we move to the evening's central topic. For fifteen minutes they argue, Karina's brother and sisters, about the relative strengths and weaknesses of the many board games in their closet. The aunt's suggestion that we play Charades instead is accidentally laughed down and she decides to watch television instead. Another round of Inca Kola, and at last what appears to be a compromise, a game called Remolino.

The board is brought, is opened on the table, and the rules are explained but not such that I am able to understand them. Both of Karina's sisters wish to use the orange marker. Mariángel steals a miniature wheelbarrow, and it is some time before we are able to convince her to exchange it for a cracker.

In the midst of this I see Karina watching me. She is smiling fully, a sort of hope or grace. Or an offering, perhaps— one kind of life. Or only happiness, and the orange marker dispute is resolved with a coin toss. Noelia wins, and Alejandra chooses scarlet instead. Then there is a sound I know. Not a sound but a tone, from the television. I listen. I stand and go.

There is the sense of others following, Karina or her brother or sisters, and the newscaster gives pictures: the road leading east toward Chulucanas, the pullout where the body was found, the blood and nakedness. A snapshot of the victim, the long straight black hair, the smile—no one I recognize, and so much like Pilar. There is also a sketch, the driver of the taxi into which she was last seen climbing, and I have seen him, I see him daily, he is every taxista, every shopkeeper, every janitor, his thin dark face dark eyes dark hair. He is every cook every plumber every passenger on every bus and my eyes, the differences, the woman's face again.

- This is what I was talking about, says Karina's aunt. This is exactly what I was saying.

I look at the aunt and the newscaster speaks: Beatriz Silvana Cordero Huarcay was on her way to the market. Her parents are interviewed at their home in Castilla. They plead for justice to be made manifest, plead with precisely the degree of desperation one would expect, plead until the father's voice fails, and there are other children, siblings or cousins or neighbors and they watch the mother, how her face dissolves.

The scene changes and there is a gang of some sort but these men are too old for any gang. For a time they all shout at the camera, and their ideas are not clear. At last all but one cease their shouting. This has gone on too long, he says. There have been too many dead women, and nothing is ever resolved. We will resolve this. We are the Resolvers.

They all begin shouting about the act of resolution. Then a roar builds from somewhere unseen, louder and louder until their shouts cannot be heard, a scream and now a passenger jet drops into the frame just beyond them. It floats lower, lower. There is the screech of wheels on tarmac.

A last picture of Beatriz, and Karina is staring at me. I most likely smile. Finding Mariángel is not easy, through the halls and each thin room and she is not here, she is gone, I call and the sisters come running, Mariángel held between them.

- We were just fixing her hair, Alejandra says.
- We're sorry, Noelia says.

I put my hands over Karina's ears and kiss her. I thank her sisters and say we will play board games together another time, take Mariángel into my arms. I walk out and hear no doors close, and taxis are passing, and other cars, and I will follow them, follow them all. The bird god knew, this is the thing that she knew, and she is the god of vengeance; Sarita Colonia, perhaps she knew as well. I will follow them all but following alone means nothing and I set the dogs upon him, watch as they rip into his flesh.

# 41.

AGAIN THE BUS BUT ALONE, AGAIN THE RIVER BUT NOW continuing east, only half an hour away if the reports were correct and the World Cup begins in three days. Many of my students wish to discuss nothing else. I am expected to have strong opinions about the United States' team and its chances, sometimes pretend to have them, and for class we watch films picked at random from the video library.

The Andes, clearer and clearer as we near. Not a hawk but litter. All license plates seen since the fall of the bridge have been wrong, but insofar as the story is true, Sarita Colonia will help. She must. It is her job to help, or would be, and I returned to the market, bought a new galvanized tub, keep it locked for now in my closet.

A dead cat on the side of the road and crows tearing at its abdomen. I wish I had kept the corpse of the hairless dog, as perhaps it truly is some sort of cure. Prayers, prayers. Certainty, yes, in all its many forms, but I do not know how this is to be accomplished.

Socorro no longer works on Sundays and my house still

stinks of paint so Mariángel is at Karina's. I dropped her off with something that appears to be a lavender toolbox but is in fact filled with materials for decorating one's hair. The twins were delighted. Karina shrugged, said they would all be fine and a hundred yards ahead there is a police car on the side of the road.

Fifty yards farther on are two more police cars, and a section of highway shoulder that is now a parking lot. It has been four days since Beatriz Silvana Cordero Huarcay entered a given taxi. I had thought the scene would be empty or nearly so, thought it a plenitude of caution to dress the way reporters dress on television, to have brought a clipboard, but all these cars and beyond them dozens of persons, some uniformed and others not. My knapsack, my camera, a pen tucked into each pocket. I make my way up the aisle and ask the driver to stop. He asks why. I look at him. The bus stops. It is a quarter of a mile back to the relevant patch of desert. By the time I reach it my clothes are thick with sweat.

A slow first circle. Oreja de león, the tracks of a chanto, and if I approach the police here they will send me away. Angolo, palo verde, and no shreds of cloth. No paper scraps, no bloodstains. Nothing, and nothing.

I approach the shortest reporter, lift my clipboard, ask if he has heard anything new. The man looks at me. He scratches the side of his face, tells me he's too busy for chitchat. I apologize, edge away and on to the next. This man is old and stooped, and I stoop as well. He asks which paper I am with.

- *El Mercurio*, I say, and do my best to look Chilean.

He tilts his head to one side.

- Santiago or Valparaíso?

- Santiago.

- I was just talking to Yáñez. How come they sent two of you?

- Who?

The man's eyes scan my shirt, and then he smiles.

- Okay, friend, he says. Okay.

He walks away. In the middle distance another man looks up. Yáñez, surely Yáñez. Already a failure, and many-colored: the credentials I lack, the information, my shoddy attempt at the accent.

Another circle, wider. No flecks of paint, no plastic shards, no tooled wood in any form. Perhaps it is only that I am out of practice but nothing and nothing and the pointless clarity of the air, the sharp gray lines of the Andes, they would have saved Pilar but were no help to Beatriz.

Back toward the highway, and another reporter. I smile, ask if she has come across anything of interest. She looks at me and walks away.

- Stupid bitch, says someone behind me.

I turn. Yet another reporter. He does not look abnormal, shakes his head, and so do I.

- I fucking hate that fucking bitch, he says.

- No shit, I say. She's the stupidest fucking cunt I ever met.

I go and stand beside him. He is staring at a candelabra, sketching its thorns. I nod and jot what will seem to him to be notes.

- Too bad about those footprints, he says.

I agree, say that I wish it had been otherwise.

- So it goes, he says. Maybe they'll get lucky, find some more.

- Here's hoping, I say.

He looks at me, keeps looking, the wrong amount. I frown at the candelabra thorns, squint at his drawing, shrug. He is still looking at me. I frown again, ask if he has heard any projections as regards the perpetrator's mindset.

- Who are you? he says.

I do not know the names of any more newspapers in

Chile and am on the verge of telling him the truth but even to me it would sound unlikely and suddenly I am sure: he believes that I am the murderer, here to revisit the scene. I nod, turn, walk away. Ten steps along I look back and he is approaching the nearest policeman. I step into a thicket of some plant whose name Reynaldo never taught me, the thorns pull and I hear footsteps, push through the bracken and the thorns catch and hold and I push harder, into a clearing and beyond it is a wall of apuntia through which they will not follow, the heavy swaying around me and the spines scratch and tear but do not drive in except one and another and now I stand and hear nothing. Blood drips from my forehead into my eyes. The spines in the flesh of my arm and they ache and I squeeze at them and prod and they will not come out but at home there are pliers and knives.

Then a thought. It may be a time before I can search here unhindered, but I know somewhere else. The clues there will be old but unsullied. Abominable thought, horrific, possible though I do not yet know how, and help will be needed. I crouch, find five stones, set the four largest in a tight square and the fifth on top: if nothing else a cairn for Beatriz Silvana Cordero Huarcay.

Lunch done and salve on my scrapes and I kiss Mariángel and go but Fermín is on the front steps. His bicycle is cleaner than seems feasible. He is already speaking of Casualidad, of a telephone call and further healing but this is not a day for Fermín. I tell him that I am very pleased for whatever the news might be and give him fifty soles.

The walk, and nothing, and nothing, and Arantxa is waiting. There are so many reasons why she might be but I do not ask, instead follow to her office. I sit down and she looks at the top of her desk and moves several papers from one side of it to the other and frowns and moves them back. She opens her mouth and then closes it, twice. She says that in an hour there will be an emergency staff meeting, that I am in charge of finding a free classroom and gathering all available professors.

Under other circumstances I would ask for additional details. Today I comply, or attempt to. Only a third of the evening-shift professors can be bullied into coming in early, but the coordinators agree to go, and the room Eugenia assigns me is small enough to seem full even with these pallid numbers.

The emergency meeting begins. Its topic is film. Arantxa has brought guidance sheets and photocopies. Beginning today, she says, all professors intending to teach lessons entailing the use of film must hand in their Video Lesson Plan Objective Sheet and three Video Lesson Exercise Templates no fewer than twenty-four hours in advance. She does not look at me as she says this. Instead she hands out a Sample Video Lesson Plan Objective Sheet and three Sample Video Lesson Exercise Templates for our future reference. Then she asks if there are any questions and does not wait to hear them.

Furthermore, she says. Furthermore, every video in the video library has been assigned a level corresponding to one of our course levels, and no video may be used at any level other than its own. Furthermore, when checking out a video, one must first sign the Video Registry. Furthermore, videos may be kept out for a maximum of forty-eight hours. Furthermore, Spanish subtitles may no longer be used at any point in any capacity. Furthermore, all illegally copied videos have been removed from the video library, and no illegally copied videos may henceforth be introduced.

It is unlike Arantxa to lean so heavily on any given conjunctive adverb. She stares at us as if about to ask for questions once again, but asks for nothing. Furthermore, she says. But there is nothing more to say. She tells us to get back to work and walks out the door.

This meeting might instead have been a confrontation, was thus a gift of sorts from Arantxa to me. To the cafeteria, and a slow coffee. Out and along the path but then quick movement underfoot and the crunch of small bones crushed.

I lift my foot. Underneath is a lizard, dead. It is three inches long, with thin brown and black stripes down its sides— the smallest species on campus and harmless to the best of my knowledge. I have never been so close to one before and there is nothing less likely than this death, not given their speed and agility, so there is hope, always hope, always.

Into class. My students ask why I am smiling but telling them would not help. The new video policies can have no bearing on a lesson planned before they existed and so I feed the cassette into the VCR. I stand back and wait. The video does not play. The cassette has snagged somehow.

I fiddle and nudge and nothing and now there is knocking at the door: Dr. Macalupú, head of the chemistry department. I ask him to what I should attribute this interruption. He looks at my students, at the floor, asks if I know Reynaldo's address in Lima. I tell him that I know nothing. My students smile at the phrase. Dr. Macalupú stares at me, thanks me, thanks my students, apologizes and exits.

The cassette will not play or eject regardless of the buttons I push or the order in which I push them. I turn the VCR off and tell my students to write an essay on the failings of technology, an essay of any length and style. My students are no longer smiling but nod or appear to.

The Cup, begun. Shouting from everywhere, at times joyful and at times less so. My friends now root for South American teams they hated months ago, cheer Brazil's victory over Scotland and Chile's tie with Italy and tonight Karina has come to my house to talk but there is another, more urgent need: the fair, I say.

Karina had not heard that the fair was in town. I tell her that it opens tonight, that it will have all the foods one expects at a fair, and the rides one expects, and the games of skill and chance. Many or most of the taxis in Piura will at some point pass the entrance, and I do not add this information.

She sits down beside me on the couch, says she does not wish to go. I tell her that the candied apples and corndogs of the Lake County Fair were the highest of high points each summer in Fallash. She does not believe me though it is nearly true. I tell her that taking one's girlfriend to the fair is simply what is done and she laughs too sharply, somehow knows that I never took anyone. She pats my hand, speaks of dust and noise, of crowds and sweat. I stand and tell her that it will be very enjoyable and that I would welcome her company and that I am leaving.

I go to the kitchen. Socorro is gathering her belongings. I remind her that she agreed to stay late. She pauses, sets her purse down, walks to Mariángel's room without looking back.

I wait for a moment at the front door, but hear nothing. I step to the street and stop the first taxi that comes by. The driver is young and broad-shouldered. Then Karina is beside me, looks at me and shrugs, takes my arm.

It is a moment before I understand that she has guessed what I mean to do, has decided to come regardless, is now part of the search. A great sad angry evil happiness surges in my chest. I was not aware of wanting this but oh how I clearly did and do.

In ten minutes she knows as little as I can usefully tell her and the traffic is no longer moving though we are still three blocks away. We walk, and the final block is packed four deep with taxis. We check all likely plates and I scan each face.

The honking, it never ceases, becomes symphonic.

As we near the entrance, Karina stumbles. I help her to stand. The exhaust fumes, so thick here, the heat, and I carry her to the gates. She laughs as I set her down, thanks me, says that she is fine and she is lying and there is work to be done inside.

The crowds are very thick as is the dust. I buy candied apples and again we stand, we eat and watch, we eat. Karina smiles at the taste, nods. Again we walk, and there are many rides, far more than I had thought. We walk from one to the next and I scan the faces of all the men in line.

When the first circle is complete we start another. Then a face almost perfectly right. The man is in line for the Ferris Wheel. I come closer, closer. He has his arm around a young woman's waist. Now he sees me, steps toward me, asks why I am staring. His voice is impossibly high-pitched. I nod, thank him, pull Karina past him and away.

A moment later her hand goes limp in mine. I turn, and she is looking at the ground. It is not sickness but sadness, I believe. I check the rides around us, and there is one, an immense metal disk, that appears to be sufficiently solid for someone of my height and weight.

I buy our tickets, and the line is not long. When our turn comes we climb the stairs to the platform, step onto the disk, sit down and hold to the railing though there is not yet any movement beneath us. Others climb on as well. They are mostly young girls talking very loudly.

When the railing is half-lined with people the door closes, becomes simply more railing, and the ride begins slowly, accelerating, spinning and the young girls laugh and shout. The disk tilts as it spins and I do what I can to hold on and the air is edged with laughter that slips toward shrieks, toward screams. There is faster spinning and faster and no laughter now, the tilting and spinning and shaking, and a girl across the disk is the first to fail, let go, tumble to the center of the disk and there one might stand if one were young and agile and strong but she is only young, strives to her feet and falls and rolls back into her friends, hits their legs and they fall as well, are swept to the center and the disk spins still harder, the twisting and spinning and tilting now violent and I think of nothing but holding to the rail, willing it not to break. The screams spin and twist and tilt and there is only the need to hold, to hold, and at last the disk begins to slow.

For a time we must sit on a bench, Karina and I. It is difficult to believe that the railing held in spite of me. When we can stand and walk we buy more candied apples, and then cannot eat them, want to but cannot.

Another circle. No faces I need to check twice. Little or no difference in smell between this fair and that of Lake County. A third circle, and there are no other rides I trust so instead at Karina's urging we try the games: three of skill, two of chance.

I work through twenty soles attempting to win a stuffed animal of any type or size. At last she takes the squirt gun from my hand. She wins the next horse race, chooses a Tasmanian Devil and looks at me, hoping. I lift it happily. I say that it is time.

She nods, looks down and perhaps I am losing her. I put my arm around her heavily. She accepts it and perhaps I am not losing her. Outside the fair again we stand and look together, the taxis, the license plates, there are hundreds, they come and go and we watch, each one, carefully.

# 42.

Black.
A slithering of armor down a hill.
Now slowly black again.

# 43.

ALONG THE DARK PATH AND GERMANY DEFEATED THE UNITED States. I was forced to feign sadness and rage and this was a very simple thing to do and the bird god must be taken into greater account. She knew, after all. I ask her about certainty and clarity, about their aspect and appearance, and she has answers but will not share them.

To the front gate, out and along, the gas station for a time. Then walking. Thickets of rebar rising from certain roofs. Karina left several messages and I would have answered them but there are too many ways tonight might go. Mexico at some point beat Korea and a mototaxi flashes its headlight. I had intended to walk. Perhaps it makes no difference.

I give the driver an address not far from where I wish to start looking. He squints at me, says that the roads are still very bad. I wait. He says nothing. I tell him that I will arrive whether he takes me or not. He nods, I climb in, and ideas come, spin and tilt and tremble, handcuffs and blowtorch, handcuffs and hammer and chisel, plastic bag. Plastic bag and coat hanger. Plastic bag and coat hanger and ax.

We jolt across a pothole and the driver swears, begs my pardon. I tell him that there is no problem though this cannot possibly be true. Colombia lost to Romania and something else is happening, something known and predicted and yet the newscasters pretend to be surprised: for two days there has been fighting in Marseille, young men from Germany and France breaking bottles over one another's heads. Elsewhere there are other alignments. In Lima young men in Argentine uniforms fight young men in English uniforms, and all the young men are Peruvian.

Slowly across the bridge, and in the dim gray light on the banks are massive tractors and cranes brought at last to reinforce the columns. Farther downriver I have seen still larger cranes removing what has fallen. To and past the Mobil station where no one now sits and watches and throws. Turning and south along the avenue, past the stadium and into Castilla, that old kingdom, those riches, this dust.

The mototaxi sways hard with my weight, nearly topples when a streetdog rushes us and the driver swerves. Past the airport entrance. A few hundred yards farther on we leave the avenue and curl along the barb-wire fence that separates the runway from a dark mass of houses. Slower, and still slower.

The houses, their tin roofs and adobe walls, a lightless corner, and here the mototaxi stops. The driver asks if this is where I meant. I nod, step down and pay, and he wheels the mototaxi around.

When he has gone, I find the street that most nearly aligns with the runway and knock at the closest door. No one answers. Up the street and knocking at the next door, and again there is no answer though I can hear children crying inside. Voices respond at the next four houses but none of the doors open; four times I am told that I am at the wrong address, four times ignored when I ask for directions to the right one.

Across to the next block, another door, and no answer.

Another, and the wrong address. Another, and the woman who calls through the door says that she has no idea what I mean. I am halfway to the next house when I hear her voice again. I turn, and her door is open, and she is pointing back down the street.

- Turn right at the corner, she says. You'll see a light. Walk another block and ask again.

Before I can answer she has closed the door. I walk as she directed. In the middle of the first block is the light she mentioned, a single working streetlight. Standing beneath it are half a dozen young men.

The circle opens as I approach. The men nod to one another and smile. I walk directly to the largest of them, say that there is no reason to smile. He does not stop smiling, is not afraid of me at all. Another asks why I have come to a place in which I so clearly do not belong. The question was meant for his friends, but I am the one who answers: In my entire life, I have never belonged anywhere so well.

His laugh sounds like razors and rust. I answer again, tell the truth this time, and ask if he can help. This is not a response they were expecting. They look at one another. Finally the largest says he will take me, and the others look away.

The sidewalks are shattered here, the walls almost bare of paint. Three blocks along the man pauses at a corner, turns down a darker side street, and I follow. From there he takes me up a still darker alley, and points at a massive hole cut into the wall.

No light whatsoever comes out through it. I look at the man, and he shrugs, precedes me in. I follow the sound of him, stumble on a stone but do not fall. Along the side of a building. A corner, and we turn, have reached some sort of courtyard.

At its center is a table. Ten or twelve people are seated around it, a few of them arguing quietly, the rest listening. Beyond them is a door, and the light mounted above it is very bright.

- Here you are, says my guide. These are the Resolvers.

Everyone at the table turns and stares. All of them are men, most my age or nearly so, but at least one is quite old, and there are a few who look to be in high school. I approach, say hello, and no one answers. I say that I have come to help. Still there is no answer. A half dozen more men come out the door, and another adolescent, and five young boys. Now the oldest man stands from his position at the head of the table. He appears to be in his seventies. He thanks me for coming, says that my help is neither needed or desired, says that I may go.

   - All right, I say. Catch him on your own then. It should not be too hard, because you have seen his face, correct? Some of you? At least one of you? No?

   - Each and every one of us, says the old man.

He holds up a drawing. I walk to the table. He will not let me take the piece of paper in my hands but lays it flat on the table that I might see. It is a photocopy of the police sketch of the taxista who opened his door for Beatriz Silvana Cordero Huarcay.

   I nod, congratulate the old man, ask him where he got it. He does not answer. I say that it is true, that the murderer looks much like this sketch. Everyone at the table nods. It is also true, I say, that there are many men in Piura who look like this sketch. But that does not matter, I say, because you have also seen him in person, yes? A few of you, at least?

   - No, says another, and neither have you.

   - But I have. And I have heard his voice. And I know part of the license plate of his taxi.

   Silence for a time. The old man asks me to stand against the far wall. I wait while they converse. At last I am beckoned back.

   - Welcome, says the old man. From now on, your name is Santiago.

In eight more minutes my students will have finished their essays and I will gather the papers and go. I walk up and down the aisles, pause at each desk, pretend to read through each text and be pleased. It has been some time since minutes took so long to pass.

This will be my fourth night in Castilla and very early this morning there was noise at my front door, knocking, Karina, drunk. I let her in and attempted to listen. She asked if I had lost my north. I said that nothing was out of the question. She said that she knows what I am feeling and this is not possible: I am feeling nothing, which is one of many essential tricks, I suspect. She shouted things about me, about her father and Italy and the green man, and finally left.

Brazil destroyed Morocco and Chile tied Austria and a French policeman is in a coma. He tried to break up a fight between one group of Germans and another, it is said, and his skull was crushed. There is talk of skinheads and cell phones and that first night we sat in the courtyard for hours. The air smelled of scrap iron and sweat. The old man's name is Segismundo. He called for another chair to be brought, and another glass, and we drank chicha de jora—all of us, even I myself—and poured the last drops of each glassful into the dirt.

Three more minutes and I continue to walk the aisles but cease pretending to read. The Resolvers are less absurd than I had thought. Some are very sad, and others are very angry, and a few are both. One or two have lost hope. I do not know why they still come.

Also there are a few who are damaged. One is middle-aged and short and fat, and I believe he is the burglar who came over my wall. There in the courtyard we stared at one another, decided as if with one mind to act as though we had never met before, and perhaps it was true. He came to sit beside me, and said that his name was Félix. He spoke to me of the taxista, of ice picks, of mop handles and battery acid and I smiled, but then Segismundo called to us, asked us to focus on what was at hand, the logistics so much like my own, the searching of bars and murder sites, the posting of flyers.

At last the bell. I walk not to my office but directly to the gate. Several taxis pass by, and I wait for a mototaxi instead, take it to the airport entrance as if headed out on business, and walk from there. It is the best way, I am convinced.

Today Mireille came to the Language Center and before she could ask I informed her that I had no possible way of knowing but would notify her immediately should there be any need. English fans attacked a reporter in Toulouse and the reporter, too, was English. The fans thought he had given them a bad name. They hurled him against a concrete pylon and broke his collarbone.

I suspect that tonight we will search in Miraflores and the Resolvers are split nearly evenly between those who knew the second recent victim and those who knew the third. Segismundo has contacted the family of the first as well. They wanted nothing to do with us, want nothing to do with anything, and this will make the evening simpler for me if no one else.

The stadium, the airport gate, walking along and in. The streetlight and young men. The side street and alley, the hole. Men call to me as I enter, know me by my size.

Miraflores, says Segismundo, and several of us nod, those who guessed correctly. This new project began last night: taxi by taxi until we find him. Segismundo reminds us each of our roles. Then there is discussion as to whether my license plate information should still be considered central. Most believe that the taxista will have changed taxis, perhaps changes them after each kill, that the man's face and voice are our best evidence. Others are certain that if we find the taxi pertaining to the earliest known murder, we will have begun climbing a chain that will lead us to the murderer though we cannot yet estimate its length.

Segismundo says that there is no reason not to consider faces and license plates simultaneously. The others stand from the table. I ask if I may speak briefly on a separate topic. Segismundo settles back into his chair and everyone else sits down, because I have seen the Face, because I have heard the Voice.

- I am very much in favor of this latest endeavor, I say. I have high hopes for its success. But there are other projects that could be undertaken as well.

I wait for them to nod, and now they do.

- Let us go to San Teodoro, I say.

The two youngest boys nod and smile. No one else reacts in any way.

- Daniela Rocío Espinoza Farfán, I say. The first of the recent victims.

- What about her? says Segismundo.

- Do you remember? Her family seized the body before the police could finish their autopsy. She was buried without anyone ever—

- No, says Segismundo.

- But—

- She has been buried and it is done. We will not be party to desecration.

- We could—

- If you wish to be one of us you will refrain from insisting any further.

I look around the table. No one meets my eyes, not even Félix. I nod, thank them all for listening, say that in that case let us proceed with Segismundo's plan for the taxistas, and perhaps we will discuss the cemetery again some other time.

We stand, walk out and along and north into Miraflores,

spread ourselves along the roadway and begin stopping taxis. Most often a glance at the face is enough and we let them go. In some cases they attempt to pull away before we have seen them properly, but already Resolvers are standing against the hood, against the trunk, against the side doors. Every so often there is one who resembles the sketch. We ask him to step out into the light such as it is, and if he refuses, I reach in.

We have been searching this way for an hour when I notice that the two youngest boys are perpetually close on my heels. The three of us stand on the curb and await the next taxi. I look at them and they look at me. I nod and they nod back and I ask for their names.

- The Resolvers call us Three and Four, says the taller boy, but our real names are Iván and Ciro.

I ask which is which and they point to show me. The shorter boy, Ciro, says that he is nine and Iván is eight, that they are Segismundo's grandsons, that they live with him in the house where we meet. I say that it is a pleasure to make their acquaintances.

- You don't recognize us, do you, says Ciro.

I look again. They are as familiar and unfamiliar to me as anyone else their age. I ask where they have seen me before.

- San Teodoro, says Iván.

I look once more, and remember.

- You carried flowers for me on the Day of the Dead.

- We would have helped you arrange them as well, but you didn't want us to.

- From now on, I say, you will carry and then arrange, and I will pay you double.

The boys agree. A taxi comes, stops when I wave, and the driver weighs perhaps two hundred pounds. I apologize, say that instead we will walk. The driver shakes his head and pulls away.

- And do you also work on the bamboo ladders,

cleaning tombs?

- Not yet, says Ciro. The older boys won't let us.

- Do you think you are strong enough to carry one of those ladders? The two of you, together?

- Of course. They are very light. And even if they were not, we are very strong.

I look at Iván. He nods. Another taxi, and the driver is in his fifties.

- Where do they keep those ladders when they're not being used?

- There's a shed behind the chapel, says Ciro.

- All right. How would you like to do a little secret ladder work tomorrow night? The murderer left clues in the cemetery and I need to find them. It will only take two or three hours. I will pay you each as much as the older boys make in a day.

The thought makes them very happy.

- But only if you can keep the secret, I say. If I find out that you have told anyone, even your mother or father, even Segismundo, the deal is off.

- His real name is Eduardo, says Iván.

- Our father is dead, says Ciro and our mother is gone.

I offer my condolences and another taxi comes.

Spain and Paraguay, scoreless to the end, and Karina sits on the couch, stares at me, says that either she is part of it or she is not.

- That is a false dichotomy. You are part of most parts of it.

- What does that mean?

- That I need you immensely in many senses but not tonight.

She waits for me to explain. When I do not she takes up her purse. I tell her that it will not be long. She asks if I think it will still matter by then. I do not know precisely what this means, and do not have to. She closes the door quietly behind her.

I set two envelopes on the dining room table. One bears Casualidad's name and one bears Socorro's and I hope it will be enough. I call to Socorro so that she will find them, leave before she has come, find a mototaxi, ride to the airport, walk.

Everyone is waiting in the courtyard, everyone except Iván and Ciro. I do not ask for permission to speak this time. Instead for good luck I give them each an image of Sarita Colonia, propose the project again, am told that there would be no point. In truth I believe they are afraid. One must never be afraid. I say that they are surely correct, that I need to leave for a moment, that if they are gone by the time I get back I will meet them on the streets of La Primavera.

Waiting at the end of the alley are the boys. We walk the six blocks to Reynaldo's aunt's house. When I ask if I might borrow her car for a few hours she says that he hasn't called. I say that he is surely very busy. She doesn't answer. I say that I know he will get in touch at his earliest opportunity. She stares at her hands, appears no longer aware that I am present. I ask if I can use her bathroom, get no response, and find the keys in a dish on her nightstand. Back in the living room I tell her that Reynaldo will be home soon with splendid stories to tell, and that I will return her car by midnight.

We stop first at my house for my toolbag. I tell the boys to stay in the car, enter as quietly as possible. Mariángel is already asleep. I go to my room, take up the bag, and Socorro stands in the doorway.

She thanks me for the money and says that it means nothing. I nod. She says that I am no longer fit to be Mariángel's father. I say that that was always the case. She says that if I do not become more of a father soon she will take Mariángel to live with her in Catacaos. I look at her, wonder how much she knows, how much Karina has told her. I say that I am so very close, that it is only a matter of days or at most weeks.

Socorro starts to cry, and I lift her gently, set her to one side. Back to the car, and out and along and up. I park along the south wall, and the three of us walk around to the front gate. There is a light on in the chapel, but I see no movement.

Back to the station wagon. Its top will not bear my weight but its hood is strong, and Ciro climbs up beside me. I take him under the arms, heave him to the top of the wall, and he scrambles over. Now Iván, and there is a small cry as he lands. I ask if they are all right, and after a moment they say that they are.

There are footsteps, and I slide to the ground, lean against the station wagon, cross my arms and hum. A woman walks by, or a man. I wait, and whisper that the tools are on their way, throw the bag and wait again. I remind the boys to take the hammer and chisel in case the shed is locked, and hear metal clank against metal.

It takes them twelve minutes to fetch a ladder and bring it to the wall. I call to Ciro to tie the rope to one end and throw it over, and he calls back that I do not need to tell him anything else, that he has not forgotten any part of the plan. The boys lift their end as I pull, and the ladder slides neatly across. I climb, and the bamboo bends but does not break. I slide over the top of the wall, pull the ladder along after me, set it in place for our climb out.

The boys come from where they stood beneath a ceibo. The darkness is incomplete as there is a slab of moon. Together we walk, and I know the number of the tomb but am suddenly unsure of the route. Around a corner and up. Dogs begin to bark and I stop, but they are outside the wall. I ask Ciro in which direction the chapel lies. He points, and Iván corrects him. They argue for a moment, at last come to consensus. Thirty yards farther along, fifty, another corner and halfway along and yes, shoulder-high, yes.

I set down the toolbag, tell Ciro to hold the flashlight steady, ask Iván for the hammer and chisel. He brings them from where they were hidden. I strike once at the edge of the frontal stone, and the boys make noises in their throats.

I turn to look at them. They do not look well. I wait, and finally Ciro asks if the woman is still inside.

- Of course.
- Dead? says Iván.
- Look, I say. We have no new clues, and this is the one place old clues might be found. You heard what I said at last night's meeting. The police were not given enough time to inspect this woman's body. They might well have missed something we cannot do without.

The boys say nothing. I ask if they have a better idea. Iván says he wants to go home.

- But I need your help, I say. How about this: we are huaqueros, the three of us, and this is the Chachapoya tomb we must rob, high on a limestone cliff.

They look at me.

- All right, I say, not Chachapoya. Have you heard of the Lord of Sipán?

Both boys nod.

- Excellent, I say. And this structure is his pyramid. I am Ernil Bernal and you are my helpers and this niche is a tomb full of gold that will soon be ours.

- No it isn't, says Ciro. It's just a woman that's dead.

I consider, and say that in truth I need them most as scouts, as lookouts, as soldiers unafraid to stand guard. They are glad to hear this. I make them pledge to alert me immediately if they hear or see anyone coming, and send them to the nearest corners.

I cover the chisel head with a patch of bark and even so make far too much noise. Ten minutes, twenty. The cement is of poor quality and slowly the stone comes loose. I ease it out and down, and there is a first scent of rot.

The end of the coffin, the burnished wood now dull, and Ciro is beside me whispering that men are coming. I ask how many. He says three, possibly four.

How many are truly needed to guard the dead? He says that he does not know, and I had not meant to ask the question aloud. I tell him that he must be very careful, must run slowly enough to be seen but quickly enough not to be caught, must squeeze out through the front gates just as the men reach for him, must circle back to the south wall, find a way up and over, wait at the ceibo. I ask if he understands. He nods, smiles, says that running is something he is good at.

We wait, wait, and I send him off. There are shouts and bobbing flashlights. I hiss to Iván, tell him to stay close in case I need him to run as well. Then I return to my work. The coffin is wedged tightly into the niche. I chip at the sides and top but cannot get it to move in any direction.

I rest for a moment, lift my chisel again, my hammer, strike at the corners of the coffin itself. It is not an expensive model, and the wood splinters easily. The smell strengthens. I work across the top and down the right side. The smell has become a stench but then a breeze rises, bears it away, brings me the scent of cypress.

I strike again and again but now mango, now sage. Her marinera dress and her tears each year and I strike. Máncora, and she nurses Mariángel, the blurred world and I strike again and again and stop, pachamanca and how she laughed and I gather it, gather it all, push it back in, deeper down, strike and stop again because there are footsteps.

I wipe my face. The men are only thirty or forty feet away. I whisper to Iván that his mission is at hand and he must not fail: be seen but not caught, slip out through the bars just in time. He sweats and nods and sprints. The men hesitate, then chase as they must. I hear Iván squeal and struggle, the tearing of cloth and more running and I strike again, again, again.

The end of the coffin is open. The breeze has died and the stench is strong but I am stronger. I reach in, have a thought of rats and pull back. I listen. There is no sound. My hands trace the smooth soles of her shoes, the knotted weave of her stockings.

Daniela Rocío Espinoza Farfán, I am very, very sorry.

I take hold of her ankles, and they are so thin; I pull, but her body is stuck to the bottom of the coffin. I pull again, and nothing. I pull much harder and something rips, scrapes, and she comes out to the waist.

Her shoes look as though once they were white. Perhaps I am not strong enough. I pull again and the body comes out and I stumble, kneel, I am holding her rigid and light in my arms, her dress is torn and I retch but do not drop her, am careful not to look, not yet.

I lay her down, work her into a canvas sack. The sack is too short and I tie it closed around her knees. I wedge the stone back into place, gather bits of concrete and throw them as far as I am able. I put my tools into the bag and shoulder it, check to see that nothing has been forgotten, kneel again and lift her.

I breathe through my mouth, and carrying her is not hard, along and around and along and to the ceibo. I set down my tools, carry the body up the ladder, balance her on top of the wall. The two boys are crouching in the shadow of the station wagon. They wave when they see me, and all is as it should be.

We load the body and tools into the back, roll down all the windows, drive slowly through the dense dark night. I park at the mouth of the alley, roll the windows back up and lock all of the doors. I lift the body, and carry it to the courtyard.

Iván stands to my right and Ciro to my left. Most

of the other Resolvers are already back from their search. They are gathered around the outside table, appear to have found nothing, turn as we approach. When they see what I am carrying they stand and curse me and shout into the house.

I set the body down on the table, ask for more light to be brought. The others surround us. Segismundo arrives last, has trouble speaking at first, says that Satan has taken hold of me. I do not argue, and ask him to help with the rope. Instead he turns and walks back into the house, and one by one the others follow, until only the five boys are left.

I hand my flashlight to Ciro, ask Iván to see if there are any candles in the kitchen. He goes, is back a moment later with a mesh bag full of white votives and a box of matches. I encircle the body with candles, light them all. If I am lucky they will burn long enough.

The boys stand in a small tight group beside me. I ask if they are sure they want to see what is to come. There is silence for a moment. Iván says he will not touch the body but wants to watch. The others nod. I untie the rope and remove the canvas sack and the boys run away, all but Ciro.

Again the stench. Her mouth and eyes are gaping, her cheeks drawn, her hair dull, her skin dark and dry. I remove her shoes and set them aside. She is wearing a long-sleeved dress, pale green and now soiled, stuck tightly to her body and stiff with dried fluid. I take out my knife and cut the dress into pieces. Even so it is not easy to remove, and in places the skin comes off as well.

Her bra and her underwear, her stockings: I slash and peel and tear. I do not know what to look for, and look all the same. The only jewelry is a medallion on a chain around her neck, some saint or other, badly failed. Her skin everywhere rough to the touch. Ciro stands close to me and holds to the hem of my shirt.

There does not seem to be anything to see except a few

small cuts on her arms and legs, one at her throat and another on her stomach. I comb through her hair with my fingers, prod her shriveled breasts. Her legs are spread slightly and I look and detest myself but must look again and do.

I check her hands and feet and there is nothing. I try to lift one arm and it will not move; I try with greater force and her skin rips open, a new wound, the purpled tissue underneath and I lower her arm quickly. I glance at Ciro, and he has seen. I ask for his assistance in rolling the body over. He shakes his head, but helps me move the candles away, then back into place.

There are flecks of blood dried black in her hair. The back of her skull has been repaired with painted plaster. On one shoulder blade are four cuts, the waxing crescent moons of fingernails dug into flesh.

It seems that no animals have been at her, not here and not in the desert, no dogs, no insects, and this is so fortunate, so unfair. I cover the body with the canvas bag and look through her clothes. Ciro lets go, steps away. Nothing in the bra or underwear or stockings. Nothing on the front of the dress, but on a piece of the back I find a hair. It is much shorter and straighter than the woman's own, is probably meaningless, most likely from whomever bathed and prepared her body for the tomb. I place it in my wallet all the same, and send Ciro for my toolbag.

I tape the underclothes onto the body, drape the dress over her and tape it in place as well. I put her shoes on, work her into the bag, wrap the rope around and call that the thing is done. The Resolvers come slowly, ask if I found anything. A hair, I say. And also some cuts that look to be from fingernails.

The men look down. I had hoped to show them more. Segismundo says I should not come here anymore. I nod, and ask Iván and Ciro if they are ready to help me put the body back. Segismundo forbids them to have anything more to do with me. I look at the old man, and know that he is right. I lift Daniela Rocío Espinoza Farfán once again, and turn away.

# 44.

Three nights, bars and streets and bridges and the bird god ruffled her feathers as I came in today at dawn. I tighten my tie, kiss Mariángel. Now back out. Turning, and past the park. The matacojudo trees have emptied and there is wind at times though never chill.

I slow, turn again. Cabeza de Vaca said something and I cannot remember and the Second Rebellion fails. Along the avenue. Manco escapes into the jungle but his wife is captured, Cura Ocllo, and she rolls in her own excrement to keep the Spaniards from raping her.

The Panamericana, gas station and hotel, and standing at the university gates is a police officer. He smiles at me as I approach. I have never seen him before and there is a rumor, Manco willing to parley. Pizarro sends two Christian natives as envoys, a black attendant, a pony as a gift. The officer frowns. Manco kills them all, even the pony. I stop and the officer comes toward me and Pizarro himself rapes Cura Ocllo. Then he has his secretary rape her. He ties her to a stake, and his Cañari cohorts beat her, fill her body with arrows.

The officer takes hold of my elbow gently, the way a friend might. Pizarro puts her ravaged corpse in a basket, floats her down the Yucay River so that Manco will find her, and the officer asks to see my identity card. I say that I am a foreigner. He asks to see my foreign resident card. I tell him it has not yet come through. He asks to see my passport, and I say that I misplaced it three weeks ago, that for three weeks I have been planning to go this very day to the police station to report its loss.

The officer smiles again but now there are footsteps, now there is a voice: Dr. Guardiola, asking if he can be of service. The officer tells Dr. Guardiola that his assistance will not be required. Dr. Guardiola claps me on the shoulder, says that he will nonetheless be pleased to accompany us until all things have been clarified.

The officer shrugs, lets go of my elbow, tells me that foreigners are required to carry identification. I say that I have never met one who did. He asks me if that matters. Before I can answer he says that I should not have waited so long to report the loss of my passport, should not have waited even a single day, and I agree, I agree, I agree. I ask if arrangements might be made, and the officer nods.

- What need is there for arrangements, says Dr. Guardiola, if everything is clear?

The officer looks at Dr. Guardiola, then back at me. Finally he shrugs, says that he will give me twenty-four hours to report the loss, that otherwise further problems will result. The three of us shake hands and the officer walks away.

Dr. Guardiola pulls me in through the gates, says that I should never pay bribes, that bribes only make things worse. I thank him for his help, and say that I agree if only in principle. I walk him to his office on the far side of campus, thank him again, and he asks if I can join him for a prayer retreat this weekend.

I ask if he saw the footage of Somalis eaten by hyenas. He says that he did. I say that God is at very best a ten-year-old boy standing over an anthill with a magnifying glass.

Dr. Guardiola shakes his head, says that he is very sorry. I say that it is not his fault, turn and walk and the police officer, why didn't he ask for my name, my address, my telephone number?

One answer only: he already knew who I was. Perhaps the Resolvers have come to trouble, and the boys gave him my address. Perhaps Reynaldo has been caught with my passport and the police are looking to take advantage. It does not matter much either way, will be settled this afternoon at the station, and now there is far movement, people at the deer pen, a covered truck. I go to see. The fencing has been repaired, and the chemist who replaced Reynaldo nods and smiles at the four deer that dash down a railed gangplank into the pen, shouts as a fifth bounds over the rail and is gone.

- Where did the deer come from? I ask.

The chemist stares at me, remembers.

- From the deer people, he says.

I nod, and he begins shouting again.

Two classes come, go, to my office and Arantxa is waiting. I smile as if I had asked her to meet me. She asks if I have a moment, and sits down in the only chair beside my own.

I put away my materials and coursebooks and tell her that after lunch I must go to the police station to report the loss of my passport, that I will be back as soon as possible, that I do not know what time that will be. She opens her mouth and closes it and rubs her eyes. I go to my filing cabinet, begin gathering the documents I will need, and she was surely about to ask how and when my passport was lost, then realized she didn't care.

- You haven't contributed anything to the resource bank in over a month, she says. You haven't finished the observation forms. Final exams are next week and your students are so worried that they have come to ask for extra grammar tutoring.

I close the file cabinet, tuck the folders into my briefcase, look at her and she looks back.

- Something is wrong, she says, and I wish you would tell me what it is.

- Nothing is wrong. What could be wrong? I am just very tired.

- Do you need help with Mariángel?

- That's not it. I'm not sleeping well, nothing more.

She doesn't believe me. Perhaps she never has in regard to anything. She is breathtakingly sad, says that if I wish to continue teaching here I will need to reconsider my behavior, stands and goes.

The walk down the path, across the parking lot, I have been this tired before and Karina will be waiting: we eat lunch together daily. Yesterday after dessert she helped me to hang flyers. We speak little but smile a great deal and it is working or appears to be.

Out through the gate. There are no mototaxis waiting. I lean back against the wall, and the police officer from this morning stands suddenly before me. He is not smiling. He takes my elbow again.

- Come, he says, and leads me toward a squad car parked up the street.

- Of course, I say, but first I am going home for lunch.

His grip on my elbow tightens and his pace does not slow. We reach the car, and he opens the passenger door, points inside.

- If you don't mind, I say, I would at least like to see my daughter briefly. She—

- Stop talking, and get in the fucking car.

As we pull away, I remove the folders from my briefcase, shuffle my papers until the edges are perfectly aligned. I say that I hope this will not take long. The officer does not answer.

Along and along and then slowing, into the market. The stalls to either side, their blue tarp roofs and loaded counters, their plastic goods and video cassettes and shoes. Old women selling charcoal. A locksmith's cart. No mangos anywhere the wrong season of course but somewhere inside perhaps grapefruit and tangerines. Perhaps pomegranates. Perhaps peaches.

Out onto Sánchez Cerro and the long white wall: the police station is only one part of a compound that takes up the whole block. To the entrance, past it and around to the parking lot gate. There we wait. The guards bear machine guns. The gate opens and we enter. This is not a part of the station I have seen before. We park, and the officer leads me in through a side door, around to a very small room with one chair, tells me to wait there for a moment, tells me to make myself at home.

I open my briefcase again, take out the folders again, look at the paperwork pointlessly. I try the door handle. I put the folders away, lean back. There is a smell to this station: mildew and ink, polyester and steel, sweat. Months since I have smelled it, more than months, a year at least, and Pilar. The forms filled in late the night she went missing. The waiting, the slow hot stream of waiting with Mariángel on my chest. Thin sleep ruptured at each siren, the officers' insistence that I leave and my constant refusal. Two days unmoving. At some point Pilar's parents had come from Chiclayo, brought us things to eat and drink, were careful to take Mariángel from me only at moments in which my hands went weak. When Mariángel and I went home, they stayed with us. Ministering, I believe, is the word for what they did.

More days of waiting, and viciously the news. Pilar's body, broken and torn and the dogs, my rage and the fight. The casket, closed. I lack documents I will need, I am sure of it, and the door swings open. It is the officer who drove me here.

- A small change, he says. You will first go and report your lost passport. He says that it is perfect in a way.

- Who says what is perfect?

- I will be near you all of the time. When you are done, you will come back to this room, and I will follow.

I nod, stand, walk out into the hallway. The officer points to a door at its far end. Out through it, the officer close behind me, and now we are standing in the station's central lobby. Nothing has changed: it is still straight lines and bad light. He takes me across to an office near the entrance and disappears.

The officer here sits at a wooden desk, and above her is a fan that does not spin. She stares at her typewriter, types with great slowness, shakes her head. There is a bench and I sit down and listen to the typing. Hanging beside the window is a calendar, and I count to make sure, and yes: Reynaldo has had the two weeks he asked for.

The far wall looks built of tiny open tombs, each niche stuffed with paper. The officer swears, pulls the page out of the typewriter and throws it away, asks what I am doing in her office. I tell her that I have lost my passport. She consults a chart, says that the administrative fees come to twelve soles. I bring out my wallet, and inside there is a bill folded oddly, lengthwise, and I remember: the hair I found on the body. I take the hair out, turn it in the light. Light brown from some angles, auburn from others. The officer clears her throat and the hair falls to the floor. She is holding out a set of forms. I take them, look for the hair, sweep my hand back and forth, find only dust. The officer asks what I am doing. I stand, apologize, pay the twelve soles. She tells me to fill out the forms as well as I am able.

When I am done she asks me to wait in the lobby. It

could be minutes or hours. I sit and wait. The officer who drove me here has not reappeared. I walk, and count dead spiders in the corners. I sit again, and wait.

Now there is shouting from an office on the far side of the lobby. I stand and walk. The door bears no sign, and inside there are no citizens waiting or filling in forms, but there is a television, and six officers yelling and pulling at their hair. They look at me in the doorway and extend their arms to me. They shout that the unthinkable has happened: Norway has beaten Brazil.

One of the officers shouts above the rest, calls for an end to the shouting. The others silence in deference to rank or volume. Everything is okay, he says. Everything is fine, because Brazil has already amassed enough points to qualify for the second round.

The other officers consult one another, and agree that this is true. The discussion turns to an earlier match, Chile tying Cameroon and thus passing through as well. The officer who shouted loudest crosses his arms and looks at me. Then a woman's voice calls something like my name.

It is the officer who took my fees and forms. She is beckoning, and still this other officer stares. I nod to him, cross the lobby, am given a thin sheaf of papers documenting my loss and a receipt for the twelve soles. She says that tomorrow I must travel to Lima, go to my embassy, begin the process of obtaining a new passport. I promise that I will, and thank her. She turns away, begins typing very slowly once again.

I step out into the lobby. The officer who drove me here is leaning against a near wall and pretending to read a newspaper. I could perhaps beat him to the entrance, but the other guards are there, and I can think of no reason to run: Arantxa knows where I am, will trace me as necessary.

The officer does not look up when I walk past, but I hear the newspaper snap as he folds it. Across the lobby to the door, his footsteps in perfect time with mine. Now the hallway, and the small room.

- So far you have made good decisions, he says. Soon you will be happy that you did. For now you may relax. He will be here in a moment.

This time I do not bother to ask. The door closes and I am alone. I wait. Karina, but the door opens again. The officer who enters is tall, heavy-set, and I recognize but do not quite remember him. Short hair, light brown eyes. He smiles. I look at his badge. He covers it quickly, then laughs and lets his hand drop.

- I am Reátegui, he says. I assisted the lieutenant on the case of your wife. I helped you with some of the paperwork.

- Yes. Thank you for that. Thank you very much.

He leans forward, lowers his voice.

- Do not be afraid. There is no reason for you to be afraid. You should in fact be very happy.

- That is what your colleague said.

- He was and is correct.

- In that case, I am as happy as you wish me to be.

- You do not look happy enough. But that is about to change.

Reátegui takes a pen and a slip of paper, writes something, folds the paper and slides it across the desk. He waits, and stares, and nods. I take up the paper, unfold it and read: Ten Thousand Dollars.

- I don't understand.

- That is how much it will cost.

- For what?

- For ten minutes with the taxista.

- You caught him?

Reátegui smiles.

- The press know nothing of it yet, but that could change at any point. The commissioner arrives this evening and the process will begin. Tomorrow your taxista will be sent to Río Seco to await trial. This is the one chance you will have to be alone with him.

- And you had me waste an hour declaring the loss of my passport?

- To give you a true reason to have been here today, should such a reason ever be required.

I nod. My chest has filled with calm, a vast dark sharp-edged calm, obsidian, but the bird god, but Sarita, and I ask for proof.

- You remember the last woman? Many people saw her get into the taxi, and one old lady got a very good look at the driver. Perhaps you have seen the sketch on television. It wasn't easy to find him, but this morning at last we did. The license plate of his taxi wasn't the one you gave us, but it was the same vehicle: we found blood traces from all four victims, including your wife. He has no alibis for any of the killings. He owns a pair of shoes that matches footprints found at the final scene, and his—

- I thought that something happened to the fooprints.

- What?

- The footprints. Something happened.

Reátegui scratches his face. He says that in truth he should not be discussing evidence with me at all. He says that I am welcome simply to return to my home if I so desire. He says that he has gone to great and excessive lengths to provide me with this opportunity, that he is running substantial personal and professional risks in so doing, that—

- Yes. And I am grateful. But I don't have ten thousand dollars. And I will need half an hour with the taxista.

- For what? You are very big, very strong.

- One is never big or strong enough.

- Nine thousand, and fifteen minutes.

- Five thousand for twenty-five.

- Seven thousand for twenty minutes, or we are done. The risks to me are—

- Yes. Yes. I'll be right back.

Again Reátegui smiles.

꙰

Seven thousand dollars is four times what a policeman here earns in a year. It is most of what I have saved. Sweat runs from my face, drips onto the front of my shirt. The line is not long and for a moment I wish it were longer.

Now the clerk. He asks if I am feeling unwell. Then he asks if perhaps I would prefer to conduct such a transaction in one of the back offices. I tell him that it does not matter, and watch as he runs the stacks of bills through the electronic counter. A second time, and the same amount results. A large envelope, and I borrow a pen to sign for the withdrawal, and the taxista, he needs to say it. I need to hear him say it.

A mototaxi back to the police station. In and in and in. Reátegui waits alone in the small room. I hand him the envelope, and he takes it, counts quickly and nods.

- Will you be needing anything? he asks. We have everything you might require.

So many imagined encounters, so many places and weapons, so many angles of light, and in fact there is nothing I need. Reátegui nods, leads out to the lobby and deeper into the station. We pass the unnamed office, and it is empty, and the television is off. Other offices, identical or nearly so. Through a double door, and out into a large open area: the heart of the compound, the center of the block. In the middle is a fulbito court, perfectly swept. A stretch of grass to either side. To the far right a large building, and to the far left a series of tiny cells.

I veer toward the cells and Reátegui catches my arm,

points instead to the building. I nod and again follow. Inside it smells of blood and mildew and sweat. He unlocks a door, leads me downstairs, unlocks another door, and down again.

There is yet another door, this one steel instead of wood. Reátegui peers through the peephole, then looks at me, takes a deep breath as if encouraging me to do the same. I nod, and he slides back the bolt.

Inside, a thin dark black-haired man is sitting in a metal chair. His hands are cuffed to the sides of the chair, and his ankles are bound to a crossbar. Reátegui leans toward me, whispers that my time started running the moment we entered the building, that he will be waiting outside. He pats me on the shoulder, wishes me luck.

As he closes the door, the air in the room goes tight. The taxista and I both flinch at the sound of the steel bolt shot home. There is a bit of dried blood at the corner of his mouth, and one of his eyes is swollen. I walk in circles around him. As far as I can see he is not afraid. I wish that I had requested a chair of my own, wish that I was dressed all in green.

I look at him, come closer, look again. Shallow pockmarks scattered high on his cheeks. Thinning hair, weak chin. His left ear slightly damaged or deformed, its lobe scarred, a skewed star of whitish tissue and I remember none of this. My memory of course less than perfect. The sky darkening the one time I saw him, too long ago.

- It was you, wasn't it?
- Mister?

His voice, too, not exactly as I have carried it in my mind: raspier, and slightly higher in pitch. I smile and ask which soccer team he supports. He says that he is a fan of Universitario. What a shame, I say.

He tells me to go fuck myself.

An advance of sorts.

There is a soft knock at the door. I ignore it, ask him

about his father. He looks in my eyes, says that his father is fine. I nod, agree that the question was absurd, turn to evidence and crime.

Yes, the taxista says, he took the most recent victim to the market as she'd requested. No, he has no alibis for the nights of any of the murders—he was simply driving. No, he doesn't know anything about blood in his taxi. No, he did not kill any of the four women. No, he has never killed anyone.

Then he smiles. There is no reason for him to smile. I look at my watch. Nine of my minutes have expired. I ask him if he knew that the evidence the police have in hand will ensure that the rest of his life will be spent somewhere small and dark and damp. He says that in that case there is no reason for him to discuss anything at all with a fat foreign fuck like me.

I congratulate him, and say that he is exactly right. Then I hit him not as hard as I could but hard enough and his cheekbone disintegrates against my fist and the chair upends. I grab him by the shoulders and drag him upright.

- Daniela Rocío Espinoza Farfán, I say. And Isabel Teresa Otero Manrique. And Beatriz Silvana Cordero Huarcay. Do you know what those three young women meant to me?

There is another knock, louder. Thirteen minutes gone. The taxista shrugs.

- Nothing, I say. Absolutely nothing. But the first victim, Pilar Seminario de Segovia—I would like to know what happened to her. I would like you to tell me. Now, please.

He stares at me. I come closer, lean down, stroke his thinning black hair.

- Tell me, I say.

He shakes his head. I lift his chin.

- Did you kill my wife?

He shakes his head again. I take him by the nape of the neck.

- Last chance, I say.

Again he smiles and I vault onto him, the chair collapses beneath us and he retches, strains to breathe and I stand and lift him and the chair, hurl them against the wall. He lands on his face and I am on him again swinging him and releasing and watching how he flies and crumples and falls and I have his head between my hands and press, not so hard at first and then harder and harder, and his eyes his mouth the wreck of his face and behind me noise and crashing and then weight and arms a mass of bodies and pulling but his skull I hear it begin to crack, my left arm wrenched back but my right arm free and I bring the knife from my pocket flick its blade open and reach but my legs fail and we fall, the taxista and I the men on top of us the knife twisting in my hand closing across my fingers blood spraying now hands at my throat and darkness.

# 45.

I WAIT BEFORE OPENING MY EYES. THERE IS A FURROWED SILENCE: our lungs pulling at the thin air. The wind is cold against my face. The stone beneath my back is still colder.

Looking now, and the sky is so bright and so blue, richer and richer as it climbs. The closest ridge is a slow gray surge of shadowed limestone. The wind ripples through the ichu grass to the far edge of this highland plain.

The highway is a hundred yards below us. Beyond it lies the Mantaro River, swift and gray, silent at this distance. Mariángel shifts on my chest, returns to sleep. Karina, stretched out on this same flat rock, also asleep. Armando's eyes are closed but I believe he is awake and listening.

We are still fifteen or twenty miles from Jauja. An hour ago the driver said that the parts needed to repair the bus would be arriving at any moment. Most of the other passengers are huddled in groups on the turnout. A few have walked down to watch the water move.

I close my eyes again. Surely there are ways not to break what one touches. The stone begins to float, and it is not only here that this happens. The world expands in the dark, then contracts, tightens around me, I open my eyes and the man I beat nearly to death had nothing to do with the murders.

The scar around the base of my right index finger is bright red, and thick as a wedding band. I woke in the back of a police car with one hand wrapped in bandages and a plastic bag in my lap. The bag was full of ice, and contained another, smaller bag, which held my finger. Reátegui was driving. He turned when he heard me move, said that the doctor would not have any questions, that if anyone else asked I was to invent an accident in the kitchen.

We drove across the bridge into Castilla, skirted the airport, passed a small clinic. Reátegui stopped the car in the darkness half a block farther along. He said that he was sorry for what had happened, and that for both our sakes I was never to contact him again. He got out, walked around, and opened my door.

A tetanus shot, an IV, surgery. I looked from time to time and immediately looked away. First the bone. Then the tendons. Arteries and veins, nerves, a final flap of skin. Half a dozen medications and I took them precisely as indicated and last week I removed the plaster splint myself.

The finger is slightly shorter than before, often grows stiff, has not yet regained much feeling and perhaps never will. I rub at the scar, bend the finger back and forth. Cold weather will not be kind to it, but the winter is nearing its end.

There is a single cloud at the horizon, a shocking white above and varied grays beneath. I watch as the wind pushes it out of sight, and the seven weeks it took my hand to heal were spent mainly in my house. At first I watched television and listened to the radio and read the newspaper each day, searched for word of the man I had attacked: of his confession or denial, his apology or alibi, his rage at the foreigner who tried to murder him.

Early in the second week a police officer came to my door. He was no one I had ever seen. My new knife was tucked into the back of my waistband, its blade locked in place. He asked me to accompany him to his car. I said that regrettably I could neither leave my house nor invite him in. He said that a conversation needed to take place, and that his car was the only secure location. I said that I would like nothing more than to be of service but sadly could not accede to his request. He stared at me, and I stared back. I waited for him to reach for his pistol or nightstick but then he shrugged, apologized for disturbing my morning, said that as I had surely guessed he had come because of the streetlight.

For a time I could not reply. The neighbors had complained, he said. He grew angry when I asked if the complaints were recent, but the matter was settled with thirty soles. I thanked him for his vigilance and closed the door and fell.

The man I all but killed was never referenced in any article or newscast, never mentioned in conjunction with any crime. Instead two other men were arrested. The first was the stepfather of Daniela Rocío Espinoza Farfán. The second had attempted an abduction, had been too slow, had given the woman time enough to scream.

This second man had a fruit stand at the outdoor market. He is young and thin and dark, has long flowing hair and the lips of a magazine model. News anchors say that each night he stayed open a few minutes longer than the other vendors, and every so often, if the final person to visit his stand met certain criteria, he would offer her a ride. If she accepted, he would close his stand, and lift her bags, and most often nothing would happen: the women arrived safely home. Except for Isabel Teresa Otero Manrique. Except for Beatriz Silvana Cordero Huarcay. Microscopic shreds of their skin were found in crevices in the rear of his station wagon.

The police say that he has admitted to those murders, and his confession was sincere or coerced, there is no way to know. He claims to have had nothing to do with Pilar, and even if this is true I now wonder at how simply I chose to look only for the taxista, to triangulate from points not yet fixed.

Regardless of whether the police charge the vendor with killing my wife, he will almost certainly be convicted of the other two rapes and murders. He will be sentenced to life in prison, and there is a fair chance he will serve his time at Sarita Colonia Penitentiary in El Callao. Of course she was his patron saint as well.

He is too beautiful to last for very long.

There have been no more murders in Piura.

- Inca Kola?

Standing before me is a girl perhaps ten years old. Bronze skin and bright red cheeks. Long straight black hair in braids. White blouse, loaded carry-cloth knotted at her collarbone, black skirt and white underskirts billowing, black rubber sandals. It is not clear where she has come from or how she knew that we were here—there are no buildings visible in any direction.

- Inca Kola? Pepsi-Cola? Sprite?

She swivels the load around to her front, balances it on a stone, removes one bottle after another. Armando opens his eyes, buys a Sprite. Karina wakes, sees what has been offered, thanks the girl and goes back to sleep. The girl swings the bundle onto her back and makes her way down the hill.

It is rumored that soon Inca Kola will cease to be the Peruvian national beverage, that the company will be bought by Coca-Cola and ruined. I told Karina that more probably nothing would change after the purchase, that Inca Kola would still be the color of urine, would still taste like bubble gum. She said that if I hated it so much I should probably drink less of it, and she is right.

Another cloud, longer and thinner. On the day I first learned of the vendor's arrest, I asked Socorro to call the police station. The officer who answered said that Reátegui was on vacation, would not speculate as to when he might return, declined to discuss the murders as such but confirmed that in regard to this particular case, there had been no previous arrests.

It seems most likely that the man I all but killed works or worked with Reátegui, that the two of them used my desire for revenge to defraud me, that Reátegui had meant to stop me sooner, and I wonder why they bothered with my surgery. Were they afraid that the loss of a finger would make me unstable, perhaps problematically so? Such a fear would not have been unreasonable.

It is also possible that the man was simply a taxista, innocent of all crimes, that Reátegui arrested him for no reason other than to give me someone plausible to hurt. If this is the case, the man cannot hope for the police to bring him justice. It will be very easy for him to learn my name, to find me, and now Mariángel wakes. I take her from the carrier, set her beside me on the great flat stone. She blinks, smiles. She pokes at my stomach. She stands, grabs at my chin, wags it up and down, kisses it. She backs away and begins turning in slow circles, her arms outstretched.

I wait until she is on the verge of falling, grab her and set her down in the grass. It takes her a moment to gain her balance on that uneven ground. She makes her way over to Karina, lifts her sunglasses, kisses her eyes.

Karina wakes, smiles, sits up. She yawns and stands, takes Mariángel's hand. The two of them circle one stone after another. Then Mariángel trips, spins, and Karina catches her almost in time, keeps her head from cracking against the rock but cannot quite prevent her from scraping her wrist.

Mariángel takes her time beginning to cry. Karina lifts her, rubs the scrape and chants the words reserved here for such occasions: Heal, heal, little frog-butt, if it doesn't heal today it will heal tomorrow. You would not think such a chant would help but it often appears to, and Mariángel finishes crying, wishes to explore something beside the nearest stone.

Karina sets her on the ground and she hunches down. When she stands back up, she is holding a fistful of tiny lavender flowers, and brings them to me. I ask Karina if she knows what they are called. She shrugs, says Reynaldo would know, and Armando snorts.

He is still annoyed at having lost his job for drinking spiked coffee in class while Reynaldo kept his with a lie about family emergencies. I sympathize but do not take sides, and Reynaldo had returned to Piura three days before I went to the police station, but was too embarrassed to see me. A week later at last he came to visit. He gave me my passport, apologized, and I blamed El Niño for making everyone insane. I said that I was glad he had not gone the way of the armadillo, and when he asked about the splint I told him the truth.

The day Socorro called the police station was the day I realized that I could never know whether the man I attacked was innocent unless he came for me. If instead he was Reátegui's colleague, then something dangerous and evil was poorly balanced overhead, and the slightest touch would send it spilling over me and everyone near me. That night I called Reynaldo, and immediately he came to help me think. By morning we had worked our way to a solution for us both: he would buy my house for less than it was worth but more than I could have gotten from anyone else on such short notice. The proceeds will support me in Jauja and then beyond. Owning it will help with any visa he might require, and renting it out will help pay his living expenses in the United States next year.

Mariángel brings more flowers, wipes her hands on the front of her dress, goes for still more, and Reynaldo was not my only visitor. Arantxa had fired me over the phone the day after the police station, for missing that last evening class with no warning, and for everything else—the films, the breaking of furniture, the story of a sea of blood though in fact it had never reached the rector's ears. She sent my personal effects by courier. Perhaps two weeks ago she called again, said that she wished to see me and to talk. An hour later the doorbell rang. I told her the story I have told everyone but Reynaldo: a cleaver, a pineapple, my clumsiness. She knew that I was lying but did not press.

I asked, and she said that allowances had been made for my students, that their final exams had been shortened, that their speeches on contemporary American cinema had been surprisingly perceptive, that all of them had passed and few grudges were held. I gave her the essays I had never returned and showed her my favorite. It was about seaweed and love and said, "The sun takes the black rubber ribbons on the sand, and makes them into colored light."

Arantxa nodded and took an envelope from her purse. Inside was a letter from the consul in Loja saying that my work visa was ready, that I need only go to Macará, present my passport and pay a given amount. I looked at Arantxa, wondered what it would be like to have that visa, to belong in that one limited sense. I asked if it made any difference that I no longer worked for the university. She said that Immigrations did not yet have that information, that I could go whenever I wished, that it would give me a year at least of peace. I nodded, and that was my best plan until the vendor was arrested.

Milk for Mariángel, mashed potatoes and steamed carrots from plastic tubs. I peel an apple, the skin rendered a single spiral as if so ordered by Oquendo, and Arantxa told me that she had resigned from the university, would soon be heading back to Spain. Nothing had happened, she said. It was simply time. She had recommended that Günther take over her post, as he was organized and focused, and the center would do well with him in charge. I agreed on all counts. She said that he was currently on vacation in Bremen but had sent me his best regards. I said that she was a marvelous administrator, and apologized for the trouble I had caused her.

She reached again into her purse, brought out something small and handed it to me. It was a piece of paper folded in complicated ways. She said that she could have made me happy. I told her that happiness was not a made thing.

That is one of the many respects in which you are wrong, she said. She leaned over then and kissed me on the mouth. Her taste was that of oranges, as if she were not from Bilbao but Seville. The folded note held her address, and Mariángel has circled back around. She is bored with tiny lavender flowers, looks up into the vivid blue, points. Another cloud has come, but she is pointing not quite at it, and now I see the hawk, hear its keen, and a van pulls into the turnout.

The bus driver stands, gestures, shouts as the driver of the van steps down. The driver of the van shouts back. More shouting, and the two men stride toward one another.

- And? says Karina.

- Soon, I hope.

- Unless they kill each other, says Armando.

The two men shake hands, and we resume waiting. Other visitors: Claudia and Concepción, Lady Diana, Juan Carlos and Fortunato, Domitila and three of the Jhons. They came as a single contingent, said I had been fired unfairly, were distraught when I said nothing had ever been fairer. They asked if I wished them to draw up a petition all the same. I thanked them, thanked them, thanked them.

Karina brings out a pad of paper and a pen, gives them to Mariángel, teaches her shapes, and Karina is no chilalo—her heart has no end of strength. She is also no putilla, no avocet or tern, is something else entirely. I have not told her what happened at the police station and do not plan to, wished and

wish her to come no closer to any of that. I have encouraged
her to believe that my brief catatonia was the result of losing
my job. She knows that I am now hers as wholly as I am able
should she so wish, that for her I have learned the names of the
jungle mammals, and at last there was time for board games: we
all played together, she and I, her aunt, her sisters and brother.
This was four days ago. It was a good goodbye.

I walked then, Mariángel on my back, and on each block
new buildings rose. Barefoot men climbed ladders of bamboo,
carried cans of wet cement on their shoulders, never wavered,
never fell, and the Piura River was a creek once again. New
shanties had been built along the walls, and new crops sown. The
metal detritus of the bridges was gone, and dozens of volunteers
from the university were gathering trash in the causeway. I knew
them all, waved from the bank, shouted my thanks.

The two men slide out from under the bus and push
to their feet. We cheer, stand and stretch, begin to gather our
things. The two men hunch over the toolbox, crawl back under
the bus, and we sit down again.

The sun nears the far ridge, and the green man has
not reappeared. Perhaps he never will—perhaps he has killed
himself, or found the right color, the necessary color, and is
free. The next goodbye was at Reynaldo's aunt's house. She has
purchased a wheelchair and rarely leaves it though I am aware
of no specific injury or illness.

The salad was served, tomato and onion and avocado,
and the avocado was perfectly ripe. Reynaldo had already told
me the best stories of his trip to the United States, now told
safer ones, his university visits, the day his heart chose UCLA,
and the main course was sea bass in crab sauce. I will very
much miss the food of Piura, miss it already though I have
been gone less than a day.

While the dishes were being cleared Reynaldo's aunt
sent him to help Casualidad find hand balm, asked me to wheel

her to the garage, and begged me to steal his motorcycle. I explained why I could not. She said that I did not have to take it with me to Jauja, that I could sink it in the ocean instead. I promised to consider it, and we rolled back to the living room where she winked at me repeatedly.

Fermín seems several inches taller than before. Casualidad is thin but reasonably strong, is now the aunt's full-time nurse. When she was done rubbing balm into the aunt's hands, she came up very close to me, opened her mouth and tilted back her head to show me the miraculous hole in her palate. I could not help but look, at the hole and then at her opalescent eye: she no longer wears a patch. Her curandero had told her that given her success against the tumor, her vision was likely to return. She has seen nothing thus far except shadows, but has not given up hope.

Mariángel points again—the sun slipping behind the ridge. There are none of Colán's reds and purples and ambers and already the temperature is dropping. We come closer together, Karina with one arm around me and one around Armando, Mariángel snug among us. Casualidad told me that Fermín's father is not buried in the cemetery in Frías, is not buried anywhere as far as she knows, is still alive, simply left one day, simply never came back. She led us to the window and from there we could see Fermín weeding in the back yard. Casualidad asked for a moment more to play with Mariángel. Reynaldo and I went to the yard, and I knelt beside Fermín, and Reynaldo stood over us, enlightened us as to the names and medicinal properties of each plant, entreated us to weed faster.

A third goodbye, the green house, Jenny. She and Ms. Alina came together to the door to berate me for not following policy as regards reservations, but I had bouquets for them both, and I kissed their cheeks, thanked them and wished them well, left them bemused and again the men come from under the bus. We watch and wait. They appear to be very pleased or very angry. Then they call to the groups of passengers around them, call to those watching the river, call and wave us down.

Mariángel does not want to return to the carrier, screams and cries and strikes me. Then Armando stumbles and she laughs, forgets what she did not want, settles into place. Together we make our way through the gathering dark.

My finger begins to ache and a fourth goodbye, Catacaos, lunch with Socorro, her husband and daughters, Oscar the Prophet. Oscar prophesied that we would begin the meal with malarrabia and was perfectly correct. He made no prediction in regard to chicha de jora though we walked past a dozen picanterías with white flags at full mast.

That day was my thirty-fifth birthday, and I had told no one. There were gifts nonetheless, but not for me: the girls had all made things for Mariángel. There was a hairpin glued with tiny shells from Elsa, a painted picture frame from Ema, a huayruro bracelet from Eva, and a crayon drawing of a monkey from Marucha. As lunch was ending I told Oscar lies about Mariángel and his painting and a hammer. I asked him to lead us to his gallery, found a triptych of seaweed splayed on sand in three arrangements, and disappointed him by failing to haggle.

Onto the bus, and the driver's assistant glares. He has not forgotten having to load our crib and playpen and unreasonable amount of luggage. Our seats once again, and as the farewells began I asked Oscar if he understood the Tallán bird god to be a god of vengeance. He said that perhaps I was thinking of a Mochica deity called Ai Apaec the Beheader. I said that I was not, that I had read of coastal islands where the decapitated skeletons of young women were found near altars built in Shi's honor. He shrugged, said that Shi was in charge of many things, that he would try to find the list, that his favorite of her tasks was this: she watched over fishermen by night.

The motor fires, roars, and the driver laughs, shouts out the window at the van driver, who shouts back and waves. We pull onto the road. Mariángel and I have a seat to ourselves, with Karina and Armando behind us. I arrange my daughter as if she were to sleep, her head on my lap and her legs stretched out, and she fights to her feet, stands facing backwards, makes faces at Karina.

The road, the dark river, the railroad tracks now visible on the far side—three lines curving in parallel. The Mantaro is dead of poison where it leaves the mines of La Oroya, but is healthier here farther south or so I have heard, and CREMPT's true name is Centro de Reposo para Enfermos Mentales para Piura y Tumbes. I still do not know how the matacojudo blossoms survived the rains, or how many stings it would take. Mireille has returned to Switzerland and the World Cup is long over, the dead buried and the wounded healing. Most Peruvians were saddened by Brazil's loss in the final but recognized that France deserved the win unless the rumors were true and Ronaldo's food poisoning was intentional.

- No! says Mariángel.

She is pointing at Karina, and this is one of our new games, abstruse orders given with real words. Her first word was at last clearly spoken during the Cup's final match. She came to me midway through the first half, smelled of oregano, had been playing with the spices. She stood beside the sofa for a moment, turned away just as Zidane ripped his first header past Taffarel. I shouted Goal! and she echoed me in accent and volume and pitch.

Finally she tires, accepts her milk, lies down and I returned to the university only once. It was midnight. I crept in through the unwalled section at the back of campus, walked to the deer pen and they were grateful, it was evident, grateful for the grass I brought them.

The valley widens, goes shallow, lets in more of what light is left. A small yellow bird flits alongside my window, perhaps a finch, and Jauja, 1564, a yanacona betrays what would have been the Third Rebellion. It was meant to begin on Maundy Thursday, the Spaniards unarmed as they wound their way to the church in holy procession, flagellating one another toward sacred ecstasy, thousand of natives lining the streets as if only to watch and falling then upon the Spaniards: an extermination.

But now the arms caches are discovered—thirty thousand axes and pikes, ten thousand bows, all useless. The curaca claims they were meant as a surprise gift for the Spaniards, a contribution to their campaign in Chile. The Viceroy pretends to believe this at first, declares it illegal for natives to own horses or steel weapons, smothers further uprisings planned for Cuzco and Tucumán. The bird disappears. I pull a folder from my knapsack, open it to the copy of the will.

May all those who read this document see that I, D. Juan de Segovia, native of Cogolludo, province of Guadalajara in Castile, and Citizen of the city of Cuzco, legitimate son of D. Juan de Segovia and Da. Juana de Buruébano, a wide bend of the river, and on the far side perhaps a dozen houses. The sky above is not yet black but the stars have begun to show. We cannot be far away and Jauja, November 1536, Alonso de Alvarado's army marches from Chachapoyas in reconquest: slaughter after slaughter, and the Inca captives are mutilated, sent to their homes as messages. Alvarado pauses to await reinforcements, seizes more Incas, tortures some of them for information and enchains the rest as porters. His Huanca allies gather, join in, murder a thousand prisoners and Mariángel closes her eyes as the empty bottle slips to one side.

Armando snores, chokes briefly, resumes snoring. I bring out my flashlight, commend my soul to God the Father who created it, to God the Son who redeemed it, to God the Holy Spirit who has lit it with His grace, and my body, sent to the earth of which it was formed, I desire that it be dressed in the habit and cord of our father Saint Francis, that it be laid to rest in the Church of San Francisco in Cuzco. Darker still, the stars brighter, a single stone peak backlit by the moon. Instructions regarding the funeral Mass, regarding the distribution of alms; in both cases the funds set aside are smaller than is generally the case and something soft brushes the back of my neck. I turn, and of course, Karina stretching forward, kneads my shoulders, smiles and leans back, closes her eyes.

Now the names of Segovia's wife and children, and no mention of his family in Spain. Next a partial catalogue of that which composed his fortune, beginning with the estate in Cuzco—there are sections here that Alexis was unable to decipher. A brief list of debts and debtors. The valley deepens again, and Magdalena Clara Coya, perhaps one of Huayna Cápac's many half-sisters but a figure of no importance within the royal family; I have not yet had enough luck tracing her to make any sense of this will, to see beyond Segovia's death.

We cross the river, the headlights of the bus splayed not quite wide enough to show the water beneath us. Jauja, May of 1536, the First Rebellion at full strength. The Siege of Cuzco has begun and Pizarro sends two expeditions from Lima in relief. Morgovejo de Quiñones leads the first to Parcos, captures twenty-four Inca elders and burns them to death. The second is seventy horsemen under Gonzalo de Tapia. Quizo Yupanqui catches them in a ravine near Huamanga, sends rockslides down upon them and they are crushed.

Sixty more horsemen are sent in support, this time not from Lima but from Jauja. Quizo Yupanqui annihilates them as well, sends a cartload of heads to Manco Inca that he might know and celebrate. Jauja all but defenseless now. Pizarro dispatches thirty horsemen under Gaete, another thirty under Godoy, but Quizo Yupanqui arrives first, slaughters the Spaniards, and their slaves, even the horses. Gaete and his thirty are attacked by their own auxiliaries—the puppet Inca he brought has switched sides. Godoy rescues the few survivors and leads his party back to Lima. Morgovejo escapes all but the final trap and the man Segovia chose as the executor of his will should have been one of his two closest friends: either Pedro de Alconchel, the other trumpeter, or Juan García, the Conquest's crier and executioner. Instead he chose a tailor named Francisco Martínez. Martínez was in Jauja in 1533 and 1534, accompanied Almagro to Piura in the course of the Quitan campaign, and I have found little else of note about him.

An opening, then a denser darkness, the valley walls drawing in, steeper and steeper above us. Jauja, 31 March 1534, Segovia's signature in halting script—perhaps the only thing he knew how to write. My flashlight fades and dies. Three months earlier Quisquis had attacked but poorly, a single Spaniard killed, the Huanca auxiliaries chasing the Incas all the way to Lake Junín.

Most of the rest of the Spaniards return from Cuzco, and in April comes Jauja's founding as provisional capital. In May the Crown sends instructions regarding the distribution of labor grants, and Pizarro ignores them, instead rewards his family members and closest friends and allies, and this is the beginning of so much here: so few with such power over so many. In June the city council asks him for additional encomiendas, and he grants them. Two months later, staring down at the endless lines of porters carrying food from the coast, he sees that it is senseless for the capital to be so distant from its port. He chooses a new site near the mouth of the Rímac. The City of Kings is founded in January 1535, Jauja begins its long decline, and already Segovia is dead.

What were Segovia's intentions when he left his estate in Cuzco? Why wasn't he given another in Jauja? Was there a falling out with Alconchel and García? Who was Martínez, and why did Segovia trust him so completely? How and when did Segovia die? Why did he leave so little to the Church and so much to Magdalena Clara Coya? How is it that she never received it, and what happened to the original will, and why was the notary's register never sent on to Spain?

And so I go to Jauja. It is possible that the answers no longer exist to be found. It is also possible that they will be too easily found, too simply explained, are footnotes to a narrative we already have. The third possibility is that Armando was right, that the answers are cracks in the surface of a story we have told ourselves for four hundred years.

I will stay there less than a month, I suspect, though I could remain longer, could travel to Brazil or Bolivia to renew my tourist visa, or return to Macará for the work visa that awaits me there. But I need only a cleaner copy of this protocol, this double, and an understanding of its layered context: of the relationships between the will and the sales records and marriage certificates that surround it in the small register; and between the small register and the larger one within which it is bound; and between the larger register and the archive as a whole. There will then be trips to Lima and Seville. At last back in Irvine I will gather all that I have found and draw borders around what it allows me to say and show, to revise and reinterpret, to think newly about and extend.

With luck what will follow is foreseeable, foresayable. I have not yet told Dr. Williamson of all that the will contains, but he has a sense for when something lays large in the field. He is leery of my past failures but pleased that I have settled on something with relatively well-defined edges, has offered to serve as my new advisor, to help arrange panels and publications and interviews.

Mariángel whimpers and turns. I wait for her to settle again. I look back, and Karina is asleep; Armando stares at or out the window, will spend a week with me in Jauja to introduce me to Alexis Ñaupara, and renew their friendship. Then he will travel the twenty miles from Jauja to Concepción, where he will research images of inherited wealth in a series of illustrated texts at the Convento de Santa Rosa de Ocopa, an eighteenth-century monastery built as gate to the jungle, its library extraordinary for the circumstances, twenty-five thousand volumes, the ceiling bright with paintings of Amazonian flora and fauna, its grounds the setting for the end of Cabello Balboa's version of Quilaco and Curicuillor. In February Armando will assume his duties as the new vice-dean of History at Universidad Peruana Los Andes. It is located in Huancayo, world capital of suicides caused by unrequited love, less than an hour from Jauja and with luck I will see him a time or two before I go.

The driver's radio hisses and spits. He mutters into it for a time, calls back that there has been a small rockslide, that we will need to circle around, to enter Jauja from the north, and Karina considers this trip both test and vacation. I have asked her to join me afterwards in Irvine and she seems inclined to go, but is uncertain how much longer her aunt will be able to care for her brother and sisters. Her father is not to be discussed and her mother not to be relied upon. Karina thinks that Irvine is thus unlikely. I hope the odds will improve when I offer her the ring. It is wrapped in a sibling immigration timetable sent to me by the embassy. Our honeymoon will be in Italy, I will say, and opening a bookstore in Irvine will not be unfeasible. Then I will wait for her answer.

My hope, expanded: that a year from now Reynaldo will arrive at the airport in Los Angeles, and Karina and I will be waiting, will drive him to Westwood, help him to unpack. I close the folder, tuck it into my knapsack between a blank pad of paper and a copy of 5 Metros de Poemas, his going-away gift to me. Your goodness painted the songs of birds, is what Oquendo says. I choose to believe that this is true.

My aunt's hip has healed and I have not yet told my mother that I am returning to California. It is best this way. I will simply arrive in Fallash, will ring the doorbell as if I were anyone else. In my hands will be flanged utensils from Jauja. My mother and aunt will love them and pretend to be furious that I left Peru before they could make the trip down.

When that is done I will walk the hills around the lake. I will visit my father's grave, and Joel's, will pack books for Irvine, and the finger I nearly lost is paler than the others, but warm to the touch. I do not understand this at all and wonder if the funds I left Reynaldo will be enough to buy bicycles for Ciro and Iván, if the instructions I gave him for avoiding Segismundo and Félix were sufficiently clear.

Thousands marched in Lima to demand a referendum on whether Fujimori should be allowed to run for re-re-election, and were ignored. I sent notes of thanks and farewell to Eugenia and Don Teófilo, a letter to Dr. Guardiola apologizing for my rudeness, have not heard back from any of them, no longer expect to. The footbridges newly hung across the Piura River were pleasingly referential, and more amusing to walk than I would have guessed. The treaty has not been signed and more troops have massed to either side of the border but Peru and Ecuador are not yet at war.

Máximo Yerlequé, engineering student and Halloween phoenix, nine months in the hospital and six operations and three days ago he died of his burns. An envelope holding a hundred soles left for Hugo the deaf midget. Cabeza de Vaca cannot get to sleep anywhere except on the floor, is uncomfortable in clothing of any sort, ends the story with the memory of a harbor, the finest harbor in the world, full of fish, a place of perfect calm with room for countless ships and we seek to extend each narrative hoping in silence that our own will likewise if not thereby be extended, that our near death will be conclusion rather than sudden cease, and here is what will happen tomorrow, or the next day, or the day after that:

Armando and Alexis and I, we are walking the cement path that crosses the Plaza de Armas. We thread through its scant trees and trapezoids of hard soil, pass the candlestick fountain at its center, continue on toward the church, the Iglesia Matriz de Jauja. Pizarro himself chose the site. The stone has been refaced with concrete that looks now gray, now beige—its color depends on the light, I suspect. The church is unbeautiful but not imbalanced, its bell tower to the left and its clock tower to the right, a vaulted niche in the center that shelters a small mosaic of the Virgin and Christ-child. Through the wrought iron gate, angels in high relief, and the small double doors are open. Through the darkened nave. Hand-carved pulpit beneath the dome, small altars in the wings left and right, and the immense central altar, its carved cedar churrigueresque, florid, Virgin of the Rosary, vast pipe organ, a small door.

Around to the parish offices. Alexis introduces me to the priest, who is seventy years old but speaks and walks as if ninety. Then Alexis and Armando remind me of where we are to meet for dinner, wish me good hunting, turn and go. The priest takes my arm and leads me to the long thin room that serves as the archive. There he presents me to the secretary. She is slightly older and slower than he is. Together they gesture to the shelves: chaotic, overfull. The priest shakes his head, smiles and says he will leave me to it, takes his leave. The air is dry and cool. There is a small table in one corner. I set down my camera equipment and knapsack, hand the call number to the secretary, sit in the single chair. The secretary works up and back along the near wall. At last she stops, reaches, brings a large register down. She places it on the table before me, says that photocopying is permitted for most materials, but not those as old as the documents I have come to see.

The leather cover is well worn, scraped dull in spots, polished bright in others. I open the register, page carefully through. The paper is in excellent condition and the secretary waits at my shoulder. I look at her, and she nods, motions for me to work deeper in. I come at last to the series of small registers at its heart. The fourth is the one I have come for. I run a hand across the parchment of its cover. The secretary smiles. I smile back, and wait. Finally she purses her lips, turns and walks to the far side of the room, opens a window and stares out at the late morning. I work slowly through to the first page of the will. There is a small bit of sand caught in the string of the binding, the remains of what was used to blot the ink, and even these few grains thrill me: Juan de Segovia stood and watched as this very sand was sprinkled across these pages four hundred and sixty-four years ago. The handwriting has faded, is all but illegible, but here too the paper is in excellent condition for its age: near-white at the center, browning to the rough-cut edges, a single small hole burned in by an unnoticed fleck of ink. I set the copy of Alexis' transcription to the left of the register, and open a clean notebook to the right. The secretary closes the window, says that she will return in an hour, that the priest is in the sacristy, that he is not to be disturbed.

May all those who read this document see that I, D. Juan de Segovia, native of Cogolludo, a cluster of distant lights and a last goodbye: I took Mariángel to the cemetery, and we stood before Pilar. I leaned down, polished the cameo with my handkerchief. Mariángel clutched at it, not as if recognizing Pilar but as if wishing to take the pretty picture home. I made her stop and she cried. We cried. I slumped against the whitewashed wall, came to rest on the ground, Mariángel walking in circles, greater and ever greater. I watched her and abhorred myself and missed Pilar so very much. Then I brought out my knife. The cameo was easier to remove than I would have guessed. It is in my knapsack as well, and home, and the telephone, I call them, Pilar's father answering, other voices in the background, Pilar's mother and brothers, their voices rising, voices, the father calming them and I say that it is time if they so wish, that they can take Pilar, take her home to Chiclayo, and they weep, all of them, parents and brothers, weep and thank me one after another, beg me to write to them from California, to send pictures of Mariángel as she grows, to come and visit as often as the world permits and the densest darkness falls away, we ride as if across the top of the earth, stars full in the sky to all sides, we are nearing the pass and I wait, wait, now the scar burns and Karina sighs in her sleep, Mariángel turns, I wait, and yes Atahualpa dead and the Spaniards leaving Cajamarca, higher and higher into the mountains, footbridges hung across gorges unlike anything they have ever seen, the horses terrified, many of the soldiers as well, helped across by small tribes who believe that the Spaniards will free them from their Inca overlords. Chalcuchima rides enchained, but there is a rumor, his army still hundreds of thousands strong and on its way, and the Spaniards ride and ride, the air ever thinner and colder, along the high spine of the Andes, at last across. Pizarro leaves the slowest troops behind, pushes forward with seventy-five horsemen, through Tarma and night falls but the men do not remove their armor, do not unsaddle the horses, there is no food, no water, no firewood, no shelter and it rains, snows, onward, piles of corpses found at Yanamarca, on and on, and now the pass, this pass, the view down a long wide valley, the mountainsides thick with Huanca villages, farther on and in, then Jauja, a lake of golden light: the city is in flames. The Incas themselves have put it to the torch to slow the Spanish advance. Now the trumpets sound, the downhill charge, the slaughter, thousands, a short sharp ascent, a curve and before us the edge, we slide to it and across and before us the same long wide valley, and Jauja, a lake of golden light, but look, the glow is steady, not fire but cradled streetlights, we lower toward them, and a thousand miles away the pacazo wakes.

## ACKNOWLEDGEMENTS.


I am deeply grateful to the following people for their help in bringing this book into being:

Matt Bell, my editor
Maria Massie, my agent
Jim Ruland, my star reader
Dan Wickett and Steve Gillis, my publishers
Paule Constant, who gave me the gift of a new myth
Victor Velezmoro and Matt Vester, for their answers and patience


My thanks are also due a very large number of people who helped in a very large number of ways:

Eric Abrahamsen, Julia Alba, Carlos Arrizabalaga, Janalee P. Caldwell, Wendy Cotlear, Gastón Cruz, David Djian, Kevin Dolgin, Dave Eggers, Pavel Elías, Arantxa Freire, Hans-Peter Fuchs, Andrés Garay, Mary Gillis, Philip Graham, Jakob Halermann, Elizabeth Hernández, Renzo Honores, Eli Horowitz, Max Houck, Dominic Hudson, Omar Hurtado, John Leary, Pasha Malla, Mary McCluskey, Shauna McKenna, Mark Miller, Alejandro Neyra, Adam Pillsbury, Karla Poggi, Marion Preest, Lelis Rebolledo, Pablo Sebastián, Steven Seighman, Lichi Seminario, David Vann and Reynaldo Villar.